Lawrence Schimel is a full-[...] who's published over 80 books [...] *The Future is Queer, Best D[...] Celebrate Gay Relationships, [...] His Tongue, Kosher Meat,* and *Vacation in Ibiza,* among others. His *PoMoSexuals: Challenging Assumptions About Gender and Sexuality* (with Carol Queen) won a Lambda Literary Award in 1998, and he has also been a finalist for the Lambda Literary Award ten other times, including for *The Mammoth Book of Gay Erotica.* The German edition of his anthology *Switch Hitters: Lesbians Write Gay Male Erotica and Gay Men Write Lesbian Erotica* (with Carol Queen) won the Siegesseuele Best Book of the Year Award. He won the Rhysling Award for Poetry in 2002 and his children's book *No hay nada como el original* (illustrated by Sara Rojo Pérez) was selected by the International Youth Library in Munich for the White Ravens 2005. He has also been a finalist for the Firecracker Alternative Book Award (twice), the Small Press Book Award (twice), and the Spectrum Award (twice). His work has been widely anthologized in *The Random House Book of Science Fiction Stories, The Best of Best Gay Erotica, Gay Love Poetry, The Mammoth Book of Gay Short Stories, The Mammoth Book of Comic Fantasy, The Mammoth Book of Fairy Tales, Chicken Soup for the Horse-Lover's Soul 2,* and *The Random House Treasury of Light Verse,* among many others. He has also contributed to numerous periodicals, from *The Christian Science Monitor* to *Physics Today* to *Gay Times.* His writings have been translated into Basque, Catalan, Croatian, Czech, Dutch, Esperanto, Finnish, French, Galician, German, Greek, Hungarian, Indonesian, Italian, Japanese, Polish, Portuguese, Romanian, Russian, Slovak, and Spanish. For two years he served as co-chair of the Publishing Triangle, a US organization of lesbians and gay men in the publishing industry, and he also served as the Regional Advisor of the Spain Chapter of the Society of Children's Book Writers and Illustrators for five years. Born in New York City in 1971, he lives in Madrid, Spain.

THE MAMMOTH BOOK OF

New Gay Erotica

Edited and with an Introduction
by Lawrence Schimel

ROBINSON
London

Constable & Robinson Ltd
3 The Lanchesters
162 Fulham Palace Road
London W6 9ER
www.constablerobinson.com

First published in the UK by Robinson,
an imprint of Constable & Robinson Ltd, 2007

A copy of the British Library Cataloguing in Publication Data is
available from the British Library.

ISBN: 978-1-84529-593-6

Printed and bound in the EU

1 3 5 7 9 10 8 6 4 2

Contents

Acknowledgments

EIGHTY BUCKS PLUS TIP © 2007 by Tom Mendicino. Reproduced by permission of the author.

TYING THE KNOT © 2006 by Robin Metalfe. First published in the magazine *BlackFlash*. Reproduced by permission of the author.

CERTAIN SHADES OF BLUE LOOK GREEN, DEPENDING ON THE LIGHT © 2003 by Marshall Moore. First published in QUICKIES 3, edited by James C. Johnstone (Arsenal Pulp Press). Reproduced by permission of the author.

ALL THE WORLD'S A GAME SHOW © 2007 by Gregory L. Norris. Reproduced by permission of the author.

THE BEST SEX BETWEEN THEM © 2006 by Andy Quan. First published in INSIDE HIM, edited by Joel Tan (Carroll & Graf). Reproduced by permission of the author.

LITTLE STEVIE © 2007 by Kirk Read. Reproduced by permission of the author.

THE DREAM PEOPLE © 2007 by Rick R. Reed. Reproduced by permission of the author.

PLEASINGLY © 1996 by Matthew Rettenmund. First published in BEST GAY EROTICA 1996 edited by Michael Thomas Ford (Cleis). Reproduced by permission of the author.

DANIEL IS LEAVING TONIGHT ON A PLANE © 2007 by Paul Russell. Reproduced by permission of the author.

EDEN © 1981, 2007 by Steven Saylor. First published, in earlier form, as a serial under the title "Blinded by the Light" in DRUMMER Magazine, #46-48. Reproduced by permission of the author.

Introduction

Lawrence Schimel

Ten years ago, I compiled THE MAMMOTH BOOK OF GAY EROTICA. The relationship between the two books is curious, since while this volume is, in essence, a sequel or companion volume to the previous one, there is in reality little other connection between them, aside from my editorship and the sheer size of both. Some of the authors repeat, it's true, but reading the previous book is not at all essential to enjoying the stories in this one. The relationship between the two is, more or less, anecdotal or accidental.

Nonetheless, I can't help feeling as if this introduction isn't half so much an afterword to that previous book a decade ago, a bridge that's meant to cover the intervening span of years.

In the earlier volume, I spent much of the introduction justifying the importance (or mere existence) of an anthology of literature about gay sex. Those reasons are still valid, I think, but the world in which this new volume was compiled is a different place.

In the wake of the tremendous success of the movie BROKEBACK MOUNTAIN and the television series QUEER AS FOLK, not to mention the growing popularity of manga comics, especially among women, the mainstream has awoken to the powerful impact of stories of homoerotic desire.

Gay characters are prominent in cinema, novels, the news. Bookstores have shelves of other collections of gay erotica, from both specialty and mainstream publishers. It's easy to feel quite complacent.

But as much as the publishing world may have changed in the intervening years, becoming more open to – or even actively pursuing – gay themes or work, legal advances have been fewer and far between; as of this writing, there are only five countries in the world where same-sex marriages are legal: Belgium, Canada, the Netherlands, South Africa, and Spain. In numerous states of the USA, sodomy laws still criminalize sexual acts between men.

And we have all, gay men and others, suffered from the past 25 years of the AIDS pandemic, as individuals and as communities.

Much work remains to be done, it's true, before equality is achieved, although many important things have been accomplished. And in many ways, it is thanks to those people who are on the sexual frontiers of our culture that has made life in the "mainstream" more comfortable for many of us, pushing back the boundaries of the social envelope.

I'm always resistant to using my anthologies to make unilateral statements or claims. One of the things I love about anthologies, as a format, is being able to bring together so many different perspective or points of view under a particular umbrella of theme or genre or subject. And given the sheer size of the volumes in the MAMMOTH series, that's a pretty large umbrella, under which can fit a lot of diversity.

It makes, I hope, a nice change from the majority of recent gay erotic collections, which seem to be grouped around ever-more-narrow subjects and themes.

At the same time, not every story will turn on every reader. That's a given. It is my hope that enough of the stories in this book will appeal to each reader, even if they're not always the same ones, and that for anything that's not floating your boat you simply advance to the next story.

Although I do also hope that you get sucked in to reading

about men exploring desires or relationships you might not have let yourself explore before, on or off the page.

Because there are plenty of fetishes and kinks within these pages, alongside romantic erotic episodes or so-called "vanilla" sex stories. Having them all rub against one another beneath the covers of this book lets the reader have voyeuristic glimpses into familiar worlds or ones he may not yet have explored.

THE MAMMOTH BOOK OF NEW GAY EROTICA is, in many ways, a document of the sexual reality of gay men's lives as much as fantasies.

This is, perhaps, a contradiction.

Many people turn to erotica as escapism from their reality, sexual or otherwise. In fantasy, the man of your dream is, in fact, attainable.

And lately, many women have been turning to gay male sex for their fantasy material. The internet has seen an explosion of this type of material, primarily written by heterosexual women for an audience of heterosexual women, whose "kinks" are often determined by the "fandom" they follow, referring to pairings of characters drawn from popular television series or films. This subgenre is known as "slash", metonym for the punctuation that determines the pairing, from the original Kirk/Spock that sparked this phenomenon years ago to numerous Rowling-inspired pairings (Harry Potter/Snape, Harry Potter/Dumbledore, etc.)

Gay men have often complained about slash that the actual mechanical aspects of gay sex are so badly written.

While this is true in many cases, it is important to realize that gay men are usually not the primary audience for this material, despite its gay sexual content. One of the most interesting aspects of slash fiction is its COMMUNAL nature.

The truth is that many women also write traditional gay pornography under male names, in large part because there is both an easily adaptable formula and a ready market for the material. Many of them are able to write this material with the majority of their male readers quite unaware of who lies behind the pen (or the pen name). I've worked with many of these female authors over the years while compiling many anthologies, and will happily continue to do so.

But in selecting the stories for this book I've restricted myself to male authors. And the majority of the stories, even those that do verge off into fantasy, are very much grounded in the reality of gay male experience, contemporary or otherwise. While most traditional pornography relies on the new encounter, here you'll find erotic stories about men at all stages of relationships: from first meetings to long-term couples – without losing sight of the desire that lingers even after the relationship is, for whatever reason, over. So the sex that happens as often happens with an ex-lover as with a new acquaintance, and only rarely with the anonymous porn magazine archetype of the pizza delivery boy. And even when searching for anonymous satisfaction, there may be a lover in the background (either literally, at the same sex club, or emotionally).

In the decade between books, many of our sexual sub-cultures have changed. Subcultures have become main-streamed, for one thing, and often they've been so over exploited as to lose some of their erotic charge.

And many of the writers themselves have changed – and not just the ones who appear in both volumes.

Many of us are a decade older, and what we look for (in sex, in literature, in writing about sex) has changed.

I think that many of us have gotten a bit more sentimental, even if often in a bitter – or, at the least, bittersweet – kind of way.

Although without losing sight of the raw sex that turns us on, in life or in fiction.

THE MAMMOTH BOOK OF NEW GAY EROTICA showcases writing by and about gay men, both original stories commissioned for this volume and reprints of exceptional recent stories. And just as desire often transcends all other boundaries, the diverse and distinguished crop of contributors comes from around the globe. The stories are as varied in subject and tone as they are in length and genre. Variety, they say, is the spice of life, so I hope you find this collection offers plenty of spicy stimulation – for both body and mind.

A History of Noah, or How I Met My Boyfriend

Shaun Levin

To be three is to be in public . . .
Elizabeth Bowen, The House in Paris

The Philosopher

We're about to come in each other's mouths when his boyfriend Daniel walks in. Noah had warned me he might come home early, but I'm still surprised, and I still feel awkward. Noah waves to him, like you'd wave to the delivery boy from your office chair when he knocks on the door with a parcel, as he holds the back of my head, fucks my face, and shoots his thick come down the back of my throat.

Rule No 1: Don't let him come in your mouth when you're not paying attention. I'm coughing so much I don't even notice Daniel undressing and getting onto the bed with us. By the time I recover, Daniel's licking the last bits of come off his boyfriend's cock.

"Stop," Noah says to him. "We need your help here."

I've never seen skin so pale, every vein visible, so hairless, and hair so red. It's down past his shoulders, and curly; he brushes it away from his eyes to look at me.

"You must be Shaun," he says.

"Enough chatting," Noah says. "Come and chew on his tits."

His mouth is warm when it lands on my nipple to suckle it.
Noah eases me onto my back, so that Daniel's head is resting
on my chest as he nibbles on the tip of my tit and fiddles with
the hair on my chest. Noah's on his knees, holding onto my
cock, inspecting it, then leaning forward to lap at the skin of
my ball sac. And I think: Oh, fuck.

"I'm there," I say.

"So quick?" Daniel says.

"I know," I say. "But I have to."

And their mouths meet at the head of my cock as I jerk off
onto their faces.

And that's how our threesomes began. I'd take the bus
from Tel Aviv to Jerusalem three or four times a month, to
the little house Noah and Daniel rented in the German
Colony. We'd cook dinner sometimes, especially if it was a
Friday and Daniel wasn't preparing for a lecture at the
Hebrew University, or Noah wasn't in Gaza with some
young Palestinian boy, selling dope to his friends after
school.

"None of the symposiads," Daniel says, some weeks later,
over dinner, his lecture on Plato's text imminent. "Not one of
them has anything to say about threesomes."

"What *do* they have to say?" Noah says, dishing up cream
and dill penne with our salmon steaks.

"Which one?" Daniel says.

"How many are there?"

"Seven," says Daniel.

"Seven?"

"If you count Alcibiades," says Daniel. "Who wasn't
really there to start with."

"Who?"

"Alcibiades," Daniel says

"Say it again," Noah says.

"Alcibiades," Daniel says.

"Oh, professor," Noah says, his eyes on Daniel's.

Daniel shrugs and smiles at me: "Pass the salad, please,"
he says.

Noah's love for Daniel was a kind of adoration, a playful submission mixed with genuine envy. Noah loved Daniel's intelligence and his background, he loved him for being what *he* wanted to be: a nice Ashkenazi boy from a well-educated, well-behaved, musically inclined family; not some farm-boy with a drug-dealer father from Syria and an Egyptian mother who cooked and washed up in silence while her husband was God knows where with his mistresses. That is where the shape of Noah's love was forged. His love for Daniel was so huge he couldn't bear to test it for reciprocity, so he diluted it with casual sex, especially with younger boys, like the yeshiva *bochers* he tells us about over dessert, when the conversation turns to fucking, in preparation for what is about to come.

"There was this kid," Noah says. "Daniel had to persuade him that I wasn't worth leaving the yeshiva for."

"Well," Daniel says. "You're not."

"Yeah," says Noah. "Especially after having your fat *goyishe* cock shoved up my arse."

"How's that done?" I say.

Because somehow it's always up to me to make the first move. Like I'm the odd one out, the minority to be respected. The move from dinner-table to futon has yet to be mastered. There is always a cue; in this case: a request for a demonstration.

"Come closer," Noah says, as he kneels before Daniel, who takes his big pink *goyishe* dick and shoves it down his boyfriend's throat.

The thing is, Daniel is actually Jewish. A Lithuanian philosophy professor with a Jewish mother and a Russian painter for a father. He grew up under communism, hadn't been circumcised, and when he immigrated to Israel in the late eighties and started sleeping with Jewish boys, realised what a novelty he was. He doesn't like being singled out amongst Jews, the way he'd been singled out amongst the *goyim*. So Noah and I aren't that surprised when, six months into our threesomes, and a year after he'd met Daniel, he pulls his cock out of Noah's mouth, lies down between us, and announces: "I'm going to New York to have it chopped off."

"Why would you do that?" I say, reaching down to stroke his cock.

"The best circumcision doctors live there," he says.

"You know what I mean," I say, pulling his soft foreskin up over the head of his cock and running my finger around inside where it's moist with spit and sweat and precome, then licking my finger. "This is how Pooh Bear must have felt with his paw in the honey jar," I say.

"Stop it," Daniel says.

"Yes," Noah says. "It's not kosher."

Which only makes me jump up and nuzzle in between Daniel's legs and swallow more of his cock. To be with the man who is loved by my friend; that is the wonder of all this. To be invited into a loving family: to be so content that every exaggeration is credible. Moments like this – Noah at Daniel's side, kissing him, both of them peering across Daniel's flat hairless stomach at me on my knees. The *shabbes* candles our only light – sustained me while I was back in Tel Aviv cooking at Skizza Bar till three in the morning, drinking vodka gimlets after midnight, then trying to write stories during the day.

Two weeks after Daniel left for New York, Noah called to say he had a letter from him: Daniel had been offered a job at Hunter College and he wasn't coming home again.

"He asked me to join him," Noah said.

"So, why don't you?" I said.

"What about you?" he said. "I'd miss you."

But we both knew that wasn't the reason. And whatever I thought then, I think differently now. It did have something to do with me, but more with me as a witness, a companion, someone to help contain Noah's overwhelming love for a man who'd never be his. And the knowledge was there from the beginning; I had been groomed for this moment of abandonment.

And then there were others.

The Married Man

I'm flat on my back with Noah sitting on my face.

"Careful you don't stick your tongue in too deep," Guy says. "He's got piles again."

So I push my face in further and spit into his arse, just to prove how well I know Noah, how deep my trust is. True friends aren't fazed by the body's disloyalties. Noah has the tips of my nipples between his fingers, and pulls on them while he pushes his arsehole down onto my tongue. One hand's pinching Noah's nipple, the other's playing with Guy's cock, and my feet are wide apart for Guy to stick a finger up my arse. He tries for more, as he leans forward – the bed a prayer mat – to suck on my cock. Guy is the greatest cocksucker; his wife taught him everything.

"My legs are getting stiff," Noah says.

So he turns around and plugs his cock into my mouth, gently, the way a friend would, the way you'd slide a pacifier between a baby's lips, without the brutality and anger so common in fucking between strangers. Noah's is the perfect cock for sucking: reassuringly pudgy and not too long. He pulls Guy's arse towards him and buries his face in it. Yes, this is Guy: IT expert, ex-gymnast, adulterer. This was all his idea; his wife knows nothing – she thinks he's on reserve duty in Nablus.

I put my hands on Guy's head and dig my fingers into his thick black hair. I pull hard and his mouth goes loose around my cock; I can feel the back of his throat, the vibrations of the drowning noises he makes while Noah rims him. From above, we're a triangle.

"Can we stop for a bit?" I say. "I need to pee."

We've been at it for almost an hour. We'd come once already, smoking our first bong and jerking off to *Nazi Youth*, a cheap pirate porn flick with skinny doe-eyed Czech boys doing callisthenics in the woods. My legs are so wobbly I have to sit down to piss. I tuck my erection under the seat and fart loudly, a wet fart, then check with toilet paper. Clean.

"Bring us something to eat," Noah calls as I flush. "I've got the munchies."

I should never have got up. I could have peed in the bottle by the side of the bed. Standing naked in the kitchen preparing a tray of strawberries and melon for two men while my lover is away – don't ask me where – I'm beginning to regret the whole thing. We haven't even negotiated sleeping around. I hadn't planned to, but then Noah called, and he's not the kind of friend I say no to. Sex with him doesn't feel like infidelity; it's an emotional attachment. He's just not very good with words; sex is his way of communicating. And mine, too, I guess, for when my lover and I are together we're more likely to fuck than to have a conversation.

When I get back to the bedroom, Guy is on a chair by the side of the bed with his feet on the edge of the mattress. His feet are wide and smooth, his nails thick and in need of clipping, and all I want to do is lick between his toes, those healthy, big-boned, reassuring toes. And I realise then that when a subject kneels before his king, a pilgrim on the steps of the cathedral, it is not an act of submission, but a desire to rest. It is an appeal for protection. So I lay the tray of fruit and Greek yoghurt on the bed, go down on my knees, and lick between the toes of the opulent 6ft 4in broad and muscled IT god.

"I love getting fucked," Guy says.

Noah guzzles the flesh of a melon while his finger goes in and out of Guy's arse.

"Try some of the yoghurt," I say.

"Are you really a writer?" Guy says.

"What else has he told you about me?" I say, eating the yoghurt with my fingers.

"That you're wild," Guy says.

"Shut up," Noah says.

I lie back on the bed and watch them kissing, Guy's lips bright red as he licks the smell of his arse off Noah's face.

I dip strawberries into yoghurt and eat them whole. I shut my eyes and fondle my cock; the sound could be anything: ripples, cunt, the wellspring of life.

"Stop drifting off," Noah says. "Come closer."

He takes some yoghurt with his fingertips and rubs it onto my lips.

"Stop frowning," he says. "Kiss me."

"Now?" I say, moving closer to him.

For we so rarely kiss. So rare are the moments of gentle intimacy between us. They were there in the beginning when we met in the army, both of us stationed in Lebanon, until the RPG missile exploded near our foxholes and blasted shrapnel and gravel into the back of Noah's legs. For those weeks he was in hospital I'd go and lick phlegm onto his wounds. We were lovers during that war in Lebanon, before AIDS came to Israel, before I knew about Daniel, whom Noah had fallen in love with in a way he and I never would. We enjoyed each other, trusted each other too much, so the mad-making, addictive kind of love we believed in back then never happened between us.

"He's loosening up," Noah says.

"I need to be on the bed for this," Guy said.

So I move the tray off the bed and onto the chair to make room for Guy on the mattress, which he crawls across, his rib-cage pressing against tight skin, the veins visible in his arms, scribbles of black hairs pasted round his arsehole, as he stretches out for Noah to fuck him.

"You're dripping on me," Guy says. "Lick it off."

"Ssh," Noah said.

They've known each other for years, since high school, I think. Noah organizes these little parties whenever Guy's in the mood. They call me when their regular guys aren't available and I agree because I miss what Noah and Daniel and I used to have and I think that somehow we'll be able to recreate something of that. But at the moment all I want is to get fucked; I don't care about anything else. I've had enough. I spit into my palm and start jerking my cock. If I ignore them, they'll go away. Guy takes a condom and KY jelly from the bedside table. He holds onto my hips and slides into me. It's that easy. From behind I can feel Noah finger-fucking Guy. I'm jerking myself off and trying to let go. Guy's cock is too comfortable to be exciting. Facing the wall, eyes wide open, I can hear Noah saying: "Fuck him, Guy. Don't be so gentle."

And I think: as long as I don't touch Guy's skin I won't have to remember him. I won't have to turn him into another man who will not love me. I jerk my cock and push my other fingers into my arse and scrape at the soft flesh inside me. I wish someone would tell me to stop. Someone tell me I don't have to do this. That my lover is ready to cradle me. That I do not have to dig my nails in deeper to tear at the walls of my arse. I am not going to say anything; it's up to Guy if he wants to bring up the subject of blood. He does, eventually, but by then I've come and my face is in the pillow, and I don't care if I'm unloved, and he's walking away, saying: Shit, shit, fuck, fuck, on his way to the bathroom. Noah's mouth is at my ear and he's combing my hair between his fingers and saying: "Hey, Honey Pie," he's saying. "Shh," he's saying. "Is this what he did to you?"

The Ambassador's Son

"The biggest ever," Noah says. "Long and fat and loads of pubes."

"I said no."

"But it's huge," he says. "I can only get about this much into my mouth."

We're on the balcony, Noah and I, naked and sweating, having both just come on my chest. We haven't seen each other in almost a year – he's been on his family's farm near the Gaza Strip; I've been trying to leave the investment banker – but we've spoken on the phone, Noah and I, filled each other in, complained about the scarcity of brave and honest men (me), and about the desire of all men to be looked after (Noah). Now he's trying to convince me to have another threesome; this time with a guy who arrived in Israel a couple of weeks ago.

"He wants to meet other writers," Noah says. "I told him about you."

"Like what?" I say. "What did you tell him?"

As the morning sun's warmth fills the balcony.

"He's dying to meet you," Noah says. "Get rid of the banker."

Noah had caught me at a vulnerable time – the investment banker kept saying he'd leave his boyfriend, then he'd ask me to fuck him in the sauna with everyone watching; those were the kinds of gifts he was offering – and now Noah was dangling this fellow writer in front of me like bait, tempting me with a man who'd been a journalist in Cambodia and Bogota, who'd spent his early twenties fighting corruption in South Africa.

"He's reading *Anna Karenina* at the moment," Noah says, on his way to the kitchen for something to eat. "If that's any help to you."

"What did you say his name was?"

All I can say is this: never mind huge, I can barely get the head of Brian's cock past my lips. Three times the width of mine. A phallic god in itself. We are impressed.

"See," says Noah.

"See what?" Brian says.

"I'd like to see him piss," I say.

"Piss?" Noah says. "You should see him come."

"Excuse me," the guy says. "It's not like I'm not in the room or something."

"He's young," says Noah.

And like all the men Noah reels in for himself or to share with others, Brian is beautiful, too. So we kiss. Just our lips at first, still dry, brushing against each other. And he smiles, and I smile, and I purr like a cat from the back of my throat. I stroke his back and kiss him until his lips give way and he swallows my tongue. It is spring again, a warm April evening, almost midnight, and the windows are wide open. The duvet on the floor and the bed a raft afloat. We face each other, Brian and I, still kneeling, too afraid to touch with more than our lips.

"So, what are you doing here?" I say.

"Where?" he says, his breath a warm wind.

"*In this country,*" I say.

"Didn't Noah tell you?" he says.

"All he told me about was this," I say.

"Yours is nice, too," he says.

"Thank you," I say.

"Thank *you*," he says.

He takes the KY jelly from the side of the bed and spreads lube between his arse-cheeks. I kiss his nipples. He tears a condom packet open and lies back on the bed. I kiss the cleft in the centre of his chest. He lifts his torso to rest on his elbows. I lick my way to his belly-button. He rolls a condom down my cock. I stroke the insides of his thighs. He lies back down. I skim his dense pubes with my open palm. He lifts his legs to rest them on my shoulders. I put lube on my cock and more on his crack. He closes his eyes. I put the head of my cock at the entrance to his hole. He reaches up to pinch my nipples. I lean forward to kiss his mouth. He says please fuck me. I say I'll see what I can do.

"Well, well, well." The words come when we do. "I might as well be holding the candle," Noah says, smiling, watching us from the carpet at the foot of the bed, his eyes peering over the edge of the mattress.

We smile, this Brian person and I, delighting in our own pleasure, my come in the condom, his on his chest, and we giggle as our joy bubbles over. What a miracle, to be plodding along, and then this. To see how a thing that began in reluctance ended in love.

"That was so beautiful," Noah says, getting up from the floor, the duvet wrapped around him like a cloak.

"Come lie between us," I say.

Merlin the matchmaker, our fairy godmother.

I didn't see much of Noah after that. The last I heard was that he'd gone off to New York to work in one of his cousin's flashy clothes stores on the Upper East Side. And Brian and I? Well, Brian doesn't really like it when I talk about him. Whenever I try to write about our love, he reminds me that Proust only wrote about his lovers when he was tired of them, or when the pain they caused him became unbearable. Proust's way was to write his lovers out of his life. And I know that. I know that the distance you need to write about anything means that part of you is always on the way out, even if your engagement with the other is absolute. So let's just leave it there, at the point where my boyfriend and I begin.

Privacy, Please!

Michael Lassell

"Lawrence," I said into the cordless, "I am looking at him right now!"

"What's he wearing?" Lawrence asked, cutting as usual to the chase without so much as a hem or a haw. The young are so refreshingly direct.

"Nothing, of course. That's what he's always wearing. If he's home, he's naked. It's the best thing about him."

"Well, if your bedroom has to face an air shaft, it's nice that the landlord provides visual aids."

"It's not an air shaft," I said, truly offended. "It's an interior courtyard with street access, and he doesn't actually live in this building. And my landlord does not supply humpy eye candy. *My* landlord supplies cockroaches and the occasional rodent we all hope is a large mouse."

Lawrence said something into his cordless that sounded like "I have to take a bowel movement," so it was probably "Why don't you move," because if Lawrence did indeed need to move his bowels, he would be unlikely to say so, thanks to WASP potty training and Ivy League schooling – and if he was going to mention it at all, he most certainly would have said, "I have to take a shit." Anyway, whatever it was, I couldn't hear it because there was a hideous explosion at his end of the line.

"What the fuck was that?" I asked, wondering if I should be alarmed.

"Oh, nothing," Lawrence said wearily. "They're shooting

another movie in the vacant lot behind my apartment. Apparently it's an action movie and they're using explosives instead of a script."

"It's one o'clock in the morning," I noted.

"I know, I know. It's been going on for three nights."

"Who's in it?"

"I don't know. Some over-the-hill heterosexual. Chuck van Schwarzenwillis or something."

"Mel Gibson?" I asked.

"He's the homophobic one who used to be cute, right?"

"Right."

"No, it's not him. It's somebody even older than that, and the girl is about thirty seconds past early puberty. I think Hollywood should be arrested for child pornography."

"I didn't realize you had limits with respect to pornography," I said.

"Well," Lawrence answered with a trace of hauteur in his well-modulated contralto voice, "I do: I hate *action* movies."

"Well, come over here, then, and I'll show you an action movie you'll like. It's triple-X rated and stars my very own new neighbor, and it is truly up front and personal."

"What's he doing?" Lawrence asked.

"Working out," I replied, but I was drowned out by the Con Ed crew digging to China at the street-access moment of my alley – er, interior courtyard. Which they had been doing for over a year that I knew about.

"What?" asked Lawrence.

"Working out," I shouted, but the cordless started squawking – his or mine, who knows? – and we hung up. We were used to it. No matter how many frequencies there are on the airwaves, there are at least ten people in any New York neighborhood with the same one, and they're all on the phone.

My new neighbor was what I would have to call hot. Steamy. Sizzlin'. He was tall, dark, and drop-dead gorgeous. Latino or Italian was clear to my ethnic I.D. antenna – although some might have guessed Greek, and had he been a little less bulky, one might even be forgiven for thinking him Persian. But he *was* bulky. Gym-bunny bulky. His shoulders swelled out about six inches on each side past his actual skeleton, and one of them sported a goofy KEEP ON TRUCKIN' tattoo just like Tony Danza used to have (or maybe still does). This made me think he had probably lived in San Francisco, since he was way too young to have lived through the 70s, and San Francisco is the one city on earth where the 70s have never died. San Francisco plus Latino, of course, meant Mexican.

He had ski-jump pecs capped by a pair of redwood-dark nipples you could use for shelter in a storm. His knotted torso made him look like he was wearing that leather armor they always have on in those Roman bible epics in the 50s (an effect heightened by his skin color, which was some unique tint comprised of caramel, camel, coffee, coconut shell, tropical sunlight about an hour before dusk, and rare gilt-edged volumes of the 16th century). Unsurprisingly, he had the legs of a seasoned soccer player. Which meant, of course, that he had one of those asses so beautifully defined and perfectly rounded that it was actually two loaflike masses of fuck-me flesh.

He was relatively hairless, which is a turn-on for me if it's natural and a total barfer if it's not. He had a patch of dark hair on his chest, nestled between his tits like a little goatee that had fallen off an idolatrous trick, and it kind of trickled over the bricks of his abs, split around his deeply sunken navel like a brook around a boulder, and came to a slightly curlicued tail, so to speak, about one kiss north of his abundant, jet-black pubic hair. He shaved his legs, from the knees down, and he did it in his bedroom – not in the shower – which is how I knew, because when he was in the shower, I could only see him from the solar plexus up.

And did I mention that he had a dick?

It's not that it was so huge, although it was definitely more dinner kielbasa than breakfast link. Or perhaps chorizo is more appropriate to the object at hand (so to speak). It was classic in shape, if you like cut sausage, and I do – maybe because I have one of my own, but also because they're less work (which is why I like summer more than winter: all those layers of clothing getting tangled up with each other every time you enter or exit a room). Which meant, I quickly clocked, that wherever his parents were from, he was probably born (a) in a hospital and (b) in the US of A, a country as irrationally infatuated with circumcision as it is with psychiatry, which may, of course, be related.

Everyone's idea of a perfect dick, is, of course, different. His was mine. Long enough to dangle and sway when he walked, but not enough to scuff his knees, and rather thick, with a slight (and I mean slight) taper before flaring into a rather more pointed than not glans. Erect, it points almost straight up along his torso as if following the path mapped out by the hair that grows along his axis of symmetry. There's an appealing curve to it that suggests the outside arc of rhinoceros horn.

Didn't I mention that I'd seen his dick in copulatory action?

Oh, yes. My new neighbor, who is probably in his mid- to late-twenties, has no shame. He not only walks around naked, but he frequently walks around hard, his usually loose-hanging balls tucking up below that divinely bouncing divining rod. And he's not always alone. I've seen a United Nations of calendar boys pass through that bedroom. I've seen his dick buried to the mustache in the greedy mouths of admiring lads. I've seen him service a procession of well-lubed assholes, pushing in until his pubes start to gleam like the raven tresses of an Andalusian starlet finding her key light, then pulling out again so the puckered scarlet tip of it cleared the welcoming butthole before he jammed back in again.

And I have seen dicks of all description, some of them larger than life, pounding his own glory hallelujah, him screaming in English and Spanish and that language of animal sounds spoken only by men in the climax moments of butt-fucking ecstasy. I've seen him knees-over-head with a family-sized dildo up his butt, and watched him wedge all his fingers into his asshole, not to mention carrots, cucumbers, zucchinis, and even a phallic lube pot. He is as erotically adroit as linguistically versatile.

Apparently he didn't realize that turning off the lights would have made it more difficult to watch him. He also did not seem to understand the principle of shades, blinds, or blackout curtains. And he certainly didn't know every spasm was being appreciated and sometimes – often – accompanied just ten or twelve feet away across an air shaft, by an admiring neighbor who – okay, I admit it – sometimes related the whole scene while it was happening to friends on the phone who were also jerking off just hearing how hot the whole fucking business was.

Or maybe he knew just what he was doing.

"That was so fucking hot," Lawrence said once when we were done.

"I shot over my head," I said into my cordless.

"No shit," he said. "I'd like to see that some time."

"Well, you can't see it unless you get naked over here," I said, following a flirtatious road that had so far led nowhere.

"What's happening with José?" Lawrence asked, for that is what we called him.

"Well, the black guy's head is kind of below the window sill at the moment, so I can't really tell if he's lapping up the come, but that certainly is what I'm guessing from the movements of those dreadlocks."

"Maybe I should come over," Lawrence said.

"I don't think so," I said, since it seemed that José was shifting himself into "Fuck me NOW!" position, a lovely profile view in doggy style that allowed me an excellent vantage point for round two. "I'm going to have to come again, and I don't think I can wait for you."

"I'm definitely coming over tomorrow night," Lawrence said.

"He doesn't do it *every* night," I said.

"I'll take my chance," Lawrence said, and a huge explosion went off on his end of the line.

"Are they still making that fucking movie?" I asked.

"No – I mean, yeah, they are, but I think that was a bomb," Lawrence answered. "I'll call you back if something interesting is going on."

Having both hands free was, of course, an advantage because I could work my dick and at least one nipple at the same time. I was on my knees in the dark watching José get hosed when it happened.

I was staring at him taking his "date's" dick up his ass, when José looked straight across the gaping gulf between our buildings and right into my eyes. And then . . . he winked. *Winked!* I swear. I blinked my eyes, as if this could not possibly be the case, as if there were no way he could be watching me while I was watching him. But, as if reading my confusion, he picked one hand off the mattress and waved. God knows what else he would have done if his top-at-the-moment hadn't pulled his head around for a near kiss.

Now, New York is a funny place. There are way too many people living in way too small a place, and we've developed a kind of privacy by agreement. We have no privacy so we agree to pretend we have it. Of course we all walk around in underwear or less, but we never, *never* "notice" each other through our windows. We would rather be guillotined than mention to a neighbor we routinely see muff diving that she has a nice butt when we see her walking her bulldog.

Watching José get hard while he curled his barbells naked in the window, watching him jerk off after toweling the sweat from his bushy underarms, watching him suck and fuck and get sucked and fucked was all sexier than shit. But none of it was shocking. The wink and the wave was unprecedented. How could I go on living here if people actually acknowledged that we were all watching each other all the time?

Now, I am a quantity shooter, and a distance shooter, too – although my second and third fusillades are usually paltry

compared to the first. But something opened up in me when
he winked. I crawled across my bed, closer to the window. I
was yanking like a madman when the black guy who was
fucking José let out a roar that José joined with a scream and
that I turned into a trio with a guttural groan loud enough to
make my ribs resonate, and I shot straight through the open
window and past the fire escape.

José turned and looked. I wondered if I'd hit his window
with my come, but that would have been unlikely for a
second shot. I vowed to see if I could make it, though –
sometime. Maybe if I stood on the fire escape . . .

"Hi," José said from behind me in the Korean deli at the
corner. I was trying to choose three perfect bosc pears from
the rotting pile on the fruit stand: Big, hard, sweet, un-
bruised.

I was taken, as they say, totally aback.

"Oh, hi," I said.

"I'm José," he said.

"I know," I said.

"You know my work?" he asked.

"Oh . . . ," I said, ". . . your *name* is José, I mean, it's
really José."

He looked at me as if I were acting strangely in some way.

"Yeah," he said. "It's not that unusual a name."

"Oh, nonono," I said, trying to cover. "It's a great name.
Spanish."

"Right," he said. "José Esteban."

I didn't know what to say, so I said nothing, my usual
mistake when my dick begins to tingle itself awake in its
auburn nest.

Some ancient lesson of civilization came bubbling out of
my genes to my conscious mind and I stuck out my hand and
said my name.

"I thought maybe you recognized me," he said, oddly
earnest.

"Oh," I said, "I do."

"No, no, not from the window." He smiled unselfcon-
sciously, as if that were a forgone conclusion. "From my
movies."

"You're an actor?" I asked.

I mean, really, when I am around a man I want to fuck I
might as well be a tourist from Oklahoma who has never seen
a city in his life. My blasé Native New York attitude goes
gurgling down the nearest sewer drain, and I become a
shuffle-footed teenager with acne and unsupportive parents.
Oh, right – that *was* me.

"No," he said. "I do porn."

"Ohhhhhhh," I said. And I meant it.

"Yeah, you've probably seen me."

"Right. Well, actually, um, no . . . sorry. I don't actually
watch it. I mean, I've *seen* it, of course . . ." Christ, now I
was insulting his profession.

"It's okay," he said. "It's not for everyone."

"No, no. It's me," I said, although I have no idea what I
meant by that.

So of course then there was the first awful empty silence. My
years on the streets of Manhattan have at least taught me this
fact of life: get past the first awkward silence, and anything is
possible; lose the moment, and you'll never get it back.

"Well," he said . . .

"No, don't go," I said . . . "Um, I mean, unless you have
to."

"No. I'm just on my way home. I just saw you looking at
the fruit . . ."

"Right," I said. "I'm a big fan of fruit."

He grinned, which kicked off the second horrible empty
pause, because I was now mesmerized by him. Happily, the
second embarrassing pause is never as bad as the first (you
already have empirical evidence you can survive silence).

"So that explains it," I managed, just because I was
wondering if he could tell I couldn't keep my eyes off his
nipples, which were bulging through a bright red, skin-tight
T-shirt.

"Explains what?" he said, jumping on his cue.

"Why you're so . . . Um, uninhibited."

"I'm not all that uninhibited," he said, almost shyly, "except sexually."

"Right," I said.

"I like it when you watch me," he said, looking directly into my eyes with eyes that I had not quite noticed before, or at least had not appreciated. They were the kind of blue that seems to exist only in children's books, not in nature: bright, light, liquid, sharp, intelligent, wild, incongruously northern in his Mediterranean face, but warm as a hearthstone. The kind of aquamarine or turquoise associated with swimming pools and parakeet feathers.

"You knew I was watching?" I said, held by those eyes like a baby chimp by its mother.

"Yeah," he said.

My mind was racing faster than slot machine wheels before they settle on bells, bars, or cherries. I was desperately trying to think of something to say.

"Don't think so hard," he laughed. "I think you're hot."

"*You* think *I'm* hot?" I said or asked or whatever.

"Absolutely," he replied. "Way. You wanna come up?"

I put my bosc pears back on the pile.

"He's really sweet, Lawrence," I said.

"You slept with him?" Lawrence said for the fourth or fifth time, the amazement in his voice growing with each repetition.

"Yes," I said. "Is that so odd?"

"Oh, no," he lied. "You sleep with dog food all the time," which was our term for those overly beefy Chelsea boys who all want more than anything to look like a meat meal. We have also been known to call them frozen dinners.

"Eat me," I said.

"Was it hot?"

"He's Chicano," I said, not by way of explanation, but to change the subject. "His father was, *is* Mexican," I continued. "His mother is half Mexican, half French – which is where the blue eyes come from, or at least that's what he says. He was born in Stockton, went to Diablo Valley Junior College and San Francisco State, has six brothers and sisters, including a lesbian, he's a few credits short of a degree in something business-y, and he's very, very sweet."

"And?" said Lawrence, who knows me better than anyone.

"And he's a porn star."

There was a silence even the bomb going off in the parking lot next to Lawrence's apartment couldn't drown out.

I started counting off the seconds, waiting for Lawrence's response, but I hadn't started right at the beginning, so I gave up counting and broke the silence for him."

"Well, not a *star,* exactly, which is a word used way too often. I mean, everybody who's ever been in a film calls themselves a star – superstar, even – but he's on the way up. And he's very—"

"Sweet?"

"Well, yes, he *is* very sweet."

"And how was the, you know, sex?" Lawrence asked, his voice rising at the end while drawing out the x-sound of sex rather longer than I would have thought humanly possible.

"Well, oddly enough," I said, because that's the kind of relationship we have, "he likes getting fucked the best, which is not what I would guess if I just saw him walking down the street, but that was fine because it is, of course, my favorite thing in the whole world to do. Sexually."

"Maybe I *should* come over there," Lawrence said.

"Well, it was very nice . . . you know, sweet and all. He's almost shy. I liked touching him. He has the stupidest tattoo that ever came out of a needle. He was a big stoner in San Francisco, although he says he's actually in AA now and totally clean and sober, and he got the tattoo one night when he was loaded over in North Beach somewhere. Actually," I continued, "I liked the kissing more than the fucking."

★   ★   ★

I had undressed him, of course. I love undressing men.

We walked through the door. He clicked a lock or two behind him, and went to pull off his T-shirt.

"Uh-uh," I said, "let me."

He dropped his arms and looked at me, eye to eye again. My dick was inching up the inside of my Jockeys. He smiled, sweetly. His gave his head a coltish toss to clear his unfashionably long hair out of his eyes.

I put one hand on each side of his waist and moved in so close I could feel the heat from his nostrils on my face. He was maybe an inch shorter than me, so he was a bit under six feet. I ran my hands up the side of his T-shirt, along the seams.

He breathed deeply, exhaling into my face.

I raised one hand and touched his lips with one finger. They were full and fleshy and parted slightly. I moved my lips as close as I could to his without touching. We were both breathing harder. I grabbed his T-shirt in two hands and pulled it roughly up and over his head. Before he brought his arms back down, I put my hands back on him, rubbing his dark-haired underarms with my thumbs, while my fingers put some pressure on his shoulder blades.

I pulled him in closer and his face moved in toward mine. Before our lips touched, I blew slightly over them and he opened his a bit more and licked them with the tip of his tongue. I ran the tip of my tongue as gently as I could on the underside of his upper lip, then moved my fingers down to his nipples.

He emitted a loud *whew* and gasped on the inhale when I pinched slightly on each one. I flicked each one with the back of my thumbnail and blew a trail of smoke down his body until I was kneeling in front of him, breathing through the denim of his Levis into his bulging basket.

"Put one of your feet here," I said, touching my chest.

He did.

I untied the laces of his boot, slowly, and then pulled it off. Then the sock. His toes were long and straight.

"The other one," I said.

When he was barefoot, I stood up again and put my fingers lightly on each side of his face, barely touching the beard stubble there. I pulled his face forward again and when his lips and mine touched, I dropped one hand to his crotch and barely touched his dick, which was already hard. I opened his belt and the top button, slid down the zipper, peeled back the fabric and let it slip over his hips.

The pants dropped to the floor and he stepped out of them. His dick sprung to flagpole position and he shuddered. He was covered in goose flesh. I slipped one hand behind him, to his upper thigh, and stroked the front of his body with the other. When I got near his crotch, I slipped past his dick and drew my fingertips under his tightening balls. Then I grabbed his balls and pushed my mouth onto his mouth at the same time.

Now, not everyone knows how to kiss. And not every mouth is made for contact. José was born oral. His hot, wet lips nearly melted away and we went at each other's mouths with our mouths until all the flesh was indistinguishable and we seemed more like kiss than kissing.

The kissing got him going and he started pulling at my clothes. I helped him all I could, because I could not think of anything I wanted more right then than to be naked and inside him.

As soon as I was as naked as he was, he dropped to his knees and took my cock into his mouth up to the hilt. God bless the gay man's gag-free throat, I thought as I started to rock my hips into a righteous face fuck. He was working me up so fast that I had to pull away before I shot in his mouth. No way I was leaving here without my dick up his ass, and I wanted that particular ejaculation first.

He was totally amenable as I maneuvered him onto his back. He reached across his bed to the windowsill without looking and got a condom in his hand, opened it with his teeth in a single gesture, and started working it onto my dick. I worked his ass with my fingers a while before slipping my dick into him. I pumped hard and fast, but not long. He was pulling on his own dick with a two-handed grip I'd only seen once before. I wondered if he knew my friend Rob.

"I'm gonna shoot," he said, and he started before he was even finished. I pulled out of him and the rubber nearly simultaneously and shot my first beautiful load of the day onto his face and shoulder and the wall behind him and onto the foothills of his mountainous midriff.

"Oh . . . My . . . God . . . !" he shouted. "You fucking shoot!"

It was the least I could do.

When I came out of the shower, José was sitting on his bed, naked of course. Behind him was his bedroom window and fire escape and the air shaft and my fire escape and my window and my bed, which was perfectly visible from here. The desk on the side of the room opposite the bed was even visible. I wondered if he could read what I was writing from here as well as I could read his body from there.

He had one leg crossed over the other, one foot almost in his lap, which reminded me of the lotus position, and he was leaning against the headboard.

"I'm sorry," he said.

"What for?" I asked.

"I wasn't very good," he said.

"You were fabulous," I said, but the truth is, I was disappointed, and wondered if he was picking up on the unspoken. It *had* been much hotter in my mind than it was in fact, despite the obvious pleasure every cell in my body had taken in the encounter: I was as depleted after a single ejaculation as I've ever been. It was like numbers two and three had pushed up their schedule to rendezvous with the early bird for a serious worm hunt.

"Something was missing," he said, rolling his head toward his window, toward my window, then quickly back. "I know sex, and I know we've got more in us."

"You have sex a lot," I said, sitting next to him on the bed.

"Do I?" he asked. "What's a lot?"

"Well, most days and sometimes more than once a day, sometimes with more than one partner."

"Well, it won't last forever," he said. "I know that. I think it's my duty to my body to use it for sex when it's still in great sexual shape, you know? I mean, it's not the only thing I do. And I'll do other things later when people stop wanting my body. I'll develop my mind. I'll join a monastery or study Buddhism."

He dropped his head to his chest like a little boy who has done something wrong.

"You're really good at sex," I said. "Really open. Undefended. It's unusual. It's . . . wonderful."

"I hope we can do it again," he said.

"Can and will," I said. "I want to." It was no lie.

"So what was wrong with it?" Lawrence was asking.

"Well, nothing was *wrong* with it," I was answering. "I mean, it was better than most of the sex I've had in my life. And he is absolutely the most beautiful man I've ever fucked – ever. But it did not rise to my expectations."

"But he wants to get together again."

"Oh, yeah. We actually went out for coffee after and had a long talk. He's not stupid. He's got a lot of ambitions for his life and career. He wants to get out of the sex business after he makes a bundle from his booty. He's actually a great conversationalist. I mean, he doesn't wax eloquent about the Jacobean Shakespeare, but he doesn't go on and on about himself, either. He's informed, interested. And there is definitely more there than meets the eye, even though what meets the eye is more than enough."

"The first time is never the best," Lawrence said with his ordinary extraordinary insight and the kind of intelligence even the Ivy League couldn't ruin.

"He's dancing at the Gaiety this week," I said.

"*Yeeww*," Lawrence responded acidly, seeming to forget once again that he was non-judgmental in all things sexual.

"Is he fucking the clients behind the movie screen, too?" he asked.

"Lawrence," I said, with mock impatience, "you can't actually have sex with the dancers *at* the Gaiety any more. You have to take them to a hotel."

"Oh," said Lawrence, with that plaintive note in his voice that signals his conviction he was born too late for all the fun stuff. "Are you going?"

"He wants me to."

"Well, then go."

"Oh, I don't know. I've sort of given up the Gaiety. It just seems depressing and desperate lately."

"Since you can't have sex with the dancers on the premises. You never were any good at postponed gratification."

Did I mention I had a huge crush on Lawrence when we met and ruined any chance for us making a go of life together by pushing too hard when he said he was ambivalent?

"Thanks for sharing," I said, "but I already have one therapist, *capisce?*"

He capisced.

"But it was fun back there behind the movie screen," I continued, "getting it on with some fantasy stud while a bunch of other couples were doing the same thing all around you, and the dancers were kind of working up their hard-ons and strutting around naked. And all for forty bucks. Now it's just . . . I don't know . . . It's like shopping for lettuce. You go in, they dance around naked, you pick one, you make a deal, you go to a hotel, they do less than you want for the money, they do more than they want to for their heterosexual self-image. Yaddah yaddah yaddah. I don't know. Maybe."

Even these days, as millennium approaches, the Gaiety Burlesk is a zoo on Friday and Saturday night, when they've got a dozen or more dancers carrying on all night long. The place is packed, humid with lust and cash, and you have to assert yourself to get what you want.

Tuesday afternoon, on the other hand – and just for an

example – is an altogether different story. There are six dancers usually. They dance. There's a scene from a porn movie. Another dancer comes out. In between they sit in the smoking lounge hoping to snag a john from the five or six geriatric tourists in the place. But Tuesday afternoon is when I had off that week, so that's when I climbed the stairs under the new canvas awning on Forth-sixth Street. *Titanic* was playing at the theater next door. The phrase "going down" kept repeating itself in my mind. And the word "disaster".

I paid my money to a young man sitting in a booth behind glass and entered a familiar dark world full of rock music.

There was a very well-put-together Asian dancer on the runway, gyrating his hips and pointing his hard-on off the stage and into the house. I counted four men in the audience. There is a no-sex policy here, thanks to an asshole named Rudy Giuliani, who managed to get himself elected mayor of New York – twice – but at least two of the old geezers were jerking off, which was kind of comforting.

I went into the lounge. A couple of men were sitting there smoking, watching one of the dancers at the ancient video game by the stage door, on which a prominent sign hung that said: PRIVATE – NO PATRONS PAST THIS POINT.

The door swung open, and José appeared, wearing sweat pants, Keds, and a sweatshirt with the sleeves ripped off. It was love at first sight all over again.

"Hi," he said, and gave me a kiss.

The two smoking elders started drooling.

"Come on," he said and led me to the forbidden door.

"You won't get in trouble, will you?" I asked.

"Nah, the old dykes aren't here today," he replied, meaning the gypsy sisters who ran the place and usually presided over the ticket booth like gorgons guarding the Golden Fleece.

Backstage was pretty much the way I remembered it. There was a bleached blond sitting on a bench in the little locker room trying to get it up with baby oil and a man-woman fuck rag.

José took my hand and walked up a couple of steps. We crossed behind the screen and down the steps on the other side. When we were alone in the little back area where I had shelled out the requisite tariff more than once, he turned to me, lifted his sweatshirt over his head and dropped his sweat pants and pushed his perfect naked body up against me. He started to get hard immediately, his stiffening dick working its way between my legs.

He planted a huge kiss on my mouth but pulled off suddenly.

"Shit," he said. "That's my music. I have to go on. Go out front and watch me," he said. "Sit right in front of the runway. I'll meet you out there when I'm done."

The blond grunted at me huffily as I left. I guessed he was about thirty. He looked fifty.

By the time I got to my appointed (and thankfully un-contested) seat at the foot of the runway, José was already on stage with his shirt and sneakers off.

I sat down and he proceeded to gyrate rhythmically, dancing only for me, stroking his dick through his sweat pants, then pulling open the waist and putting his hands inside.

He twirled around and showed his butt to his audience of one, slipping the pants down off his ass cheeks and flexing his gorgeous gluteus maximus muscles. He bent over far enough, spreading the cheeks with his splayed fingers, to give me a unobstructed, spotlighted view of his happily hospitable hidey-hole in its nest of sweat-sleeked hair.

Then he stripped the sweat pants off and turned around. He'd already worked himself into a beautiful boner and he dropped himself to his knees at the end of the runway, pulling on his dick and pumping his hips directly at my face. He was smiling and licking his lips and giving me the hypnotic limpid eye all at the same time while sweat started dripping out his pores and down over the muscles of his belly.

I was as hard in my jeans as I ever get in my jeans, and I

was rubbing my sweaty palms on my thighs when the music ended and the lights went down to the sound of two or three entranced old-timers applauding limply.

I was still sitting there when the movie started up again and José came into the house wiping the sweat off his trunk with his sweatshirt. He was ignoring the man trailing him and gave me a gesture to follow him.

"Sit with me a while," he said, and led me to the back row of the theater, where three seats sat in virtual darkness between the projection booth on one side and the corridor wall on the other.

We sat down. I put my arm around the back of his chair and he put his hand on my thigh. I was still hard, which he found out almost instantly.

"Very nice," he said. "Did you like it?"

"You were very, very hot," I said, which was the God's honest truth.

"You're pretty hot, too," he said, still stroking my throbbing dick. I was starting to breathe heavy.

"I'm in this movie," he said suddenly.

"Really?" I said.

"Oh, yeah. The evil dykes always try to show the movies of the guest dancers," he said. "I'm in the next scene."

I thought I couldn't get harder, but I certainly wasn't getting softer.

He leaned over to kiss me, deep, the way we both like it.

That's when the scene started on the screen.

A behemoth of buff beef was lounging beside a pool with a hard on the size of a baseball bat.

"We made it in L.A.," José said, which I took to mean the movie.

José was playing the pool boy. He was wearing tiny cutoffs and was rubbing his crotch salaciously while watching the satisfied homeowner fondle his most prized possession.

Their eyes met. José turned and looked me right in my eyes. He was fondling his own crotch as well as mine.

Up on screen he was approaching his employer, who was

slathered in oil from head to foot and was glistening in the southern California sun. He spread his legs, putting one foot on the patio stones on each side of the lounge chair he was sprawled on. José slipped off his shorts on the screen and then slipped his sweat pants down to his ankles in the back row of the Gaiety beside me.

"Here?" I said kind of panicked, my heart beating with fear and anticipation at the same time.

"Nobody will watch us," he said, but I wasn't so sure. I also didn't care.

Movie José was sucking the daddy's dick. Real-life José was on his knees between my legs, pulling my easily opened jeans down off my hips. He had my willing dick in his naturally lubricated mouth right on down to the throat. Up and down he rode in the dark as his image on the flickering screen did likewise.

"God," I whispered.

"No," he said, stopping his mondo suck job long enough to grin, "it's just me."

"Same thing," I said and he went back to work.

Meanwhile, the brutish brunet had turned his water boy around and was massaging his butt cheeks, which José seemed to know without ever looking at the screen. Because, when he turned around, he stood up, leaned his hands on the back of the seat in front of us, and tilted his asshole in my direction. Bluto was playing with starlet José's pretty pucker, and I saw no reason not to join him. I spit on my thumb and started making little concentric circles around his dark asshole, pushing in at the same time.

José was groaning in stereo now, and so were his screen companion and I. I took my cue from José's co-star and put my tongue to his asshole, which was twitching like a sea creature. I was sucking and probing that friendly orifice as greedily as my celluloid counterpart and way more into it than I had ever been before when one of the other members of the audience managed to find his way back to our corner.

"Could you leave us alone?" I hissed at him when I saw him standing there with his hand in his pants.

"It's okay," José said, but pushed the man's hand away when he reached out to touch him.

Up on screen an adorable young slip of a FedEx driver was standing behind an oleander bush watching a gigantic dark-haired hulk poking his dick at the asshole of a breathtaking Latino with a KEEP ON TRUCKIN' tattoo on one inflated bicep.

"I don't have a rubber," I said, beginning to get into it, but José had thought of that, too. Bending over (and backing his sweat and spit drenched ass crack against my raging cock) he pulled one out of sweat pants and handed it to me with a small vial of lube. I cracked the lube open and spread it right onto my target, pushing it inside him with the fingers of my right hand while working the fingers of my left up the knots of his spine while José held his cheeks apart.

When the host of the impromptu pool party started pushing at José's asshole with his safety-sheathed bat, I rolled that condom onto my dick and slid it into as welcoming an asshole as I've ever slipped into. Dark-haired actor-man and I pumped in and out of José. Up on the stage, a thousand Mylar icicles that formed a kind of curtain were reflecting the merciless filmed sunlight of Los Angeles. The FedEx guy had his dick out and at full mast by now, and so did the guy who was watching us at the back of the theater. He made a grab for José's dick, and my neighborly neighbor pushed his hand away.

"*No touching,*" he said insistently to our silent witness, yanking on his own dick with one hand and pulling a nipple nearly off his chest with the other since I had both of my hands on his hips pulling him forcefully onto my dick over and over again. I was Vlad the Impaler and he was a unfortunate prisoner of war.

Up on the screen, the big bad dark guy pulled out of José and let his come fly.

"You call that coming?" I said out loud, and – in a totally

characteristic spasm of competitiveness – I whipped out my dick and put a thumb back in its place, ripped off the rubber, and started jerking to the finish line while my rival's meager come was shown in slo-mo a half dozen times.

The FedEx man was splashing his joy juice all over his parcel and so was our voyeuristic friend, who was dribbling his own love liquor and making a last grab at José's egg-plant colored dick.

"Would you please give us some privacy?" I said, and José turned around to face me, his dick stretched to the breaking point.

We were slamming our dick-filled fists at our bellies and started to let fly at the same time.

"Oh my GOD!" I growled back into my throat, not wanting to make a spectacle of myself, and shot clear over José's shoulder and onto the gray presence in the corner.

"Go, baby, go," José was shouting out loud, drawing the attention of every other dancer and client in the place. And because I am an agreeable fuck, I did. I shot more than I ever had before. It was cascading off José's drum-tight torso, and I still kept coming, and then José started to come, and a couple of other gents started circling around and José just started screaming "Oh . . . oh . . . oh . . ." with each spurt of hot heavy syrup, and the circle of interested observers started tightening and José was nearly convulsive, practically shouting "Give . . . Us . . . Some . . . Privacy . . . Please!"

But I was not at all sure he meant it.

The other men – realizing, after all, that all was, indeed, over – started to disperse. José and I wiped ourselves off with his sweatshirt, pulled up our respective clothing back into its recommended configuration for normal use, and cuddled back into our seats.

"Now that," said José, "is what I call sex. A hundred percent."

"Absolutely," I agreed, although just before the film was interrupted for the next dancer, José, his boss, and the grateful FedEx man were swimming around in the pool, paddling around into what would doubtlessly be a clumsy three-way. José was licking my neck, totally satisfied, apparently. I felt as if a light switch had gone on as an idea began to hatch in the incubator of my post-coital mind. I'd have to call Lawrence and see if he was game.

I was on my knees on Lawrence's lovely king-sized bed, my dick buried to the short hairs in his tight, compact ass. He was kneeling, too, his mouth full of José's lollipop. José was on his knees facing me across the small expanse of Lawrence's back. José was working my left nipple with his right hand; I was giving him a bit of loving tit torture with my own. Perhaps because we'd completed the sacred circle, we'd managed to get a lovely rhythm going. The sexual energy was flowing to every inner nook and outer cranny of my body. My ears were red, my asshole clasping and unclasping its own heat as I clenched my ass and leg and stomach muscles with every thrust.

José had just taken my thumb in his mouth when all of us heard a baritone voice somewhere outdoors below us yell *"Lights!"* – and a million candles' worth of floodlights flicked on outside the window, which was conveniently located next to the rumpled bed. I could see a light spring rain falling in the light and behind the clouds the Empire State Building lit up red and green for Cinco de Mayo.

"Camera," the same voice shouted, as José looked at me with grateful glee spreading all over his face.

"And *action!*"

Lawrence, who was used to the film crew camped outside his building, never missed a beat; José arched his back in total ecstasy, pumping a bit harder into Lawrence's throat; and I kept up my end of the bargain, although I admit I was biting down on my lower lip to keep from breaking out into a roar of laughter. And I did take a peek at our images, flickering on the walls of the apartment like the antics of Javanese shadow puppets. And I did think I caught the faraway sound of a chorus of male voices hooting and woofing and otherwise cheering us on to the finish line as I felt the lava starting to erupt from my buried volcano and a series of earsplitting explosions went off all around us.

The Best Sex Between Them

Andy Quan

They know that they shouldn't. But the things that we know don't always help us.

"Would this be all right?" Geoffrey looks at Max searchingly.

"It's up to you." Max looks neither happy nor sad.

"Why is it always up to me?"

They step towards each other, not without hesitation, and kiss.

Sex had never been great between Geoffrey and Max. Their physical attraction to each other had been but it didn't seem to translate to the right chemistry. Geoffrey may have been in his forties but his body was boyish and thin with soft skin and barely a hair on his torso. For Max, it was a perfect combination of the sex appeal of wisdom and a fantasy of a young university student.

Max, on the other hand, was thick: solid neck and shoulders, a jutting chest covered with salt and pepper hair, and barrel-shaped thighs.

"You make my throat dry," Geoffrey told Max the first time they had sex. He was often given over to extravagant statements; he was an ad man who wanted to write novels.

The words didn't make sense to Max but the context did. Kissing was good. In fact, it was excellent: the shape of their mouths a perfect match; they would take turns naturally, licking the outside gums of the other, sucking on the other's tongue, nibbling the other's bottom lip. They lost themselves in that motion.

But the first weeks, unusually, Max couldn't come. He couldn't explain why, but he liked Geoffrey so much that it made him nervous. It short-circuited the simple order of being aroused, sexual play, and a burst of semen from the tip of one's cock.

"You don't mind, do you?" asked Max and Geoffrey admitted that if this is the way sex was going to be between them that it might be a problem.

"I like some sort of equality. It's not just about me wanting you to come. It's that I think you'll be more satisfied if you've had an orgasm too."

"But I don't mind."

Max was telling the truth but Geoffrey was unconvinced.

Geoffrey pulls up Max's rugby shirt and balances it up onto the shelf of Max's chest while he takes a great mouthful of the body that is revealed. He licks and softly bites Max's pectoral muscles, these broad round shapes. If they were vessels, they would be made of metal, thick-walled, and unable to be easily lifted when filled with water. A great chest has always been an obsession of Geoffrey's. Will he ever again find one as beautiful as this: one you can grab onto, that makes you think of strength, and makes your cock stand out sharp as a salute? They stay like that for a time before Max stretches up to lift off his shirt completely, then reaches down and eases Geoffrey out of his. It's already unbuttoned so Max eases Geoffrey's arms back, pushes gently at the fabric of the business shirt, and it wrinkles down onto the floor, Geoffrey's mouth never having lost contact with Max's chest.

The problem of orgasm (or lack of one) didn't last but instead changed into something else. It was Geoffrey this time, and at first he thought it was mental. It was the first time that his combination of antiretroviral therapy was failing and though his doctor advised him not to overworry, he found it an

impossible state, like failing to clear your mind when med-
itating because you are thinking the whole time about clearing your mind. So Geoffrey thought it was stress that was
causing a pronounced lack of sexual drive. But after weeks,
when the doctor assured him that the new medication regi-
ment was working, he wondered if the dip in his libido could
be due to his new meds.

He knew that Max was frustrated and he knew that only
months into a new relationship was not a good time to draw
away from sex. But he couldn't seem to do anything about it.
He and Max would masturbate together; they would kiss too.
But the level and intensity of love-making was underwhelm-
ing.

When they came back – desire, energy – the problems were
resolved only for a time. It was like a singer who didn't have
time to warm his vocal cords properly before a performance.
He sings his way through stumblingly but the orchestra plays
its final notes before he can find his way. They were never in
synch.

"Have you talked about it?"

Geoffrey was seeing a counsellor. He'd never done it
before but he'd worried about things not working with
Max. He didn't want to quit therapy unless he knew he'd
put in a good effort. He was too old to give up too easily and a
relationship that had only lasted a year seemed trivial. Plus he
couldn't be certain that the problem wasn't something deep-
seated and invisible to him but an issue that came from him
rather than being mutual.

"Well, what would you like him to do? Really. Is there
some situation that you can describe, some way that you
would like him to be when you're having sex?"

He liked this counsellor. He liked the questions which
poked and prodded and made him think and talk or come to
sudden revelations like this one:

"I'd like him to take charge. I'd like him to throw me onto
the bed and make love to me instead of me making love to
him." Geoffrey thought about big, strong Max: the odd

juxtaposition of his size, and his gentle disposition. Was he hoping for something that Max just couldn't give?

Max has closed his eyes. Geoffrey is still working on his chest. It's a long foreplay before they'll get to crotch level. Geoffrey treats it as a separate sexual act, as if sexual orientations were divided into a much wider spectrum than homo, hetero and bi and he's discovered that there are only certain men with chests he can make love to. It helps when they are broad (just like it helps, frankly, to have a large penis) and it also depends on the shape and size of the nipples. Small and flat doesn't really work; the mouth glides over them, there's nothing to bite, there's little to differentiate them from the surrounding skin. What works is jutting. What works is fleshy. Of course, Geoffrey has also met men who have the perfect chests for worship but aren't interesting in participating, being focused on other body parts, other motions, or being the active partner. With Max, Geoffrey's pretty much found nirvana. He can make patterns of his soft bite marks on Max's chest, the hairs of the chest brushing over Geoffrey's lips like a comb. He can suckle for long minutes the round coins of flesh with small fingertips pointing out of them, protrusions just large enough to nibble, to inhale. He licks and nips at them until the whole area of these parts of Max's chest have turned the pink of roses.

It's a blow job of a different type but has a similar effect on Max, a direct pleasure circuit between what is happening on the surface of his pectoral muscles and the tip of his penis, out of which pre-come is forming, enough to coat its head but not enough to actually form a drop that falls onto the floor. If Max could ask for more, he'd ask to be bitten harder, a real clamp-down. But Geoffrey seems too afraid to do it. He backs off just when things are getting good. Still, Max's cock is hard with blood. He's responding to pleasure.

Geoffrey can feel this pleasure in the grip of his hand and is excited by it. The thought comes to him (which he loses, purposefully, moments later) that this may be the most magni-

ficent chest that he's ever made love to and that he may never be able to do it again.

Sex was easy, Geoffrey told himself, though the truth was that it was plentiful, but not simple. Still, it could be found in saunas and sex clubs, in cruising grounds, in the locker rooms of swimming pools and gymnasiums. But someone to fall asleep with, someone to lie beside, and someone whose arms in which you can awake – how often do you find that? Geoffrey thinks that he's found quite a lot of sex in his forty-some years. But partners have been few. Trade-offs, he thinks. Everything is a trade-off.

In this case, the items are sleeping together and having good sex. If he was challenged on this, he would have to back down. They did have sex. They sometimes had good sex. Sex and sleeping together were not opposite things. In fact, they were quite complementary. So, he would have been forced to clarify: in this relationship, what was important to him was waking up in Max's arms, the intimacy of shared sleep, falling asleep to his partner's breathing. Really hot fucking wasn't something that could be expected or demanded. Maybe, in the end, it wasn't even that important. At least that's what he told himself.

The pre-come is flowing for both of them now, Max more than Geoffrey. They've rimmed each other, then Geoffrey has inserted one, then two fingers into Max and is now feeling the smooth walls of the rectum while his other hand plays with the hair on Max's belly.

They'll return to habits soon. For Geoffrey, it will be to lie on his back, with Max kneeling over him with his balls positioned over Geoffrey's mouth. Geoffrey will suck and lick and look up at Max's great form: the most beautiful view of a man, Geoffrey thinks. If he's not careful, Geoffrey will come right then, Max's hand reaching back to jerk him off. But he'll be able to restrain himself enough to slide his body and head down, one last suck on Max's balls, a lick of his arsehole. Then, he'll flip himself

*around and get up, push Max down onto his hands and knees and
fuck him slowly while reaching around and massaging his belly,
especially between his belly button and crotch, the way that Max
likes and requested the first time they fucked.*

*They will feel delicious and comfortable that they know each
other's bodies, customs, and fantasies so well.*

It was Max who was frustrated with the sex. But it was
Geoffrey who decided to end the relationship.

"Are you happy with this?" he'd asked angrily one morning. They'd snarked at each other for days.

"No, I'm not," replied Max.

"Then you'd better figure out what you want out of this."

But that was the problem. Max didn't know. He was in
love with Geoffrey – frustrating, crazy-making, annoying
Geoffrey – and that was enough. He didn't demand the
future. He didn't want something out of it. The present
was enough to deal with with its imperfections and lop-
sidedness.

Though Geoffrey didn't exactly know what he wanted
either, he knew from the weight felt across his shoulders, that
he didn't want this.

*Geoffrey is an awkward bottom, sometimes finding it hard to relax,
unable to be penetrated if a cock is too thick or too long. So he has
always marveled at how open Max is, how relaxed and flexible his
anus is. Not only that but his flexibility in general. Such a big man
but he can lift his knees up so they touch his shoulders and then even
stretch his legs out nearly straight from there.*

*The condoms are out. A wrapper falls away easily. Lubricant
is pumped onto a palm and then smeared onto latex, and onto
skin. Geoffrey enters Max easily in one plain motion, simpler
than speech, quicker than argument. The slight friction between
their body parts creates heat like swallowing a mouthful of
whiskey.*

*He fucks him for a while in Max's favourite position, kneeled
over with Geoffrey's hand on his belly. But this time, they're*

really going to make it last, they'll fuck as long as they can, as hard as they can – in no particular order:

lying on bed from the side, one of Max's legs lifted and resting on Geoffrey's shoulder;

standing, Max's right hand balancing against the corner of a wardrobe for balance, Geoffrey behind him, his hands on each side of Max's shoulders, thrusting;

Geoffrey lying on his back, Max on top facing him, leaning down occasionally to kiss.

Like a concerto that returns to the theme of its opening bars, they return to their first tableau: the same action and postures. Max squeezes all of the muscles inside of him, like holding in laughter. He feels his sphincter and anus constrict around Geoffrey's cock. Geoffrey gasps and moans at the same time.

It's as good as it's ever been. Why couldn't sex have been as unencumbered when they were together? Geoffrey is free of a dozen worries and a dozen insecurities – among them: Do we always have to do it the same way? Do I always have to be the top? Am I enjoying this? Worst of all but perhaps hidden, even to Geoffrey himself: if it's good, really good, does it mean that we should be together forever?

Max feels the same liberty and joy. Gone is the worry of whether Geoffrey loves him as much as he loves Geoffrey. Of whether Max is attractive enough. Or whether he is truly the ideal lover that Geoffrey wanted. He's happy, so very much so, to fall into the motion of truly great sex; that Geoffrey is not holding back; that there is force in these thin but strong arms, grabbing him and making him into an object of pleasure.

They shouldn't really be doing this in any case, this forbidden act of sleeping with one's ex, of making the messy messier, of complicating matters considerably and doing what all your friends say you shouldn't do. Breaking taboos can cause even more excitement. Not that they'll do it again – in different ways, they both know that. It makes this last time all the more sweet.

It was just a visit to pick up the last of his possessions but Geoffrey senses that he won't return. He doesn't feel sad but there's an empty, unreplied feeling, like wandering into the entranceway of a run-down old home, and calling out to see if anyone is there.

With some difficulty, he opens the front door to leave Max's apartment building. His hands are each carrying a few large plastic bags, and on top of this he's balancing a small box of miscellanea. He manages to put it all into his car then frets – *there he goes again* – turning circles in his mind:

Will what they did make it harder to be . . . friends? Is that what they'd be? Cordial ex-boyfriends? In contact?

Yes, he decides, it will make things more difficult. But – his heart beating fast and at an erratic pace – it was worth it. Well worth it.

Max doesn't think as much, or at least, he pretends not to. There are things that he's putting out of his mind already: the lead-up, the background story, the dialogue. It won't happen right away but eventually he'll be left with just memories of the physical act and the windstorm of emotions that accompanied it. Now, he remembers Geoffrey's head, the dead weight of it, on his right side on top of where his chest and stomach meet, resting on his torso after this last sex, this best sex they've ever had. He knows that it's ridiculous but honestly it feels like there's still an indentation there, as if in a down pillow after a deep, motionless sleep. It will take time to fill in again, for his body to regain form.

Independence

Lawrence Schimel

It was that subtle mysterious moment when cuddling became foreplay. Javi tilted his head from where he nestled into Carles' shoulder as they watched TV on the couch, and looked up at Carles. And then they were kissing, their hands flying to each other's face, thigh, shoulder, neck. After-dinner drowsiness was forgotten. CRONICAS MARCIANAS was forgotten, though Xavier Serdà kept talking and making jokes for all those many viewers across Spain who were not currently distracted. But in Carles' apartment, only the two of them existed, and their mutual passion and desire for one another.

Carles released Javi's mouth only long enough to lift Javi's shirt over his head, then began kissing him again, tongue seeking tongue while Javi's arms were still stretched above him, caught in the fabric. One hand fell free, and sank to cup Carles' cheek and pull him forward, as if they might somehow become joined more closely through sheer force of will. The other hand came free, and Carles let the shirt drop behind him.

There was a clank, as a spoon hit the floor, knocked over by the falling shirt.

The lovers paused, laughed, looked at what had happened. The remains of the dinner Carles had cooked lay on the table, waiting to be cleared away and washed up. A bowl from which they'd eaten ice cream had been tipped over, and Javi reached out to right it, but that was all. Carles stood and slid the table back from the couch, then undid the drawstring on his shorts and let them fall to the floor. Summer clothes were so convenient that way. He removed his shirt and stepped free of his clothes, but before he could rejoin Javi on the couch his lover had grabbed hold of either hip and began to lick from Carles' navel out toward his flank. Javi threw one arm about Carles' back, squeezing him gently, while the other hand forced Carles' legs apart and lightly feathered its way up and down his inner thighs. Carles groaned.

What was it, he wondered, that made something so simple feel so good just because Javi was the person doing it? When had he ever had so many nerve endings in his belly, just where Javi's tongue was moving? How had they all lain dormant for so many years, until just this moment? What had he done to deserve to be so lucky?

Carles bent, pressing his lips to Javi's, slowly sinking down until they were both again seated on the couch. He clawed at Javi's pants, wanting them off, rubbing Javi's cock through the fabric while he waited for his lover to unzip them, to be naked as he was, to be ready and available. Javi's body was wonderfully familiar to Carles, but it had never become comfortable; simply to touch it, to hold him, still sent a thrill through Carles. No matter how much he worried about his lover's other affairs, when they were together the chemistry always overrode all his concerns. Carles hoped this would never change, even though he didn't understand it. He wanted always to find Javi so exciting, so alluring, so desirable. Which wasn't difficult to imagine; he couldn't contemplate ever failing to find Javi sexy.

Because they were so familiar with each other and each other's bodies, there was neither order nor score keeping to their lovemaking. That was one of the wonderful things about an ongoing relationship. It wasn't like a new encounter, where if he sucks your cock there's a social obligation to return the favor. There wasn't that feeling that he was doing you a favor. It was simply pleasure. And if Javi remained dressed, either partly or in full, while giving Carles pleasure, there was no rush to finish him off, for his turn to follow. It would come when it came, or not, and that was all fine. They could go from foreplay to sex and back again, doing only what they liked and wanted to do just then. So often, Carles thought, when you picked up someone new, it felt like you were following a script or trying to complete a scavenger hunt, having to pass through certain acts in a certain order before allowing yourself to claim the goal of orgasm.

Javi still hadn't removed his shorts. He pushed Carles back and began to suck his cock, no longer the coy teasing licks of Carles' abdomen a few moments earlier. So much of sex was anticipation, teasing, offering, but holding back. But that was only one side of sex. There was also the more animal urgency, the grunting, thrusting, physical lust of sex. Of losing oneself so completely in another person that the two bodies became one.

It had been difficult for Carles to learn how to accept pleasure. To just enjoy it, without offering anything back, which was his stronger instinct. To accept that Javi might be enjoying the act of giving him pleasure more than anything Carles could do to him just then.

He still struggled with himself over this issue. Especially with Javi. With other men, it was easier to accept if they wanted to do all the work, as it were, for a while. But with Javi he wanted always to show his devotion, to be the one giving pleasure, making his lover feel special.

Carles stood and lifted Javi with him, unzipping Javi's shorts and pulling him into the bedroom. They lay down on the bed and reached for each other. Carles rolled atop of Javi, interlocking their legs as he kissed his lover's neck and shoulders. Soon would come that decisive moment, when one or the other of them would assume a role, even if later they flipped. It was one of the aspects of gay sex that always fascinated Carles, the fluidity of dominance and submission between two essentially equal entities, as opposed to hetero-sexual intercourse where the man would always wind up topping the woman, from biological necessity. With two men, the dynamic was always changing, even if one (or both) partners had a strong preference for one position or the other. But everything was possible.

Javi held Carles' cock and squeezed it tightly. "I want you to fuck me," he said.

There were condoms and lube in the nightstand. Carles reached for the drawer, grabbed a foil packet, tore it open. But before he put it on Carles reached for Javi, dragging him forward so that Javi's crotch was positioned by his head. He took Javi's cock into his mouth and only then, sucking gently, did he begin to unfold the condom onto his own dick. Without releasing Javi's cock, Carles then squirted a dollop of lube into his hand and began to work it into Javi's ass, spreading it over his fingers and then slowly, one by one, poking them up inside Javi, loosening him up. Javi's body always responded instantly; Carles, on the other hand, often needed more time to relax, to get used to the width of one finger, then two, working upward before he was ready for someone's cock. As a result, he liked to go slow, giving his partner time if it was needed. For one thing, it gave Carles time to think about, to get ready for, what was to come.

Javi pulled back, straddling Carles' chest and then sliding backward, toward Carles' cock. And in a moment they were joined, Carles thrusting upward as Javi sank back onto him. They both paused, as if the shock of connection had overwhelmed their senses, then Carles began to grind his hips slowly, gyrating. Sometimes Carles would lie utterly still as Javi lifted himself up and then down along his shaft, sometimes it was Javi who remained frozen mid-squat as Carles pushed his hips upward again and again. Sometimes one or the other asked for a pause, to catch their breath, to not come too quickly. But soon they'd start to move again, building up to that inexorable fall into bliss.

"I'm going to come," Javi said, as he drew too near to the precipice of orgasm. Carles grabbed Javi's cock and began to tug on it as he thrust up inside his lover. Suddenly, Javi's cock convulsed in Carles' grasp, shooting out a jet of white semen across Carles' chest. Its hot wetness, falling against his skin in spurts, sent Carles into orgasm as well, and he cried out as his own come shot into the condom's plastic reservoir tip.

They lay entwined in a sweaty heap, Carles' cock still lodged inside Javi. He began to soften, but still stayed more than half-hard. He worried that he should pull out, and take off the condom properly, wipe himself off. But he didn't want to move. His cock was so sensitive, even Javi's gentle breathing sent shivers through him, as their bodies shifted slightly.

Carles smiled with delight, and kissed Javi desperately, as if he were afraid that it was all a dream that Javi was his boyfriend and he would soon wake up. Javi returned the kiss, and suddenly their bodies broke apart. They lay together, caressing one another's bodies and kissing.

At last, Javi pushed himself off the bed and stood up. "Do you want to shower with me? I promised I'd meet JuanMa and Victor by 2:30."

"You're going out?" Carles asked. He tried not to feel hurt. But he couldn't help asking himself, why wasn't he enough for Javi? What was Javi looking for, that he wasn't satisfied with what they'd just shared, the way Carles was?

Carles stayed in bed while Javi showered and got ready to go out with his friends. They would go drinking, they would take drugs of various sorts, they would go dancing. Would Javi have sex with someone else tonight? Carles tried not to think about that, but after he'd brushed his teeth and climbed back into bed, he couldn't help returning to the subject, his mind refusing to stop worrying and let him sink into sleep.

Javi might wind up having sex with someone in the back room at a disco, high on ecstasy and alcohol and letting feelings take control. He might go back with some man to the guy's apartment and have sex there, maybe spending the night but probably not. But as upset as Carles might be by these possibilities, they didn't really mean anything, being simply actions of the moment than anything more serious.

But now that he had his own place, Javi could bring someone home with him. And if the man spent the night, they'd perhaps talk the morning after. As if it were the beginning of a relationship.

"I've never had a chance to be on my own," Javi had argued, when he told Carles that he was moving out from his family's home. "I don't want to just trade living with my parents for living with you. I need to see what it's like to have my own place."

Intellectually Carles understood, but he still felt hurt. On one level it felt like a rebuff, both of himself and their relationship. He had to keep reminding himself that Javi was nearly a decade younger than him, and wasn't necessarily ready for the same things that he was.

It was also difficult to be too hard on Javi when his reason for moving out were so altruistic: Javi's older sister Lola had returned home unexpectedly with her eighteen-month-old baby. She'd been unable to put up with her husband's abuse any longer, especially when in a drink-enhanced foul mood one night he'd actually raised a hand at their daughter because the baby wouldn't stop crying. She'd put herself between his fists and their child, and the following morning, when he was supposedly out looking for a job, she took little Brenda and a suitcase full of clothes, and took the bus back to Madrid. Her parents had, of course, made room for her, but it was cramped with all of them living there; it simply wasn't set up to accommodate so many people, the way the larger apartment they'd had when Lola and Javi were younger had been.

The evening following her return, Lola and Javi were sitting in Chez Pomme trying to figure out what she would do with her life now. Much as her mother would've preferred that her children stayed home to eat dinner, they couldn't really talk with their parents around. Lola had needed their comforting and acceptance, but she also needed a less judgmental point of view on how to rebuild her life. And she'd needed a break from constantly tending the baby. So their parents had agreed to watch Brenda, and the siblings had set aside their rivalry and sat down together over a meal like two adults – albeit young ones – trying to come up with a practical solution.

Javi offered to give Lola his room and look for an apartment, saying that it would be necessary for her to have their Mother there to take care of the baby, especially if Lola was thinking of working, which she'd have to do at some point.

One of the waitresses overheard them and mentioned that there was a room suddenly free in her apartment, giving Javi the telephone number of her roommate Igone in case he were interested in coming to see it. This was the kind of thing that always happened to Javi. He seemed to evoke that sort of response from people, strangers even, as if he were a lost puppy that needed protection. It was easy for them to fall under the spell of his good looks and easy charm. But more it was that situations seemed to resolve themselves for him without any apparent effort on Javi's part. He put his faith in the world, and the world, unexpectedly Carles thought, treated him with good faith in return. He was touched by a glamour. Sometimes Carles couldn't believe his own good fortune in being Javi's boyfriend. He was often shocked by his own jealousy of Javi, a sense of envy for his beauty and his manner and the way people responded to him, which tried to express itself by a desire for Carles to control his lover. Which was often hard for Carles to fight against.

It was a constant internal struggle: to be Javi's loving boyfriend but not try to possess him too much. Because Javi was one of those elusive beautiful creatures that would be smothered by a cage, be it emotional or physical. So Carles tried to give them as much space as possible in their relationship. They had an open relationship, sexually, even though Carles was horribly jealous of every man who Javi even spoke with. But as an ex-lover of his had explained once, when Carles was newly coming out himself, how could he deny someone he loved anything, especially pleasure? And for all the torment each new liaison evoked in Carles, his elation each time Javi returned to him was all the more intense.

Carles had his own little adventures and histories on the side, as well, sometimes out of desperation on nights when Javi was off with other men, sometimes out of a sense of moral determination to live a modern, plural lifestyle unconstricted by the antiquated heteronormative ideals of mainstream societies. Sometimes simply because the sex was convenient and appealing.

But he would give it all up for Javi, he knew. Without a moment's regret. If only Javi would make the same sacrifice for him. But Javi wouldn't even consent to live together. Not yet, at least . . . Carles hoped that eventually Javi would change. Once he'd had time to spread his wings and fly on his own for a bit.

When he thought about the future, Carles often liked to imagine his life like a page out of the IKEA catalogue: two handsome well-dressed men in a domestic ecstasy. They have nothing overt in the adverts to signal that they're gay – no pink triangles or rainbow flags – but you can feel the subtle sexual tension between them, the knowledge of each other's bodies. They're domestic without losing their masculine edge. That's what made the images so sexy for Carles.

Carles had gone with Javi to IKEA to help him select items to furnish his new place. Because Javi was moving into a flat where other people already lived, he was only furnishing a small part of an apartment – basically just his own rooms. But they wandered the entire store, to get a feel for possibilities and prices. To make sure there weren't any low-cost gems hidden further along the path, strategically placed so that one had already made a more expensive choice earlier on . . . And then they went back, and looked again at the items they'd made note of on the special sheets of paper that were so handily provided everywhere.

Shopping for furniture is different than any other kind of shopping. Furniture is so much about the future. Food is so temporal, even the canned stuff – technology has forestalled decay, but the products have their expiry dates clearly labeled. And clothing, too, has a lifespan; even something "classic" in style is not expected to last forever without wearing out. But one doesn't really think of using up one's furniture or outliving it, mostly one sheds it whenever one moves. Otherwise, it seems almost impossible to get rid of. Carles thought of the hideous red chair in his parents' home, that had belonged to his grandmother. All the little knick-knacks his parents had accumulated over the years and never pared back.

Fashion is about what's new, what's hot. It's a constant out with the old, in with the new cycle. And when it ran out of ideas, it had no shame about going back to whatever had been trendy a few decades ago, and calling it retro, and charging top prices for it.

In a way, it hurt Carles for them to go shopping together, as if it were their shared future they were shopping for, when it was actually Javi's independence they were setting up. Especially watching countless pairs of gay men of all types – gym bunnies and well-dressed pijos and pathetic dweebs and even the occasional leathermen – buy "family sized" comforters and mattresses and the like, while Javi wanted everything in "individual" sizes.

When it came time for Javi to want things in "family sizes", would Carles be the man he wanted to share those items with?

Suddenly Carles remembered the man on the motorcycle he saw Javi riding with the other day. The one who never took off his helmet. The one who, at the time, he'd felt certain was David Beckham, since he'd just been listening to Miguel Angel go on about a rumor he'd heard that David Beckham was having a gay affair.

It was one thing to gossip about whether or not a celebrity might be gay, but Carles hardly ever tried to imagine Beckham or anyone else actually engaged in the act of sex with another man. His fantasies usually involved memories of sex he had actually had, or imagining sex with his lover or men he'd already been involved with. Miguel Angel, on the other hand, was sure to have done so; Carles sometimes wondered if Miguel Angel could think about any man without imagining what he would be like in bed. He wondered, sometimes, if Miguel Angel had had these same thoughts about Carles himself. It seemed strange, given Miguel Angel's aggressive sexual appetite, that they hadn't ever wound up having sex together, but their friendship never seemed to take that particular turn. Maybe because of Manfred. Manfred wouldn't have been upset if they had sex, but because Manfred was always there, even if in the background, as Miguel Angel's boyfriend, Carles had never considered Miguel Angel as truly being available. Not in the sense that Carles needed. Because he couldn't easily separate sex from the possibility of something more, and Miguel Angel didn't offer anything more; anyone might get sex from him, but Manfred had all his affection.

Miguel Angel sometimes joked that Carles was the one man left in Madrid who he'd not had sex with, although that was perhaps debatable. One night, a few months after they'd met, he and Miguel Angel had wound up in a curious threesome at the Strong Center. There had, of course, been some sexual tension between them – was it ever possible for gay men to be friends without some tension? – but they'd never acted on it. In the back room, each had gone off in pursuit of his own pleasure, in separate areas. But they'd run into each other again, in the darkness, and were comparing experiences when a flash of light revealed a man standing nearby, with his cock in his hand. It was an impressive cock, and they each felt moved by it.

Miguel Angel immediately sat down and took the man's dick in his mouth. Carles, feeling awkward at watching his friend fellate this stranger, began to play with the man's nipples. He felt almost as if he couldn't just leave – not that Miguel Angel would notice or be upset – but they'd been in the middle of conversation and it just didn't seem . . . polite.

Besides, the man's cock truly was impressive.

The stranger began kissing Carles, and when Miguel Angel stood up and told the man he wanted to go into a cabina for the guy to fuck him, the stranger grabbed Carles' hand and pulled him along, too. Carles didn't really do much, mostly just encouraging the other two. At one point, Miguel Angel was rimming the other man, who in turn unzipped Carles' pants and began to suck his cock. But Carles didn't have any sexual contact directly with Miguel Angel, it was all via the other man.

Carles was pretty sure Miguel Angel didn't really consider him as a sexual possibility, not any longer. But he was equally certain that Miguel Angel did so for just about every other man he met, and this would hold especially true for any celebrity, even ones he only saw in photos.

But Carles lacked the practice of such extrapolation; when he fantasized, he usually remembered sex he'd already had, or sex he'd seen, whether as a voyeur in real life at a sauna or in two dimensions in videos and magazines.

Would Beckham be a top or a bottom? The rumors never mentioned that when they said someone or other was gay, which probably proved that they were just rumors; a gay man wouldn't leave out important details like that when he was gossiping about who – and what – he'd done.

Carles tried to picture Beckham having sex with his boyfriend, Beckham wrapping Javi in his broad embrace and kissing him, Javi responding. What would it be like? How would it be different from the sex he and Javi had just had? That was the question Carles always came back to: What did another man give Javi that he couldn't?

To his surprise, Carles found that his dick was painfully hard, even though he'd just come so recently. He began to stroke himself slowly, imagining Beckham's hand on Javi's cock.

A moment later he was coming again, short white spurts falling across his belly.

He felt guilty for a moment, as if his fantasy had been unfaithful to Javi. But that didn't make sense, since Javi had been part of the fantasy. The sex had been between Javi and Beckham, Carles had merely been watching. What did that mean? He was too tired to think about it. He leaned out of bed and kicked the light switch off.

Eyes closed, exhausted after two orgasms so close together, Carles let himself drift off, conjuring a vision of Javi's beautiful face to sweeten his dreams. "Javi," he whispered, and for a moment he wasn't sure if it was his own voice or Beckham's who'd uttered that name. And then sleep claimed him, and he no longer worried.

Unsent

Greg Herren

Dear Greg,
   I hope you don't mind I'm writing this letter. You said you didn't mind so I'm guessing you don't.
   I wanted to thank you for being such a nice guy . . . it's funny, I've been wanting to write this letter for a long time; I started writing you so many times and I just ended up throwing the letters away every time. I know you probably think I'm just a goof; a dumb kid who doesn't know what he wants or needs or anything, and that's true I guess. I don't know what I want to do with my life . . . if I live through this. I just wanted to fly planes, and now I am flying them . . . but this is different.
   I guess I was just naïve and stupid when I joined the Air Force. All I wanted to do was fly planes . . . it never occurred to me I'd be flying planes and killing people . . . pretty dumb, right?

He was just a boy.

He couldn't be more than fifteen, was my first thought when he walked into Lafitte's that Tuesday morning. There was no one in the bar besides me; it was twelve thirty. I was working the 5 a.m. till 1 shift, covering for Mike. This shift sucked. The only hope to make any kind of money was leftovers from the previous night when you start, and they're gone by nine . . . so for the last four hours of the shift it was just me and the cleaning women, and they were gone by eleven.

He stood for a few seconds in the doorway, hesitating. I looked up from wiping down the bar for the thousandth time in the last twenty minutes, and smiled to myself. I recognized the hesitation – an underage kid steeling his nerve to sit at the bar and ask for a drink. Well, kid, I said to myself, prepare to be carded.

He walked in and sat down on a barstool right in front of me. He was cute, still with a little babyfat in his pale freckled face. His hair was military buzzed, reddish-blonde, and his eyes gray. He was wearing a red sweater and a pair of blue jeans.

I put my rag away under the bar. "What can I do for you?" I asked.

He looked around the bar, not meeting my eyes. "A beer?"

"You got ID?"

He reached into his back pocket and pulled out a worn black wallet, pulling out a military ID which he slid across the bar to me. I picked it up. The picture was him, all right, looking maybe ten years old, innocent and young. The birthdate was August 12, 1968. Yeah, well, so I was wrong about his age. "What kind of beer? A draft?"

"Yeah." He nodded and smiled at me. His whole face lit up when he smiled, his full lips pulling back over slightly crooked, yellowed teeth. I got a plastic cup and filled it at the tap, my back to him. I placed it on a napkin. "Dollar fifty."

He handed me two ones, and I gave him his change. He left the quarters on the bar, which I slid into my hand and tossed into my tip bucket. "Not very busy, huh?" he said, looking down at the bar, not touching the beer.

I shrugged. "Nah, we're never busy – don't even know why we bother being open."

"Yeah." He toyed with his napkin. "Do you mind talking to me? I don't wanna be a bother."

I laughed and gestured to the empty bar. "Not like I got anything else to do."

He smiled again. "Good." He sipped the beer, looking down at the bar again.

"Where you from?" Standard New Orleans bartender opening – when in doubt, ask where they're from.

"Laurel." Mississippi – that explained the sweet accent.

"What's your name?" I held my hand out over the bar. "I'm Greg."

"Tommy." He shook my hand. His grip was strong, sure, even though the palm was moist.

"What brings you to town?"

"I'm flying out tomorrow morning." He looked down again. "Going back from leave."

Ah, the military. "What branch?" My stomach dropped a little bit. Saddam Hussein had invaded Kuwait, and the world stood on the brink of a war.

"Air Force."

"You fly jets?" I grinned at him, leaning on the bar.

He grinned shyly back at me. "Yeah."

"You going over there?"

He nodded, his smile fading. "Yeah."

I didn't know what to say. I just stood there, looking into his sad gray eyes. Finally, I said, "You'll be okay." It sounded lame to me.

"Thanks." He laughed. It was a sweet sound, boyish, the kind of laughter you heard in the locker room after a football game. "'Preciate that, man." He looked around the bar again. "I've walked by here so many times before but never had the nerve to come in." He shrugged. "And now, I figured, what the hell, right? I might die over there, so what could it hurt? And no one's here."

I think about dying all the time. All of us over here do, even though we don't talk about it. It's like the Grim reaper is always outside our tents, you know what I mean? So we play cards and watch some television and write letters and read books, trying to take our minds off what we are going to have to do . . . the risks we'll be taking. I write my mama, I write my sisters and my brothers, but there isn't anyone I can write to and be honest with, you know? I

*don't want my family to worry . . . and the only friends I
have are my squad, and we can't talk about any of the
things I want to talk about . . .*

He laughed again. "Just my luck, right?"

"Are you gay?" I couldn't believe I'd said it, after the
words had come out.

He looked at me for a long time, our eyes locked. I
wondered if he was going to slug me, get mad and
storm out of the bar. He smiled, the corners of his
mouth turning up in a shy way, and his eyes went down
again. "Yeah, I think so." He half-whispered. "I joined
the Air Force cuz I thought it'd make a man out of
me."

I looked at his boyish face and tried to remember what it
was like for me at that age, my first time in a gay bar, how
nervous but exhilarated I'd been, how disappointed I would
have been had I been the only person there. I didn't know
what to say.

"Guess it didn't work." He sighed, shredding the edges of
his napkin. "You know, I try. I go out with my squad to bars
and meet women . . . but I just don't feel anything for them,
you know what I mean?" He laughed. "All the other guys
think I'm this heartbreaker stud because I don't ever want a
girlfriend, just keep playing the field, but . . ." his voice
trailed off and he looked down into his beer again. "I didn't
tell my mom I was shipping out tomorrow . . . I told her it
was today. I decided to come down to New Orleans and
spend the day here . . . and maybe . . ." He shrugged. He
looked back up at me and smiled. "Thanks for talking to
me."

"You know, I get off work here in about half an hour." I
don't know why I said it. He'd gotten to me in some way.
"I'd be happy to show you around."

His smile was adorable. "Really, I just want to spend some
time with someone. I don't care about going to bars or
whatever. I just don't want to be alone today." His voice

broke momentarily, he swallowed and looked down. "I really don't want to be alone."

I put my hand on his. "Okay, Tommy."

I feel so alone here. The guys play cards and read their letters from home out loud, you know, just trying to kill time until we get orders to start. The desert is kind of pretty . . . it's like a long beach where you can't see the water. At night you can see all the stars . . . and I look up and wonder if you're looking at the same stars on the other side of the world, and I wonder what I'm doing here . . . what's a boy from a small town in Mississippi doing halfway around the world? I shouldn't be here, I don't belong here . . . but then I never belonged anywhere. I love my mom, I love my family, but I never belonged in Laurel . . . part of why I joined the Air Force was to belong somewhere . . . but this didn't take either. I never really knew what to do with my life . . . and now I wonder if I've made some big mistake . . . maybe I should have just moved to New Orleans or Atlanta or someplace . . . San Francisco or New York . . . somewhere where it would have been okay for me to be myself . . .

After I got off work, we went back to my apartment so I could take a shower and make some coffee. I wasn't a morning person, never have been, and I was tired. All morning long I'd been waiting to get off work so I could go home and go back to sleep, but now I couldn't. There was just something about him, I couldn't quite put my finger on it, but I wanted to take care of him. After I got cleaned up and changed my clothes, we sat in my little kitchen and drank coffee, and he told me about his life growing up. His daddy had died when he was only ten, and his mama had to support him and his brother and two sisters. It was hard, there was no chance for college for him, and he wanted to get out of Laurel, wanted to be a man, wanted to be what he was supposed to be. He'd liked the Air Force, he liked his squad, but he listened to

them talk about fags and queers contemptuously, and knew
they'd turn against him if they knew. So he went with them
to bars and picked up women, joined them in talking about
pussy and tits and fucking.

"Have you ever been with another man?" I asked finally.
He sipped at his coffee. "No."
"Do you want to be with me?"
He looked down. "I'd like that, very much."

*. . . but then I think about what it would do to Mama, if
she knew, and how hard it would be for her in Laurel if
anyone else ever found out . . . and I wonder if I made the
right choice . . . sitting here at night listening to the wind
and looking at the stars I can't help but feel I made the
wrong decisions, every step of the way. All I've ever
wanted was to be loved, and to love someone else, to have
what Mama had with Daddy . . . can two men have that
kind of love? I'd like to believe so . . . and I've realized
that it would be wrong for me to keep living this lie, to
marry some woman and have children, all the while
wanting to be with another man . . .*

I undressed him.

He kept trembling as I pulled the sweater over his head.
His skin was pale, his shoulders speckled with freckles. His
body was lean and hard, his nipples round and pink on the
hard muscles of his chest. I held him as he trembled, my bare
chest against his, and then we kissed, his mouth tasting of
cigarettes and coffee, but still somehow sweet. I took him by
the hand and led him over to my bed. He took his boots off,
and then I undid his pants, sliding them down over pale
muscled legs covered with thick blond hair, and then his
white Hanes underwear came off. His cock was long but thin,
pinkish and hard. I pushed against his chest gently until he
sat back down on the bed. I undressed and sat down next to
him.

"Are you sure you want to do this?" I whispered to him.

He swallowed and nodded.

I began kissing his neck, moving my lips down to his right nipple, which I licked and sucked on. He groaned, his whole body going rigid then trembling. I hugged him tightly, then began working on his hard cock. He was just a boy, after all, and he came almost immediately, but stayed hard.

Ah, youth.

. . . so I've made up my mind. When my time comes up for re-enlisting this fall, I am going to leave the service. I'm going to come back to New Orleans, and maybe go to the University on the GI Bill. I've saved up almost all my money since I've been in, and I think it's the right thing to do.

And I'm going to tell Mama the truth, even if it hurts her, because I love her and want her to love me for who I am, not for who she thinks I am . . .

We made love together the rest of the afternoon, never leaving my apartment. We ordered dinner in, and we just held each other for most of the time. He told me about his hopes and his dreams, and how scared he was of the coming conflict. He slept in my arms that night, holding on to me like a baby with a teddy bear.

In the morning, I called him a cab to take him to the airport.

"Do you mind if I write to you?" he asked. "I don't really have anyone I can write to . . . it would mean a lot to me."

"Of course you can." I wrote my name and address down for him, and he folded it carefully and placed it in his wallet.

I walked him to the door. The cab was waiting out front. He wrapped his arms around me and held on to me like a lifeline, and then he smiled and walked out the door and got into the cab.

. . . I think about you all of the time. Whenever things get rough, or get scared, I remember the way you held me that

last night, how sweet you were, how kind, and I don't know, Greg, maybe I'm in love with you . . . I close my eyes and I can see your smile, and remember the way you touched me so gently, like you were afraid I'd break or something, and it gets me through . . . part of the reason I want to come back to New Orleans is to see you again . . . I miss you all of the time . . . do you think there's a chance we might be able to be together? That's what I hold on to, what I'll hold onto through everything that's coming. Whenever I get scared I think of you . . .

The months passed, and Kuwait was free. Like everyone else, I watched CNN every chance I got while I went about the business of living my life, of getting up and going to work and slinging cocktails, going to bars and meeting men. And sometimes, when they were hurriedly throwing their clothes back on and getting out of my apartment as quickly as they could, I remembered a sweet little boy from Mississippi who'd wanted to stay and held on to me as hard as he could, who didn't want to leave.

And I said a little prayer for him.

. . . it's been really hard for me to write this letter. My friends are always bothering me about it, because I won't let them see it, won't tell them who I'm writing to, and they all think I've finally found a woman to love . . . they've noticed the difference in me and they tease me about it. If they only knew . . . it kills me not to be able to share this with anyone but you . . .

Greg, do you think you could love me?

It was a beautiful May morning. The weather had started getting hot and sticky again, and my air conditioner was running 24/7 to keep the damp out of my apartment. It was my day off, a Thursday, and I was going to stay home and clean the place. I'd really been bad, letting the laundry go, not cleaning or doing anything I should, and I'd finally had enough.

I was sorting the laundry into big piles on the living room floor when someone rang my doorbell. I walked over and peeked through the curtains, and saw a short woman I didn't recognize. I opened the door. "May I help you?"

"Are you Greg Herren?" she asked. She was maybe five foot tall, wearing a black sweater and black stretch pants. She was overweight, maybe in her late forties, and she looked tired – her eyes were red and watery. She was wearing too much make-up and her thick hair was dyed black, but she'd probably been pretty when she was younger. Her accent was thick.

"Um, yes."

"I'm Ila Mae Harper." She looked into my face. "Tommy's mother."

At first I didn't know what she was talking about, and then I remembered my little Air Force pilot from so many months before. My heart sank. The last thing I needed was a confrontation with his mother. I invited her to come in, apologizing for the mess, and cleared a space on the couch for her to sit, offering her coffee, anything, wondering how to avoid this, how to get her out of there.

She clutched her black patent leather purse as though for dear life as she looked around my apartment. She smiled weakly. "Thank you, but no, I don't need nothing. I just want to talk to you for a minute."

I heard Tommy's voice echoing in my head. "Is he okay?" I asked, and once the words left my mouth, I knew.

Her eyes filled. "Tommy was shot down over Baghdad." For a moment she was overcome, then she got control again.

I felt like I'd been punched in the stomach. I just stared at her in shock.

She was opening her purse. She pulled out an envelope, and held on to it, staring down at it. She took a deep breath. "When the Air Force sent me his things, this was in them." She held it out to me.

I took it from her. My name and address were scrawled on the face of the envelope. It was fairly thick. I just stared at it.

"Mr Herren, I'm sorry, but I read it . . ." she swallowed. "I want you to know I loved my son. He was my baby, my first. Nothing would have changed that." She wiped at her face. "It breaks my heart that he felt, that he could have possibly thought, anything would have changed that. Since I—" her voice broke, and she looked away from me for a moment before continuing. "Since he was killed . . ." and she started to cry.

I moved over to the couch and took her in my arms. My head was spinning, my stomach lurching. My hands felt cold.

She leaned into me. "Since he was killed, I've wondered what I ever did, how I failed him as a mother that he thought he couldn't tell me the truth. I would have loved him, Mr Herren, no matter what . . . I want you to know that."

"Call me Greg," I said.

She went on as though I hadn't spoken. "And when I think he joined the Air Force because he couldn't . . ." a sob rose in her throat. Her entire body shook as she sobbed. She stopped, wiping at her mascara smeared cheeks. "You know, even when he was a little boy, I knew he was special, different, and I loved him all the more because of it. He was just the sweetest little boy, so thoughtful and loving and considerate of other people . . . everyone just loved him, you know? And when they called me to tell me he was—" She bit her lip. "I thought, when I tried to make sense of it all, that maybe I could sense all along he wasn't meant for this world for long, he was just too good for this world, you know what I mean?"

"Yes." I did know, thinking about a scared but sweet little boy in a man's body, holding him all night long before he went off to war. My own eyes filled.

"Anyway." She got to her feet. "I wanted you to have that

letter." She moved toward the front door and I followed her. At the door, she paused, and reached up and kissed my cheek. "Thank you for making my boy happy." Then she was through the door and walking up the street, a broken hearted little rural woman from Mississippi who might not ever regain the light in her heart.

> *So, that's what gives me the strength to get through this all . . . the chance of seeing you again. I hope you don't mind . . . but when this is over and I get leave again, I'm going to come see you. I sometimes get scared, and think maybe he won't want to see me again, or maybe he doesn't even remember who I am, but I'm willing to take the risk.*
>
> *I love you, Greg.*
> *Tommy*

I cried while I read his letter, as he poured out his heart to me. I cried over what might have been, what could have been, what should have been. I cried for a sweet boy with a thick Mississippi accent wearing blue jeans and a sweater sitting at a bar, shredding a napkin. I cried for the lost potential. I cried for the letter in my hands, never sent, for never having the chance to write him back, to let him know how special he was. In my mind I could see his face in his cockpit, knowing he was going to die. Did he cry, I wondered, as his plane fell out of the sky? Did he think about me? Were his last thoughts of me?

I laid down in my bed, my laundry forgotten, and I remembered lying there with him in my arms, holding him and kissing the top of his head.

I just lay there, until the sun went down, and then I roused myself and had to get out . . . to get away. I walked down to Lafitte's. The bar was empty when I walked in, a few people scattered here and there, the music loud.

And for a second, I saw him sitting there at the end of the bar, and he smiled when he saw me.

And then he faded away, like he'd never been there.

It's been fourteen years, but I still have his letter, carefully folded in a metal box where I keep things like my high school football letter and medals from track meets. Once a year I drive up to Laurel and lay roses on his grave.

I don't think I'll ever forget that shy, sweet smile.

Bless the Blue Angel

Daniel M. Jaffe

What's the difference between the animals in the pet hospital and those in the Los Angeles sex club beside it? The dogs and cats don't know they're animals; we men do. And that's why I'm here. Again. Another Saturday night after Jimmy has fallen asleep.

Sure, I'm here partly because of the Johnny Appleseed theory of sex – isn't it in men's nature to spread our seed as widely as possible? But mostly I'm here because Jimmy encouraged me to go. I'm here so that he doesn't feel guilty and so that my resentment doesn't grow. I'm at a sex club in order to save our twenty-year relationship.

You might laugh, but it's true.

I show my ID and membership card, pay the $12, clomp down the narrow hallway, stuff wallet and keys into a locker, then go out back to the courtyard water fountain. I pop a Viagra. While waiting for the blue angel to work his way from belly to crotch, I sit in a beige plastic chair and stare at flames dancing in the fire pit. At fifty, I need the blue angel in order to get it up with strangers. With him in my belly, I can stand on the glory hole platform, give a quick couple of rubs and get hard, stick my seven inches through a hole and fill any mouth, old or young, handsome or not. I can slip a condom on and fuck away in the dark. But without the pill, not even the hairiest bear, the smoothest twink, the most well-proportioned of muscle men can perk a stir in my jeans. (Maybe if someone sucked me long enough, my sluggish blood would flow; but, even under the best of circumstances, we're talking sponge here, not rock.)

I need no medication with Jimmy. Never have. A touch from him, sometimes even a look, is all I've ever needed. It's not that I don't see the changes in his body – if I were to pass him now as a stranger on the street, I wouldn't look twice what with his sunken cheeks, fat jowls sagging beneath his chin, fatty lump between his shoulders. The toothpick arms and legs on bloated torso make him look almost like a poster child from some famine-suffering country. But he isn't from elsewhere, he's from here. And he isn't a stranger, he's Jimmy, the only man I've ever loved. A light graze of his fingertips along my thighs and ass, and even my eyelashes get hard. A tongue kiss from him and I leak.

In front of the fire pit, my eyes burn just a little and my forehead feels suddenly thick, and so I know the blue angel's about to fly. I gently rub my jeans until my basket bulges. Now I'm ready to make the rounds.

I saunter through the courtyard, walk into the corrugated metal porn room, watch a couple of average Joes licking and sucking some young guy on the room's sofa as well as on the screen (life imitates art imitates life). I tweak the young guy's nips and he moans, but he doesn't reach up to me, so I leave.

Into another corrugated metal room where I push open the wooden door of a cubicle and see a skinny guy on his knees pressing his face through the metal prison-like bars. I smell the faint aroma of poppers. He looks up at me, opens his mouth, sticks out his broad tongue. I step in, latch the wooden door closed, unbutton the jeans and thrust my crotch. He takes me deep into his mouth and sucks. He moans as the blue angel turns me into granite. He pulls my balls out of the fly and licks them gently, the way I like. Experienced, this one, knows how to keep the teeth off. Deep throat. His tongue laps my balls each time he goes all the way down. He's grabbing the prison bars, and I am too. Up and down, up and down. He pulls back for a breather. I chuck him under the chin and leave the cubicle. I'm just getting started.

I watch a few more random sucks, linger at a cubicle with a sling, watch a guy in a leather vest pull his fist out of the slingee's ass, apply more white grease, slip his hand in again up to the middle of his forearm. The slingee lets out one of those deep, soulful howls that come only from being fisted. Maybe we men have extra voice boxes up our asses.

The dogs next door bark in response.

Jimmy's ass was a sizzler when we first met at the baths. I spotted him showering, and even though I'd just washed, I took off my white towel, hooked it and stepped in beneath the shower head beside his. I soaped up my hands, reached down, caressed his fleshy globes. Yeah, an aggressive move even for the baths, but I couldn't resist. He turned, looked my face over – the stubble and the square jaw – and he cupped my balls gently, leaned in without even saying a word. I reached around and pressed him close, all the while caressing that smooth ass and thinking how sexy he was, how handsome with that red hair and freckles and tiny nips and ass so spherical it could be used for a geometry lesson. He leaned up and pressed his thick lips to mine, which is when I stopped thinking about his ass, stopped thinking about how handsome he was, stopped thinking, just felt my tongue fill his mouth, his hands slip to my shoulders, his tongue fill my mouth, his fingers squeeze my shoulders and my chest and tug just right on my thick nips, and I pulled my face back and he understood the look of surprise in my eyes and said, "Me too."

We froze there in the shower while two side-by-side sprays rained on our shoulders and heads, the two of us clinging together, afraid to let go even for a second because what if this was one of those coincidence passions that clicked only then and there and in that one second but never again not even a second later not one foot away? I swallowed hard and he swallowed hard and he rested his head against my shoulder like we'd been comforting each other for years, and we swayed and sort of waltzed right there in the shower until some asshole said, "Get a room, lover boys." A killjoy in every crowd.

"I've got a room," Jimmy whispered, so we stepped out, grabbed our towels, and I followed him up two flights of stairs, hoping he'd still want me and still knock every damn thought out of my head with a kiss. He fumbled with his key, a sign of shyness so cute, I wanted to cradle him. He lay down in bed with the towel draped over his crotch, which I also found endearing and incredibly cute, given that we'd just been dancing pressed together naked. I dropped my towel to the floor, pulled his off him, then puppy nuzzled his big balls and cock with my nose, sniffing in the scent of him mixed with coconut soap. I licked him and sucked him, then slid up and held him and kissed him and held him and kissed him and felt him start to pull back as if preparing to go down on me, but I didn't let him go because all I wanted was to hold him and kiss him and stare into his eyes and kiss him. His eyes turned glassy wet, and I knew this was more than coincidence passion.

Finally I let him pull away to see what he would do. He shoved me onto my back and slid down to lick beneath my arms and to suck me, then he slipped a condom on me and rode while tugging my nips, leaning down and kissing me, groaning and humping faster and jerking himself when I told him I was close and he shot hot and I shot and he shot more and I shot more and he dropped onto me while I was still inside him and holding him and he kissed my neck and face and did the unforgivable in the baths, the unbelievable in the baths, the unthinkable in the baths, and said, "I could love you." I forgave him and believed him and thanked him and said, "Me too."

After listening to a few more howls from the slingee, I move out of the corrugated metal room into the night air, cool in LA September, take another drink from the water fountain and saunter inside past the lockers to the main play area where everything – wooden cubicles, walls, ceilings – is painted black. And it all smells like piss, even though the piss room is behind black curtains in the corner.

I stand for a while by a row of cubicles, wait until a short muscular guy steps into one, makes eye contact with me, then shuts and latches the door. I step into the cubicle beside his, latch the door, and look through the glory hole – he's already on his knees. My fly's still unbuttoned from before, so I just tug out my half-hard dick and stick it through. This guy, too, knows what he's doing. I think how risky it is to stick your dick through a hole in the wall. What if the guy on the other side likes to bite, or if he's a psycho with a knife? Slice! At least then I wouldn't have the option of stepping out on Jimmy.

Enough, time to move on. I pull out and leave, wash myself in the bathroom sink. I meander to the piss area and see a fat guy lying naked in one of the white tubs. I stand over him. "Please, sir," he says, and I piss all over his belly and chest while he plays with himself. "Thank you, sir," he says when I'm done. I like respectful boys.

I wander some more, squeeze into a backroom packed with shirtless guys. It smells like armpits. I yank off my T-shirt and stick it through my belt. Immediately, hands grope my chest. Yeah, I'm fifty, but I work out and it shows in the dark where my eye wrinkles hide in shadow. Some mouth in the dark fastens onto my left nip and suckles like a newborn while another mouth leeches onto the right nip. I wrap arms around their shoulders – Daddy's boys – and stroke their heads. Jimmy and I used to sit like this sometimes on the living room sofa, his head on my lap, me bending over him, one of my nips in his mouth. He'd suckle for half an hour, an hour, as we listened to jazz and I held him and caressed his red hair and kissed the side of his face. My Jimmy. He's only three years younger than me, but when we're alone, he always calls me Daddy. I like that. Makes me feel all protective and strong.

One of the backroom tit-suckers moves away to vampire some other guy, and the boy who's fastened my other nip to me bites too hard so I shove him away. He lunges back and clamps on even harder, probably thinking it's all part of the game. Get that testosterone pumping and Hell knows what guys'll do. I grab him by his curly hair and yank him off. He moves to clamp on yet again, so I slap him a good crisp one this time, smack across the cheek. He mutters, "Asshole," and squeezes his way out of the room.

I leave, too, and lean against a wall, watch men pass, avoid eye contact. His medicine cocktail sent Jimmy's libido into a coma years ago. At first, I pretended I didn't mind. "It's enough for me to lie beside you and jerk off," I said. I did this a few nights, pressing my naked thigh against his, using my right hand on myself, holding his soft dick in my left. A few nights later he took to falling asleep before I even finished.

I stopped jerking off in bed. Instead, I shut myself in the bathroom before bedtime and did the adolescent thing. Here I was, a grown man back to pulling his pud in the toilet. What's wrong with this picture? At least I was humiliating myself in private instead of beside Jimmy. But let me tell you, macho posturing aside: coming does not necessarily equal achieving satisfaction.

A few months later, after he commented that I'd become all grouchy, Jimmy took my face in his hands and told me to start going to sex clubs. "You need to do it," he said. "We both need you to do it."

"I can't," I replied, liking the idea, wanting to do it, but feeling like a traitor. We'd never spoken the words, "For better or worse," but I'd intended them nevertheless. How could I dishonor him or what we had?

We argued for weeks until he said, "You're still hoping my desire will return. It won't."

Yeah, Jimmy was right. I'd been hoping he'd somehow wake up from the libido coma and want me again. How long could I live with the sex life of a twelve-year-old? How long before love turned to total resentment and anger, or worse?

I don't do it every Saturday night, just sometimes when the pressure's really bad. I take my best boy out on the town, my blue angel. I can't bring myself to tell any of our friends. Besides, who'd give sympathy to a guy whining that he's got permission to fuck around?

I step up to the central platform surrounded by glory holes, and I stand in front of a hole where some mouth is open. I can't even see the face, just a mustache on an upper lip. I bring my crotch close and wait for him to stick out his tongue, which he does. It's long. He licks the denim. I get hard. I take it out and feed him. He's one of those vacuum guys who could Hoover up a dam.

Jimmy never sucked me like that. Instead, he'd start real slow with licks all around the base and then up the underside and down the topside, then he'd tease around the tip and slowly suck me in until I gasped. He always made me gasp just as our eyes met, just as he filled his mouth with me and stared up so intently I felt Cupid-pierced by his baby blues. He'd glide me in then, all slow and deep, and he'd ease me out, and in again and out again while he gently cupped my balls and slid a finger behind them and he'd stroke, Jimmy would, in the right spot, my spot he discovered early on, knowing when to flick that finger, when to rub and when to press, sensing as my muscles contracted just so, speeding up his mouth and tongue then, adding pressure to that finger, speeding up and pressing, speeding up and pressing, speeding up and –

"Ah!" I let out a grunt there on the glory hole platform. My head snaps back and I let out a second grunt. And my pelvis bangs against the wood around the hole and I spasm three times, and a fourth. For a second, just a second, I nearly succeed in imagining that I see Jimmy's eyes in the dark and feel Jimmy's eyes. And for a second, I nearly smile.

I silently bless the blue angel – not for the hard-on, but for the moment of Jimmy fantasy.

Pull out and zip up. Deep breath. Bathroom. I wash myself, then stomp over to the lockers, get wallet and keys, and I leave. I plunk into my car. I pull out of the parking lot and head for home, hoping Jimmy'll still be asleep when I get there, so that I can slip in beside him and hold him like I used to after we made love. So I can lie in the morning and tell him I hadn't gone out at all. Even though he'd understand the truth and wouldn't mind.

Because I mind.

Eighty Bucks Plus Tip

Tom Mendicino

His email had taken me by surprise:

> *Hey, Robert – I'm doing nude massage again for former clients. Let me know if you're interested. Hope all is well. – Michael.*

I waited a week to respond, wary of frightening him off. Michael can't be pursued. He must come to you.

The light is low, a concession to modesty, both his and mine. He kicks off his loafers and drops his pants to his ankles. I stare at the floor, knowing he's shy and not wanting him to feel like he's performing a striptease. I ask if he's cold and he says no, lying. I tell him I'll shut the window anyway. "If you like," he says, smiling. Out of the corner of my eye, I see him fluff his shriveled penis. I touch his shoulder before I lower myself on the bed, a friendly gesture, nothing sexual.

"I like it," I say.

"What?" he asks, confused and a little wary.

"The goatee. Very flattering."

"It's starting to itch."

"You should keep it."

Compliments make Michael self-conscious.

"Sorry I've gotten f . . . f . . . fat," he apologizes.

He's put on five pounds, tops, but they've all settled around his waist.

"You look fine," I laugh. "Where do you want me?"

"On your stomach," he orders, "with your head at the foot of the bed."

He says it's a pleasure to work for clients like me, men who stay in shape, who don't need to pay for companionship. The obese, the elderly, those afflicted with psoriasis or halitosis or anti-social personalities: they want him for sex. He thinks I can get that anywhere, that I hire him because he's a talented masseur, that the "full release" is just an afterthought. Yes, I can still compete. Middle-age hasn't yet banished me to the sidelines. A small investment of my time and energy – a late night at the bar or an hour or two online, a few drinks to give me a buzz but not enough to leave me with a hangover – still pays off in erotic dividends. But masseurs and escorts are more convenient. No need to primp or obsess about the gray at my temples or the bald spot spreading across my crown. Sixty minutes of physical contact and emotional detachment. Why risk the possibility of complications and expectations when an email or text message and a withdrawal at the ATM will get you instant gratification?

Sure, not everyone comes as advertised. Some of their photographs must be ten years old and their hair is thinner and their muscles aren't as toned. The picture posted on Michael's website promised a sweet face and a smile that would be the envy of a Hollywood icon. It doesn't do him justice. He should sail through the world, disarming everyone he meets with his beguiling, soft brown eyes. But life has played a cruel trick on Michael. The fates decided to amuse themselves by tossing roadblocks at the thoughts racing through his head. Michael is constantly frustrated by his inability to speak in paragraphs. His sentences crash land in a jumble of vowels and consonants. The world condescends to him, assuming he's stupid and incapable. Two months ago, he'd stuttered that it would be our last time. He was retiring. He had only eighteen hours of training left before he was eligible for certification. He was certain good employment opportunities as a massage therapist awaited him in hair salons and chiropractic offices, but the bone-crackers and stylists dismissed him without inviting him back for a second interview. Michael has taken solace among his old clients, few of whom require him to speak.

He oils my skin and slides his palms between my shoulder blades. I ask if he's still living with his roommate, a girl he's known since grade school. They're best friends except during one of their frequent intense fights. They never remember what started the argument when they finally make up.

"No . . . no," he says.

"Find your own place?" I ask, wondering how he found the scratch for the deposit.

"Not really."

I sense he doesn't want to talk about his living arrangements. I'm seized by irrational jealousy. One of his clients must have taken him in. Envy is morphing into anger. Why hadn't he asked me?

"I moved home," he confesses, sensing my agitation. "My mom, she has cancer. Not too bad . . ."

As if there is a good cancer?

". . . but she shouldn't be alone. I can drive her to chemotherapy."

"That's sweet of you," I say, knowing Michael is too irresponsible to be a caretaker, too fragile to be any help during a crisis. Michael's mother has taken him in because he has nowhere to go. He's a burden, especially now that she's battling lymphoma, but I'm sure she doesn't mind. Of all her children, he's always needed her most.

Over time, I've pieced together the fragments of Michael's life. The runt of a large Irish litter, he grew up the youngest of eight, adored by his sisters and protected by his brothers. His puppy eyes and nervous stutter made him an obvious target for bullies from first grade well into high school. Inattentive, unable to concentrate, he struggled to graduate and fell into the family tradition of collecting paychecks and earning seniority at the post office.

At the age of twenty-two, the husband of his favorite sister introduced him to the pleasures of recreational drugs and anal penetration. Once the door to the cage was kicked open, Michael fled Glen Burnie, Maryland, drawn to the club scene and sexual opportunities in Our Nation's Capital. He found a job as a bar back in a New York Avenue dive where the dress code forbade cologne and shirts. He hated emptying ash trays and hauling cases of beer through the surly crowds, but the schedule accommodated his growing affection for mind-altering substances.

He'd been working at the bar almost a year when the press secretary to the Governor of Colorado, in D.C. to chair a mid-term Republican strategy caucus, wandered in, drunk and horny, looking for a little out-of-town debauchery. He'd whisked Michael off to the Ritz Carlton where they partied until daybreak, flying high on crystal meth. Back in Colorado, the press secretary called two, three, times a day, unable to get Michael out of his head. A month later, Michael watched his face melt in the mirror as he tumbled from the peak of another thirty-six-hour high. Terrified of dying of an overdose, alone in a rented room, he gratefully accepted a one-way first class ticket to Denver.

Michael discovered his talent for massage in the Mile High City. The press secretary suffered from rheumatoid arthritis and Michael, who couldn't gossip about politics and scandals, could at least rub his joints and muscles to soothe the pain. He immersed himself in web sites and text books, learning the full range of techniques, Swedish and Sports, Deep Tissue, Reiki and Holistic. As the weeks went by, he started to feel he'd traded one prison for another. Resentful of his dependence, he created a screen name and solicited clients, promising a "sensual solution" for the stresses of daily life. Three weeks later, he'd collected enough cash for a ticket back to D.C. He left the press secretary a note, thanking him for everything, apologizing for not being able to fall in love, and promising he'd be in touch as soon as he was back on his feet.

"Hey," I say, rolling over on my shoulder. "Show me your foot again."

He giggles as I pinch his toe. I can still make him laugh.

"What's it called?" I ask, knowing full well the clinical name of the anatomical aberration of a second toe longer than the big one.

"Morton's toe," he says.

"You know that it's a sign of high intelligence, don't you?"

"Yes," he answers, pleased and proud.

My friends are skeptical when I tell them Michael is nothing like the hard-bodied, cruel-eyed mercenaries for hire through the internet or the classified pages of the weekly gay newspaper. They think I've collected another Bambi and mock my attraction to wounded birds that have tumbled from the nest. Whatever happened to Kyle and Christopher and Kevin and Tony? they ask, reminding me of other lost boys who were ultimately exposed as heartless opportunists without a soul or a conscience. I insist Michael is different, a good kid scrambling to make ends meet until a better opportunity comes along. His time may not come free, but he's not a "professional" who arrives flush from a dose of Viagra with an eye constantly on his watch.

"Am I too heavy?" he asks as he settles his weight on my ass.

"No. Of course not. You feel great."

Michael believes that success in his profession requires a smooth body, a trait that genetics and heredity have not selected for him. He stopped shaving his body hair after a staph infection from a razor nick left a fiery crescent moon scar under his left nipple. Now he simply runs his clippers along the contours of his body and the bristly stubble makes me squirm when he uses his forearm to smooth the knots in my back.

"Are you all right?" he asks.

"Just ticklish. Don't stop."

Some of his clients require audio enhancement, either horrid New Age instrumentals meant to evoke elves and spirits or ghastly environmental sounds like crashing waves and forest breezes. I prefer the sound of Michael's heavy breathing. There's nothing erotic about his panting; it's only the sound of his body working to deliver oxygen to his bloodstream. He gives his all, no holding back, and it isn't long before I feel sweat dripping from his armpits.

"Wow," I say, responding to the pressure of his hands.

"Too hard?" he asks.

"No, no . . ." I whisper as he rubs the oil into my skin. "Coconut?" I ask, catching my breath.

"Papaya," he says, stumbling over the word. "Do you like it?"

"Very tropical."

He works the muscles at the base of my spine and his hands slide across the round cheeks of my ass. His fingertips tease my balls. My erection presses into the mattress. I feel his penis, neither hard nor completely soft, against my thighs.

"Are you okay with this?" I ask.

"Yes," he says. "Yes, I am."

He won't work at the bar again. He's drug free now and he's trying to stay away from alcohol, allowing himself only the occasional cocktail. He's been picking up work as a house painter. I tell him I hate the color of this room, that it makes me feel like I'm sleeping in a tube of mint toothpaste. He laughs. What would he suggest? Raspberry, he decides. Black or red? I ask. Red raspberry, he says, or maybe cranberry with a white accent wall. We should talk about it, I say. I have a fantasy of Michael being fucked on a canvas drop cloth. I ask if he can work up an estimate. When could he start? He doesn't respond, pretending to be absorbed in the muscles of my left calf. He cradles my foot. The thick crust of callus soaks up the massage oil. He works methodically, gently tugging and popping each of my toes.

"Roll over on your back," he says.

I could close my eyes and let him work unobserved, but his intense concentration, his desire to please, is endearing.

"What?" he asks, blushing at the attention.

His hands linger on my biceps and pectorals, his soft touching acknowledging that he appreciates well-defined muscles.

"Why are you smiling?" he asks.

"I'm thinking."

"About what?"

"Nothing," I say. "Just something stupid."

I could never tell him my thoughts, that he's haunted me since the first time he was here, that I was disconsolate when I closed the door behind him after his last visit, knowing that he'd slipped into the void, that I would never see him again, that his fate would remain forever unknown. How would he react if he knew how my heart soared when I read his email? He's told me about the stockbroker with cash to burn, enough to hire Michael two, three, times a week. The broker finally confessed he'd developed feelings, an attraction deeper than the purely physical. *That's not what this is about,* Michael cautioned, refusing to respond to his emails when the broker refused to accept that the attraction could never be mutual. I consider myself warned.

"Now comes your favorite part," he promises.

Michael places his hand on my stomach and traces small, tight circles. He knows that I'm morbidly self-conscious about the soft pile of my belly. I'd flinched reflexively when he touched my abdomen during our first session. Good for the digestion, he said, not withdrawing his hand. I'd laughed and told him no one gets near my stomach. He asked why I was letting him touch it, no hint of conquest in his voice. Because I feel very comfortable with you, I'd said. I feel comfortable too, he'd responded.

I know he is. He is the one who sought me out. He says he's available for hire again, but he's taken down his website. Maybe he's not being totally forthcoming, afraid of how I might respond if he were to tell me I am his only client. I try to ferret out the truth with a few casual questions.

"You tired tonight?" I ask

"A little."

"Busy day?"

"Yes."

Why am I deluding myself? I'm probably his fifth session since noon. He better be up for this. I'll never hire him again if tonight ends with his flaccid penis and a few obligatory jerks of my rod. It will be the last time, I swear.

"A lot of massages?" I ask, emboldened, wanting to confirm my worst fear.

"No. You're the only one."

What about yesterday? Tomorrow? I don't dare ask.

"I spent the day with my mother. The chemo is making her sick."

"You should have cancelled. We could have rescheduled," I say, chastised.

"No. No. I wanted to come."

Because he needs the money, I expect, to supplement what he's earning from his painting jobs.

"I needed to get out of the house."

He could have gone anywhere. A bar. The movies. To visit his friends.

He chose to come here.

We're heading into the home stretch. We haven't talked too much tonight, not like most nights, not like I know we will again. I'd like to hear about his Christmas plans, how his favorite sister is coping with the single life, how his mother is responding to chemotherapy. But not now. Now is not the time to talk.

He dribbles massage oil on my erect penis, gently moistening the plump head with this thumb and forefinger. I extend my hand and he squirts the oil into my palm. He's not quite hard, only half way there, and I reach between his legs and cup his small balls. He snorts when I press my knuckles into the soft, vulnerable mound behind his testicles.

It's been a while, too long, and I'm already close. We're already long past the allotted hour and a whore would be rushing to get me off. Michael doesn't resist as I gently roll him on his back and crawl between his legs. We've come to the part of the session when I take control or, more accurately, when Michael and I pretend I'm in control. My body is on high alert for subtle messages and signals. I release his balls and grab his piece, a nice one, neither big nor small, and squeeze. Michael closes his eyes and gasps. I pump several times, feeling his legs slide up my torso. I rub my thumb against his asshole and he squeezes down on my finger as it slips inside. Michael opens his eyes and I know I can do anything I'd like to him. He spreads his legs and lifts his hips. This isn't on the eighty-buck menu. I'm sure he's never offered this to another client. I roll on a sheath, then a second, insurance against shooting too quickly. I penetrate him easily, no resistance. He grits his teeth, moaning, when I bury my shaft in his rectum.

But there's something more I want. Something he's given me before. Something I'll never ask for. Something I wait for him to offer. The one thing that's never for sale. The proof that I'm more than the outcall rate plus tip. He throws his arm around my neck. I lean forward slightly, waiting. He's breathing heavily now. Awkward as it is, I slide one hand behind his neck and stroke his cock with the other. His precome slicks my fingers. "Oh, God," he whispers, and I squeeze his penis again.

Michael pulls me towards him. He closes his eyes and his mouth slackens, still hesitant, unsure of whether I'll accept the invitation, unaware that I feel something close to euphoria race through my body. I wait a long moment, then nuzzle his neck before letting my lips graze his. He slips his tongue into my mouth and I open wide enough to suck up his soul. We kiss for both a brief moment and an eternity and, my hips grinding into his pelvis, we come together and collapse on the bed.

"I needed that," he says, flopping back on the mattress, his arm flung behind his head. I expect that tonight, for the first time, he'll linger, maybe doze off, wake up a few hours later and decide he might as well stay the night since Glen Burnie is an hour away. But he stands up and walks to the linen closet. I like that he knows where to find fresh towels without asking. Of course he has to leave. It's selfish of me to want him to stay when his mother needs him. I dress while he showers and count out four twenties and a very generous tip. I decide I'll broach the subject carefully, casually, as if it's a mere afterthought. I'll let him know I'm open to suggestions: same time next week, maybe grab something to eat before or after, a drink, maybe dancing.

He dresses quickly, not waiting until he's completely dry. Doubts about his intentions creep back to taunt me. I ask if he wants a glass of water, a beer, and he declines, zipping up his jacket. I follow him down the stairs, growing angrier with each step, first with him, then, realizing he's done nothing wrong, with myself for being such a fool, a cliché of the ridiculous middle-aged man. Then, at the door, he spins on his heel and grabs my face, forcing my mouth open with his insistent tongue.

"Thank you," he says. "Thank you for everything."

I know he doesn't mean the tip.

"I'll see you next week," I say, reassured.

"Sure," he says, flashing his biggest smile. "Oh wait. I may be in Philadelphia next week."

"Philadelphia?"

"I met someone last weekend. He's really cool. He asked me to come up and hang out."

My face freezes, every muscle determined not to reveal my reaction.

"I'll email you when I get back and let you know which night I can do it."

He practically skips down the street, two hundred dollars richer. I pour myself a single malt and turn on the computer. I send his saved emails into the recycle bin, like those of Kyle and Christopher and Kevin and Tony before him. I pour another drink and crawl into bed. Half drunk on disappointment and Scotch, I bury my face in the pillow and take a deep breath. Tomorrow I'll throw the sheets in the laundry and what's left of Michael and papaya will be washed away.

Daniel Is Leaving
Tonight on a Plane

Paul Russell

"I don't know about you," he said, "but I have this really bad feeling our Mister Elton John might just be going gay on us. What do you think?"

Surely we must have spoken before, but those are the first words I remember Darryl addressing to me. He held up a copy of "Goodbye, Yellow Brick Road" he'd plucked from the record bin – presumably as evidence – and grinned broadly. He had badly crooked teeth.

I'd taken a job at a record store in the new mall in hopes of hastening summer's end, and my eagerly awaited departure for college in another state. "I can't work *enough* hours," I'd told the manager my first afternoon, even though Raleigh Springs Mall was halfway across town from where I lived. "You should give me everything you've got."

He was happy enough to oblige, being basically a lazy s.o.b., and I found myself in the store six days a week, from eleven in the morning till we closed up at ten at night. It was dull work, not particularly enlivened by my co-workers – Jennifer the pothead, jolly overweight Denise.

Then there was Darryl with his plaid bellbottoms and overstacked platforms and sunburst-yellow shirts with flamboyant collars. The year was 1973; even I had occasionally affected such outlandish costumes when dressing up for school dances. The thing was, Darryl dressed like that all the time, as if one day he'd got into costume and then couldn't figure how to get out again.

I didn't know what to say to his question. Whether Elton John was going gay or not was of absolutely no interest to me one way or another, though I suddenly realized that the store always seemed to be broadcasting his music whenever Darryl was around. My own tastes, such as they were, tended more to Led Zeppelin and Pink Floyd, music I could get stoned to. I liked nothing better than to come back from a long sweaty run, step in the shower, and then cool down in my bedroom with a joint and the music cranked up on the headphones. It never occurred to me, back in those days, that I might be running *from* something; I just enjoyed the pull of my muscles, the almost holy sense of lightness in my brain, the vague euphoria of accomplishment afterward. I was still a little bitter about the cross country finals, the nagging sense I'd let my buddies down.

My lack of response — I think I managed a shrug — didn't seem to faze Darryl a bit. When we closed up that evening, he was waiting for me by the palms in the concourse as I pulled down and locked the metal security screen. With the mall nearly deserted, only a few last employees heading for the exits, you could hear the fountains splashing — a sound you never noticed during the day. I always liked that moment; the fluorescent lights and the palms and the echoing emptiness made me feel faraway, a kind of foretaste of the time when I'd have put all this behind me.

"So where're you from?" His voice brought me back to the tedious here and now.

"What do you mean, where am I from?"

"Like, what high school?"

I told him I'd just graduated from Memphis Prep.

"Ridgecrest," he said, pointing to his thin chest. "Aren't we supposed to be rivals or something?"

I told him I had no idea, though in fact Ridgecrest's track team wasn't half bad. There was something well-scrubbed about him, as if he'd just come from a long, furious shower.

He sported a mop of straw-colored hair. A fiery spatter of acne daubed his cheekbones. He was really quite pathetic, I thought.

"Make love not war is my philosophy. Do you think we'll be drafted?"

I told him I was heading off to college.

"I see," he said. "Around here?"

"Far from here," I told him. "This is just my summer job."

"Mine too," he said. Then: "Endless summer for me."

The night, when we stepped outside, was muggy. A blurred moon floated low to the horizon. My motorcycle was parked, for security, beneath a streetlight.

"It's cool that you ride," he said. "Kawasaki?"

"Yeah," I said. It was a touchy subject, actually. I'd bought the bike back in the spring – sort of on the spur of the moment, with money my grandfather had given me in advance of graduation. My parents had pointed out, less than helpfully, that I'd just have to turn around and sell it when I left for school. "So I'll sell it," I'd told them. "I'll enjoy it while I can." But it was clear they thought buying a bike was frivolous. All my life I'd tried hard not to disappoint, but one way or another, lately, that was all I seemed to manage. "Senior slump," my mother diagnosed, pointing out that at least I'd gotten into a good school, and with a good scholarship, too.

The weeks passed. Humid June became sultry July. I had a calendar on my desk at home, and I gratefully marked off each bleak day that had separated me from what I saw as a long-deserved and fully-earned freedom. I tried to imagine the life that awaited me at school, but besides hoping I'd be assigned a fantastic roommate, somebody smart and athletic and interesting, my hopes were distressingly blank.

Darryl sang the first line of Elton John's "Daniel", nearly matching Elton John's smooth British voice as he skittered along the aisles of Stellar Records. "This is the best song ever," he announced to me and Denise, the only ones in the store at the time. "Actually, it makes me want to cry whenever I hear it."

Denise rolled her eyes. "You're admitting to something like that?" I asked him, sorry at once that I'd spoken. When he'd held up "Goodbye, Yellow Brick Road" I'd said nothing, only looked at him coldly.

"Why not? See, it's about two friends, very close friends. And something tragic's happened, and one of them's missing the other one something crazy. I think maybe it's about the war."

Customers had come in; at least he had enough sense to cool it when customers were around. I hated it that he felt so comfortable around the other employees. Sometimes I fantasized that Al the manager would lose patience and fire him, but Darryl always behaved himself when Al was around, and Al was around as little as possible. Whenever he'd been in his little closet of an office, where Jennifer sometimes visited him for protracted spells, the rear of the store reeked of marijuana.

Annoyed but not in the least bit jealous, I watched as, in Al's absence, Darryl teased those two girls, draping an arm around them while he confided some inane something or other, or playfully swatting their fat butts as they walked by. They had little enough to say to me; I told myself it was because I intimidated them a little, an effect I'd sort of enjoyed having on the girls at my school. Truth be told, I was always reluctant to stop and analyze that enjoyment too carefully. It kept my teammates off guard. "Jeez," Mike Spalter said once. "You sure don't have to pick and choose among them, do you?" I wasn't sure what that meant, but chose to take it as a compliment.

I'd gone to the senior prom with my longtime friend Sara, who I guess was unofficially my girlfriend. How much nicer, I thought, to have sped away on my Kawasaki from the downtown hotel where the prom had taken place than to sit with her in my parents' car in her driveway, wondering as the windshield fogged up in the cool night air whether or not I was expected to finally make a move. When Sara slipped her tongue between my lips I was a little startled, and even more startled at where her hand got to, but I went along with everything easily enough. For my part, after trying to get my own reluctant hand inside her prom dress, all I managed to do was prick my finger on her corsage, which I took as an excuse to cease and desist. Since then we hadn't seen much of one another, though she'd intimated on more than one occasion over the phone that a repeat of our rather ludicrous exercise would be just fine with her.

I wasn't so naïve as to fail to connect my lack of interest in that proposal with certain bleak recognitions that came to me from time to time, usually in the middle of the night when I couldn't sleep. But then every guy, I reassured myself by the welcome light of morning, was attracted to other guys just a little.

I was most certainly not attracted to Darryl.

Still, you had to feel sorry for his persistence. He actually seemed to think being friends with me was a possibility. Pity leads to bewildering gestures, I suppose. One night after closing, I took him up on his suggestion that we grab a slice of pizza.

One thing he'd told me, among many unwanted items: he was vegetarian. Thus I was surprised when he ordered a slice of pepperoni.

"Are you kidding?" he said when I called him on it. "This is *synthetic* pepperoni. It's made from plastic, not meat."

I rolled my eyes.

"You should get real meat," he went on. "Like sausage."

"You think I'm a real meat kind of guy?" I asked him.

"Absolutely." He wolfed down his slice. For a skinny kid, he had quite the appetite. He reminded me a little of this freshman, Harry Lewinsky, Lebovski, something like that; Mike and Gabe and I used to torment him in the showers during P.E. Harry who'd transferred to another school after freshman year. I'd totally forgotten about all that.

I was a little irritated with Darryl for dredging up pointless memories. By the time I'd finished my slice, I was more than ready to get out of there.

"I've never ridden a motorcycle," he said as we stood awkwardly in the parking lot. "Come on. You should give me a ride. What about it?"

"You crazy? You've got your car."

"No, I mean just up and down the street."

I tried hard to think of a reason not to, but it was dark, and I didn't care a thing about his safety, so why not?

He was clumsy getting on behind me. "Grab hold," I told him.

"To what?"

I hesitated. "Put your arms around my chest," I instructed. "No, like that. Under my arms. There you go."

What the fuck had I gotten myself into? He clung tight, even though we weren't going anywhere yet. "Ease up a bit," I told him, and when he did, I took us out of the parking lot. That made him tighten his grip all over again, but what could I say? Instead, I tried scaring him a little. I raced us through a yellow light just as it changed red. I weaved us in and out of traffic. I could feel his body pressed against mine, like we were frozen in a moment of wrestling while the thick night air streamed over us and the lights of the strip blurred past. "Whoa-ho!" I heard him yell next to my ear. I kept thinking we'd had enough, and I should turn back, but something, maybe it was his unexpected fearlessness, kept me going. Traffic was light, and soon we were past the developed areas; dark empty fields spread away from us on both sides. I pushed our speed till we were definitely unsafe – if a deer bounded onto the lane, we were goners. But it was a rush; it was somehow what I'd envisioned the future to be. I wouldn't have my Kawasaki at school, but I'd have my roommate, I'd have my new friends, good-looking guys in white jeans and black turtlenecks, and even though we wouldn't be going eighty-five miles an hour, still it would feel exactly like this.

All at once the thought that it was Darryl who was clinging to me for dear life was so depressing I knew I had to bring this stupid charade to an end. Without alerting him to what I was up to, I braked suddenly, skidding out onto the shoulder. The move caught him by surprise, and as we turned in a tight circle and came to a halt, off he tumbled.

"Jesus, you were supposed to hold tight," I said, though my tone belied my concern. What if I'd actually gone and hurt him? But he was laughing, already pulling himself up off the ground.

"Don't worry," he told me. "I'm really very resilient."

"Sorry about that," I apologized. "We must've hit a patch of gravel."

He was holding his left elbow and grimacing.

"Are you really okay?"

"I'm a bit skinned up is all. I think I ripped my shirt sleeve. I didn't like this shirt much anyway. But that was all pretty exciting. Do you always speed like that?"

The last thing I wanted to admit to was having gotten carried away – and yet that's what I'd done. My actions, frankly, perturbed me.

"So what do you want to do now?" I asked. "Should I take you to the emergency room?"

He laughed. I'll never forget that laugh – high and bold and resigned, the way someone might laugh as they stepped off a cliff into pure airy nothing and below, like a heartbeat, the surf pounding, pounding on the shore.

"Oh," he said, as if it was nothing, "if you really want to know, what I'd love right now is to kiss you."

Maybe it was only my own treacherous heart pounding.

"You've got to be kidding," I told him. "You didn't just say that, did you?"

"One surprise deserves another. I didn't exactly expect you to try to kill me just now."

"Forget it," I said. "It's not gonna happen. Not even in the realm of possibility. What were you even thinking?"

"Well, I do think you owe me. I could've died there."

"I can't fucking believe this," I said.

"Forget it. I'll walk back," he said.

"You can't walk back. We've gone miles. It's the fucking middle of nowhere."

"You're upset," he said.

"No I'm not," I yelled. "I just don't like people playing games with me."

"What? You're the only one who gets to play games? You know you've had your eye on me."

"This is ridiculous. Get back on the bike. We're getting out of here."

For a moment he stood there, recalcitrant, a spoiled little kid who hadn't gotten his way. Then he shrugged – hopelessly, it seemed. Despite itself, my thundering heart went out to him a little. "Okay," he said. "Have it your way."

"No funny stuff," I told him as he climbed on behind me, but before I knew it his hands had gone straight to my crotch.

"My, my, my," he observed, his breath hot on my neck. There was no denying I had a hard-on.

"I'm pretty good at what I do," he murmured. His lips grazed my ear. "If you'll just relax and let me do it. Come on. We'll push the bike into those woods there. Nobody'll see us. Nobody'll ever know."

There hadn't been a single car come by since we'd been stopped; as if on cue, far up the straight road, a pair of headlights glimmered. But in the shadows of the trees all was still – though hardly quiet. A cacophony of tree frogs pulsed and ebbed and pulsed again with ever-renewed fervor. Led Zeppelin was never so noisy nor mad. It turned out Darryl hadn't lied; he was exceptionally good at what he did, not that I had anybody to compare him with. Though I groaned fair warning, he didn't let up till he'd taken my load in full.

I'd been clutching his hair, and now when I moved my

hands around to his face, I was disconcerted to feel tears on his cheeks.

"Jesus," I said. "What's wrong with you?"

"I just happen to feel really happy right now, you know? I'm just wishing you feel half so happy as I do."

I didn't feel happy at all; I felt empty and ashamed and freaked out. "Why shouldn't you be happy?" I accused. "You got lucky. You hit me in a moment of weakness. Every guy has a moment of weakness. And you – you took a one in a million shot and it paid off. You should be fucking delirious. But don't think for a minute I'm celebrating, because I'm not."

"Come on. You don't have to think of it that way," he said. "Really you don't."

"Let's get going," I told him. "This stupid little mistake is over. No, actually, it's not over, because it never even happened, okay?"

"Who'd believe me anyway?"

"You're right," I told him, unconsoled. "There's nobody would believe you." Except I knew deep down, with secret dread, that Sara would believe him – but of course Darryl didn't know Sara, he didn't know anybody I knew and he never would.

Still, I couldn't believe I'd given in so easily – and with somebody like him. That was what I found so humiliating. Sure, I'd imagined it before, those awful middle-of-the-night surrenders, only I'd pictured the first time going so very differently – a bit of horseplay with one of my track buddies slowly, gorgeously unfolding into something else, or better yet, some good-looking, tautly muscled runner from another county I'd met at a meet. We'd be cool together, we'd be discreet. When I'd bought the Kawasaki, I'd fantasized winging my way to a rendezvous with my secret, yet-to-be-met friend in some place where nobody would know either of us.

I dropped Darryl off in the parking lot of Pizza Hut. I was glad he hadn't tried to kiss me on the ear or neck or anything on the ride back; I was grateful at least for that bit of restraint. I was only sorry his arms had felt so good around my chest.

"Don't get any stupid ideas," I felt I had to warn him as he walked to his car. Did I detect a sort of triumphant lightness in his step?

"Who's saying anything?" he said as he slid, with a self-satisfied smirk, into his faded old Dodge. I swear the radio, when he turned on the engine, was playing "Goodbye, Yellow Brick Road."

I contemplated not showing up for work the next day, even quitting my job altogether, but in the end decided, via some very convoluted night-time logic, that the best course of action was to show him that, as far as I was concerned, it really was true that nothing had happened. Since I almost never talked to him in the store anyway, it would be easy enough to avoid eye contact as well. My one fear was that he'd come over and try to chat as if nothing had happened, but soon enough it became clear that he had no intention of trying that tactic. After several days I had to grudgingly admit to myself that, if nothing else, I admired his discretion.

I thought sometimes about his accusation that I'd been eyeing him. Maybe it had been true, a little. I couldn't quite remember. But now I did catch myself glancing at him from time to time when I was sure he wasn't looking; I was oddly sorry, as the days lengthened into a week, then two, that we hadn't somehow done more when we'd had the chance. I was beginning to think of it as a wasted opportunity. Not that I really wished all that much to reciprocate. Still, I did find myself, wretchedly awake and restless toward dawn, wondering– with less and less certainty that my curiosity was purely "scientific curiosity" – what it might feel like to have a penis in your mouth. And those times when the physical tension became just too much, and there was nothing left but to release it, how disheartened I was to find Darryl shouldering aside, at the crucial moment, the more muscular phantoms of my teammates with whom I usually preoccupied myself in those messy nocturnal ordeals.

I watched him kidding around with Jennifer and Denise, touching them playfully, making them squeal with laughter at some off-color comment about a customer or a band, and I realized, seeing all that rapport, that my presence here among them was merely temporary, that I didn't, in some fundamental way, count with them. Come September, I'd be gone, and they – well, hadn't Darryl said, boasted almost, "Endless summer for me?"

I found it hard to believe he didn't want more, too, and the possibility that he'd gotten everything he wanted from me and was satisfied secretly angered me.

On my rare free evenings I usually tried to hang out with Mike and Gabe; both of them, however, were proving unusually busy that summer, and not always easy to make plans with. But several times the three of us managed, as in bygone days, to go for a long, deliciously exhausting run through the leafy streets of midtown and along the secluded, winding paths of Overton Park. How good it felt, at the end of one of those jaunts, to give my decent, normal buddies a quick hug goodbye, smell the musk of their bodies, feel their strong arms enfold me likewise. Then home to a shower, a joint, some Stones or Jethro Tull on the headphones. Those were the only nights that summer I seemed to find my way to any kind of sleep.

July came to an end, and my calendar, that had shown such a host of blank days, revealed barely two weeks' worth left to scratch off before freedom and the world. Meanwhile, I received in the mail my roommate assignment: with plunging heart I beheld in the accompanying photograph a squinting oriental fellow burdened with coke-bottle glasses and an unpronounceable last name.

That very evening, as we were closing up (Darryl had taken to leaving promptly at ten, prudently vanishing before I'd even finished rolling down the security gate), I opted to break our long silence.

"So," I said as he made to leave, "feel like grabbing a bite of pizza by any chance?"

He stopped mid-stride, looked at his watch and hesitated. "Sure," he said, after a maddening pause, "I could probably do that."

There are times, in a race, when you think you've gauged your opponent, when you're sure he's going to make a move to pull ahead of the pack, and you're timing it, waiting for him to make his move before you then make yours. I was pretty good at psyching out the opposition. Darryl was, in his way, a formidable adversary.

"Still a vegetarian?" I observed as he ordered his slice of pepperoni.

"You bet," he told me.

If he took it as some kind of allusion, or maybe double entendre, as I secretly hoped, he made no sign of it.

Pizza Hut was crowded. A sense of futility descended on me. I realized I'd been depending on Darryl to somehow help things along, but he seemed nonchalant – even, had I not known better – clueless.

"Gosh, time flies, doesn't it?" he remarked, wiping his mouth with a napkin. "I can't believe August's already here. You'll be going away to school soon."

"Yeah," I told him. "Soon."

"That's too bad, I guess."

"Can't be soon enough," I reminded both of us.

"I guess so."

If I were him, I told myself impatiently, I'd see my best chance and take it. Instead, we finished up our Cokes in silence. I told myself I absolutely refused to offer to take him out for a spin on my bike.

"We could, you know, if you wanted to, go for a . . ." I could hear my voice peter out amidst the din of the room. Once again he looked at his watch – a tactic clearly meant to annoy me, I thought.

"Sure," he drawled thoughtfully. "We could do that. Only if you want to . . ."

I remember looking around at the other booths and tables, parents with their kids, guys out with their girlfriends, in a corner an old couple who must have been married fifty years, and I thought, with chilling clarity, I'm seeing all this for the last time. I'm bidding all this goodbye.

"Yeah," I said. "I guess I want to."

As soon as we were safely past the lights of the strip malls and roaring into the dark, his hands shifted purposefully from my chest to my crotch. I sighed, and flushed, and drove us on to a secluded farm road I'd idly scouted out a few days before.

"Don't worry," he said. "I know the rules. No kissing. No funny stuff. Shall we get straight to business?"

I'd always loved hugging guys, always tried to slow-motion and savor those moments with my buddies and teammates, though I also knew better than to try to do that anywhere except in my head. "Come here," I told Darryl, opening my arms and folding him in an embrace and yes, for the first time in my life actually slowing down time for real. I think it completely surprised him – certainly it surprised me– but he adjusted. He hugged me back just the way I hugged him. I almost felt like crying, though crying wasn't something I did.

"So, hi," he said quietly. "I thought you'd never get around to asking."

"Shut up," I told him. "Just do what you have to do."

And so it started. How many times did we tryst during the next two reckless weeks? Altogether, probably only six or seven, certainly less than ten. As if enacting some secret, solemn ritual, we'd take my bike out to that same secluded bit of farm road. I don't know why we never came up with some better alternative, or even thought to vary our routine. We weren't particularly innovative, either; it took several occasions before I finally yielded to that ravenous curiosity that had consumed my nights.

"Really," he said, as I dropped to my knees and unbuttoned his fancy trousers. (What had he worn on his prom night? Had he even gone?) "You don't have to. I'm okay with . . ."

"Shut up," I told him, "and look at the stars."

His cock was slenderer than mine but longer; as I buried my nose in his pubic hair the odor was faintly sweaty, a little funky, a desperate and gratifying whiff of that jock stench that came off my buddies when I embraced them at the end of the course, no matter whether we'd won or lost.

His voice came to me from above my head. "There's not just stars," he said. "There's planes. I count two, three. All heading out from the airport. Heading for Spain – like in the song."

I half-expected him to start singing, but he didn't. I couldn't have cared less if he had, to be perfectly honestly. I was doing my own traveling, where I'd never thought I would go.

I hadn't stopped to consider that his shaft would make me gag. He laughed appreciatively. "Don't worry," he said with such gentleness. "You'll get the hang of it. We all do, eventually."

After a while my jaw began to feel a bit tired; he must have realized this, being the more experienced. His lemon-yellow trousers were around his ankles. Taking my right hand by the wrist, he moved it between his thighs. "Put your finger in me," he instructed.

Hardly had I accomplished that rather unexpected favor when he groaned and I felt his warm seed spurt into my mouth. I wasn't completely surprised by the taste and texture; I'd experimented with touching my coated fingertips to my tongue on a couple of desperate occasions. Still –

I wasn't exactly happy I'd become a cocksucker – more resigned to it than anything else. A phase of experimentation, I told myself, though we barely progressed beyond putting our penises in each other's mouths. And I wasn't at all sure I wanted his finger where he wanted mine, so that never happened. We never kissed, either, at least on the mouth, though I allowed him to smooch my neck, and shoulder, and belly, and I allowed myself to nuzzle, on occasion, the pleasing curve of his collarbone. I liked to run my fingers through his longish thick hair.

By daylight, in the record store where we never spoke, never acknowledged one another in any way, his crooked teeth bothered me. Why hadn't his parents gotten him braces? At eleven and twelve I'd endured the curse of braces, and now my smile was for all intents perfect. It seemed like such an obvious thing to have left undone, though I suppose they perhaps couldn't have afforded it. About his parents, his home life, his time in school I knew nothing. I told myself I preferred it that way, and that, besides, it was necessary, safer somehow. I knew he wasn't anybody I could ever let myself be seen with; his life, whatever it was, wasn't something I wanted to be associated with.

Rather perversely, I never told Darryl when I planned on leaving. I thought since what was happening between us was, by common consent, *not* really happening, what better way to mark that than by just vanishing into thin air? He knew I was going away to school, he knew perfectly well September approached: he could put two and two together, and see just how numbered our days were.

To be quite honest: I felt relieved that it would soon be over. There were times when I told myself I had walked into something I never should have walked into, that I had made a very bad mistake, and the only thing that kept my despair at bay was the reassuring thought that soon, soon, I would have moved on, and put the episode harmlessly behind me. It had been a sorry kind of practice, I told myself, for much better things to come.

"You seem to like how this feels," I said, removing my mouth from his cock and twisting my finger in his rectum. It had been, unbeknownst to him, my last day at work; it would be our last lovely bit of misbehavior together.

"I do." He sighed. "A lot."

Inspired by his response, I screwed a second finger in.

He groaned appreciatively. "We could, you know . . . If you wanted. I brought some lube," he said.

"You what?"

"Some lube. In case you ever decided to graduate with me to the next level."

He pulled from his pocket a half-scrolled tube of vasoline.

"You use this stuff often?" I asked.

He grinned that grin full of crooked teeth. "I'm not a virgin, if that's what you're worried about."

"I'm not worried," I said, though I wondered what he meant, exactly: what other escapades he was alluding to.

"I'm also not a slut," he said. "Here, put some of this on your dick."

"I never said you were."

"Go slow," he cautioned as I nudged my way in. "Give me time to adjust."

But I didn't give him time to adjust. The sensation was so unexpectedly exquisite that I grabbed him by his slim hips and thrust myself fully inside. It took him by surprise, and he yelled "Ow!" – which excited me, and I thrust again, gratified to be having this effect on him. Gradually he did adjust, and his cries evolved into a satisfying series of yelps and whimpers. I liked that I was hurting him like this, and his own apparent enjoyment of the pain I was bestowing on him both bewildered and moved me. I reached around and gripped his rigid cock, all the while keeping up my stupendous rhythm, and soon I had him squirting, which set me to squirting as well. "Oh," he said, in what sounded like wonder. "You came inside me."

"Sorry," I said.

"No," he said. "It's great. One for the road."

"What does that mean?"

He looked at me over his shoulder. I thought about kissing him just then – but of course that would never, never do. "You tell me," he said.

I eased myself from him. We'd both worked up a copious sweat. The whole thing, from beginning to end, had been much messier than I'd imagined, and a whole lot more exciting.

"If I'd known," Darryl said, "I'd have brought a towel. But you never do know, do you? That's what I love about my life."

It had never occurred to me that Darryl might love his life.

As we sped back dangerously along the dark highway to deposit him at his car in the mall's empty parking lot, I thought angrily that he'd *better* have loved every minute, because after tonight he was never going to see me again. Still, I couldn't get Darryl's remark out of my head, audacious and nonsensical as it was: "That's what I love about my life."

A couple of evenings later – I was leaving for school the next morning–I walked out into my front yard and saw the late light glinting on a silver jet as it sped across the clear sky, con trail in its wake. The first line of "Daniel" ran through my mind. That mellifluous, stylish little song had insinuated itself into my head. At that point in my young life I'd never flown in an airplane before, and the sight of that star-bright vessel heading for Spain or some other faraway place equally remarkable filled me with a pointless longing that turned, all at once, into a very pointed longing for none other than unbeloved Darryl, whom I had so resolutely abandoned along his goofy smile and abundant seed and unexplored life; I actually groaned aloud in a kind of sorrow and desire and regret all confused together like the notes of a difficult, altogether unsingable song that wasn't Elton John's at all, but wholly, alas, my own.

After a moment, though, I recovered, and the next day went forth unhesitatingly into my bright, broken future.

Tying the Knot

Robin Metcalfe

According to their tickets, the young couple in lower 4 had still had different last names when they booked their fare on the Ocean Limited. They boarded my car in Montreal as Mr and Mrs, newly minted, heading for a honeymoon back East. Wearing matching outfits, modish for that era, as understood by small-town Nova Scotia. Each wore grey slacks, a pink shirt, and the groom wore a grey knit tie. Light brown hair, falling over his collar in soft curls, a fresh, blank face on which time had not yet decided what to write. His bride was a more rounded version of the same. They must have come straight from the reception, looking barely old enough to be going to the prom. They – almost – seemed to regret the prospect of taking off their party clothes later, to celebrate their nuptials in a narrow lower berth behind a heavy wool curtain.

That's the quick impression I jotted in my journal that evening, after getting the beds down, while a few last passengers straggled back from the bar car and the lights of Québec rippled across the Saint Lawrence. On the same page are quick verbal sketches of men I had ogled earlier that day in Montreal. My scraggly handwriting preserves them, like ripe fruit plucked from the sun, sensual memories to be stored away and tasted again later. The line of a back, a jaunty walk, a handsome face, a round firm butt.

For some reason, there is a distinct graphic sensibility in the record of my erotic responses that week, alert to bold contrasts and qualities of line. On Crescent Street, from a terrace in the hot summer afternoon, that last day of August, 1984, I'd been struck by a young Asian man, ferociously beautiful, with stiff black hair and wedge-shaped eyebrows like two fierce brushstrokes. Later, on Sainte-Catherine, a small man with a billowy shirt, its immaculate white linen bracketed by ink-black hair above and black pants below.

That aesthetic severity did not make me averse to the pastel charms of the new groom. While I would not sing to him, each spring to him, I *might* worship the trousers (polyester blend? almost certainly) that were clinging to his shapely buttocks. His pink slinky shirt tapered neatly from wide, lean shoulders to an Endymion waist, one that had yet to register a history of too many beery barbecues.

Why do hets go all nelly when they get married? I wondered. No-one does frou-frou as exuberantly and badly as couples at their weddings. (It would be another twenty years before Canadian queers joined the bandwagon of bad taste and buried the world in a landslide of rainbow wedding invitations.) The bridesmaids, who know it is their job to look fat and hideous beside the dazzling bride, wrap themselves in tents of lime or eggplant-coloured satin. Young studs who normally wouldn't be caught dead in ruffles suddenly preen and fluff themselves like the less reputable sort of tropical bird.

As a porter, I observed the outfits of others from the sartorial security of a uniform. The classic CN monkey-suit had been similar to that of a bell-hop: a short-waisted red cotton jacket with lapel collar over a white shirt and black tie; close-fitting charcoal trousers that crisply defined both basket and butt, with a racing stripe of black piping down the side. It was a combination well suited to show off a trim young gay body, particularly while doing the gymnastics routine involved in making down open sections. I've known car men, of no apparent queer bent, to linger while squeezing past me in the narrow corridor, drawing out the moment when they brushed past my uplifted ass.

After Canadian passenger services were combined under VIA in the late 70s, however, we got new uniforms. A formless jacket of purest acrylic (blue or red) that melted at the touch of a cigarette. It ignored the shape of the body beneath, hanging sullenly over my best assets fore and aft. If we were the ugly bridesmaids, who were the brides we were supposed to make look good? Perhaps the Passenger Service Assistants, who strutted around in natty grey suits, handing out brochures while I sweated in my plastic tunic to put away the linen.

The top and bottom of the outfit had changed the least. The black porter cap was still a short pill-box with a shiny visor, although the band had changed from CN red to VIA yellow. The black shoes, carefully polished, remained the same. Dress shoes with steel toes, since portering is an industrial occupation as well as a form of personal service.

Tidying away the beds the next morning, I saw that the groom had carefully removed his swanky new tie without untying it, keeping the knot intact, as he looped it over a light fixture. This is not the way to care for a tie, I noted to myself. Probably he did not trust himself to achieve the knot a second time; probably an older male relative, or, worse, his mother, had tied it for him. Now he's stranded on a train in the middle of New Brunswick with no father or brother or mother to turn to. The dimpled swell of a Windsor knot, removed from the neck it adorns, will crumple like a soufflé removed from the oven and leave the tie creased, not suitable for retying. Someone would have to have a talk with that boy.

Working as a porter, I took pride in my care of masculine appurtenances – what haberdashers would call "men's furnishings". Buried in the bottom of my bags was my kit. A fine horsehair shaving brush and the razor my father has used for forty years (Schick injectible, brass with an ivory cellulose handle). To protect my work shoes, a pair of red shoe socks that I had found at a flea market, sporting the outline of the lower 48 states and the words "American Trailways" in white.

Whenever I unwrapped my shoes and began to cram myself into my uniform – in an empty roomette in the Point Saint-Charles coach yards, weeds blowing in the hot dry wind outside, along rusty tracks where the old CN colours (black grey red) flaked off derelict Pullmans – my kit helped me to remember who I was. Like the lace undies of a fetishist, whispering one story to my body while my drab uniform prosaically stated another.

The bridegroom nicked himself in the morning, shaving. His girlfriend – no, his wife – came to me in search of a towel. He had gone into the next car to find a washroom that had running water, the tanks on our car having run dry. He returned, shirtless, through the heavy steel doors between the cars, giving me a good view of his hairless torso. His chest was boyishly smooth but with nice definition. The line between his shoulder blades described a pleasing S-curve into the small of his back before disappearing under the waistband of his pants.

We were passing through Rogersville, ablaze with Acadian flags. I had just finished tidying up a vacated bedroom when the young husband poked his head beseechingly around the door frame. He had staunched the cut and put his shirt back on, and from his hand hung the tie, unknotted. Could I help him? He had apparently tried to pull yesterday's knot on over his head and all had come unravelled. Did I perhaps know how to knot a tie?

Come into my parlour, said the sleeping car porter to the groom. His helplessness made me feel very suave and mature for my thirty years. The young man placed his tie in my outstretched hand where I examined it, frowning slightly. Leaving it knotted overnight had left the fabric twisted. I smoothed it between my thumb and forefinger, letting the cloth relax back into a smooth fullness. My passenger stood facing me, his collar up and his hands at his sides, waiting for my help. His eyes stared guilelessly into mine, his lips slightly parted. I could easily have kissed him.

As pleasant as it was to look into that innocent, expectant

face, I was accustomed to knotting my own tie, not those of other men. It was all backwards. Turn around, I said, and taking him gently by the shoulders I rotated him 180 degrees to face the triple mirror over the bedroom's tiny porcelain sink. Now we could each see the two of us, the (older, more experienced, more dirty-minded) porter standing close behind the young man who had sought his help. I pulled the tie straight, giving one last tug to ease out its wrinkles, and reached my arms around him from behind.

Dear reader, you can take it from here, if you are so inclined. I have given you the set-up. The privacy of an empty bedroom, on a train (the romance of travel, far from the habits and constraints of daily life, ships passing in the night – provide your own cliché). A lovely young man, just married, in his sexual prime, perhaps not fully sated from the previous night's exertions, his unmoored libido perhaps drifting towards other shores. A slightly older man, sexually self-aware, more knowing of the ways of the world. The young groom has placed himself willingly in this man's hands; is standing, now with the older man's arms around him, his butt gently pressed into his groin. (I almost groan at the thought, just hold myself back from pressing forward to firm up the connection.) The older man is in uniform. (Okay, it's a porter uniform, but work with me here: the cap is not bad.) He has some authority on this little vessel, this sleeping car. He has a tie in his hand – he is apparently good with knots. Surely you can do something with that.

Did I rub my hot hands down his torso, cup his cock and balls manfully in my hand, crush my own swelling bulge into the crevice of his muscular ass? Did I take his jaw in my hand and turn his lips to mine for a smouldering kiss? Do you think I should tell you? Or should I leave you with that tantalizing moment, like an iridescent bubble of lust, holding its breath before the three-fold image in the mirror?

I will tell you that I stood, his body a breath's distance from my own, and tied his tie as if it were mine, as if his reflection in the mirror were my own. Teaching him what I hardly knew I knew; improvising an instruction manual for an action I did wordlessly every day. Over, under, over, up and through. Do everything with the fat end, I said; hold on to the knot so that it doesn't fall apart until you are done.

It is not the alienness of the homoerotic that sets some straight men's nerves on edge; it is its very familiarity. Men can only learn to be men from other men, in a pedagogy as intimate and tender as the bond between lovers. That day in front of the mirror was one of my earliest inklings that I could be one initiating another into the masculine rites.

That day also taught me something about my own masculinity. It opened up the prospect that I, who grew up a notorious sissy, might grow into that manhood that all men seek in one another, gay or straight. Age, that capricious conjurer, bestower of breasts on grizzled old men, might also confer masculinity on those men who have learned to live without it, as their mildness mellows into quiet authority. A gentle boy is called a sissy. A gentle man is called . . . a gentleman.

A porter is a gentleman's gentleman. Not to be confused with a man's man, or a man who is for men – although he may be either or both. A personal servant, he is also a man in uniform – even if it is made out of acrylic. In common with military officers, teachers, haberdashers, priests and valets, he is called upon to evince authority, discretion, reserve and good grooming.

Are regular ties easier to knot than knit ones? asked the young husband. Yes and no: smooth fabric slides more easily into place; knit fabric holds its place more securely once you've got it there.

That's it. I was done grooming the groom, teaching him how one man ties another man up. Young fellow went on with his marriage, happily or unhappily, had lots of kids or came out or both. As for me, one week later I allowed myself to be filmed on a beach in Acadian Chezzetcook (near where my grandmother's people came from) performing fellatio on a banana. My journal records that I saw a man in Halifax, at the Silver Spoon, with short coal-black hair, a little spiky and brushed forward in the centre. He had incredibly full black eyelashes, hard to achieve even with mascara, and several days growth of beard; a full mustache and very white teeth. In his New Wave-ish grey bomber jacket, I wrote, he was "dazzlingly sexy".

Alaska

Trebor Healey

He came to Anavik in August. He didn't know anybody here and took a room in Curtis Shandley's boarding house for the fall term. He was young and tall, rangy. He looked like the typical young man from the states who came up this way – likely a mountain climber of some sort. He'd come, ostensibly, to teach school – fifth grade – at the Anavik grade school.

He kept to himself generally, though he was friendly in an aloof sort of way. Not really standoffish, he projected a public persona that you suspected wasn't the whole story, but was all you were going to get. He related in order not to relate. He let you know he was there and was harmless – you could safely ignore him. It seemed he was in a sense asking you to ignore him with this ritual superficiality he displayed.

He ate with the other boarders at Shandley's, made the usual small talk, but never made any attachments to anyone there. They were a mixed crew as it was: stoic Eskimos working the fishing fleet, gruff loggers and truckers, pipeline workers. He was the schoolteacher – he was supposed to be the talker. But he didn't assume that role. He washed the pots, cleaned up, kept himself busy that way in the idle hours when men socialized.

But if he wasn't terribly social, he seemed to take a great interest in the trees. He was often seen standing under one – a Douglas fir or hemlock – staring up into its branches or circling its trunk with a kind of wonder and curiosity in his gaze, almost as if he'd never seen a tree before.

He wasn't a mountain climber as it turned out. He had none of the gear for it. All he'd brought with him were a laptop and a duffle bag of clothes. Curtis Shandley told us all this one night at the Hoot Owl, where I was line cook. Shandley drank and Shandley liked to spin tales. One never trusted Shandley completely. He was a fisherman, and like most fishermen, full of stories from the vast and voiceless sea that consequently could never be verified. He'd nearly died of pneumonia more than once and had infected his wife with it one fateful winter, killing her, and in his grief, putting an end to his fishing career. Since her demise, he'd sought to become both of them in a sense, keeping house – sewing, even – cooking meals for his boarders, while still splitting wood, fixing cars, repairing boats and re-roofing houses. Many people thought when she died, his spirit went with her body, and that her spirit jumped into his, so that he was in a sense both of them, but really more her now than himself. The manly things he did were things his body did from memory. The things he did that were formerly hers came to him in an oddly facile manner that fed superstition and wild supernatural speculation.

Shandley told us the man was writing a book of some sort.

"On trees?" I inquired.

"I don't think so. Some kind of novel."

"About Anavik?"

"I don't think so. He seems to be nearly finished with it."

"Why is he here?"

"I don't know. To teach school, I guess; finish the book."

I nodded and said nothing more.

But I wondered. Why Anavik? Why come here? A hard place. Why come here to write a book? Other than the isolation, which was something, I suppose. Something writers valued I'd heard. Whatever the case, his being a writer explained his social reticence as far as most people were concerned; allowed them to forget him; to give him his place and return their attention once more to their own lives.

*   *   *

One night, after closing, I saw him climbing a tree. A big spruce, next to the post office. He was about halfway up it when I spied him. It was summer and the middle of the night, so maybe he was after the sunset. It was going purple and pink and it was messed with all number of clouds that gave it yellow streaks. It would be very beautiful to a stranger. It would be worth climbing a tree for.

I stood and watched him, in my stained white uniform, my parka, in the fatigue brought on by another eight-hour day frying burgers and making soup from moose and caribou stock. I liked being a cook. In a place so difficult, so cold, that required so much hard work just to survive, making food was a sacred thing. My father didn't and wouldn't understand that. He worked with heavy equipment, was all tied up with the lumber and oil companies. He was "hooked up" to Alaska, he would say. Right down to the Eskimo wife and mixed-blood son. My father was here in a certain way, and it wasn't my way. There was nothing to be done about it, though, so we'd grown estranged.

I sat on the bench in front of the hardware store across the street and watched him, waiting for him to stop, turn around, come back down. But he kept going, slowly and surely up, through the cracking branches, starting and stopping, making a racket as he found footholds. It was a big tree, a hundred feet at least.

I was cold; he had to be cold too. After 45 minutes, I was too cold to sit any longer and watch this strange spectacle. But I couldn't pull myself away. I needed to understand something about it, or if not that, I needed to watch over his work, witness it. There was something important, meaningful in his climbing that tree. But I wasn't one to fret or push things too far, so I retired, went on home, turning now and again, in the lonely street – visited at this hour only by idling lumber trucks and the occasional pickup – to look back and see the disturbance in the high branches that indicated his struggle; listened for the continual snap of the dense twigs he busily furrowed through.

The next morning when he walked into the Hoot Owl, I gave him the cursory look I do all customers until it dawned on me who he was. I didn't know his name of course, had never been formally introduced. He still had spruce needles in his hair, smears of sap on his parka. There were only three other people in there, sitting at the counter: Nana, my aunt, who was the owner, having her breakfast; Katak, the fisherman; and Griswold, the postmaster. The first two weren't big talkers and the other two didn't know each other, so it was quiet. It was 5 a.m., and it occurred to me that the sun rising outside, yellow and pink, looked much like it had when it went down the night before.

I brought him coffee and placed it before him. He gave me an appreciative grin, looking up from the menu, which he afterward put down. I didn't smile back because I don't smile at anyone. I don't like the way people use smiles, getting in the way of who they really are, what they really mean. His perfunctory little smile nearly put me off my curiosity about him. Of course, he's a school teacher. He must smile. Childhood is terrifying after all. The smile of the older ones is really all that gets you through it.

He ordered eggs and pancakes, without smiling this time. He said thank you in a flat way, a straightforward way, when I put his food down in front of him.

Griswold turned to him then, raised his voice over the three seats between them: "Teaching school over there, eh?"

"Yes," he said

"Where you from?"

"Down south."

"Well, I figured that much!" And he laughed as if he were with a whole group of people in on some joke, but Katak and Nana didn't even blink. "Where south?"

"California." And he said it quickly, almost shamefully.

"Getting used to our weather?" And Griswold looked to Nana, who ignored him, and to Katak who just looked right through him.

"I like it here," the young man said. And he beamed when

he said that. "It's a good place. I like the children at the
school. I'm Thane." And he reached his hand across the
seats. Griswold fumbled with his napkin, wiping his face and
hands, a bit put out by the sudden enthusiasm of the young
man's response. He clumsily grasped Thane's outstretched
arm.

"Leonard, Leonard Griswold, postmaster."

"I'll see you around then," Thane said, pulling out his
wallet and looking toward me. I came and told him he owed 5
dollars and 45 cents. He gave me 7 dollars, said thank you,
again without smiling, and departed.

This was how his friendliness worked. He'd respond to
whoever talked to him monosyllabically at first. Then he'd
warm up in time to introduce himself, but only just before
leaving, which left the impression that he was a nice person,
that perhaps you could get to know him later. But it was
always this way. Standoffish at first, then warm just before
leaving. From then on you were an acquaintance, someone
he'd gotten out of the way and no longer needed to converse
with. Just a nod or a quick hello would do.

So no one got to know Thane. I figured we were probably
just characters in his book. That was his world. But I was
wrong about that. That morning, when he left, having come
down from the tree he'd spent the night in, something
between us turned, and he became curious about me after
that. I could tell. He watched me for a split second too long as
I poured coffee, and later when I wiped the counter. He had
noticed I did not appreciate smiles – had noticed that right
away, and respected it. He was careful never to smile around
me after that. He knew that about me. I knew he knew other
things because of that.

"Why did you climb the tree?" I asked him one morning
after pouring his coffee.

I looked at him in such a way that he would know I wanted
a concise answer; I didn't want to have a conversation. I
realized I was interested in his strangeness, his different-

ness, more than in him as a person. I'm not that interested in individuals actually. Not really. I'm only really interested in what they do, what their motivations are. What they know about things.

"I like that tree," he said. "It's a nice tree." And there you have it. I wanted to ask him if he'd climbed other trees, but that would have entailed a conversation which I didn't want to have. It wasn't necessary besides. Others spoke of his passion. Even Griswold. "I was fishing up at Clay Creek, and that teacher fella – he was in a tree. I called up to him, but he wouldn't answer or didn't hear. He was way up there. I was there a few hours and he never came down." Griswold had just shrugged his shoulders, slurped his soup. Nana told me she saw him sleeping in a tree once. It was a fir tree, leaning onto another larger tree. "Like a child leaning against its mother's hip," she'd said. "He looked sweet there, curled up like a little boy. Something lost about him, I think," she said, before changing the subject to the meat order.

I chanced upon him one day, finally, myself. I liked tracking badger, much to my father's consternation, who had tried to make me a big game hunter like himself. I was going up a steep ravine when I heard it. That snapping sound – cacophony really. Distinctive. It wasn't graceful what he did. He wasn't like a badger. Or any animal out there really.

He was clearly not made for trees. Not of this place.

I didn't immediately investigate. It seemed a solitary thing for him. I wanted to respect it as such. Besides, he'd likely scared off any badger. So, there was nothing to do but find a place to sit and watch for awhile.

I located the rustling leaves and could see he was on the opposite side of the tree from where I sat on a boulder. I looked around, saw some birds flitting about, a butterfly, listened to the grasshoppers click, the flies buzz, the mosquitoes drone. I heard water falling as the nearby creek quickened through the gorge. And Thane. Thane was like some new, awkward animal who hadn't found a way yet to blend in. His racket was all discord and dissonance in a scene that had found a balance over millennia, that made of it one sound.

It seemed hilarious all of a sudden, and I laughed at his clumsiness – at the clumsiness of a man up a tree. Bears made such a racket too, I remembered then, but they didn't make a habit of climbing trees generally, so I hadn't considered it. Perhaps though, he was no less a part of all this than a bear. Which made him very much a part of all this. I laughed for a while, and as I wasn't one to laugh, when it came it burst out of me like water and flowed for a good long while.

He must have heard me because the rustling in the fir suddenly quieted, then stopped. I still couldn't see him and wondered if he now saw me. Like a bear. This too made me laugh: the sudden wariness of him. Like a bear. I picked up stones and began throwing them at the tree, attempting to hit the branches near him. Then I thought to hide. If he hadn't seen me yet, he'd have no idea who I was. Who knows what he'd think? He might become afraid and shimmy down. I could track him then through the woods, follow him like a badger, full of stealth and mischief. I felt suddenly like I had as a child, teasing a cat or a dog.

But he didn't come down. Nor did he resume climbing. I was in the bushes now, under the branches of a thicket. I knew he couldn't see me, and I knew how to remain still. I wondered what he was thinking up there.

It got colder, darker, and still nothing. No snapping branches, no rustling about.

There was only waiting. That was always what it was with most things. Waiting.

I would wait.

The stream grew louder in the dusk, the crickets diminished. Shadows were the things I saw now. I began to worry a bit about bear. I had my pistol, but I really should have brought a rifle if I planned to spend the night. A pistol was pretty useless against a grizzly. I suppose I should have just left. I should have known that he'd not come down. I'd seen this before, his spending the night in a tree. And now, what was the use of my mischief? A test of wills. Or so it seemed to me. But how could I know if he even suspected I was still there? Or had ever been there? How could I be sure it was my laughter that had stopped his climbing? How could I know if he hadn't just stopped coincidentally at the same time? It was possible.

Then again, perhaps it really was a bear, and not Thane at all. A test of wills with a bear was something.

I fell off to sleep all the same, and I slept then for a long time. And I dreamed about my mother. Remembered her waving goodbye from the ferry. She was going to a funeral. The whole group of them going to the funeral of a great aunt of mine. All of them went down with the boat, as if with the relative they'd gone to mourn. For many years afterward, I waited for her. Not in the way my father did, who looked at boats in a funny, stupefied way after that – but here, out in the forest. I understood that she would come this way when she returned.

When I awoke, the little canyon was loud again with grasshoppers and birds. The water sounded fuller. The sun was high, high enough that I knew it must be past seven, well after sunrise. I looked at the tree, but detected no movement. I went over to it and circled it and looked up into it as I'd seen him do. Eventually, I figured he was gone. He never stayed late in trees as far as I knew. He was a teacher; he'd be at the school by now.

So I headed back. I needed to work that night as well and hadn't planned on spending so much time out in the woods. I was surprised he hadn't awoken me. I didn't really believe he could get out of there quietly, or if he had, that I was so tired that I wouldn't have heard him.

And then I noticed something; something different ahead. Along the creek. The rocks looked different, the dirt was all exposed like some great beast – only a bear could do it – had fouled the bank on its way down. But when I looked down there, toward the stream, I saw Thane. Propped up against a rock, he was massaging his ankle and shivering terribly.

"Hey," I said, and scrambled down the embankment. He looked frightened and I wondered how long he'd been here like this; how long he'd been shivering. He'd fallen into the creek and his clothes were drenched. Why was he still in them? How long had he been sitting here? I knew what needed to be done and I did it quickly, dragging him out of the creek, stripping off his wet clothes, and then my own, and rubbing my hands against his chest to warm his heart; pressing my body to his in a bear hug to give him my warmth. But he kept on shaking.

I needed to get him into the sun, which was difficult as we were in a ravine and he had sprained his ankle badly. I would have to carry him back up to the clearing, to the tree he had climbed, where there was a small meadow and sunshine. He was heavy, but not very, perhaps only 150–160 lbs. But I was only 140 lbs myself, so it was awkward. I carried him piggyback, and thusly I plodded determinedly up the trail, huffing and puffing, while he shook. When we reached the clearing, I knelt down and rolled him off me. Still he shivered, and again I embraced him as fully as possible, in the sun now, rubbing my hands across his chest and back, moving my legs against his legs, breathing my breath into his mouth – anything to generate as much heat as possible. I hadn't brought my clothes back up with us, and perhaps I should have as it might have served as a blanket to warm him up still faster. I thought to go back for them, but I couldn't leave him there, even for a second, shivering. It wouldn't be right and it wouldn't be wise.

Next I would need to make a fire, and something hot for him to drink. But first I had to stop his shivering. I was getting worried. There isn't much time in such things. I wouldn't have time to make a fire and tea I realized. We were fortunate only in that it was warm in the sun.

What happened next didn't come from me. It came from the sun. Or fire. I didn't really make a decision about it at all. It just happened. I kissed him. I kept rubbing him too, and then I gave myself over to this effort completely. Perhaps I remembered how much heat it could generate. From Kita and Anna, from Valerie. Even on cold nights, we'd sweated as we'd struggled to give ourselves to each other.

Nana had told me when I was just 15: "Sex is a gift you give someone." She said that, "People get lonely, lost, confused, unable to remember certain things. They make horrible mistakes. They get hurt. Then you chance across each other. You are a piece of good luck for one another. Sometimes a child is born. All children are lucky. They know they are, but they forget. Maybe when they grow up and have sex, they remember." And she'd giggled then, before sighing: "So much is forgotten. Remember this much."

I thought of my pistol then because I was afraid, and that it was what I'd brought for safety. It was worth nothing in this fear. I wasn't saving myself now. I didn't need good luck. I was *his* good luck; I needed to act like good luck and give him a story to tell of how the sun saved him once, when he fell out of a tree and into a river. Because the sun is what saved him, though later he'd thank *me*. But I was just chance, something that had happened along.

If there'd been a boat, my mother might be alive. My mother couldn't have lasted long out in the sea. No clearing there, not even sun that day. No warm bodies anywhere around. No boats. But if there had been, would she have thanked them? They too would have been just chance, like I was. It would have been the fire in the boat, or the blankets, or the land of it in the vastness of the sea. It would have been their own bodies and the earth that saved them.

He saved himself perhaps. He responded to my kisses, to my caresses. He came alive, his muscles, so stiff and cramped before, elongated now, moved like waves far out at sea. We were squirming together, almost wrestling, and I felt myself smile because I knew now he would live. But this realization did not stop me, nor him, and as we rubbed ourselves together I felt my gift leave me, and then his a moment after, warm and mixing against our pressed-together bellies.

We panted, laughed, caught our breath. He searched my eyes, but I simply smiled.

I knew I had to get the clothes for him now, to keep him warm.

"Wait," I said, and hurried down the trail to fetch my pants and shirt and jacket; the old construction boots, the sweaty socks.

I dressed him quickly on the ground, like a child, as he couldn't stand for the ankle. I kept the jockey shorts for myself, and the boots, so I would have something to wear, walking back down the trail.

I hoisted him again on my shoulders and told him: "You rest now."

All the way back down the trail, how my back ached, how my feet burned on the stones and pine needles for I'd put the socks on his feet for warmth and the boots were stiff against the skin of my own feet. And it was five miles to the road, and from there another several miles to town if no trucks came along to give us a ride. But it was midday, there would be someone. I knew. A road was by nature a thing of good luck.

Sure enough, an old Eskimo trapper named Kapush came down the road almost the minute we got there. I was glad an Eskimo had come upon us and not one of my father's people, who would have wanted all the details, the facts of the story; who wouldn't understand about the sun. Kapush – he understood.

"Too cold," he said. And looking up into the sky, he smiled. "Lucky for him."

I did not run into Thane for several weeks after that. I did not see him in the trees of course, nor hear about him being seen in them. It was September now, and there was little time left to wander up the canyons for tree-climbing anyway. The snows would be coming. You'd die for sure if you fell in a creek then, if it wasn't frozen, which might then save you so long as the surface of it didn't crack. You could be saved by

the cold just as you could be killed by it. The same went for
the sun and the earth and the air. Men even. All things really.

When next I saw Thane, nothing was different. We didn't
smile at each other, as was our way. It was as if that night in
the canyon was in some other world, separate from this one.
A dreamplace of sorts. We didn't speak of it at all. This felt
natural. He came and went like he had before, thanking me
and paying me. Then one time, in January I think it was, he
left an envelope under his money at the counter.

"You forgot this," I called to him.

"No," he said. "I didn't forget it." Then he turned and
left.

I read the letter later that night in my room in Nana's
house. In it, he talked too much. He thanked me first for
saving his life, which would have been enough, even though I
did not think it was so. But then he chose to explain. Why he
had come to Anavik; why he did not like the places he was
from; why he had felt it necessary to make a choice and tell
people of the choice he'd made. Which wasn't really a choice
he told me. It was his nature. But many did not see it that
way: parents, politicians, priests. I did not understand why
that was so important to him. And he talked a great deal of
beginnings and endings. When he came and when he would
leave; when this and when that; how this had changed him,
made him new; where he would go next, and what he would
write about when he got there. He wondered what I thought
about all this – about his feelings, about being the kind of
man he was. He wondered what kind of man I was in this
way. How clumsy it all sounded. How my father's people's
whole culture was that way. At the end of the letter, he said
he had thought often of the clearing. Of that place we had
been together.

I didn't write back; I threw the letter away.

Instead, I went up to Curtis Shandley's the next afternoon,
and to his room. He looked excited to see me, and secretive,
like we were partners in some crime. But I did not see it that
way. I saw that he was still cold inside, had been very cold for

a long time. I caressed him and kissed him again like I had in
the clearing. We took off our clothes and we made love in a
similar fashion to how we had before. I liked the strength of
it, like two things crashing together – a river and rock,
lightning and a mountain, a bear up a tree. It was different
than with a woman. A different place where different things
met. But there was nothing new about it. Not really. How
was this thing we did, then, in his mind, a new thing,
unaccustomed to the world? He seemed to me like Eskimos
I knew who drank, who couldn't square their world with the
world of my father's people; who wouldn't live in peace or
make peace with it. Who sacrificed themselves to it instead.

Before Thane, I hadn't known that they did it to their own
kind. Truly, they had a different way.

We lay together for a long time afterward, caressing, and I
told him a story. It was a story that Nana had told me once
about a caribou that lost its herd. For a long time, it followed
a creek through a wide plain, knowing intuitively that the
stream flowed downward and that they were all heading that
way last time he'd noticed. But he never came upon them and
began to worry that he had lost his way, and that perhaps
they'd gone in another direction entirely. He got strange
ideas then, and climbed over mountains and waded through
lakes, no longer paying attention to the facts, but letting each
thing he came across suggest itself or something to him. And
so, when he saw a solitary tree in a meadow, he thought to
climb it. This was a ridiculous notion for a caribou, but he
had gone past such prejudices and so he approached the tree,
circling it. He slept below it for two nights, hoping that a
method might suggest itself. On the third day, a grizzly came
along and killed the caribou. He ate a good deal of him then
and there, and then dug a hole to bury him in. At some point,
the bear must have forgotten about the caribou or lost
interest. Winter came and snow covered the animal's remains. In the spring, a mound of grass grew there and
flowers. Small animals cleaned what was left of him from
his discarded bones. Birds carried pieces of his hide for their

nests high into the branches of the tree, and insects carried parts of him up its trunk and across its branches. And the rest of him sunk into the ground where he was received by the roots of the tree and then carried by them up through its trunk and branches high into the sky where he'd first thought to go. High enough so that he could see far off and was able to locate his lost herd. And in this way, the caribou was not lost anymore.

In June, at the end of the school year, Thane left. He had not climbed trees that spring. I did not know why he climbed trees when he first arrived, nor why he no longer climbed them that spring. And I did not ask him.

But I found myself wishing I would find him climbing one again.

He did not say goodbye to anyone specifically, but he was civil, even friendly to those he ran across on his way to the ferry. He came as he'd arrived, unannounced, unobtrusively. He did not say goodbye to me, and this made me smile, in the same way his not smiling had made me happy nearly a year ago. It satisfied me because it made me feel he knew things.

He did not come back. Not ever.

I did not expect him to; did not wait for him; or for a letter. I did not watch the boats. Sometimes I watched the trees, that is true. I knew if he returned how he would come.

I think about him from time to time. I'd been only with women before him, and only with women afterward. I had never met a man like him before, where that was possible – that place, that piece of luck, that way that the sun could touch the world. But I didn't think about it in the way he talked of it in his letter. I did not think about it as a nature or a choice to be made, or what anyone might think of it. It was not a beginning nor an end of anything just as it had not begun, nor ended. I thought of it as Nana had explained it: as a gift, some luck, a way of remembering something that in any other way would be lost and forgotten.

He had brought me something. Something from high in the trees.

I had given him something as well. Nana said sometimes a baby came from that kind of luck. But it was not a baby in our case – it was a place, and a lucky place, like how children are lucky. And like a place, it was permanent that way, even if I were never to visit it again. It was there. I knew this as I knew other things. And this satisfied me and made me smile.

The Dream People

Rick R. Reed

Do you ever wonder where the dream people come from? Do you know what I mean? Those people who appear in our dreams that we've never seen anywhere else? They're fully fleshed-out people with their own voices, actions, and physical characteristics. But yet, we know we've never seen them during our waking hours. Where do they come from? Are they, as some might say, people we've seen and registered in our subconscious? Or are they real people, appearing in the dream realm to us?

Since I'm more of a romantic soul, I like to think that these dream people are real and they've somehow made their way into our dreams. Maybe they have something to say to us . . .

I awoke that unbearably hot August morning twisted in damp sheets and struggling to grasp for the dream imagery that always scattered the moment I opened my eyes. The bedroom was sun-dappled, dust motes floating in shafts of light. My dream had been erotic and, as I sat up in bed, throwing off the sheet and exposing the physical evidence of the sexual nature of the dream, I tried to remember what had caused my blood-engorged state.

There had been a time in my youth when awakening in this state was an everyday occurrence. Now, at 42, morning wood was a less frequent thing and it made me yearn to discover the cause. I wiped sweat from my forehead and stared down at my withering erection, as if an answer awaited me there.

I closed my eyes, listening to the sounds of traffic outside my bedroom window, the sirens, the whine of the garbage truck as it made its rounds, and an image came to me. I was in a room I had never seen before and I was alone with a man. As I jogged my dream memory to provide details, certain things emerged. The room, for one, was a place I knew I had never seen before. I forced myself to psychically survey my surroundings and figured I was in the bedroom of a run-down apartment building. The walls were old; the paint was peeling; the curtains at the window looked like they were once white, but now were yellowed with smoke. I moved to the lone window and looked out: directly below me were the tracks for the train line we Chicagoans called the "L". I couldn't see a stop, so I wasn't able to pinpoint my location exactly. But as a train came rumbling down the track, I knew I was in the city I called home: Chicago.

I turned and looked toward the mattress on the hardwood floor. A man lay amid the cream-colored sheets, his dark skin a contrast to the color and texture of the linens. His eyelids were at half-mast, looking both sleepy and lustful at the same time. The lids shadowed the palest green eyes I had ever seen, all the more brilliant in contrast to his dark (Latin?) skin. He smiled at me, and his perfectly-white teeth and full lips lit up his stubbled face. He patted the bed next to him, inviting me to join him. I hesitated, the window at my back, feeling a strange sense of foreboding. He certainly looked inviting: his hard, muscular body sculpted from a tawny granite and dusted with coarse, curly black hair. He cocked his head.

"Come on, sweetheart." His voice was deep as he sang a lyric from an old reggae song, "The bed's too big without you."

The confounding thing about the dream was not so much its obvious eroticism and the man lying there. He was the embodiment of my filthiest fantasies. Perfect in every detail, he was a vision of masculine glory. I looked down at myself (not nearly the perfect specimen of my dream man: a body gone a bit thick around the waist, freckled and too pale) and saw that as I thought of my dream man, my dick had engorged itself again.

I got busy with my hand and a dollop of the Wet I always kept in the nightstand and forgot all about the truly confounding thing about my dream: that I was not only aroused by this man and this early-morning setting, but that he represented something I could never have. What that something was is mysterious but in an odd way, exciting to ponder.

It was two weeks before it happened again. Or at least that's what I thought: how many dreams are squandered with the morning light, leaving our brains before we have even the chance to consciously remember them? This time, though, I awoke in the middle of the night with a start, heart pounding, and my chest hair slick with sweat. I knew the sweat wasn't from the heat. September had arrived and with it, relief from the heat and humidity that had made Chicago seem more akin to New Orleans.

Again, I grasped for the scattering dream images. And again, it came back to me in bits and pieces. First, there was the setting. This time there was no run-down apartment, with a view of the L tracks. This time we were in a back alley. I strained to recall details, and suddenly they came rushing in. The back alley was one I was familiar with: this brick-paved route ran parallel to the L tracks and was in the near north suburb of Evanston, just south of the Davis Street stop. On one side were the high back walls of business buildings, on the other, the train tracks were above, supporting the weight of the rumbling trains as they made their runs. The illumination was a sickly yellow, cast from the sodium vapor of a street light at the alley's entrance on Davis. I knew this spot well because I arrived and departed from it each day on my way to and from work.

My fantasy Latino man was there again. This time he wasn't naked, but he was no less alluring. He leaned against a brick wall, his body partially obscured by shadow but clear enough for me to get a glimpse of something that could leave me breathless. His face was almost hidden by shadow, but his dark, well-cut features superseded the darkness: again, the stubble and the pale green eyes, the perfect smile. He had pulled up the ribbed cotton of one of those shirts referred to as a "wife beater" by the politically incorrect to reveal a perfectly flat and defined brown stomach, glistening with sweat. A treasure trail of black hair snaked downward; my eyes followed. His frayed jeans were pushed down almost to his knees and with his other hand, he was stroking himself. He paused to let a gob of spit slide slowly from his mouth onto the purple head of his cock and then began pumping his hand up and down. His cock was long and thick, with a loose, dark foreskin that alternately revealed and hid the shiny plum of his cock head. My mouth watered.

A cigarette dangled from between his lips; the cherry alternately glowed and darkened as he jerked his head, beckoning me closer. I cast a look behind me; people hurried past the alleyway entrance and I guessed we were too far back in shadow for them to see us. None appeared to take notice of the two men by the Dumpster at any rate.

My heart was pounding as I moved closer. He thrust his hips upward as I neared him. I could see the want in his face. He threw the cigarette on the ground and whispered, "Please."

I moved quickly and positioned myself on my knees. I pushed his hand away from the cock before me and replaced it with my own, guiding it toward my mouth. I was already starting to savor it, knowing it would be salty and fragrant with the smell of perspiration and something darker and more organic.

Then day arrived, a traitor. The sky cleared abruptly from darkest blue to bright, cloudless sun. It was the kind of time passage that could only occur in a dream. I didn't take his cock out of my mouth as I turned my head slightly to see a crowd had formed around us. There was my mother, a disappointed frown on her face. My two sisters leaned close together, clutching one another for support, their mouths open in horror. There was even one of my teachers from high school, a man who had taught me world history and who had encouraged me to study history myself at university. His dark eyes sparkled in the sun as he slowly shook his head back and forth. A group of teenage boys, wearing punk skater uniforms, pointed and laughed.

And making his way through the crowd was a police officer, his clean-shaven face red with fury.

It was at that point that I awakened, finding myself now alone – and I had to admit – a bit relieved. The darkness of my room was doubly strange in contrast to the bright sunlight of the final scene from my dream.

A pool of come slicked my stomach and groin. Again, I wondered what the man was trying to say to me beyond a lustful come-on. What did the dream symbolism mean? Was I not as comfortable with myself as a gay man as I believed? Was there some secret wellspring of shame I had never acknowledged? Why else would the disapproving face of my mother have appeared?

It was not until the tail end of fall when my dream man came back. I had just dozed off on my living room sofa. The TV was still blaring out a late night rerun of *The Golden Girls*. I had fallen asleep with my feet up on the coffee table, the remote control still clutched in my hand.

When I awakened (or at least thought I had awakened . . . my first clue that this was not reality was the fact that the TV was making a low humming noise and all it displayed was a black and white test pattern; I would have to reach far back into my childhood to recall that pattern), the apartment was still and the lack of sound outside my living room window made me think it must be very late at night. I wiped a line of drool off my chin and sat up straighter, stretching. My back complained and shot tight pains all the way up to my skull. I rubbed my neck and vowed to myself I would get myself into bed before allowing myself to fall asleep in such an uncomfortable position again.

I stood and pointed the remote at the TV, hit off. The test pattern went dark, dwindling down to a tiny circle of gray light that finally winked out.

And then I heard the sound . . . a soft scratching. The sound was coming from my kitchen and I headed that way, wondering if I was being revisited by a mouse or two, drawn inside by the cold temperatures of late autumn. It had happened before. As I neared the kitchen, though, I could tell someone was scratching at my back door.

Why would they be scratching? Why not just knock? I felt the hair on the back of my neck rise as I moved closer to the door and cautiously lifted one of the mini blind slats to peer out into the gloom.

I saw nothing. No surprises there; the sound was emanating from low down on the door, beneath the window. Should I open the door? Maybe a stray dog or cat had wandered up my back stairs and had mistaken my home for its own? What would be the harm?

I opened the door and there he was: my dream man. He was on all fours at my back door, one hand still raised to scratch at the wood. He looked up and me and grinned, revealing that smile that made me ache with longing, and then he barked at me. Yes, barked.

I would have laughed had the situation not been so odd. For several minutes I simply stared and watched as he looked up at me with imploring eyes. The puppy routine was in contrast to the obvious signs of sexual arousal. His dark cock was ramrod straight between his dark and muscular thighs. A drop of precome glistened at the tip of the head.

I didn't know what to do. I reached down to pat his head. As I stroked the black, stubbly hair, he pawed at me, finally wrapping his arms around my legs (I was wearing boxers) and began to slowly lap at my thighs.

I think it was Errol Flynn (or at least that's who the quote is most commonly attributed to) who said something along the lines of God only giving men enough blood to use for their brain or their penis, but not both at the same time. My penis took over for my brain and even though there were vague admonishments in the back of my mind, I did what I really wanted to do, which was to step back into my kitchen, so he could come inside with me.

I closed the door behind us, slid out of my boxers and lowered myself to the tile floor to be with him. Gently, he pushed my back against the cold tile and covered my body with his own. The heat emanating from him was like a furnace. He pinned me down on the floor and began licking me all over. I arched my back when he got to my crotch, wanting him to linger there, but that was not to be: he grasped my calves in his hands and pushed my legs back against my chest, lowering himself to my ass.

And that's when the licking began in earnest. Everything was blotted out: the hum of the refrigerator, the steady drip from the kitchen sink faucet, and most of all, common sense, as I surrendered to the pleasure his tongue in my hole was bringing me. I squirmed, certain I would come from the delightfully invasive ministrations of his probing tongue.

But again, *my* desires were not necessarily what this bizarre scene was all about. All at once, he stopped and rose up to look down at me. His face was slick with his saliva and he smiled . . . and not kindly. There seemed to be sadness in his gaze, and I imagined the look was telling me he didn't quite want to go through with this, yet things had spun wildly beyond his own control. In a very real sense, an animal had taken over. I let my gaze roam lower and saw his erection sticking up between my legs; it was eclipsed by my own tumescence, which he wouldn't allow me to touch.

I felt him press the head of his cock against my opening. I strained against him, never wanting anything inside me more, but he held back, teasing, that same mystery grin playing about his lips.

"Please," I whispered.

And then, slowly, he began to enter me. I forced myself to breathe as the thick length of him pushed deeper. It wasn't painful; his tongue had warmed me up too much for pain. All I wanted was him buried inside me.

But that was not to be.

Suddenly, bright lights came on outside and the air was alive with the shrieking of sirens.

I awoke on my couch with a start, just in time to see an infomercial for a truly spiffy rotisserie oven, suddenly realizing where I was.

For good or bad, I had no visits from my dream lover until the following summer. I had not quite forgotten him, conjuring him up in my most lonely moments and his attentiveness – and savageness – had provided many happy releases. But the man of my conscious fantasies never had the erotic pull of the rapid-eye-movement literal dreamboat. That man was as real as anyone I worked with at my job as a loan officer at First Chicago or the guys I ran across at the bars on Halsted Street. He had his own mind and his own being . . . he may have been in my dreams but I swear to you he was not of me. You know what I mean?

I live not far from Lake Michigan and on warm summer nights like this one I like nothing better than to wander down Lawrence Avenue to the lakefront. I like walking through the park that borders the lake, checking out the rollerbladers, bicyclists, and runners.

If you go to the lakefront at dusk, it begins to get a little quieter and as I made my way east on Lawrence Avenue, the sky ahead of me was already gone almost full dark. Behind me, to the west, that same sky was a riot of pink, lilac, and grey as the sun set.

I was hoping things would be especially quiet tonight in the lakefront park. I wanted to walk a while, maybe even as far south as Fullerton, where an incredible view of the Chicago skyline rose up. But I also wanted time to sit and think . . . to ponder once more why I was still alone at age 42.

Such ponderings had become common for me lately and I was rapidly coming to the conclusion that I would always be alone. Oh sure, there were outlets for sex, some even superior to my own imagination and expert hand, but there had never been any true connection with another man, not for a long time, anyway.

I sat down on a bench facing the lake and looked out at the churning waters, which broke and reassembled a full moon that had just risen. My dream man came back to me and I thought how wonderful it would be if he were real. All my dreams – literally – fulfilled.

Weariness delivered me from depression and I stood up to begin the mile-or-so walk back home. Sleep would provide blessed deliverance from worrying about the pitiful state of my love life.

I turned and exited the lakefront park and found myself on the thoroughfare bordering the park, Marine Drive. The quiet and peace I had found by the lakefront was shattered immediately by the traffic rushing by: cars with loud exhausts, groups of chattering teenagers . . . the city teeming with life. It only served to make me feel more alone.

Up ahead was a bus stop and as I neared it, a charge passed through me, like an electric current. At first, I couldn't pinpoint what caused the abrupt racing of my heart and the tingling in my toes and fingers. It was almost as though I had perceived him subconsciously first (like in a dream?).

There was a little group gathered at the bus stop, waiting. They appeared to be a family: two small children, a six-year-old absorbed with his Gameboy and a little girl, even younger, maybe three, tugging at her mother's hand. The mother looked tired, her pretty features pulled down with exhaustion, black hair yanked back from her face and secured with a rubber band. And then I saw their father, who was looking right at me.

When our gazes met, it was electric. It was a reckoning, an epiphany, one of those magic moments one thinks only occur in the movies.

Of course, it was a recognition. We knew one another. He was the man from my dreams. I stood, staring, the background noises of traffic and conversation suddenly muted, almost falling into those dark eyes I thought had existed only in the realm of dreams. He stared back and the connection was so pure and real, I had to restrain myself from running up to him, from collapsing into the arms I had imagined and dreamed of being enfolded by countless times.

It seemed like hours passed, but I'm sure it was only seconds. My dream man started toward me, as if he was about to speak. The little boy finished his game and slapped at his father's hand, annoyed with him for not paying attention. "Papi, what are you staring at?"

And the words were like a magic charm, breaking the spell and causing the moment to scurry back where it had come from . . . a dream. My dream man looked at me for only a moment longer, then turned back toward his family.

The bus pulled up, brakes squealing and sending foul-smelling exhaust into the air. There was a pneumatic hiss as the doors opened and I watched the family board. I stood waiting as the bus pulled away. My dream man moved to the back and sat in the very last seat. Just before he was out of view, he turned and our eyes locked.

He pressed his hand against the glass.

I started walking toward home, snorting out a bitter laugh. Wasn't it just so typical for a gay man to wish for a hot companion over one that might offer more intellectual and emotional support? What was the difference? This man was no more real than the porno hunks I watched late at night when I felt restless and horny. Hot Latino or not, I was never going to meet him. I felt myself aroused as I thought of his dark gaze, black hair, and lean build. And the something else: wetness on my cheeks. What now? Tears? Was I crying because of something as stupid and sentimental as the knowledge that, for some, dreams never come true? I brushed angrily at my tears and began striding quickly, toward home.

I still don't know where the dream people come from. Had the two of us, both hungry for something we had never found, met on some fantastic dream plane that stood in place of the denial the real world condemned us to? Worst of all, I worried that now that our paths had crossed in real life some spell had been broken and those paths would never cross again. Not in real life. Not in dreams. Maybe dreams stand in for a reality we can't have. But I like to think the dream people come to us with a promise. If I didn't believe that, I wonder if I could ever sleep again.

13 Crimes Against Love, or, the Crow's Confession

Alexander Chee

6.

He had a name everyone had. He was my friend's boy-friend and in the dark on my bed as I held him he was like a poem about a beautiful naked boy in the dark. Very pale, easy to see. All the light in the room ran to be on him. There wasn't much, as it is very dark inside the crow's wing.

He'd needed a place to stay the night as he lived out of town, and I don't remember why he couldn't stay with my friend, but he couldn't. Something about roommates.

We shouldn't do this, he said, inside our kiss.

You're right, I said, against his mouth, and turned it into the kiss again. We went on with it. He was afraid and so was I, but somehow we felt it was brave to do something wrong. Outside, the screech of the night wind on the glass that I know now to be the Fates, yelling at all the work we were making for them. Asking us for a rest.

He of course told my friend the very next day, who came to find me at work. He had the look of someone who'd been stolen from, which I thought odd of him at the time. I am pretty sure I apologized, but it wasn't with any of the sorrow I feel now. I lost them both, of course, and they lost each other. And now the former friend is a friend of Crime 3's ex-boyfriend (yes, ahead). I ran into them once together and after they left I wondered if they compared.

1. & 2.

How did the crow become black? He saw Apollo's lover cheat on him and repeated news of it to him, and took the crime's color on in the repeating as Apollo, listening, grew angrier and brighter and burned him black. He was white before, like a page can be, and black after the story.

Apollo is the god of poets.

Think of California days dusty with waiting, spent casing the joint, the shiny blue-eyed poet serving cup after cup of coffee to me at the cafe where he worked. Freckles spot the smooth planes of his hips as he leans and his shirt rides up. I am very young, in love with a poet who is in love with a scholar. The scholar has a boyfriend, a nice man I know, and sees the poet on the side, and I hate him for doing both. The poet works at this café to be near the scholar. I go to the café to be near the poet.

He is a boy with a taste for something sweet, and I am a boy with a short supply of sweet, a motorcycle, and a wide streak of anger. A long time ago something burned out the middle of me, something someone else had set on fire and set down in me. That crime is a matter of public record, court transcripts, etc., all available. These are not, until now. See the police map, the pins marking victims, the search for a pattern.

The poet accepts my courtship in the hours free when the scholar is with his boyfriend. I know now we're not particularly compatible but I am obsessed with the idea that the scholar is in my way. He tells me the scholar's name, thinking we'll never meet, perhaps, or because it's modern, or both. And then at the gym I see someone who looks like an underwear model speaking to someone trying to bench-press. His name comes out. He looks at me and smiles, and I know what he wants.

A short while later, after I had dragged him around my

apartment, taking him even on my backstairs so the neighbors could see, so that even the sky might know that I had won, I told him who I was as he lay under me in my bathtub, shiny from what we'd done. He looked up, and smiled with those underwear model teeth, improbable, untouched.

We can't ever tell him, he said. He shifted around and tried to take me back inside him. I pulled back, like he'd flashed a knife. Right then I knew we'd both lost, had all lost, in fact.

Everyone broke up with everyone by the end of the year.

3.

A man loved me as his first love, but my inability to clearly remember or speak of the crime committed against me kept me resisting his efforts at lovemaking. The senses on my body would wink out at the touch of him and his love.

I understood sex and love as fear at this time. The problem: I didn't fear him, and so couldn't, at the time, have sex with him. But I wanted to. With him, I felt like a blind man in front of a painting.

He went to others. Meanwhile, I met someone visiting town with his boyfriend. Thunderclap of something, love, I think, me unable to look at him for how much I want him. Burning. The black fell off my eyes. Why him and not the other? The first lover watched it happen from across the room, as did the boyfriend of the new love. Sheets of light surround most of what happened to us and between us, and prevent it from being told, but one thing I do regret: I still spent nights with the first man, both of us clueless, stuck, all that love glaring, glaring, stuck in place, bodies still, minds moving. On one of those nights, I write a letter to the new love, while the man sleeps. I write, explain how I would do it to him, what I would show him, what I would use to clean him with afterwards, and send the letter to him. He sends me what I told him I would use. I tie it to my motorcycle handlebars, my prize. I drive with it, fluttering, proud as a crow. Keep the new love for three years.

Other things happened between me and the new love, but those weren't crimes.

The boyfriend, his, is left behind. The first lover also, goes on to do over what was done to him by me many times, crisscrossing the city like a fire I'd set and left untended.

4.

I meet a couple out one night near the end of my time in San Francisco. I know them both, one I hate, one I like. They are newly in love but also want to have sex with me. I go home with them and find myself with condoms on my fingers, while they 69. I feel like I am attending a surgery on Siamese twins, oddly non-erotic. The one I like falls asleep after they come, and I stay, fucking the one I hate beside him. For the reason of the crime, during this part of my youth I can stay harder with hate.

I went back for more from the one I hated, called him a few months or weeks later and told him I was coming over. I took him all over his floors – bathroom, kitchen, bedroom. Scuffed his back in doing it. Why did I need so many angles? As I dressed, he looked at me from the floor where he lay, still breathing hard. You're a sociopath, he said.

Perhaps, I said. And left. I had started to have a feeling of some kind when he said that. But his enjoyment had been thorough. It's dangerous. To try and reform thieves. Only when they want something they can't just take do they stop.

5.

Why do thieves start? Because they feel they are starting with less than nothing. And that this will never change. A black crow with a memory of having been white.

At work at the bookstore, a boy at the counter stands with a copy of Jeanette Winterson's *The Passion*. He had read my letters to his friend and fallen in love with the writer of them. He knew as a result my favorite book. This is the trap he set

for the crow, a book in the snare. He is a Missouri Rimbaud,
fox-faced, tall and athletic. When he tells me later of his
Chinese grandmother, brought to Missouri by his missionary
grandfather, I understand why he looks so familiar to me and
me to him. You remind me of an uncle, he tells me. Fox, he is.
Fox meets crow. Two thieves. Who will win?

We sink into each other, stabbed through by with what we
find later in my bed. It feels like the first time ever with a boy,
he says to me. All my burning no preparation for this cutting.
He said this and I watched it cut into me but would not feel it
until later, when he returned to his NY boyfriend.

Years later I meet the fox's boyfriend. He didn't know
about me but remembers that the fox returned changed.
They didn't last the summer after. Did you know how much
damage you did in NY from San Francisco, he asks. For he
also, it runs out, knows the letter-recipient's boyfriend from
Crime 3.

No, I say to him.

7.

An astrologer with a son. Meets me at his front door in
sweatpants, no shirt, no underwear. Summer drone, cut-
grass smell everywhere, air thick, the swing of his dick in his
shorts, skin the color of tobacco, all hypnotize me. He dreads
his hair small and pulls it back. He reads my chart down in
the basement while his young son watches television, his
girlfriend, the mother, at work. He tells me that in a past life I
was a temple whore who was also a spy and betrayed many
men to their deaths, and that in this life I have to meet them
all and help them on their way.

This seems both completely understandable and unfair.
And, a come-on.

Weeks later, I meet him out at night downtown. He is
housesitting for his mother, asks me to come over. On his
mother's bed in her apartment I take off his clothes and do
what I want with him; he is oddly pliable, as if by obeying me

he's not at fault. He has done only what I wanted and not
what he wanted. He asks that we not come, so as to make a
tantric bond between us. I agree at the time, and then go
home and jerk off about him after. The crow doesn't wear a
leash. I don't want his cord on my soul.

8.

Infidelity is violence. At this point I am a hardened criminal,
headed out to do more. I am walking through the parking lot
of other people's love with my car key out, cutting into the
painted exteriors. I don't know what I cut any more or why,
just feel the clean scrape along the side right in my teeth as I
smile.

I find myself at a party, after the astrologer. Making out
with a boy who I'd thought was straight. He is known for
getting drunk and taking his penis out, walking around and
asking people to touch it, other men especially. If you ignore
it, sometimes he puts it in your beer. It's very large. He often
gets what he wants. We're on the stairs and a girl comes up
behind him. She puts her hand on his shoulder, eyes wide
with disbelief. Uh, you have to go outside RIGHT now, she
says. Or Crystal's never going to speak to you again.

I'll be right back, he says. One minute, and he holds his
finger up for emphasis.

He returns. I have to go, he says. Here's my number, call
me.

Crystal, of course, is his girlfriend. He had the same name
as Crime 6. Literally, so many people have that name.

9., 10., & 11.

Having done what I could to New York from San Francisco,
I move there to get closer.

A short-story writer in a long-distance relationship. He
tells me when we meet, I have a boyfriend. So, I ask. His
boyfriend gets so upset when he hears about us that he gets

into a car accident. He survives just fine. The story-writer hops away. Still doesn't like to see me. A designer with a friendly smile laughs when I tell him I like him but am emotionally unavailable. Perfect, he says. So am I. I have a boyfriend. Okay, I say. We have many nights of incredible sex that summer, and he opens to me in ways that move me. But we never speak of it. Then, he tells me one night that he has a present for me. I can see the crack right down the middle in the air as he says it. I break it off shortly thereafter, and don't get the present for years. We run into each other and he mentions it here and there, and eventually I have lunch with him, a confirmation that we won't have sex again. It's a hardback of *Franny & Zooey*, J.D. Salinger. I'd told him it was my favorite book. It still is one of them. I now think of it being akin to the trap the fox set with The Passion, back in Crime 5.

After breaking up with someone else, I am in his friend's apartment, having sex with him one more time. He has another boyfriend now, someone I resent enough that I am here having sex with him again. I have to go to the bathroom. On the way there, the door to his friend's bed-room is open, where the friend is having sex with someone else. I watch them from the door, go back to my ex, sinking back into him again and again, feeling like a nail that won't stick. It isn't the right way to say goodbye to what we had. But it's what we do.

12.

This one was the most dangerous.

He's kneeling on the floor of his West Village apartment, by the door, asking me to leave. He first said he saw someone once a week. But what he means is that they sleep together every night, as they live together, and spend their Sundays together. We're in the apartment he shares with his lover, a chef, who has just called asking him to come down to the restaurant for dessert. I know I have to leave. But I know

why he's kneeling. He'd changed into these flowing medita-
tion pants and then from just how I looked at him, he got an
erection. We both watched it rise until it was sticking straight
out, pulling his sheer pants up his ankles. Now he is kneeling
to hide it. He's a sweet 23-year-old boy, looks younger, even,
and he's irresistible in pain.

I walk over to stand in front of him. He turns his head to
the side. I kneel down, and I say, What is this? Reaching for
what I know is there. I lay my hand gently along the surface
of it. I can feel his pulse racing there against my fingertips.
It's large enough to scare a great many people. I am pretty
sure it's larger than his heart. This on a boy who's as tall as
my shoulder.

Please don't, he says.

I'll leave, I say. But, what is this? I ask him with my mouth
right in front of his, his breath, shallow, crossing my lips. I
breathe it in. His cheek trembles against mine. I'm sure it
belongs to me, this thing in my hand. Sure of it. If you can't
hold their heart, you can hold this and hear the heart.

He was a student of Alexander technique, a theory of dance
movement. He'd volunteered to give me a lesson and so I'd
come over. Taught me that the spine ends inside the head,
not underneath it, that skulls are firmly mounted on the neck,
the top vertebrae behind your eyes, inside you. Taught me
that a repeated pattern of wrong movement, while not painful
at the time, can create greater damage than a single cata-
strophic injury. A shoulder that breaks heals. A shoulder
worn away by wrong use must be replaced.

I can hear the Fates screaming again, stop, stop, stop. And
for perhaps the first time, I do.

I let go. I stand and he looks at me from the floor, sad, and
then looks down. I kiss the top of his head.

I remember on the stairs how I had once before tricked
myself into thinking I was brave, which is what I felt, holding
his dick, him unable to stand for shame, desire. But this
wasn't bravery.

On the street, later, I thought about it. I didn't want to

meet the chef at some party a year later and hear from him how his lover had broken his heart by cheating on him with some guy. And I felt, if I went on, this would be ahead of me. I wanted to heal what hurt in me. It couldn't be replaced except through death and rebirth, really. And apparently I'd done that many times. I didn't want to have to see the astrologer again, in some other lifetime. So, healing. How?

Things can burn black. And then white again.

13.

With twelve you get one free.

He worked in flowers. Argentinean, green eyes you could see through windows, and would watch me from inside his store with an expression that suggested I had something he'd never eaten but had always wanted to try. We met up some weeks later, he was drunk at a bar, newly graduated from college. He checked his messages. Ten, he said. I'll be right back.

Ten messages suggested to me that somewhere was a boyfriend anxious to speak with him. I sat and waited. He returned and we left, him asking me to walk him home. You ought to, he said. I'm very drunk and we don't want anything bad to happen to me. He sat down on the Brooklyn sidewalk then, in someone's stone garden and he pulled me onto him. We lay there, kissing. He tried to undo my pants. No, I said. So we stood and went to his front door, where he kissed me again, and his dog from inside began to bark as if he knew there was a crow in the hall.

Won't that wake your neighbors, I said.

It'll wake my boyfriend, he said.

Instantaneous anger. My heart. Awake, it turned out. Right there. Is this what it's like to feel? I asked myself, and went down to the sidewalk, deciding it was. He followed me up the street with his dog on a leash and then under a streetlight a block from his house I let him kiss me one last time. He reached into my pants and pulled my dick out. I put it back in. No, I said. And left.

I can't steal again if I don't know how to put back what I stole. If it leaves me once I steal it. Shake out the nest, dump all the shiny things in the road to be found by whoever wants them.

The crow is white again, salt-white. Hang this in the wind, ask the sun to visit me.

Someone Like You

Jameson Currier

At thirty-six Tom thought it was time to be more serious about his personal life, though it wasn't until three years later when he woke up one morning and felt the twang of a tendon above his kneecap, the ache of an upper molar that would need a root canal, and a heavy sinus headache from the one beer he had drank the night before that he felt something should change. It wasn't his physical decline that created this idea, however. Tom felt another decision was imminent. For more than seven months he had been dating two guys at the same time and sooner or later he would need to choose one to stick with. Peter was forty-eight, six inches taller than Tom, had a lanky, runner's build, and was HIV-positive, which Tom felt accounted for Peter's rather flushed and reddened complexion. Dylan was eleven years younger than Tom and sero-negative, with a strong, swarthy jawline and a stocky, hairy physique. Tom's dates with Peter were always calendared and planned: dinner out at a good restaurant followed by a movie, drinks at a new bar before going to a comedy club, a holiday weekend trip upstate antiquing with them staying at a recommended B-and-B. Dylan was more spontaneous, calling Tom on his cellphone from the corner and saying, "I'm on your block. Wanna get together to do something?"

Two boyfriends meant that Tom now kept his apartment clean, a bottle of wine chilling in his refrigerator, and a landline and cellphone with caller ID. Obsessively, he kept his hair cut, his teeth brushed, his breath fresh, and his nightstand drawer full of condoms and an extra bottle of lubricant. On the days before he got together with Peter, he would shave and groom his body so that any nicks or scratches would have time to heal. For Dylan, he spent an extra ten minutes at the gym working on his stomach. Dylan might be a beefy and bearish sort of guy but he appreciated that Tom was not.

Tom's physical decline continued in the form of spasms: a nervous twitch of his eyelid, an anxious twinge in his rectum, panicky butterflies in his stomach. While Tom appreciated and enjoyed dating two men at the same time, he had long ago realized that he was a serial dater – a one-man-at-a-time sort of guy. Two guys at once was not too ethical to his conscience. Whenever he spent time with one of his two boyfriends there was a moment of guilt over his belief that he was deceiving the other one. Peter did not know about Dylan and vice versa, and while Dylan might be cool to the notion that Tom was dating another guy – Dylan was always telling Tom about a recent trick he had hooked up with online – Peter would have been heartbroken and discouraged. Peter had long ago left behind his tomcatting days; he wanted to settle down in a relationship and live together with a guy. Dylan only wanted a security blanket, a lover without any jealous demands.

To compensate for all this, when Tom was alone he meditated, stretched his body as he had learned to do in a yoga class, and listened to new age Celtic music. Sometimes he even lit a scented candle. He also confided in Suzanne, his co-worker at the law firm where they were both securities attorneys. Suzanne was a tough, shrewd business woman and a terror to her staff. But she had a pretty face – dark eyes and dark hair – and a pearish body, more thighs and rump than breasts and cleavage, which she kept camouflaged with dark, tailored business suits. In turn, Suzanne confided in Tom about her own dates set up through an online dating service, one guy after the next who was a "loser", "dork", or "jerk" and who often knew nothing of her reputation in the office but could tell that there was something a bit too off-putting or aggressive or disquieting about her personality.

"Why can't I meet someone like you?" she would ask Tom when they sat together for lunch.

"Like me?"

"The straight version of you."

"There's no such thing as a straight version of me."

"Okay. Someone conflicted. Like you. Someone who has a Dylan and a Peter."

"You want a straight boyfriend who dates two guys at a time?"

"As long as he's conflicted about it," Suzanne said. "That would at least mean he has a conscience."

Suzanne was in her late thirties and Tom often heard her biological clock ticking. He enjoyed telling her what he had done with Dylan the night before or what his plans were for the week ahead with Peter. He never asked Suzanne for advice, though he always enjoyed witnessing her reactions of his narrow escapes if Dylan had called while he was seeing Peter, or if Peter phoned while he was having sex with Dylan.

"You'll never guess where I am," Dylan said when he called Tom at his apartment on Sunday night.

"Some kind of party," Tom replied. In the background Tom heard loud dance music, a techno thump and a wailing soprano's voice. Dylan wrote about the city nightlife circuit for several gay magazines and newspapers; he was always covering a book launch or a film preview or a drag act at a bar. Sometimes Tom went with Dylan to a theater opening or a cabaret performance at a nightclub because Dylan did not like going alone, the invitation usually arriving at the last minute, as if Dylan had just gotten the assignment himself. Other times Dylan stopped by Tom's apartment for a late night visit on his way home from a dance club or an after-party. They would chat for a moment at Tom's kitchen table, sometimes sharing a beer or having a glass of wine, then suddenly stop talking and begin to grope each other. Tom never considered these stopovers as real dates, though he didn't complain about them either because he felt Dylan was the best sex partner he had ever had. Dylan enjoyed being versatile, an eager bottom or a willing top, whatever Tom was in the mood for. In bed, Dylan never failed to make Tom feel desirable, masculine and yet vulnerable, empty of neediness and full of yearning.

"Ship of fools," Dylan said, with a laugh crackling through the static of his cellphone. "A boat full of porn stars. We're all circling the island, trying not to look seasick."

"Any autographs?"

"Honey, there's a line for the toilet," Dylan said. "Some tired old queen's locked herself in there with some shirtless hunk and won't come out."

"Be sure to get details," Tom laughed. He enjoyed hearing Dylan's stories from his parties, and he loved reading how Dylan converted or disguised the gossipy details for his columns. Oddly, Tom was never jealous whenever Dylan wrote about "locking himself in the toilet with so-and-so" or "last night I was out with a trick from last week". Sometimes it gave Tom a little thrill to discover himself as Dylan's "BF" – or "BoyFriend" in print: "Last night the BF and I went to the opera," Dylan might write about their trip to the Met. Or "enough parties this week – I just want to spend the next three nights in bed with my BF."

"One of your favorites is here," Dylan said.

"Who?" Tom asked, his left eyelid suddenly twitching. Sometimes during sex Tom and Dylan watched DVDs together – porn that Dylan also reviewed under a pseudonym – and they were always commenting about the particular attributes or physical features they liked about one star or another.

"Red hair. Big arms. Tats. Know who I'm talking about?"

"Yep. How does he look?"

"Hotter than hell," Dylan said. "Made me think of you."

"No way," Tom answered, playing along and feeling aroused.

"Made me think of how good the two of you would look together in bed. His arms on your butt."

"And where would you be?" Tom asked, a twinge rattling through his rectal muscles.

"Enjoying you both," Dylan said. "Maybe I'll bring him over later."

"I bet we could all have a good time together."

"You'd like that, wouldn't you?"

"Not as much as you would, I bet."

"Maybe I shouldn't." Dylan said, his voice sounding faint and earnest.

"Why not?" Tom asked loudly, raising his voice as if their connection was about to fail at any second.

"I enjoy having you to myself too much. I don't want to share you."

Butterflies fluttered through Tom's stomach as he thought of Peter. "Don't tell me you're getting serious," he said to Dylan with a light-hearted, mocking tone.

"I know a good thing when I see it," Dylan said. "And I know how good it is when I get it from you."

Though his life was complex, Tom tried his best to keep it compartmentalized. Work was work and his personal life was personal. The only overlap was Suzanne. Together, they celebrated birthdays, work anniversaries, and an occasional bonus, raise, or holiday. At home, Tom told Dylan and Peter that Suzanne was like his office wife; he kept no secrets from her. She knew all about Dylan – or Peter – depending on with whom he was spending time. In truth, Tom knew he spoke a little too much about his boyfriends with Suzanne and a little too much about Suzanne with his two boyfriends. Some days he felt that this made him a bit less than the perfect boyfriend and co-worker. Neither a good catch nor a good employee, what he had become was a good gossiper.

This fault made him think of his other faults: his crooked

bottom teeth, his thinning hair, his often gassy stomach. Sometimes he wore the same suit, shirt, and tie two or three days running, too bored and lazy to try to match another shirt with a different tie. At work, he had a list of vendors he liked and disliked using, and often found himself annoyed at having to double-check Suzanne's work. She had a good grasp of concepts and theories and how to interpret the law, yet little skill at managing the details of checking dates, adding numbers, or even using the proper grammar.

At lunch on Tuesday, Suzanne unloaded a weepy tale about her blind date the night before with an overweight man who did not ask her anything about herself. "He talked about the Yankees," she said. "How they had bungled their lead in the last inning. I sat there the whole time thinking why can't I meet a guy who wants to have a glass of wine at the MoMA café?"

"A straight man?" Tom asked.

"I'd settle for a breathing one."

Tom was also sensitive about playing too affirmatively into Suzanne's ideal of a perfect boyfriend or even assuming the role of a substitute. Of course, he would love to spend a day at the museum with Suzanne and then drink a glass of wine at a café. But Tom's own past history of women with ideas of who he might be for them haunted him. His best friend in high school, a funny, highly strung girl named Melissa, had attempted suicide when Tom refused to profess love for her and he told her he thought he might be gay. Since then, Tom had been cautious of being too friendly with women, though he was always aware he had never had the special kind of bond with a man (gay, straight, or otherwise) as he had had with his close female friends.

After work on Wednesday, Tom met Peter at a supermarket. Peter had a recipe and a list of items he needed in order to cook dinner at Tom's apartment.

"Do you have a garlic press?" he asked Tom.

"Of course not," Tom answered with a good-natured

laugh, but felt his eyelid twitch. He seldom cooked in his apartment. He'd only gotten a salad spinner and a pasta strainer since dating Peter. Tom and Peter seldom spent time at Peter's small studio because it felt like being inside a closet. Peter loved the fact that at Tom's four room railroad-car apartment he could be cooking in the kitchen and not even hear Tom watching television in the bedroom.

"We should probably get a grater, too," Peter said. "Do I dare ask you if we have a grater, too?"

"Greater than what?" Tom answered, proud of his pun even though he felt a shudder of guilt move through his rectum as he thought of Dylan.

Peter liked talking as the collective unit of "We". Peter worked as a manager of a photographic studio downtown. He loved reminding Tom about how his job had evolved, from chemicals and darkened labs to computers and disks. "Think of all the things we are seeing changing in our lifetimes," Peter said. "Faxes, e-mail, DVDs." It made Tom think of how lucky Peter was to be alive, to see in their lifetimes how a virus might morph from a death knell to a manageable disease.

Back at his apartment, Peter unloaded the groceries while Tom checked his answering machine. After listening to a solicitation for "three free nights at Disneyland", Tom discreetly unplugged the phone so he would not be disturbed while spending the evening with Peter. Not that he expected Dylan to call, but in case he did, or in case Suzanne, weepy and weary from another bad date, decided not to wait until the next day at work to share her misery. Sometimes Suzanne called just to rehash their stress in the office with a client or their boss (an aging partner who still believed he was in the military) as much as to reiterate the misery of her most recent bad dates. There was no need to aggravate Peter. Peter could often be jealous over what he did not know of Tom's life and a long, placating phone conversation with Suzanne would give Peter the exact kind of cause Tom was hoping to avoid.

"Put on some music," Peter said from the kitchen. Peter and Tom had fallen into a habit of seeing each other twice a week. On Tuesday or Wednesday night and again on Saturday night. Tom was lucky that Dylan seldom liked to spend Saturday night together because it was the best night of the week to go to a club and dance, or so Dylan said, which in Tom's version translated into the pickings and tricking were best on the weekend when there was no real need for an occasional BF. Tom couldn't fault Dylan for this. He'd been just like him when he was Dylan's age.

Once, Tom had seen Dylan and Peter back to back on a late Saturday afternoon when Dylan was passing through the neighborhood and before Peter had shown up at the apartment before they went out to a new restaurant. The close call had delighted Suzanne when Tom had told it to her the following week.

"The lube was out and the porn was still playing when Peter buzzed," Tom told her. "I had just stepped out of the shower and had forgotten I hadn't cleaned up. Luckily, Peter opened a bottle of wine and I had enough time to get rid of all the incriminating evidence from Dylan."

In the kitchen Peter came behind Tom and squeezed him, his arms embracing Tom's waist and his flushed face nuzzling against Tom's neck. Peter loved being romantic; he often brought Tom flowers or wine or a CD he thought Tom might enjoy. Sometimes Tom loved feeling trapped in Peter's world, a shiny object of affection coated with heat and cologne. Peter never wanted to rush right into sex; he preferred to hug or nuzzle or cuddle. Sometimes he gave Tom backrubs or a slow massage that ended in a release (and that Tom was not expected to reciprocate). Sex was never Peter's real objective and Tom, in fact, was relieved when it did not happen. Tom was always conscious of body fluids and the items they shared when Peter was with him or staying at his apartment, perhaps because Peter was always so conscious of the next pill he needed to take. He traveled with a week's supply of his HIV medications in his knapsack, not about to let a terrorist attack or an Act of God send him off schedule. Tom always changed the sheets and threw the damp towels in the dirty clothes hamper right after Peter left in the mornings. At the back of his mind was the idea that no matter how safe they were together, there was still the possibility of a slip-up and Tom could become infected.

"You're going to love this dish," Peter said, as they unraveled and Peter addressed an item that was cooking in the skillet on Tom's stove. "It's full of garlic. I love it when we stay in and do these sorts of things together."

Tom smiled and now it was his turn to embrace Peter and revel in the warm, delicious odor of cooking garlic. He knew Peter was testing the waters. Love wasn't the smell of garlic or the size of Tom's apartment or keeping their sex life a little too safe to even call it sex *together*. Sooner or later love was going to land against his skin, ring in his ears, and try to settle into his chest. It happened after dinner, when they had settled into Tom's bed and were watching a DVD Peter had brought, a film made in England with English actors pretending to live and work in an English country estate. Peter fell asleep before the movie was over, though Tom enjoyed watching the plot unfold. When the deception was uncovered – an actor pretending to be a servant but really the son of the wealthy landowner – Tom felt the familiar twinge of his eyelid, which he took, now, not as being from guilt over deceiving both of his boyfriends but from exhaustion and a desire to fall asleep. Dylan seldom spent the night with Tom, preferring his own bed and his own space. Peter loved to sleep over at Tom's apartment, their bodies entwined, his long slender body encircling Tom. Peter stirred when Tom turned off the TV and the room floated into darkness.

"I love you," Peter whispered.

Tom responded with a kiss, butterflies startling across his stomach.

Eight years ago Suzanne's husband was killed in a motor cycle accident on Long Island. Pregnant, she carried their baby to term, but the boy died in the delivery room, strangled by the umbilical cord during a long, complicated labor.

Suzanne sued both the physician and the hospital and was awarded a large settlement, which was money she added to the payout of her husband's life insurance, but the year she took off from working did little to ease her sorrow and she felt the best thing she could do was return to the workforce. Six years ago she moved to Manhattan and began her employment search, hardened and toughened and ready for a corporate job, starting as a new attorney at the firm at about the same time Tom was changing jobs.

Tom, at the tail end of an affair with a married man (and another attorney who refused to divorce his wife and move in with Tom), was the one who urged her to start dating again, to keep herself focused on her work and distracted from her grief. At the time, Tom was bouncing between tricks and first dates and possible pick-ups on the rebound from his married attorney ex-boyfriend. Suzanne had met her losers, dorks, and jerks through dating clubs, singles nights, support groups, and Catholic and Jewish matchmakers (though she was neither Catholic nor Jewish; raised a Methodist, she no longer went to church, but had found her way into both dating circles courtesy of a friend-of-a-friend). She had never "given up the hunt", as she liked to call her great dating quest, though she was savvy enough not to expect anything more than a few minutes of boredom over a cup of coffee, or a last-minute proposition for a quickie if the guy had liked her enough to want to have sex (and which she always refused, or so she told Tom).

Peter and Stuart had been lovers for nine years. They had both been diagnosed as positive at about the same time, but it had been Stuart who was the first to get sick. Stuart's decline had lasted several years; there were several months of disability and numerous trips to the hospital. Stuart had not responded well when the new cocktail medications became available and, after his death, Peter had resisted the temptation to find a new lover quickly. There were three years of abstinence between Stuart's death and Peter's meeting Tom in the locker room of a gym on Eighth Avenue.

Dylan had never had a lover before, though he had fallen in love with the first guy he slept with after coming out in high school in Florida. Mike was still his closest friend – they had moved to New York together and shared a studio apartment in the West Village. When Dylan wasn't writing about going to the theater with his BF, he was usually writing about his BF (Best Friend) Mike. Mike was thin and blond and often in competition with Dylan with scoring a trick. Tom had slept with Mike first before he had had sex with Dylan. Mike had been Suzanne's temporary assistant for a day, and had given her the nickname "Dragon Lady" because she had made him retype a contract more than sixteen times in the space of two hours. Tom had run into Mike the week following his abrupt dismissal during happy hour at a gay bar on the Upper East Side. Tom had bought Mike a beer before bringing him back to his apartment. He met Dylan on a second date with Mike. It was Dylan who called first, to ask Tom to get together, after Mike had decided to pursue dating another guy who was younger than Tom.

Sometimes, Tom told Suzanne, he wished he could have the best of both boyfriends: Dylan's sexuality and Peter's domesticity, Dylan's spontaneity and Peter's romanticism. The morning after Peter said "I love you", Suzanne insisted at lunch that Tom tell Peter about Dylan. And vice versa. "You're playing with fire," she said. "Someone's going to get burned. And I'd hate to see you go up in flames."

"I know I should choose," Tom said. "But what if I pick the wrong one?"

After lunch, the fire ignited by itself. Spontaneous combustion. Dylan phoned Tom at the office. "I tried calling you last night," Dylan said. "All I got was the answering machine. Where were you?"

"I was out of town," Tom lied. "Suzanne and I had to go to Washington. FCC meetings for a client. I came back this morning."

"Want a visitor?"

"Sure. When will I see you?"

"In about fifteen minutes."

"*Here? At the office?*" Tom said, his voice rising nervously a pitch higher. Dylan had never been to Tom's office. (Nor, for that fact, had Peter.)

"You're not ashamed to show me off, are you?" Dylan answered.

Tom's sexuality was known and accepted by his co-workers, but other than what he shared with Suzanne, the details of his romantic and sexual life were kept private and confidential and certainly out of the workplace and (he hoped) out of the office gossip.

"Of course not," Tom answered.

"Good," Dylan said. "I thought it was time I met the Dragon Lady in your life."

Fifteen minutes later, Dylan appeared at Tom's office, just enough time for Tom to prep Suzanne on why they were in Washington the day before and not in the office or at their apartments last night, and that Dylan, in fact, was a friend of Mike's, her former temporary assistant who had given her an unpleasant nickname. Suzanne was wounded, not by the nickname but by the fact that Tom had never told her about sleeping with Mike and how he had *really* met Dylan, and she told him so, which set up the tension for the forthcoming introductions. When Dylan entered Tom's office, he introduced him to Suzanne, and Dylan said, "Glad to meet you. I've heard all about you."

Tom confided in both Dylan and Peter about Suzanne's horror stories of dating, as if reminding both boyfriends, as well as himself, what they could expect to face if they let each other go – blistering, bad dates with men who were dysfunctional and without scruples. Dylan linked Suzanne's inability to find a boyfriend to her inability to keep Mike as her assistant. Tom had never brought up with his boyfriends Suzanne's personal trail of sorrow, though sometimes Tom talked about Suzanne and her miserable dates when Dylan talked too much about the fabulousness of his anonymous tricks, as if by changing the subject away from Dylan, they also might change the subject from being exclusively about sex.

Suzanne scowled and reddened, as if she were Tom's other lover and knew exactly the kind of dysfunctional and scrupleless man Dylan was, and said, "Glad to finally meet you too." They shook hands as if they were about to step into opposite corners of a ring and begin to fight. Luckily, Suzanne's corner was in another office and she retreated, banging the door shut on her way out of Tom's office.

"And to what do I owe this pleasure of your visit?" Tom asked. He was seated at his desk. Dylan was still standing where he had greeted Suzanne. He was dressed in a black T-shirt, black jeans, black sneakers, black stubble on his jaw, inappropriate attire for an office visit, and Tom, in fact, *was* embarrassed at Dylan's appearance. He looked like a messenger boy eager to make an extra buck with a blow job. Tom was dressed in a suit, as he was most days in the office.

"Are you sleeping with her?" Dylan asked.

"Of course not," Tom answered. "Why do you even ask? I've never slept with a woman."

"You weren't home last night. I tried and tried."

"We were in Washington."

"She seems very protective of you."

"She works with me. I work with her. It's called teamwork."

"Let me see your eyes," Dylan said.

Their eyes locked and Tom hoped that Dylan would see the truth in that fact, that he was not sleeping with Suzanne, and not notice the twinge of his eyelid because he was thinking that moment of Peter.

"I've been thinking about you," Dylan said, a bit more relaxed, as if he had discovered some kind of truth behind Tom's eyes. "I wanted to see you. There's a lot I don't really know about you. I realized that I had never seen your office."

"Not much to report about," Tom laughed. "It's an office

with a desk and a computer, too many books, and a view of the next building, like most in the city."

Dylan walked to the windows and looked at the next building. "Do you ever see anything going on? Office romances?"

"Over there? Of course not. I'm too busy over here to look to see what's happening somewhere else."

"I'm not keeping you from something, am I?"

"I've got a few minutes," Tom said. "It's good to see you, though I wish we were somewhere else and not in my office."

"I don't know. It's kind of hot to me. Seeing you all dressed up. Working. You ever have an office romance?"

"You've been watching too much porn."

"No, I mean it. Ever had an office romance? Sex in your office?"

"No," Tom answered. "Of course not. And it's not appropriate to start."

"Come on," Dylan said, suddenly standing beside Tom's chair. "I came all this way just for you."

"You said you were in the neighborhood," Tom answered, but just as he said this, Dylan dropped to his knees in front of Tom's chair, as if he were about to ask Tom to marry him. "I thought you wanted to *see* me."

"I *do* want to *see* you," Dylan said, his hand reaching out and kneading Tom's crotch. "I *love* seeing you. I *love* getting you all hot and bothered. It means you care about me."

The blow job lasted five minutes. There was a fierce aggressiveness behind Dylan's technique which made Tom feel both powerless and extraordinary.

On his way out, Dylan stopped by Suzanne's office to say goodbye and she gave him a weak, disgusted smile, as if she already knew what Tom would eventually tell her.

Tom escorted Dylan to the elevator and the lobby of the building. "Now you won't forget me," Dylan said. "I'm the one you'll think about in your office."

*　　*　　*

Tom, in fact, thought about Dylan when he returned to his office. He felt both disgusted and proud. A good catch and a bad boy. He thought so much about Dylan that he could not help thinking about Peter. And the more he thought about the both of them, the more his head began to hurt. First, above his twitching eyelid. Then the ache stretched across his forehead and rested behind his left ear, a bright burning spot that grew and tightened the muscle below his shoulder blade.

He left his desk and lay down on the small sofa in his office, closing his eyes and slowing his breathing as he did when he meditated, but the ache brightened beneath his eyelids and the pain moved from below his left shoulder blade to the center of his back. When it began to blaze and burn down his spinal cord, Tom decided to get up and take a taxi home.

In the taxi, he felt relieved to be out of the office and the ride across town to his apartment eased him, in spite of the traffic and the workday congestion.

Upstairs, in his apartment and lying down on his bed, he fell into a deep sleep – he felt unusually exhausted because of both the energy the pain had consumed and the tension Dylan had created and released while in his office. When he woke four hours later, the pain was back, this time burning in his stomach and flushing up into his chest. In his sleep Tom had started to sweat, and his forehead and underarms were soaked with perspiration. He coughed, remembering reading somewhere that it might jump start his circulation if a heart attack was imminent.

The pain continued, burning in his chest. He decided to call Peter first. Peter would know what to do about the pain. He was always full of common sense when it came to aches and pains of the body; he knew about antidotes and alternative therapies or homeopathic remedies. He'd be able to quickly assess what was happening, make a recommendation, and offer the appropriate concern.

Tom looked at his clock and wasn't sure if Peter would still be at work. He dialed the photographic studio, but Peter was not there, his voicemail picking up after the fourth ring. Next

Tom tried Peter's home number and then his cellphone, leaving urgent messages to return the call as soon as possible.

He waited thirty minutes, till the pain was brighter and harder and making it more difficult to breathe. He tried calling Dylan on his cellphone. When there was no answer he left a message, then left another message on Dylan's home answering machine. Dylan might not know what to do, but Tom thought Dylan's voice might simply offer some kind of calm and reassurance.

After fifteen more minutes and a growing tightness at his chest, Tom became frightened. Neither boyfriend was around when he was desperately needed. Tom was adrift in pain, caught in the burning tower of his body. He'd always thought it would be work that would do him in. Not a boyfriend. Or two of them.

It was Suzanne who came to his rescue, doing what neither of his boyfriends could do – getting Tom's spare keys out of his desk drawer, taking a taxi across town to check on him, climbing the stairs of his apartment, finding him sweating in bed, and calling an ambulance to take him to the hospital.

"I promise I'll make this up to you somehow," Tom said to Suzanne as he was carried down the stairs of his building and into an ambulance. He was grateful he was not alone, that someone was around to go through the next steps with him.

"Stop worrying," Suzanne answered firmly. "Or I might hold you to your promise. Then you'll be sorry you ever called me for help."

At the hospital, Tom was given blood thinners and admitted for observations and tests. A cardiologist was consulted. Tom was under too much stress. The possibility of open heart surgery was discussed. Another procedure for clearing his veins was considered. Suzanne stayed with Tom in his room or waited with him for results, helping him to ease his fears. Her work from the office was sent over by messenger. She only used her cellphone in the hallway by the nurse's station.

Tom thought a lot about Suzanne. If he could love her. If he weren't gay. How he would make this up to her. How he could not live without her in his life. Her toughness disappeared, replaced by a motherly, or sisterly, concern. Tom felt that she deserved to find a good man, that, in fact, she truly deserved someone better than him. She deserved a *truly* good man, not someone who could date two men at the same time. If he wasn't good enough himself for her, then he would make a stronger effort to help her find someone who was.

The following day both boyfriends called Tom.

"What are you doing in the hospital?" Dylan asked.

"Tests," Tom said. "I needed a test. Where were you? I tried calling."

"Are you okay?" Dylan asked, avoiding Tom's last question.

"Better. But I'll be here for a few days. Will I see you?"

"I can't come by today. I'm on deadline and I promised to take Mike to a screening tonight."

"Can't break your promises, can you?"

"I'll visit you tomorrow," Dylan said. "Promise. Do you want a visitor tomorrow?"

"Ask me tomorrow," Tom answered and hung up.

"I can't do this," Peter said, when he called. "I can't visit you. Ever since Stuart died, I get panicky when I think about a hospital. It makes me too worried about myself. I have to think about my own health. I'm stressing out just thinking of visiting you. My herpes is back."

"I wouldn't want to be the cause of anything that made you sick," Tom said.

"When will you be out?"

"Ask me tomorrow," Tom answered and hung up.

When Suzanne arrived at the hospital with work, he told her about both calls. She nodded and said true colors were often displayed in times of a crisis.

"You're too good to me," Tom said. "Why don't you have a boyfriend? Why aren't you married to someone?"

"I'm working on it," she answered. "I have five dates pending."

"What? How did this happen? Why didn't I know this?"

"I didn't want to say anything, because I thought I might turn out to be a big loser myself, and you were too self-focused about your boyfriends and it didn't seem right to tell you about my plan after Dylan showed up at the office."

"Where did you meet these guys? And *five*? How did you ever meet five guys to date?"

"Speed dating," she said. "The less they know of you, the more they want to see you."

Surgery was not performed, though Tom was released from the hospital with a pad of prescriptions he needed to fill and take on a daily basis.

Dylan did not visit Tom at the hospital and stopped writing about Tom in his weekly column. Peter called again and apologized, but avoided visiting Tom because of his herpes outbreak, then simply stopped calling and faded away into Tom's list of ex-boyfriends. At lunch, Suzanne began to talk about two of the five men she was interested in becoming more serious about. Will, a psychiatrist, who was a little too interested in getting inside her head, and Vic, a construction worker who was the best sex of her life.

Later, months later, well on the road of recovery and spending way too much time working on work, Tom took Suzanne's advice and went to a speed dating night at the gay community center in the West Village. "One desperate guy after the next," he laughed and told her the next day at lunch, about the men he had met for all of two minutes the night before. "Why can't I meet a guy like you?"

"Like me?" she answered. "What do you mean?"

"Someone like you. But gay. The gay version of you. A gay man who cares a little more than expected."

"Are you sure?" she asked. "Why would you ever want someone with a hardened heart?"

Daddy Lover God

Don Shewey

Sunday is often a busy day, but yesterday was slow. Two sessions, neither of them strictly speaking a massage. It was an afternoon with what I call my client-husbands. There are several of them now among my regulars, men with whom the work has gone beyond erotic massage and into the realm of sacred intimate work, where anything is possible. Sometimes it's a dilemma when more than one of my client-husbands call to book sessions on the same day. They take up a lot of energy, and I prefer to see no more than one a day.

But these two yesterday, Eugene and Lester, were so vastly different that I didn't mind seeing them one right after the other. In fact, it made the afternoon really fun.

Eugene is one of my most intriguing clients. A handsome, rich, and successful African-American book publisher with two kids and a soon-to-be-ex-wife, Eugene turned 44 recently and decided it was time to do some of the things he'd always dreamed about but never done. Being with a man was one of those things. He'd gotten massaged at his health club, but he called me for a private session out of curiosity to see what might happen. I quickly discovered Eugene's pleasure spot was his butt, especially the tender pink skin around his butthole, stroked by a finger or a tongue or the firm head of a hard cock. What really surprised me, though, was how eager Eugene was for hugging and kissing and friendly affectionate interaction. He didn't seem to have a shred of sex-shame or body-shame. I couldn't bring myself to think of him as heterosexual; he was just sexual, period.

Our first few sessions set a pattern. I would stretch him out and massage his back thoroughly, relaxing him and working out the kinks. Eugene was fairly relaxed anyway; he took care of his body and always stopped at his health club to shower and groom himself before a session. I would work my way down his body to his butt and legs, applying firm pressure when kneading his buttocks, sliding my warm oily hands lightly over his inner thighs (always producing a beautiful cherry-red boner), working on his feet to let the erotic energy subside, then stroking back up the legs to spend time on his butt.

After some stretching, stroking, and rocking, Eugene would be loosened up and ready for further exploration. At first I put on gloves and gave him a full-scale internal prostate massage. But after a few sessions we discussed it and I learned that Eugene preferred the external butt stroking to penetration. What he really liked was for me to lie on top of him, resting the full weight of my body on his back, and tease his butthole with the head of my dick. I would wrap my hands around his pecs and pull him close, nuzzling the back of his neck with my lips and teeth, while he writhed and pushed his butt back against my hips. Sometimes I would get so hot doing this that I would squirt prematurely onto his back, which he never seemed to mind. In fact, he said it turned him on. Inevitably he would roll over and pull me on top of him for some deep tongue-kissing. He would let his huge warm hand slide down my body until it rested over my hairy butt, and we would proceed from there until he was ready to climax. I didn't bother trying to convince Eugene to contain his erotic energy. He was so highly charged, there was no stopping him from coming.

Eugene was full of euphemisms. I enjoyed hearing them and liked to torture them out of him by asking point-blank, "What is the experience you would like to have today?" Eugene was much too polite and respectful to say, "I want you to chow down on my joint" or "Put it up my ass, baby, the way you know I like it." No no no no no. He'd say things like, "Well, I like part one of the massage, and then I'd like to move to part two." Or he'd say, "Depending on how you're feeling, I'd like to have an 'interesting' session rather than a conventional one."

Yesterday, when I asked the question, Eugene dropped the expression "role play". This puzzled me. In the gay world, role-playing generally takes place in SM relationships and the roles are severely defined. Master and slave are the most common, but they can also be as benign as big brother/little brother. Somehow I didn't think that's what Eugene had in mind. Then it dawned on me that for a straight guy accustomed to taking the initiative with women and always dominating, simply to lie back and have someone else take care of you is a role-reversal. What to me seemed like a natural, reciprocal interaction – two guys rolling around together, alternating top and bottom – Eugene considered a psychologically risky abdication of male gender behavior. Ideal recipe for good sex.

The breakthrough session with Eugene came when I asked him to close his eyes and think for a minute and tell me exactly what experience he wanted. Eugene hesitated and very shyly said, "I want to make love." I rejoiced that he had stated his desire so directly. That night we abandoned the massage table. I pulled down the comforter on my futon, and we spent a lovely hour in bed together. It was the first time Eugene ever had a penis in his mouth. Looking up from between my legs, where he'd been attentively stroking my cock, he murmured, "Can I taste it?" When he got permission, he was trembling. I ran my hand across his wooly hair. "Take your time," I said. "Enjoy it. Really taste my cock. Feel what it feels like in your mouth."

Getting blowjobs from novices isn't the most exciting thing in the world, especially when they get hasty and frenzied and their teeth get in the way. That's why I like to slow them down, to get more tongue, more spit. There's a sort of regression that takes place. Sucking dick is like nursing, and it takes a few minutes to relax and get into it, to go back to the infantile pleasure of sucking for the sake of sucking. For grown men, I notice, infantile feelings often bring up a lot of shame. It feels too good to be that helpless, and that's not permitted. It's a macho thing, too – the man has got to be in control, and one way that shows up in cocksucking is the sucker feels he has to work really hard to make the guy come, so the pleasure of simply sucking gets lost in the mechanical function and the power struggle.

I watched Eugene sucking me with the peaceful detachment of a mother watching her child nurse. "This is what it's like to be a sacred intimate," I thought. "I don't feel the urgent need to come or control the situation. I'm content to be present and let Eugene try on this behavior. There are harder ways to make a living."

Yesterday we had one of our "interesting" sessions. Eugene called earlier in the day than usual and arrived for an appointment at noon. After a brief conversation about his latest skiing trip with his children, we undressed each other and proceeded to sprawl on my bed. The early afternoon sun joined us. In the direct sunlight his skin changed colors. Where I licked his thigh, the wet spot shone yellow against brown. I loved seeing the clear sparkle of precome on the tip of his undying erection in direct sunlight. And the blanket of skylight added a layer of warmth to the crush of our hairy chests together.

"I missed you," Eugene murmured in my ear as he lifted his knees and wrapped them around my waist.

For a fleeting moment I wondered how I really felt about Eugene. I know this will sound funny, but I try not to have personal feelings toward any of my clients. It's specifically because I have no future with any of the men I see that I can bring to them a radical presence. In a way, all my clients are the same man – a combination of Daddy, lover, and God. Sometimes I get lonely after they leave. Sometimes I entertain fantasies that a relationship with a client could expand into something larger and more unpredictable – if not a domestic partnership, then some kind of glamorous or romantic partnership of courtesan and patron, with free trips to exotic destinations. But I know I can only get hurt if I expect anything from them. The last time Eugene had visited, he was on his way to a blind date with a famous black opera diva. When he didn't call for three weeks, after a pattern of coming to see me every week, I assumed that Eugene had clicked with the diva and decided to terminate his exploration of mansex.

So my heart lifted and opened at Eugene's tender confession.

"I missed you, too," I said.

In some ways this is the best kind of lovemaking on earth. Both of us set aside time to be together, devoting ourselves to pleasure and connection. All the sex manuals and marriage counselors advise couples to set aside time for lovemaking, but how many people actually do that? In my experience, scheduling lovemaking usually creates anxiety and resentment and imitations of arousal. In the context of a sacred intimate session, both parties rise to the occasion. Of course, there is a financial transaction – the client wants to get his money's worth, and the professional wants to earn his keep. Marxists might call this the commodification of desire, and Puritans might frown on the sale of what should properly be given freely. Sometimes I feel cynical about the work and observe myself going through the motions. I'm performing work-for-hire masquerading as unconditional love. I'm peddling counterfeit romance to men too deprived or depraved to complain. Those are the accusations I fling at myself.

But in the best of times, the work feels not like consumer carnality but focused ritual. Ritual in the sense of creating time out of time with a specific intention. We are here not to talk about the weather or the stock market, or to run power trips on each other, but to do something we don't get very many opportunities to do – open our hearts and bodies to someone else.

I must have been getting a little corny and overly spiritual in my reverie, because Eugene suddenly raised his head and looked me in the eye. "When are we going to go all the way?" he asked. Then I remembered that I really was dealing with a straight man, whose experience of sex centers on intercourse-to-ejaculation, in contrast to which everything else is hors d'oeuvres.

"Going all the way" with Eugene tempts me. If there is any scenario that justifies fucking without rubbers, here's a pretty good one – a "straight" guy who's never been fucked, a wealthy businessman with no drug habits. I'm as certain as I can be that I'm HIV-negative. What would be the harm of going in bareback? He'd love it. I'd love it. Skip that awkward moment of freezing the pelvis while struggling with the condom pack (not easy to rip open with lube-smeared fingers), trying to stay hard while putting the rubber on, inevitably putting it on upside down to begin with, reservoir tip UP so the rest of it rolls DOWN the shaft, and then aiming for the hole and hoping it yields immediately so the friction of sliding in and out can rejuvenate any diminishment of erection . . .

I wondered what Eugene did with the women he slept with. Did he use rubbers? Did they insist? Eugene clearly has no trouble staying hard. He's usually hard the entire time he spends with me.

The angel choir of Safe Sex Precautions and Professional Integrity danced in my head, with some semi-legal language about the "slippery slope". I have a responsibility! To educate guys who are out of the safe sex loop, exactly like Eugene! At the moment, I didn't feel like educating. So I avoided the whole question by positioning myself so he could feel my cock pulsing against his butthole, and I rocked my hips against the back of his butt and thighs, for that all-important first chakra awakening sensation. For me, hardly anything feels better than butthole-surfing. Still, I knew Eugene craved the sensation of penetration, if only out of curiosity.

Maybe it would happen another day.

*   *   *

When we were done, Eugene dressed slowly, chatting all the way. I didn't want to rush him, but as soon as the door closed, I had to rush around like a madman. I didn't have to put fresh sheets on the table, because we'd skipped that part. But I saged the room, hopped in the shower, closed the curtains, and then changed clothes. Out of my sweat pants and T-shirt, into my leather pants, white tank-top, leather vest, and high-top Timberland boots: an outfit that predictably brought a sigh of pleasure from Lester when he came in the door.

Lester looks more like Humpty Dumpty than anyone I've ever met. A middle manager in his late 50s, he recently shaved his mustache and cut his white hair short, so his large head looks paler and more egg-like than ever. Over six feet tall, he probably weighs 250 pounds, including a big soft white underexercised belly.

He walked in the door and handed me a black plastic shopping bag. Inside was a white plastic shopping bag with the handles tied in a knot. In addition to his usual wrist and ankle restraints, he brought some new toys that he'd picked up cheap from a one-man bazaar at the Eagle: a black leather dog collar and a black Spandex hood with a single mouth-hole for breathing.

"Have you tried them out?" I asked.

"Yes," he said.

"How do they feel?"

"They feel great. I can see through the hood, though."

I instructed him to remove his black turtleneck, and I fastened the dog collar around his neck. I pulled the hood over his head and then went to my bureau drawer to get a foam-padded blackout blindfold and strapped that over the hood. I restrained his wrists behind his back, noticing drops of anxious sweat already trickling along his flabby sides. Unfastening his belt, I roughly yanked his denim pants to his knees and smacked his ankles until he spread his feet wide. Then I tugged his white cotton underpants down as well, freeing a big fat smooth-headed boner (already drooling precome) and giant balls. I walked across the room to fetch a length of clothesline from a drawer, and when I turned back I stopped for a minute to take in the sight in front of me: a giant schlumpy black-hooded Igor with a deserted lot of scraggly graying hair on his droopy chest standing with his pants around his knees, sporting an erection, wearing a dog collar with his hands tied behind his back, and gulping shallow breaths through his goldfish mouth. This is truly sacred work, I thought.

I stood in front of him and tied the clothesline to the largest ring on his dog collar. I let the other end of the clothesline fall to the floor and then wrapped it around his cock and balls several times, which made his dick bob toward the ceiling higher and harder. Now a long line of liquid dripped from the tip of his dick down to the carpet. (Good thing I'm not very Suzy Homemaker, hysterical about spills and stains.) I grabbed the rope at chest level and plucked it gently, tugging his neck and balls at the same time. I let myself enjoy playing with Lester in this state. No rush.

I knelt at his feet and one after the other lifted his legs and removed his trousers. Then I walked behind him and, sliding a hand down one arm after the other, I unsnapped the wrist restraints. Walking in front of him again, I unwrapped the clothesline from around his balls and said, "I want you to get down on your knees."

As he lurched forward, I added, "Slowly!"

Grunting, he dropped first to one knee, then the other.

"Okay, now get down on all fours." I adjusted the dog collar so the ring the line was attached to slid around to the back of his neck. "We're going to go for a little walk."

I led him across the room, steering him with slight tugs on the rope. When I got to the hallway, I didn't say anything but let him find his bearings between the radiator (going full blast) and the wall. Leading him down the hall, I realized we would be passing the window in the hallway and wondered if anyone in the adjacent apartments happened to be standing at their windows looking this way. If so, they were getting the kind of show urban voyeurs long for and rarely find.

I herded Lester into my small bathroom. I pushed the toilet cover up against the tank with a loud ceramic crack. Then I pushed the toilet seat up so it also made a distinct sound.

"Are you thirsty?" I asked the figure on the floor.

"No, sir," came the faint reply.

"Are you sure?"

"Yes, sir."

After a few rounds of boot-kissing and sitting-up-and-begging, I walked him back to the living room and had him kneel on a pillow on the floor while I attached the wrist restraints to the end of the massage table. I took my wide leather belt off and gave Lester the strapping that he eagerly anticipated at every session. This turned out to be a good position. Usually I tie him down to the table on his belly. On his knees, he could stick his butt way out – a sign of pleasure and a request for more – and lengthen his back for the strokes on the upper back and shoulders that he seemed to like even more than lashes across his expansive white butt. I also noticed the strapping made him rock hard, a fact that lying on the table usually concealed.

Finished with that, I had him crawl up onto the table and lie on his back, still blindfolded, hooded, and manacled. I opened a bureau drawer and took out my braided nylon bondage ropes. I secured his feet to the end of the massage table and pulled his arms up over his head. Then I wound the longest rope I had around his mountainous belly and under the table and tied it up tight. Then I brought his arms down and secured them to the ropes. I got out a set of Walkman headphones, plugged them into the stereo system, positioned them over Lester's ears, and turned on some spacy and vaguely sinister electronic music quite loud. His shiny red apple of a dickhead pointed straight up to the ceiling.

I stood back and examined my work and saw that it was good.

My experience in tying people up is laughably limited. Lester would have been surprised to know that he was my only SM client. He repeatedly marvelled at my ingenuity and expertise at taking him on journeys through intense body play. If the truth be known, I surprise myself almost every time I see Lester. Although the practice of massaging someone centers on being radically present and paying attention to the individual body on the table in front of you, most of my massage sessions follow the same routine, touching the same spots in the same order each time. Even lovemaking sessions with my favorite sex partners tend to follow the same pattern after a while, once we've worked out what we like. These sessions with Lester, though, permit and even require much more spontaneity than I'm used to.

It actually terrifies me. I hate having to be spontaneous. I much prefer having a script in front of me, a road map. But more and more I find myself having fun in these sessions with Lester. Working with someone who is blindfolded, restrained (no touching back), and often sound-sealed, I can operate without being seen. Sometimes I feel like a scientist working in a laboratory, mixing this chemical with that chemical and observing which makes the liquid turn green and which produces clouds of vapor. There is a lot of Frankenstein involved, too – I measure the effect of my actions by how much the creature on the table twitches and jerks.

I often find myself thinking, as I'm feeding Lester a ripe strawberry or a teaspoon of his own copious precome, or as I'm stroking his engorged penis with the blossom of a rose, this is as intimate as I've ever been with anybody. I've never done this even with a lover.

I had about 15 minutes left to play with Lester in this state. I rummaged around in my basket of playthings and pulled out a handful of clothespins. I fastened one to his right nipple, which made him jump, and then another to the left. He rocked slightly from side to side, and his fleshpole danced with pleasure. In quick succession I attached three clothespins to his scrotum, starting at the bottom near his perineum up to the base of his shaft, the wooden clips forming a kind of peacock's fan spreading out over the top of his balls, which were as big as a juice orange. Very aesthetically pleasing.

After a pause, I stuck a few more clothespins on some other sensitive areas: the sides of his belly, just below his armpits, his inner thighs. Then I hung back and let the endorphins kick in. I knew that, far from being tortured, Lester was having a ball. Not only was he feeling sensations in parts of his gargantuan body that usually spent their days numb and dead, he was also being closely attended by a hot studly leatherman. It was like having a Broadway show performed just for you.

I reached over and fiddled with the stereo system, hiking the volume up and fucking with the fast-forward button so the music sped up and slowed down.

It was getting to be time to stop. I quickly pulled the clothespins off of Lester's body in reverse order. At each removal, a shudder would ripple through his system. When I got to the nipples, I squeezed each clothespin harder until I got a whimper of response, and then unfastened it. I walked into the kitchen and plucked a pink plastic-handled feather-duster off a hook. I took it to the massage table and lightly brushed each of the spots where a clothespin had been. I lingered at Lester's balls. Brushing up and down the scrotum, barely touching them with the feathers, made his slightly drooping dick harder and redder. I returned the feather-duster to its hook and began untying the ropes. I took my time, coiling each rope and knotting it for storage before going on to the next. Cleaning up while I go saves me time later, and it gives Lester a few more minutes to stay in his trance. I could tell that he had gone pretty deep this time, because his body was very relaxed and his breathing was quiet.

Once the ropes and restraints were removed, I had him sit up on the table. "I'm going to count backwards from five to zero, and when I get to zero, we'll be done." As I counted down, I kneaded his shoulders and unhooked his dog collar. I slid the blindfold off, and as I got to "Zero," I pulled off the hood.

He looked up at me with the docile, shining eyes of a newborn chick. A puddle of gratitude and satisfaction, he seemed more like a five-year-old child than a middle-aged man.

"Sometime," he said, "you're going to have to figure out what your overnight rate would be."

Lester almost always makes a comment like that when the scene is over: he wants it to go on and on. He once even proposed marriage, pointing out the excellent health benefits his company offered the spouse equivalents of employees. I take these comments as compliments to my work, but they also make me a little nervous. I guess I recognize in Lester my own aggressive instinct to concretize my desires. Sometimes, though, fantasies are more potent when they remain in the fantasy realm. That's why I've never taken off my clothes in front of him and never given him a "release". I want him to consider me a guide along the journey of coming out (as a gay man and as an SM practitioner), not the destination.

When he made his half-joking request for an overnight session, I felt a little badly, because I knew that as much as Lester enjoys the SM play, he really wants to be held and loved. What are the chances of a fat bald middle-aged man who's just come out of the closet finding a lover? It is not impossible, but it takes as much inner work as getting out there and hunting. I wanted to give Lester a pep talk about self-esteem, to urge him to look inside himself for validation rather than outside. But that seemed tricky coming out of a session that revolved around wearing a dog collar and having clothespins fastened to his nipples.

I recently flipped through a paperback book of SM fantasies called Sir, looking for new ideas of what to do with Lester. I was getting a little tired of the routine we'd established – dog training, strapping, bondage. I read through the stories. They weren't very interesting. Most of them involved teenage or college-age boys having their first experiences with a man. None of them involved a fat middle-aged bald man seeking experience in the hands of a professional masseur.

I tried to remember what I'd been like as a kid, full of yearning for experience. When every physical encounter felt like a judgment from heaven on my worth as a person. In high school I knew for certain I was queer. I was in love with two of my friends: tall and talkative Lenny Meltzer, whose mother was the art teacher at school, and dark, handsome Ron Garrett, whose father was a general and who wanted to be a priest. I would go for long walks in the woods with Lenny, talking about the pseudo-philosophical stuff young intellectuals discuss, while fantasizing ripping off his shirt and holding him to my heart. Ron and I would sit in his family car late at night after play rehearsals, talking for an hour when, to my mind, we could have been making out.

My fantasies about Lenny and Ron were less sexual than romantic. It was the jocks at school who stirred up my beastly fantasies. Listening to them brag about the number of times they'd fucked girls, I conceived hot scenarios in which I'd be alone in the locker room when tall, long-legged football star Jack Mundy would wander in from his shower with half a boner and sit on the bench drying his crotch over and over again, looking at me with an attitude of pugnacious challenge mixed with a vulnerable curiosity . . .

I was 19 before I ever had a dick in my mouth, and I felt like I was years behind then. Imagine being 57 and never having sucked a cock. "Why bother coming out?" Lester complained, and I had a hard time arguing with him on that point.

When I began my massage practice, I unthinkingly assumed that everyone in the world had the same images and associations with being gay that I have. For me, coming out as a college student during the mid-1970s in politically active Boston meant entering a community, gaining self-knowledge, finding a place in the world, and enjoying almost limitless sexual opportunities. Seeing so many clients who are married, closeted, or coming out late in life, I've come to realize that their associations with being gay are much more negative and frightening. Embracing a gay identity for them means jettisoning another that, for better or worse, has served them for a lifetime. Being gay is just as likely to conjure a sense of loss and shrinking horizons as to spell freedom and expansion. And for many of them, sexual satisfaction will only occur through encounters with professionals. Admitting these realities makes me sad and angry, and it increases my compassion for older guys who didn't have the same chances I had – a compassion I'm not always able to show. It does make me wonder what my life will be like when I'm 60. I assume that I will be partnered and sexually satisfied, but for all I know I'll be just like Lester, investing my emotions in unrequited affairs with young erotic masseurs.

After Lester left, I decided to give myself a sacred intimate session. I turned off all the electric lights in the apartment, leaving the candles flickering on the mantelpiece and on the ancestors' altar. I put on my favorite ambient music, a spacy disk with unpredictable eruptions of bass-heavy sex-groove riffs. I peeled off my Tom Petty and the Heartbreakers T-shirt and my black drawstring sweat pants. And I gathered supplies. One bottle of coconut oil was still warm from the last session. I dug around in the middle drawer of my supply bureau and brought out my personal-use dildo, which was slightly smaller, more friendly, more human than the somewhat imposing dildo I used with clients. Grabbing a tube of K-Y, I climbed aboard the massage table, still slightly cool and damp with oil.

I lay on my back and slid the cushioned face plate under the middle of my back, which pushed my chest out while my shoulders relaxed backwards. I took deep breaths. For all my coaching of clients, I knew I didn't breathe as much as I could either. Breathing brings up all kinds of feelings and sensations. It opens you up to the possibility of pleasure, but it also makes you acutely aware of aches and pains in your body as well as whatever emotions you've been avoiding all day. I registered the dull ache that usually shows up in my lower back on the right side at the end of a day. I felt the heaviness in my balls and wondered if it was related to my lower back pain. Kidneys? Backed-up jizz? I hadn't come for two weeks and had experienced raging hard-ons practically every day. Sure, some Chinese practitioners could go for ten years without coming. But I felt quite certain that my own body was getting a little fried with frustration. I am my own cocktease, I thought. My cock had been gearing up to shoot every day now, all the neurons and pistons and hydraulics on alert and ready to spring into action. I had a moment of understanding why the United States was always getting drawn into conflagrations abroad. If you spend half the national budget on defense, employing a million hot-blooded American males to be ready to fight, they're going to get very antsy if they don't get to blow off some steam every now and then. Hey, maybe I should write a grant application to the Pentagon, proposing a giant annual orgy, a week-long sexual Olympics, in lieu of invading some tiny foreign country populated by non-white people. This would primarily be aimed at servicemen between the ages of 18 and 25. There would be physique competitions, how-many-times-can-you-come contests, how-far-can-you-shoot matches, circle jerks, blowjob booths. I would personally volunteer to supervise the festivities. Yes, I would write that proposal.

Later, though. Right now I was oiling up my half-hard cock and thinking about Jacob. He was one of the few clients I had crossed the cocksucking barrier with. It was an extraordinary experience to play with Jacob. I always gave him a good thorough massage. He was relaxed, tanned (maintained by frequent trips to South Beach and the local tanning salon), and well-groomed. He trimmed his body hair closely. I prefer untrimmed body hair, but the way Jacob attends to his seems to have no purpose other than erotic. I'm pleased to inspect the careful way he shaves his balls and razors his pubic hair up to the top of his beautiful fat dick, which begins to swell as soon as I lay my hands on his body.

The routine is that I don't introduce any erotic touch for the first hour, until Jacob has gotten stretched and pummeled and all the kinks worked out of his back. Then when I roll him over onto his back again, I lightly stroke the tips of his close-cropped body hair, from his clavicle to his big toes and back. After stroking the full length of his body, I do another length with one hand while using the other to lightly brush his nipples, which I know sends him through the roof. Before long, his cock is rock-hard and pointing at his chin. I stand at his head and brush both nipples while breathing quietly into his ear, encouraging him to fill his body with oxygen, to feel the erotic energy all over his body. He has a tendency to catch his breath, hold it for a while, take in a little bit at a time. I have to keep reminding him to breathe all the way down to his toes.

I lean across his face to stroke his chest and his belly. The curly hair on my chest and torso tickles his nose, and he begins to nudge my body, keeping his eyes closed, like a newborn puppy blindly finding its way to sustenance. I climb onto the table, carefully kneeling on either side of his head, and proceed to plant a line of very, very soft kisses down his belly, to his shaved balls, and eventually to the dripping, bouncing head of his dick. Opening wide, I invite his cock into the warm wetness of my mouth. After a couple of preliminary strokes, I take him all the way into my throat, like a key going into a lock. And I rest there, lying flat on top of Jacob, our warm hairy bellies smushed together, and I breathe through my nose, while he moans softly, his cock twitching, the full length of it buried in my mouth. I've almost never experienced this ecstasy before. It's a cocksucker's dream: the Perfect Fit.

I replayed this scene, lying back on a maroon bedsheet, my oily cock in one hand. It didn't take much to get fully stiff, thinking about Jacob. If only he were here right now. If only he and I could permit ourselves to indulge in an hour-long blowjob, rather than a few minutes snatched at the end of a massage session. I felt down between my legs and ran a fingertip around the bulging pucker of my asshole. I snapped open the fliptop tube of K-Y and squeezed a drop onto my forefinger, and then smeared it over my butthole and easily slid the finger in up to the first knuckle. It wasn't so often that I played with my own butt, so I decided to go all the way.

I got up on my knees and faced the mirror over the fireplace. I extracted another gob of lubricant from the long white tube and slathered it on the head and shaft of my rubber husband. Then I positioned the dildo at the opening to my butt. It immediately slid in just past the head. I stopped and took a breath. My cock had wilted a little bit during these maneuvers, so I stroked myself again. My hands were gooey from the K-Y. I wiped one hand on the sheet and returned it to my cock. With the other hand I pinched first one nipple, then the other. Concentrating on my breathing, I opened my ass to receive more of the dildo. Suddenly, a rush of heat spread all over my body, down my legs, through my hips and butt, up my spine to the back of my neck. I slowed down my cock strokes, then sped them up. I was so close. I loved this fullness. I thought of all the cocks I'd loved sitting on, and the ones I'd fantasized sitting on, filling me up and rocking and rocking and holding and pushing and heat hot full hot gasp stop stop can't stop oh oh oh oh. I spilled a torrent of thick white juice onto the blood-red sheet. It looked like a map of all the Great Lakes: Lake Michigan, Lake Huron, Lake Ontario, Lake Erie, Lake Superior.

Little Stevie

Kirk Read

Spike, by this point, was doing two shows a day at the Beacon
Cinema. He was filling in a slot by one of the headliners,
who'd gone missing. Those guys did four shows a day, which
is like being deployed to a country riddled with genocide. He
had a lot of different names and he was gone. Everyone
assumed crystal, because, I mean, come on, she was a mess.
Those last few weeks they'd cut him back to three shows a
day, then two, then moved him to a single prime spot at noon
with all the businessmen on their lunch breaks. That's where
you get all your hooker business. Private shows. If you're a
really good stripper, you might make $100 for a 30 minute
shift. But that's a long time to dance and most guys make
around $25. It's about the lap dances later. You stay 30
minutes after your shift. Last Tuesday, that was the last time
anybody saw Steven. He was sitting down for a lap dance and
lost his balance and fell over. All these patrons rushed over to
catch him so he didn't hit his head on the railing of the stage.
They lifted him up high above their heads and put him back
on the stage. They looked like pallbearers or chorus members
in "Godspell". You shouldn't pass out right after your shift.
Everybody's got problems, but that's tacky.

I don't know why Lyle the manager liked him so much. In
gay businesses, all you have to do sometimes is strike a
nostalgic chord in the guy hiring you. Maybe you're wearing
a striped sweatshirt and when he arrived in the city thirty
years ago, a striped sweatshirt was the only warm clothing he

owned. Say what you want, but gay guys who've been down
where you are – they're a loyal breed of animal. I'm talking
about traditional gay businesses – bars, video stores, sex
clubs. The kinds of places where you can find a job when
you're young. There's a sympathy – guys want to help you
out. Maybe they talk to you like you're a piece of ass sometimes, but they still want to help. I'm not talking about new
gay businesses. Real estate companies and trendy restaurants
and boutique stores. That's a whole different thing. And
places that are corporate-owned, forget it. I'm talking about
places owned and run by the same person, some country fag
who smokes Salem 100s and started calling himself an old
queen the day he turned 37. The guy owns the place but he
still works the front desk. That's what I'm celebrating.

Anyway, Lyle, the manager at the Beacon, he was one of
those fags. Traditional. Moral. He would find kids in the
street, leaning up against buildings to steady themselves
while they shot up heroin through their toes. Dirty kids,
the ones who'd started rotting from their blood on out. He'd
get those kids right after they did their hit, when they were
dreamy. He'd carry them home, literally carry them. He's
enormous, bigger than you think they make gay guys. For
years the theater didn't have a bouncer at all because Lyle
was working the door.

One time this grad student type was doing a shift at the
theater. He had a big dick and had some good boy stuff to
exorcise. He came into the theater with his anthropology
vocabulary, telling Lyle he wanted to do an "ethnography"
of the theater and its "workers". He started calling Lyle
Horatio, as in Alger, because of his tendency to retrieve
urchin boys. Nobody knew what he was talking about and a
decision was made that this guy was stuck up. He was gone in
a couple of days. Not fired, but he knew it was time to go.
The other guys got nervous when he started talking about
doing his thesis on them, their class background, social
capital and structural violence. He used words like this in
the dressing room! Guys are trying to get their dicks hard and

he's asking them were their parents on welfare. What happened was, they told patrons they didn't like the guy, patrons complained to Lyle and the whole place was strangely unified. Every now and then you see that.

Point is, Steven, the one who went missing, might have had a concussion or something. Maybe he was confused. Maybe he was shooting heroin and speed – goofballs – and crackin' on in some downtown hotel. Maybe he went home to his parents in Oklahoma. People thought Oklahoma because that was where Steven had his tax forms sent. Lyle didn't tell any of the guys that but one day when Lyle was downstairs, Brian, a former assistant shift manager, had seen the W-2 forms sitting on the desk. He had terrible boundaries, which was one of the reasons he didn't work there anymore. It had only been 11 days, but at the theater, that was a really long time. Lyle was about to file a missing persons report, although that was a last resort because he hated the police. You know that feeling you get when you're watching "Cops" and they're dragging some woman out of a trailer, practically beating her as they mug for the cameras. Lyle identified with the woman, not the cops. He wasn't into censorship, obviously, but he felt like that show was a sign of the Endtimes. Cops were some of the soldiers of the apocalypse, as far as he was concerned. Their vehicles were the white horses and he didn't want any of his boys swept up into their dirty rapture. You get a couple of cocktails into Lyle, after closing, and you could hear the entire book of Revelations, point by point. The creatures with millions of eyes, the floods, the serpents. Lyle had figured out the corollaries for every symbol, right in the neighborhood. That was the problem with most people, he'd say – they were waiting for dragons and the dragons were already here. "It's a code, that's all," he'd say. "Revelations is a poem."

Steven had a whole bunch of names. When he made porn movies, it was Cody Brandon, but who can take that seriously? Lyle didn't like putting that on the marquee, even though he could make money by selling a few of the DVDs at

the front desk. Guys love buying a movie with someone
who's just touched the other end of their five dollar bill. It's
nature. His street name was Sky. That's the one he used with
friends, other hustlers, dealers. But he'd kind of grown out of
that. To street customers he was always Kevin. When Lyle
found him, he was probably 110 pounds. It was raining hard
and the rain added probably five more pounds. All his stuff
was soaked through because it was in bags he'd stolen from
the Army surplus store on Market. That night he told Lyle
his mother called him Little Stevie. So that's what Lyle
called him from then on. That's how people figured out his
real name. He danced under Jake Winston, which sounded
every bit as fakey as Cody Brandon, but up it went on the
marquee. Lyle was up on that ladder, a long cigarette hanging out of his mouth, lining up the letters. He was missing the
W, so it became Stinson. After Steven started getting clients
from dancing, he told them his name was Mitch. It's a good
thing he was so cute, because he confused the hell out of
people. But when you've got that kind of pretty that isn't
going to last, you can get away with just about anything.

Lyle had called the police several times that morning, then
hung up. He wasn't hearing anything from his usual sources
– the outreach workers from various needle exchanges, the
other dancers, patrons he knew who frequented Steven. He'd
walked the neighborhood over and over at different times of
day. Steven was an early bird, known for waking up at 5am
and going to bed by 10. That was one of the things about him
that you could smell, his wholesomeness. Of all the kids Lyle
pulled off the street, Steven had the easiest time kicking. Lyle
would set them up on his pull out sofa with a quilted mattress
pad to catch the moisture from their sweats. Depending on
their habit, it could take up to a week of fevers and puke and
mess. Since Lyle lived upstairs from the theater, they were
never left completely alone.

　　Lots of times boys wouldn't be ready to kick, so they'd try
to take something, a VCR or a stack of CDs. Lyle was a light

sleeper, so they'd barely get the thing unplugged before Lyle was standing there in his boxers, lighting a cigarette and saying "Maybe you should go." He'd hand them five bucks and ask if they had a place to go. Not kicking them out, really, but making a call. Once he'd seen that dishonest impulse, something clicked off for him and he knew it wasn't going to be a match.

Steven had only been shooting heroin for a month when he met Lyle, but the speed he was doing to stay up and turn tricks had melted weight off him. He was a teeny thing, probably five two. The little ones really got to Lyle. He couldn't resist picking them up.

Lyle was six eight with fingers too big for most keyboards. The theater had a cash register with massive buttons. For years, there was no cash register, but it made stealing too easy by employees. You have a cash business, there's going to be stuff taken, no matter what. Finally, Lyle broke down and ordered a cash register made by a company that catered to disabled people reentering the job market. Lyle took the bell out so it didn't make noise when the drawer closed. He said he hated the idea of people associating this sound with their dicks.

That first night, Lyle brought a propane space heater into the bathroom and warmed it up, then ran a bath. He helped Steven out of his clothes and put them in a plastic trash bag to wash. He lifted Steven up, naked, and carried him from the toilet seat into the bathtub. He'd seen too many boys fall down, and there's not a more unforgiving room than a bathroom. He'd seen boys do permanent damage. Lyle sat on the toilet seat and smoked a cigarette while Steven lay shivering in the hot water. Lyle soaked a washcloth with hot water and put it on Steven's head. That was when Lyle asked him his name. He said "What does your mother call you?"

Steven said "Little Stevie."

And Lyle said "Okay." And they had an understanding.

Lyle shampooed his hair and scrubbed Steven's scalp lightly with his enormous fingers. Some boys were jolted

when Lyle did this – they'd tense up like a cat who wants to
be put down. Steven sank further into the tub, letting the full
weight of his head settle into Lyle's hands.

As the bath was draining, Lyle picked Steven up and
hoisted him to a standing position. He dried him off with
an oversized beach towel, the only kind Lyle could reason-
ably use himself, and carried him into the living room. He
dressed Steven in a set of Boy's Large thermal underwear
and green wool socks. He wrapped Steven in three blankets
and pulled a knit cap down over his ears. It was white with
red snowflakes on it and it made Steven look like he'd just
been born.

That first week, Steven ate nothing but chicken broth.
Lyle'd heat up a saucepan on the stove – he didn't trust
microwaves at all and only grudgingly put one in the dressing
room. The dancers had been complaining about it for weeks
and one day a new boy held up a packet of instant soup and
said "I'm *hungry*." And that did it. Lyle was at Goodwill
later that afternoon, buying the biggest one they had. But
upstairs, it was an old gas range he lit with a match. The
flames were sometimes jumpy so he'd stand there and stir the
broth slowly with a big wooden spoon. When it approached
ready, he'd take a slurp out of the spoon and say "All right,
little one. Who's hungry?" And Steven would play along,
saying "Me, me," like a baby bird shifting in its nest. That
first night, Lyle fed it to him with a turkey baster, since
Steven was shaking so much. Lyle didn't want him to hit his
teeth on a metal spoon, so he said "Here goes," and Steven
opened his mouth a little. Lyle looked down at him over a
pair of reading glasses. As he stirred the soup, he was reading
the newspaper under the stove light. Local news. Missing
people. Murdered wives. Kidnapped babies.

Lyle fed him like that for a few days, until Steven was
steady enough to hold a sippy cup, then a mug with a straw,
then, after a few days, just the mug. Lylee would have used a
baby bottle, but he didn't want to freak Steven out. Later
that night, when Steven was sleeping, Lyle dipped his thumb

in chicken broth and sucked on it while he jerked his cock. He crouched in his bedroom so he could catch a glimpse of Steven's head, covered in red snowflakes. Lyle thought about fucking him the old way, just spit and patience, but he thought it might tear him up too much. Lyle had to be careful with people. He'd been told that too many times. He had to let boys sit down on him so they could control the first part. What Lyle really wanted, eventually, was to get to the part where he'd be standing, lowering Steven onto his cock, one hand cradling the boy's head, the other bracing the small of his back. Lyle wanted to be so far inside Steven that his pubes got sucked in, until his balls popped in, until the vacuum was so strong that the entire room was shaking with wind. Like a tornado on the inside. Lyle stroked his load onto the shirt he'd worn that day. Why gum up a clean towel?

Steven didn't snore, thank goodness, but you could hear a whistle through his nose when he exhaled. It was quiet enough to be sweet, like a timid tea kettle, and Lyle fell asleep, having adjusted his breathing to match Steven's.

Two Hearts

David May

*If men could live all their lives as virtuously and intro-
spectively as when they're in love, we'd all be gods, and
there'd be no need of promises of heaven or of hell.*
                                        – John Horne Burns

1. Butch Bottom

A year before Craig died, he and Jon had moved to Seattle, a
place where it was easier to be over forty than San Francisco
had been, where they already had some friends, where they
both found jobs, and where more condo could be bought for
the same money. Then Craig died so suddenly that Jon's
initial response to the announcement was, "But his CD4
count has been great since he's been on the cocktail!" Forgetting, as all his friends had forgotten, that one could die of
things other than the plague that had haunted them for
twenty years, he was dumbfounded. To have beaten the
odds for so long and then to die of heart disease: The irony
did not escape Jon, but neither was it appreciated.

Jon's life was, now that he was well into his forties,
relatively placid. He lived almost alone in a large condo on
First Hill with a view of the Puget Sound, the kind of view
they never could have afforded in San Francisco. He had also
found the proverbial dream job that paid him well for the
benefit of his experience. That he should get paid more
money for less of his time amused him, and would have

made Craig laugh, he often thought. And Ben, too, for that matter.

"Why do you stay in such a large place if it's just you?" someone had asked.

"I have a lot of ghosts," Jon wanted to say.

Instead he just shrugged his shoulders and mumbled something about resale value. But the ghosts were there: Ben, his first Sir; Craig, his second; the two muttly dogs that had been Ben's and then his and Craig's; countless friends. Sometimes he wandered from room to room, most of them half empty, looking at his Museum of the Dead: Photographs on the walls, paintings and books left to him in wills, odd pieces of furniture from the estates of friends, souvenirs of his lives (for there had been two very distinct lives) in Los Angeles and then San Francisco, boxes of theatre programs, magazines, and mementos from marches and rallies, dance parties and festivals: Relics from a lost world.

Over all of it presided a magnificent mackerel Maine Coon named Schrödinger. He sat on high in whatever room Jon happened to be in, presiding over his dominion, guarding Jon from his ghosts, licking away the silent tears when they came. Content to be alone all day with a warm place to sleep and the radio left on NPR, somewhere to watch the rain and a table lamp to sit under, each evening Schrödinger greeted Jon quietly with a raised head and soft meow before stretching awake and asking to be picked up.

"How was your day, Schro?" Jon would ask, as he used to ask Ben's dogs. Having not been raised with animals, he hadn't understood their mysteries or their importance before living with Ben. Now he understood the comfort and company they offered. Now he appreciated, more than ever, the pleasure of not being alone in an empty apartment or, worse, an empty bed.

Jon was a Top as much out of necessity as out of desire. He had always been a switch in the field but a bottom at home, having found not one but two Sirs to love him in turn. But being alone and over forty, meant being a Top – at least if he

wanted to get laid, for, as always, boys were plentiful and
Daddies fewer. Boys came and went, boys of all ages, all of
them poz: Boys he could flog and fuck, boys he could beat
and breed. A few tried to reach out to touch Jon's heart only
to find it shielded, unreachable behind an armor made from
loss and regret. Jon appreciated the effort but knew it unfair
to let them pursue their course. These boys he stopped
welcoming to his playroom, sending them away as much
out of kindness as out of self-preservation: For he was never
satisfied unless there were tears were in a boy's eyes. To
demand this of someone who wanted love would have been
nothing short of cruel – and cruel in a bad way, he was quick
to add while explaining his dilemma to his friends over beers
and ciders at Six Arms.

"I've only just learned to take care of myself again," he
told his friends. "I'm not going to start taking care of
someone else, too."

His friends refrained from pointing out the obvious, that
Jon was already taking care of a cat as devoted to him as he
was to the cat, that his heart had never stopped beating but
only retreated in order to heal. Why else 50s and 60s jazz,
upbeat and sad, bitter and sweet: music that ran the gamut of
love lest any nuance be misremembered or forgotten. This
was a heart, Jon's friends well knew, preparing to love again.

Typical of the boys he fucked was Danny. Scruffy and sweet,
a shy smile and flawless body, a beautiful mouth perfect for
both kissing and fucking, and big brown eyes that glistened
with tears when the pain became unbearable, winning Jon's
attention as few had since Craig's death. Nothing was as
sweet as a salty kiss, as tear-stained lips, as grateful surrender. Nothing got his cock so hard. The teary kiss was
followed by a fast, furious and brutal fuck that left Danny
sobbing with gratitude, often climaxing without touching
himself – his hands bound behind him the whole time – and
as spent as Jon. But Danny, for all his charms, wanted
nothing more from Jon than this. Jon was one of many

men he surrendered to on a frequent basis, each man knowing that the man who would some day own Danny had yet to enter his life. But he warmed Jon's heart with his sobs and tears, his agony comforting Jon time after time, giving him a peaceful night's sleep.

Jon was on a date with a man he'd met online, someone close to his age who claimed to be both "versatile and masculine, UB2". Like most men who insist on their masculinity, the need to do so sprang from the world's apparent blindness to the exact degree of his machismo. Jon was ambivalent as the rest of the world within ten minutes of their meeting face to face but, not wanting to be rude, suggested the man accompany him to Chop Suey to see a new queer band he'd heard about from Danny.

They arrived just as the band was starting, the handsome lead singer (bearded and golden, green-eyed and amber) singing a song Jon had never heard before, a song about some stranger's Pretty Mouth. The rest of the crowd was younger than Jon and his date, but Jon found himself nodding to the boys in the crowd he already knew sexually and otherwise. He handed his date a drink just as the band started "Stony End".

"I can't believe he's singing a Streisand song. Is this supposed to be ironic?"

"Streisand wasn't the first one to record the song, and, no, it's not irony."

"Isn't it about getting knocked up?"

"It was, but not when he sings it."

"I'm sure you're wrong."

"I know I'm right."

Jon stepped forward, and away from his date, to better hear the lead singer explain how he got knocked up, but knocked up as he heard the boys in the gym use the phrase: "Did you hear about Lance? Dude, the condom broke and he got knocked up. Sucks to be him." Jon knew at once that the singer was poz, and that he sang about his sero-conversion and the accompanying fear, and Jon understood the familiar

lyrics as he had never understood them before. Then the
singer segued into "Wedding Bell Blues".

"Why the fuck is he doing this old number?"

"Don't you get it? It's a protest song when he sings it. This
is where the irony comes in."

"I'm bored," said his date.

"Well, please don't let me keep you. I think these guys are
great and I want to hear them."

Jon gave his date the perfunctory kiss goodbye and moved
closer to the stage to better see the singer. Jon was entranced
with the band, with the singer's beauty, with the lyrics to
their original songs, to the choice of old songs interpreted in
new ways. The singer's masculinity was unquestioned as
sang about sex with men, about heartbreak and desire.

"Great, huh?"

Jon turned and saw the familiar face of Danny, shirtless
with the top button of his 501s undone as they rode down his
hips.

"Hey, baby."

Jon gave Danny a kiss and let his hand migrate down
Danny's spine to his ass.

"And he's famous for wearing fewer and fewer clothes as
the night progresses. See, he just took off his shirt."

Jon looked at the muscular body covered with fine silky
hair and slick with sweat. Another song started, slow and
familiar.

"Oh, this is so cool, Dad. This is when the straight boys
dance together."

Danny pulled Jon to one side and, true to Danny's word,
the straight boys left their dates and paired up, some dancing
cheek to cheek, others nuzzling each other affectionately.
One pair, as if on a dare, even kissed. Jon recognized the old
show tune, now being sung as a rock ballad, as "You're My
Romance" albeit with a B inserted before the last word. The
song ended and the crowd cheered. The boys, some of them
still arm in arm, went back to their dates. The girls, excited
by the sight of two men together, threw themselves at their

boyfriends, partly to reclaim them, and partly to reward them for the public foreplay.

Jon's hand slipped inside the back of Danny's jeans and fingered the moist hole.

"You're already wet."

"Afraid so. Turn you on?"

"Fuck, yeah."

They kissed, embraced, and sucked face for several minutes before Jon guided Danny out of the club, his hand on Danny's ass the whole time. They were unaware of the sad envy in the singer's brilliant green eyes as he sang, *sans* irony, "He's a Rebel."

A few nights later, Jon and several of his friends congregated at Purr. Ordering drinks, it was several minutes before Jon saw Leo approach the tiny karaoke stage after being introduced by one of the staff. It was few more minutes before Jon recognized him.

"Hey isn't he the singer from that band, the . . ."

"Butch Bottom and the Absent Daddies?"

"Yeah. Isn't that him?"

"Must be, no two men could be that handsome in the same way."

Jon leaned forward, his face with its salt and pepper beard framed in the reflected light from the stage. Hearing Leo croon "It Had to Be You". Jon forgot his drink, let the ice melt in the glass and dilute the liquor as he nodded with the music.

"What's his name again?" Jon asked the cocktail waitress bringing a refill he wouldn't touch.

"Leo Lourea. Cute, huh?"

Jon nodded.

Reluctantly, Jon left with his friends just as Leo's song ended. When he got home, he held Schrödinger close, wondering what had just happened to him. A few days later, as if the gods conspired with more coordination than customary, he found out.

They reached the door of the Eagle at the same moment.
There was a nod, a short greeting, and some mutual admiration as Jon assessed Leo's interest. Face to face, it was easy to
see that they were about the same height with similar builds,
though Jon had the weight of maturity, the grizzled beard
and chest hair that said "Daddy". Still, each man having
friends to meet and greet at the bar, it was a almost half an
hour before they ran into each other again, drifting to that
dark corner by the pool table found in every bar called The
Eagle. There was another nod and their mouths met without
hesitation; their hands grappled beneath each other's gear to
grab the glory of the other's manhood. They kissed and
groped for an hour or more, unable to free their selves from
the embrace, not wanting to escape except into each other.

"We'll go to my place," muttered Jon between kisses.

"Yes, Sir," was all Leo managed to say before dropping to
his knees nuzzling Jon's crotch.

"Good boy."

"By the way," whispered Leo between kisses. "I'm poz."

"I figured. Me too."

They left hand in hand, kissing occasionally until they
turned up Terry Street.

"No fucking way, Dad. You live here too?"

And now they laughed to discover that they had lived in
the same building for more than a year but had never met
until now, the gods guarding Jon from seeing the one he
would love before he was ready.

Kisses continued in the elevator. When the door opened
and they moved into Jon's too-large apartment, their en-
deavors to undress each other became frantic, their breath
caught in quick gasps. Jon tried to move Leo towards the
bedroom, but they never made it there. Soon Jon's face was
buried in Leo's ass, then Leo's face buried in Jon's pubic
hair. There were cries for relief from the anguish of tumescence, tiny howls from deep within, primal grunts and growls
they were unaware of making until Leo grabbed Jon's thick
cock and eased it towards his hole and whispered.

"Please, Sir, no jacket. Just fuck me, Dad."

Jon complied with just spit for lube, felt the sudden joy of penetrating the perfect tawny ass, a luscious pink hole sprayed with the light dusting of red-gold fur. He held Leo down as he fucked him, slapped his ass, a stream of expletives coursing from an otherwise gentle voice. He rammed into Leo as hard as he could, eager to have him, eager to embrace the profound beauty squirming beneath him, eager to leave his mark of ownership. He came with a scream, with the primal call of man taking man, of a man making another man his own, the ancient cry of the conqueror that echoed back so many millennia. He collapsed on top of Leo to recover his presence of mind. He reached underneath Leo to see if he was hard only to discover that while this was indeed true, Leo had also come. Jon rolled off of his sudden conquest, pleased with himself and the one who had so quickly become the vessel of his seed.

"So," asked Leo, breathless between each word, "what's your name, Dad?"

As if on cue, Schrödinger walked into the room with an almost human cry to announce his presence. He greeted Jon with a lick on the nose before introducing himself to Leo and accepting the newcomer's homage. When satisfied, he took his place on a nearby ottoman, watching them through half-closed eyes.

"Excellent cat."

"Yes," agreed Jon, happy to be relieved of the burden of self-disclosure by the cat's presence. "I inherited him." And from those three words came the story of his life, elicited from the inevitable question:

"Who from, Sir?"

It came like a torrent, the tale of life with Ben followed by widowhood in Los Angeles, meeting Craig and moving to San Francisco for twelve happy years grabbed from the Fates that ended after their move to Seattle only a few months before the same Fates, as if making the cruelest of jests, struck Craig down with a heart attack. Leo heard all this with an open heart, leaned over Jon's handsome, bearded face and kissed him with more tenderness than Jon had known in years, bringing him as much pain as comfort as the shell protecting his heart shattered like an eggshell. A few minutes later they were showering together, continually kissing as if for nourishment.

For the first time in more than two years, Jon dared to hope.

"This is ridiculous," Jon told a friend the next day. "He's barely thirty, and I'm . . . a lot older than him."

"But how does he make you feel?"

"Alive," confessed Jon for the first time. "And happy."

Their courtship proceeded without pause. They saw each other every day, if only for a meal. They made love, fucked, and played constantly. And kissed, desperately. Jon went to hear Leo perform either alone or with the Absent Daddies. Leo took to dedicating songs to "my sweet Daddy", making Jon blush with pride and embarrassment. When Leo crooned love songs alone at Purr, he looked right at Jon as he sang, his voice taking on a timber, a new authority that, for all his experiences with men before Jon, it had lacked until now.

That they were both desperately happy was evident. Schrödinger now expected Leo as well as Jon, apparently pleased that order had been restored with the presence of two men in his bed instead of the mere one.

"You can't argue with a cat," Craig had said when Schrödinger had selected him at the animal shelter years before. Remembering this, Jon turned to the cat for guidance.

"Is this really what I need, Schro? Is this what I want?"

Cats, however, tend to be inscrutable when presented with a direct question and Jon had to observe Schrödinger's behavior for an answer.

One morning in late summer, Jon found himself alone in bed. He got up to pee, wondering if Leo had already left for his day job. He opened the bedroom door and saw Leo, naked and facing the early morning sun as it flashed off the sky-scrapers of downtown Seattle. He was rocking back and forth, softly singing, as if in prayer. Jon cocked an ear and listened carefully. He recognized the Hebrew hymn, for it had been sung at both of the funerals that had marred his happiness. When Leo was finished singing, sobs, soft manly cries of honest pain and loss, emerged from the trembling, naked figure.

Jon came up behind Leo, wrapped his arms around Leo, and kissed the back of his head, his shoulders.

"Baby," he whispered. "Sweet, sweet baby boy. What's wrong?"

"I woke up and remembered that this is the day Uncle Ori died."

Leo turned around in his lover's arms, facing Jon with tear-stained eyes.

"He died when I was fifteen. He and Uncle Cary used to look after me all the time. And then they both died."

"Baby, I'm so sorry. I didn't know. Should we visit their graves today?"

Leo nodded the affirmative, almost smiling.

Jon kissed away Leo's tears, tasting their salty sweetness with a new kind of appreciation as Schrödinger wended his way between and around their legs, making small cries asking for inclusion in their affection, or maybe for breakfast, but probably both.

"And now?" ask Jon's friends when he told them this story.

"Now do you believe this is right?"

"We all think so."

"In fact, if you break up, we all plan on keeping him as a friend."

"We're all crazy about him."

"The question is, are you?"

Leo demonstrated his devotion in so many ways, ways that said, "You're the Daddy I've always wanted. Be my Sir, and

I will love you for the rest of my life." He cooked for Jon, looked after him, gave him space to spend time with friends, never asked him where he'd been on the rare occasions Jon hadn't been there to hear him sing, was always willing to be used by either Jon or any man Jon chose, and only asked for the occasional beating. He never spoke of love to Jon, only murmured the words to Schrödinger, just to make his intentions known.

Everyone waited, Jon, Leo, and all their friends, for the dam to break. They waited as summer turned to fall, as the rains returned to the Puget Sound, and a wet frigidity settled over a city with covered in fallen leaves.

Snow fell, and was the habit with this city, most people stayed home from work. Only the essential commuted into or out of the city. Even though Jon walked to work, he knew there was no urgent need to get there since nearly everyone else would stay home. He would work from home today, taking care of anything urgent but leaving the mundane until tomorrow.

Snuggled beneath the down comforter, Jon felt Leo's arms wrap around him. He moved closer to Leo only to feel Leo's fat cock searching for Jon's fuckhole, an orifice nearly forgotten for a year or more. Leo moved closer, the slick head finding and poking the hole, softly piercing the hairy maw. Jon cried out in pain but didn't resist. He let Leo take the lead, let him find the secret soft place deep inside him, the hard knot that would make him cry out in pleasure. It hurt. Jon bit the pillow, submitted to Leo's assault, silently begged for more because the brilliant fire now searing through him touched his heart, burning away that final residue (like the membrane of egg beneath its shell) and sent Jon into the sweet oblivion of pleasure and pain.

"Sweet ass, Dad."

"Fuck me."

"You want your boy's come inside you? You want to be your boy's bitch?"

"Fucking breed me."

Leo obeyed. He forced his way deep inside Jon.

Jon could feel a small trickle of blood trailing down his balls but didn't ask Leo to stop. Instead he pushed back when Leo pulled out. Leo bit the back of Jon's neck, held Jon down as Jon had held him down so many times. The bed covers fell to the floor. Leo slapped Jon's ass just to feel Jon's hole quiver around his cock, just to get closer to his goal. He'd come the night before while getting fucked by Jon, but he was young and a morning hard-on demanded attention.

"Bitch Daddy!"

"Fuck me, fuck me . . ."

"I'm gonna come, Daddy. You want your boy's come inside you?"

"Yes, yes, please."

Leo cried out his final pleasure, the momentary eternity, as he marked the man he loved with the liquor of his manhood. A moment passed and they were back in bed together, both coming to as if from a blackout. Then Jon realized that he was weeping. For one desperate moment, he thought he'd been unmanned, made less of the Dad he wanted to be for Leo. But Leo rolled him over and kissed him. His silent tears, they both knew, were tears of joy. There was a pool of jizz on the sheet where Jon had come while Leo fucked him. It was not until then that Jon realized that he'd climaxed, that he had let himself feel pleasure and pain as he had not let himself feel anything since Craig had died. It was true then, and Jon had no choice but to tell Leo that truth:

"I love you, baby boy. Please stay with me, baby. Stay with me forever."

So many seconds passed before Leo answered, each second a beat of his heart, each an eternity.

"Oh, Daddy, Sir, of course I'll stay with you. I love you so much. I love you so much it hurts."

And as they kissed again, their kiss the seal on the bargain that would be their future together, Jon wondered: Which is saltier, tears or come? And which the sweeter?

2. An Absent Daddy

Leo was fortunate not only to be born at a time when ethnic ambiguity was fashionable, but in a city where it was almost inevitable. Descended from African nobility sold into slavery, Swedish peasant farmers raised to the status of gentry, Snohomish elders that lead their nation, and once-wealthy Sephardim with bloodlines so ancient they might laugh at American *poseurs* like the First Families of Virginia, Leo was strikingly handsome with features that suggested rather than demonstrated his ancestry. As a result, his lovers (and there were many) saw in him what they wanted to see, and embraced that part of the world they most desired. He was as tawny as his name's sake, with bold features and high cheekbones complimented by a dusting of freckles, wavy auburn hair and a luxurious beard, his hard, muscular body covered with red-blond hair. Able to blush, his golden skin was set off by the delectable pink of his lips, nipples, butt hole and cock head. Best of all, he had no idea how beautiful he was.

When he was eight years old, Leo took to singing "It's Raining Men" as he danced around the house. His parents, left-wing intellectuals, assumed the obvious and arranged that Leo should spend more time with Uncle Ori and Uncle Cary (who were already in the habit of spoiling Leo and his older siblings) so that Leo might grow up with the expectation of finding love. Leo's favorite memories were of falling asleep on their couch, snuggled between his uncles, as they watched *The Wizard of Oz*, *Auntie Mame*, *Mary Poppins*, or *Gentlemen Prefer Blondes*. In the morning he'd wake up in "his" room with Sheba, his uncles' dog, stretched out at the foot of his bed guarding him (so Uncle Cary insisted) from any nightmares.

When the uncles died within six months of each other just before Leo turned 16, he was almost inconsolable, finding solace only in the music and movies they had shared with him. His entire family, equally bereft, pulled on their multi-

ple traditions, providing the many kinds of spiritual comfort
that Leo came to rely on later in life. He learned to pray to
Whomever it seemed most appropriate, repeating prayers in
languages he might not know, finding in the rhythm of the
syllables the solace of a mantra. And as a result of his parents'
insight, Leo never Came Out with a declarative statement
but rather with the introduction of his first boyfriend, Seth,
less than a year later. That Seth was so fearful of sex and
infection that he confined their physical expressions of affection to dry kissing and mutual masturbation might have been
a relief to Leo's parents (had they known) but it was frustrating to Leo who knew (if only from finding his uncles'
stash of pornography) that sex might be so much more.

After Leo's break-up with Seth (just after their prom), he
sought more of what had looked so appealing on video. Now
in his majority, he was able to pursue the adult men he
actively desired. Soon he was experimenting with men he
met online or at the baths. Willing and able to try just about
anything, he found he enjoyed most of it, taking and giving
whatever pleasures were presented to him. There was no love
at first, or the need for it, only affection and respect – and for
a while, that was enough. His boyfriends came and went,
rarely becoming anything too serious, for when they did Leo
felt forced to abandon them to their own devices. He was
neither needing nor prepared for True Love as long as there
were more men ready to do him than he had time for each
weekend. He loved the Circuit and had more fun than he was
able to remember after each party in Palm Springs, South
Beach, San Francisco, New York, or Chicago. Although
conscious of being something of a star, Leo also knew that
he didn't want to be on the Circuit too long. He feared
becoming one of those fossils desperately dancing in a
drugged daze pretending to be something he no longer
was. Someday it would be time to retire and build a nest.
With each birthday, the itch to settle down, to be done with
the Circuit, increased. Each weekend party, he promised

himself, would be the last. And then, after one particularly
profligate weekend in Palm Springs, Leo realized that he had
at last gone too far and that it was time to find The Man Who
Would Take Him Home, a man, whom Leo now knew,
would have to be poz.

Thus, his sero-conversion was the impetus for many
changes in his life, including abandoning the Circuit while
he was still young enough to be missed. He blamed no one
but himself – for no one had forced him to swallow the X that
weekend just as no one had forced him to bend over and take
all and sundry uncovered cocks up his cleaned and prelubed
ass. After the bad news (hardly unexpected), the Circuit lost
its glamour and Leo focused on finding the kind of life his
uncles had shared. Now it was time to nest; now he was the
same age as his older siblings had been when they married.

First he focused on his band, Butch Bottom and the
Absent Daddies, which gave him the voice he wanted to
share with the world. They became well known for singing
original songs like *Bad Touch*, *Show Me on the Doll*, and *Jack
Daniels Tastes Like Daddy's Kisses* as well as standards like
Jailhouse Rock, *I Sold My Heart to the Junkman*, and *Love
Potion Number Nine* that took on new meanings when performed by the Absent Daddies. On other nights, he sang
karaoke in cocktail lounges like Purr, crooning the same
ballads his uncles had danced to around their living room.

His day job, laying tile in the posher homes of the Puget
Sound, was an art he'd learned from his much loved paternal
grandfather. Having done it most of his life, Leo didn't think
much about the gift passed down to him through the gen-
erations; instead, he just enjoyed his work, singing to himself
all the while, finding the perfect phrasing, the right cadence,
the proper *cris du coeur* to make each song his own. The
demand for his talent as a mosaic artist (for that was what he
was) allowed him to make his own hours, and his clients
granted him all the privileges due creative talent.

Shortly before his thirtieth birthday, Leo moved to a small
but stylish condo on First Hill. From his bedroom he could

see the Space Needle piercing the heavens – the same heavens
his Snohomish grandmother had once told him were raised
high above the trees only when the native nations surrounding the Puget Sound came together and pushed the sky up
high above the trees with their combined strength. On his
first New Year's Eve in the condo, he invited friends to watch
the fireworks ejaculating from the Space Needle at midnight
before they headed to the Eagle.

His bedroom was now his nest high above the world, the
private domain he now hoped to share with the man he'd yet
to meet.

One night at Chop Suey, when the band still had third billing
below Loss of Function, Purty Mouth, and Tractor Sex
Fatality, two straight girls came up to the stage between
songs.

"Hey like we made our boyfriends promise to dance
together so could you guys do like a slow song?"

"Only if you make them kiss, too."

"Ohmigod that is so awesome yeah!"

"Totally awesome, they gotta do it, even if it means we
have to blow 'em later."

"Totally!"

Assured that a kiss would be part of the deal, the band
played *My Buddy*, a song they often did as a rock ballad,
slowing it down a notch for the occasion. Sure enough, the
boys danced together, cheek to cheek. When the song ended,
they kissed each other perfunctorily on the lips, mouths
closed, to the delighted squeals of their girlfriends. From
this grew a tradition for the band, one that not only assured
its increasing popularity among a generation of young adults
who found the display of boy-on-boy dancing not only
titillating, but proof of machismo for the young men dancing.
From then on, when the band sang *My Buddy*, the straight
boys danced together, some looking desperately for a partner
when the song was announced for fear of being thought less
of a man for being unwilling to participate. So popular did

the song become, the band added *You're My Bromance*, a pun that delighted the young men as much as their dates. Sometimes single straight men even brought their gay buddies so they could be seen dancing together and so solicit the attention of the young women they wanted to meet.

Leo would always remember the time he first saw Jon. He was at Six Arms, sitting with the Absent Daddies after a gig, when Jon walked past him, joking with his buddies about the wet wind lashing the windows of the pub and that real men didn't need umbrellas. Leo had never seen a man more desirable than Jon, salt and pepper hair and beard, and (despite the inevitable tummy) the naturally hard, muscular body of a man who had been pumping iron for decades without the benefit of chemical additives. Leo watched him leave as his friends teased him.

"Leo likes his Daddy Bears."

"Huh?"

"Wipe the drool off your beard, Leo. He's gone now."

Leo forced a weak smile.

"A man's dick has a mind of its own, you know."

Only a few nights, later, singing his song for the straight boys, Leo saw Jon in the audience talking to a young man Leo knew only in passing. When Jon left with the other boy, Leo thought his heart might break. It was only when he saw Jon again at Purr a few nights later that Leo thought the gods might be on side after all. Jon's face was blissful in the reflected light, eyes half-closed as he nodded to the music. Leo sang to Jon, wondering if Jon knew what was happening between them, that Leo had made love to him with words and music, with a heart that needed a home.

It seemed an eternity to Leo, but it was less then two weeks between the first encounter and the moment Leo found himself bent over Jon's leather couch. When Jon ejaculated inside him, Leo squeezed hard with all his interior muscle to milk every last drop of jism, to keep it all deep inside him for

as long as possible so that he might feel owned by Jon. He had
no idea, just yet, that Jon was just as enamored of him. It was
only when Jon spilled the story of his life, so quickly and with
so little time to breathe for fear of sobbing before this
suddenly intimate stranger that Leo understood how vulnerable Jon was. In that vulnerability Leo found the foothold
that would lead to the capture of Jon's heart. He relied on
every love song he'd ever sung to win Jon, on every kiss, and
on each cry of pain he could convince Jon to elicit from him.

Their courtship began with an immediate invitation to
dinner followed by Leo making their breakfast the next
morning. It felt natural to Jon for Leo to be rattling the
pots and pans in his kitchen, too normal for comfort even,
and Leo sensed Jon's simultaneous appreciation and dismay.
Leo, with the inner wisdom of the Lover, said nothing and
made no demands. He left Jon's side the next morning
knowing that Jon would call him, that his absence would
feel as wrong as his companionship felt right. Just to be sure,
though, he held Schrödinger a moment before he left, asking
the cat's permission to love the man they had slept with the
night before. The cat, pleased with Leo's manners, assented,
and Leo left it to the cat to work the needed *mojo*.

Before the day was over, Jon called Leo's mobile phone
and Leo asked him to meet him at Purr. Jon came and sat as
close to the karaoke stage as he dared, drinking little except
Leo's voice, Leo's song a spell that wove itself around Jon
like a net, forcing him to breathe the air that he had for so
long avoided, and so find himself renewed. After singing,
they sat in a corner of the club kissing, touching, each unsure
of the other's tangibility. Leo had become a vessel with their
first kiss, a cavity that longed to be filled with Jon's kisses,
cock, come, and affection. Now he let his kisses speak for
him, as his song had done before. He had not known how
much he wanted to live his life with a man until he met the
man he wanted to live with, until he understood how deep
desire can run in a man's soul.

*　　*　　*

"You love him," said the drummer, the only female Absent
Daddy, an athletic baby dyke frequently mistaken for a boy.

"I think so," admitted Leo, afraid to say anything more
definite.

"Yeah, you are. And he's a babe, too."

"You think so, too?"

"Oh, yeah. What are you waiting for?"

"For him. He's been widowed twice."

"Broken hearts heal," said the drummer reaching across
the table and taking Leo's hand. "You just have to give him
time. I see how he looks at you. He wants you bad, real bad,
and I'm not just talking about that sweet butt of yours."

Leo blushed, started to disagree but didn't. He'd seen the
same look in Jon's eyes. Each time he saw it, his heart danced
in his chest and he felt short of breath, hoping desperately
that Jon would say the words Leo wanted to hear. Then Jon
would look quickly away, suddenly fearful as he been hopeful
a moment earlier, and Leo knew that he had to wait until pain
gave birth to joy – or until Jon started making excuses for not
seeing him. One or the other would have to happen.

Even on that summer morning when Leo woke up and knew
without looking at the calendar that it was his uncle's *yartzheit*,
even when Jon had been so sweet and understanding, even
after all those months, Leo waited. He didn't dare push, didn't
dare ask Jon how he felt. When Jon made plans without him, he
told Leo ahead of time but hurried home to call Leo as soon as
he could. Leo made a point of going out without Jon. Sometimes he played *Mah Jong* with the men he met through Jon,
spending an afternoon or an evening away from Jon but well
within his field of vision. Jon's friends, most of them now
regular members of Leo's audience, gently prodded him,
asking for more information than Leo had to give.

"You're still an item?" asked one of the men at the table.

"I hope so."

"Will there be a wedding?"

"We'll see. Mom and Dad said they'd host one if I wanted
it."

"Have they met Jon?" asked a second man.

"Yes, he came for Passover. They loved him. He's a lot like them."

The friends nodded.

"And he'll come for Thanksgiving."

"And Hanukah?" asked the third.

"And Christmas and Kwanzaa."

"Is there anything you family doesn't celebrate?"

Leo thought for a moment before answering, playing his tile with cool deliberation.

"Sure there is: The Feast of the Immaculate Conception."

The snow came early that year, a few inches piled here and there across the Puget Sound's many microclimates. First Hill was without snow at first, not accumulating any on the streets until most of the surrounding neighborhoods had succumbed to it. Leo and Jon made love by Jon's fire as the snow fell outside. They made love and Leo felt closer then ever to Jon. Jon was alternately gentle and cruel, hurting Leo as much with a caress as with a blow. An open palm might lead to orgasm, a kiss to unspeakable agony. It was only when it was over that Leo realized that Jon had never been the receiver in their erotic exercises. He had come countless times in, or on, Leo, but never had Leo been allowed to do more than suck Jon's ample cock, and even then Jon held the back of Leo's head and took control. Leo's ministrations to Jon had been limited because Jon no longer allowed himself the luxury of abandon.

Schrödinger approached them with a small meow, simultaneously disclaiming on the icy debris falling from the sky and suggesting that they all head to the bed.

"He knows when you're coming, you know."

"Really?"

"Oh, yeah. He runs to the door before you're even out of the elevator. That's how I knew you were a keeper. You can't argue with a cat."

As they kissed, Jon felt the cat's paw press on his back as if urging him to take the needed step. When they were all in Jon's bed again, safe beneath the covers, Schrödinger curled between, his face looking towards Leo. Stroking the cat, Leo felt a small nip. He looked at the cat and saw his green eyes almost glow as he slowly closed them before falling asleep. Leo understood the cat's assessment of the situation. The cat wanted them both for his companions, for having two men in his bed was the norm. Leo knew what had to be done.

Leo woke first the next morning. Looking around he saw Jon sleeping peacefully and Schrödinger sitting in the doorway, blinking slowly in greeting. Wordlessly he got up and followed the cat into the kitchen. Feeding his friend, Leo knew better than to ask for more instruction than had already been given him. Silently, he thanked the cat and headed back to bed.

A moment later he was rubbing his hard cock against Jon's hairy ass, letting it slide between the muscular butt cheeks. Jon drowsily reached back to hold him closer. Leo smiled to himself, kissed his lover's neck, and let his fat cock find Jon's bunghole.

"I need your hole, Dad," he whispered urgently.

He heard Jon gasp in pain as he pressed forward, and paused a moment. Then afraid he might lose his nerve, Leo pushed in. He felt Jon open up, felt Jon's desire for more despite the anguish of the assault. Leo forced himself in until the entire length and girth of his manhood was incased tightly in Jon's flesh. Now Leo moved slowly, murmuring encouragements, promising to take Jon to the other side of desire:

"Sweet ass, Dad."

"Fuck me."

"You want your boy's come inside you? You want to be your boy's bitch?"

"Fucking breed me."

Jon rolled his head back and forth, clutched at the sheets, bit the pillow. Leo knew the signs of a man on the verge, knew that Jon was very close to abandoning any hope of solitude, to breaking every promise he'd made to his grief-hardened heart.

"Bitch Daddy!"

"Fuck me, fuck me . . ."

"I'm gonna come, Daddy. You want your boy's come inside you?"

"Yes, yes, please."

Then Leo heard Jon scream his joy, felt Jon's hole clench tight as Jon ejaculated against the sheets. Then Leo came, marking Jon as Jon had marked him countless times. Now Jon would be as much his as he was Jon's. Now Jon waited, an eternity of moments for the words he wished to hear. Staying inside his lover, Leo held him close, kissing Jon's neck until their flesh disengaged of its own accord. Jon rolled over, facing Jon, silent tears staining his stubbled cheeks. Leo kissed the tears away, wondering what havoc he had wrought in fucking his Dad, in letting his need for love get the better of him – but then came the words:

"I love you, baby boy. Please stay with me, baby. Stay with me forever."

Leo took a breath and held it, repeating the words he'd just heard in his mind's ear over and over again before he answered.

"Oh, Daddy, Sir, I love you so much. I love you so much it hurts."

And Schrödinger watched from just outside the bedroom door, purring loudly, slowly kneading the carpet and working his *mojo*.

Aegis

D. Travers Scott

Soon, Ian thought.

The razor glided across his scalp, leaving a smooth, pink wake in the lather. A chill followed the razor's swath, cold air touching exposed skin. In contrast, a warm burn glowed. The hot/cold juxtaposition reminded Ian of raves: flushed Ecstasy-forehead heat against cold menthol jelly on lips and eyelids.

Hot and cold make tornadoes, he thought.

Stevik was steady, careful.

Ian shifted his concentration from top to bottom as the razor made another pass.

Feet flat against the floor tiles, back braced against Stevik's goal-post legs, Ian held himself as still as possible. The tattooist's knees jutted out through torn black denim: the cotton fray and kneecap hairs tickled Ian's earlobes. Ian's arms circled back around Stevik's calves, the hard swells from years of bike messengering wedged solid inside Ian's elbows. Stevik's shins ran down his bare back in sharp verticals.

Ian focused on the tactile sensations underneath his fingertips and sweaty palms. Stevik had put him on a regimen of L-arginine, niacin, pantothenic acid and choline to heighten his sense of touch. Boots and jeans flooded his system: rough canvas cord, cold metal eyelets, supple leather, smooth spots on frayed laces, and rough denim.

Focusing on these sensations kept Ian motionless. Stevik

could work around a nick, but Ian knew he'd prefer perfection from the onset, and Ian wanted to give it to him. He opened his eyes. The sun, low on Belmont, shot orange verticals of August evening through the windows of Infinity Tattoo. Stevik's boots glowed black-red; the silver ring on Ian's fourth finger gleamed in bright contrast. The oblique light carved deep shadows into the inscription, "BOY."

Ian fought a shudder. It would take several sessions to do a piece as elaborate as Stevik had promised, as elaborate as the work he'd done on Rufus: the outlining, fill, shading, color.

Finally, they were in the home stretch. Once Stevik had marked him, it would happen.

"So," the pierced guy with dreads drawled, "who gave you the ring?"

Ian turned around, surprised.

"No one." Ian's eyes, burning underneath thick, furrowed brows, darted around the club. They lit on the dreaded guy. "Gave it to myself."

The man held his gaze, unblinking. "Self-made 'Boy'?"

Ian looked away.

"Someday—" Ian glanced at his half-peeled Calistoga label. His eyes danced briefly onto the pierced guy, gazed past him out into the pit.

"Someday someone'll give me one to replace it."

The man curled out his lower lip thoughtfully.

Ian scowled into his bottle.

The man with the dreads rose, took one of his two singles from the counter.

"Yeah. Someday," he muttered.

Ian's eyes trailed his dissolution into the crowd.

"There."

Hot/cold prickles ran over Ian's clean scalp, down his neck.

"OK, Ian. I'm done."

Ian stared at the ring, and his pale fingers gripping Stevik's black laces. He didn't want to let go. He'd waited so long for this – and what would follow – he almost feared its arrival.

"Ian, I gotta get you into the chair to do it."

Ian tilted his freshly shaved head against Stevik's lap, looking up into his eyes. Stevik's brown dreads circled down around his face like curtains. His face was a series of long shadows and gleaming sparks from the stainless piercings: septum, eyebrow, labret below the lips, Niebuhr between the eyes. Ian traced them with his eyes, drinking in the details of the man's face. His black goatee curled down in a point; scars striped his eyebrows. Two dark brown eyes terrified Ian, their enormous potential energy, poised to spring deep into him.

Ian smiled. Stevik's lips curled into a fond snarl. "Fuck," Stevik sighed. "I get so hot thinking about marking you."

Ian nodded. He squeezed Stevik's ankle and laid his face against his thigh. He breathed in sweat, dirt, and crotch-funk through the stiff denim, nuzzled the coarse fabric, sighed.

"I know," Stevik murmured. "Won't be much longer, boy. Not too long. And it'll be worth the wait. You'll have earned it."

Ian exited into the gelid night. LaLuna's neon splashed cobalt across the wet street.

Town always looks like a fucking car commercial, he thought.

Assorted young queers drifted past with affected chattering, unlocking station wagons and Buicks, strapping on bike helmets, revving motorcycles, stretching into raggedy sweaters and backpacks.

Ian kicked around the corner, disgusted. Another wasted night. Tweakers, smoked-out grooverats, slumming twinks. Even at the freak convention, he felt the freak. The kids, his peers, had all been babbling about the Psychotronic Circus coming down from Seattle, trashing a new all-ages called The Garden, comparing notes on which of the street kids arriving for spring were fags and which ones would fuck around anyway, for money or a dose.

And the older guys: trolling, married, shut-down, falling asleep . . . fuckfuckfuck.

What I'd give for one fierce guy.

He cut through the alley, staring at his black Docs scuffing the gravel, listening to the regular jangle of his wallet chain. *Chink-chink-chink.* Another regular beat, some low-fi changa ambient thing. Mix in a little tabla or chant, maybe, and it could've graced the clove cigarette smoke in the chill room.

Chink-chink-chink—

Juh-jangle.

The dissonant beat startled Ian. He stopped, looked up.

The dreadlocked guy, one hand supporting himself against a dumpster, stood across the alley from Ian. Facing the club's rear, his suede jacket glowed a scabby red in the halogen streetlight.

The man looked over his shoulder. "Oh – you. Hey." He turned away and spattered piss against the mossy bricks. Ian stood silent, watching the froth pool around his boots.

The dreaded man again looked over his shoulder. Ian didn't move. The man's boot-heels ground into the muddy gravel. He pivoted to face Ian. His piss-stream, spewing a circular arc like a suburban lawn sprinkler, rained across the alley between them.

Ian met his gaze. The man frowned. Ian dropped to his knees, immersing himself.

The man shook off the final drops, tucked, buttoned. Ian's jaw dropped, the dour drops hitting his tongue. Ian's eyes stung. His T-shirt was cold and soaked. The bitter piss dripped from his forehead, shoulders, and chest, gathering and falling from his face in swollen round drops, splattering on the earth.

"Come on," the man whispered. Ian followed him out of the alley.

"We'll just aim for starting the outline tonight. Just see how far we can go."

"I can take it."

Stevik's hand sifted through Ian's hairy chest, calluses stretching out a nipple like fleshy caramel. "I know you can. I know you can."

He jerked out a couple of hairs from around the areola. Ian stiffened, inhaled briskly. "I'll give it to you," Stevik said. "All of it and more. You know I will. But not till you're mine." Ian's hard-on thumped against his belly, disconsolate.

Stevik unlocked the door to the metal Quonset hut. Ian followed him deep into the high-arched space, filled with only a few chairs, a couch, some cinderblocks. Eight-foot sheetrock walls set off a room in the far back corner. In the ceiling's dark recesses, rain splattered against the corrugated metal.

A light clicked on beneath the furthest wall. Ian shut the door behind him and twisted the deadbolt. He felt his way toward the light.

He stood in the doorway, blinking in the light. Stevik sat on the edge of a bed that descended from the ceiling on heavy wooden braces.

Stevik looked up, almost surprised.

"What?" Stevik stopped, holding one boot in his hand. "What do you want?"

"I, ah —" Ian struggled for a response. "Well, why'd you bring me here?"

Stevik rolled his eyes and yanked off the other boot. "Why'd you follow me here?" he shot back, tossing the boot onto the floor.

Ian shrugged. He took a step toward the bed.

"Look!" Stevik barked, "I don't want to *touch* you, get it? Little fuck; I don't know shit about you, if you're even worth it. I just – You can stay here, tonight, if you want." He jerked his thumb toward a pile of dirty clothes in the corner. "There. Sleep over there if you want."

Ian stared at him. Stevik rolled away, still in his clothes, and yanked a plaid comforter up over himself. He clapped twice and the lights went out. Ian found the pile of clothes in the dark. He could smell them.

Ian climbed off the floor into the chair. He stared ahead at the screen Stevik had set between the chair and the store's windows.

"Bet you've been dreaming about my dick every night, all these months," Stevik said, rolling open his station's drawer.

Stevik pulled out a rustling sheaf of carbon papers. Ian had seen him working on them, it was the design, the tat for his scalp. Stevik hadn't let him see it finished.

"What it feels like, how it smells. You've only seen it pissing. You don't even know what it looks like hard, how it feels in your hand, all hot and heavy."

At the apex of the Broadway Bridge, Stevik told him to stop.

Ian stared at Stevik, a few feet before him, hands across chest. A curtain of vertical lights rose behind Stevik, a skyscraper-light mirage that made Portland look, at night, like the metropolis it wasn't. The verticals of lights were only expensive houses rising up along the West Hills, but it had fooled Ian that night, years ago, when he'd leapt off the freight train beneath this very bridge.

"Take your clothes off, jack off, and don't look at me."

Stevik sauntered over to the walkway's railing and leaned back.

Ian pulled off his T-shirt, unbuckled his belt. He was elated to have run into Stevik again, but wondered where things would go this time. He kicked off his sneakers, pulled down his jeans.

Just the boxers left. If someone comes along –

"I said don't look at me, dogshit!" Stevik kicked Ian's shirt out over the bridge's lane gratings.

Ian scuffed off his shorts. He leaned back against the cold metal girder, its single-file row of rivet heads pressing into his back like a formation of soldier-cocks. He licked his palm and rubbed his shriveled dick, trying to coax a hard-on. He kept his eyes moving to avoid Stevik: the tiny scythe-blades of moonlight on the Willamette River, the splintery wood planks of the walkway, the kitschy yellow lily of the Suicide Hotline sign.

A dull roar grew. Cold whiteness rose up his bare side; Ian kept a steady rhythm pulling on his soft dick. A breeze whipped against him as the truck plowed by; the bridge vibrated against his back and ass and feet. Silence. Ian was raging hard.

Relaxed, he stared up at the stars. Orion guarded him above, bow drawn. Ian stared at his jeweled belt, and came.

"Good," Stevik said. He was standing right at Ian's side, holding Ian's shorts. "Here."

Ian slipped them on, his jeans, socks, shoes. He looked over at his tire-tracked shirt stretched across the grating.

Stevik set his jacket on the girder and pulled his own T-shirt off. "Here. Yours is trashed."

Ian swallowed and pulled the shirt over his head, Stevik smell surrounding him.

"You don't always have to wait to just run into me, you know," Stevik said as they descended the bridge. "You can just come by the shop."

Stevik sprayed disinfectant onto Ian's scalp, minty-cool mist dancing across his raw skin as it evaporated dry.

"I bet you dream about it in your mouth, going down your throat, swallowing all my load."

A sticky bar ran across his head, leaving residue. Ian smelled Mennen Speed Stick, a cloying musk of misdirected macho.

Ian waited across the street at Subway, watching Stevik work. He chewed pepperocini thoughtfully. Watching Stevik from a distance afforded him moments of striking lucidity, quite distinct from the blind heat saturating his mind in the man's close proximity.

This is so weird, he thought. It was one thing when it was so – casual, but now. Fuck, Ellen's already rented my room out to that sculptor-guy.

He's never hurt me, though. He's never done anything I haven't loved.

"And your ass just itches, don't it? It hurts – don't it hurt so bad, the way you want it? You think of me up there, my arms crushing your chest, my tongue in your ear and my dick, that dick of mine you dream about just ramming away up inside you, plowing into your hot gut."

Stevik pressed the carbon against his scalp, the design transferring to the adhesive deodorant.

"Put some music on," Stevik muttered as they entered the long metal building. He wandered into the kitchen for a beer. Ian flicked on the living room light and rifled through the CDs.

"Wanna Sheaf?"

"Yeah, that's great." Ian hummed happily. Stev had never asked him to pick out the music before. Some old Skinny Puppy would be fun, he thought. Or maybe more mellow, that Moby ambient album. He clicked through the CDs: Marc Almond, Everything but the Girl, Annie Lennox, Edith Piaf, Billie Holliday.

God, I've gotta unpack my discs soon.

Stevik walked into the room with the two brown bottles of Australian stout.

"God, Stev," Ian quipped, scowling at the track listing on *Billie's Blues*, "you got anything besides all this diva-queen crap?"

Stevik set the bottles down on the floor. His fist plowed squarely into Ian's gut. Ian collapsed to the floor, gasping.

"Put on the headphones – and listen to that CD," Stevik said through gritted teeth. "Don't go to bed till you get it." He picked up both bottles and stalked into the bedroom, slamming the door behind him.

4:03 am.

"Stevik."

Stevik rolled over, blinked.

"Can I go to sleep now?" Ian was crying.

"Yeah."

Ian knelt to spread out his blanket.

"No –" Stevik pulled off the sheet, stretching out in a black T-shirt and shorts. "Get in here. You ain't gonna get anything, and don't cling on me all night, but – just go ahead and get up here. You don't have to sleep on the floor anymore."

"You think of me fucking you and you get all weak, doncha? Like your knees giving out."

Stevik peeled off the paper and set it on the counter. Ian stared at the ceiling, feeling the vinyl and chrome of the chair beneath him. Stevik spoke in a steady monotone as he set out his supplies. The ink bottles clinked against the individual glass wells as he dispensed and mixed the colors.

Ian waited on floor beside the chair.

"So you're Stev's new boy, huh?" The woman looked down at Ian, balancing her water bottle on the shiny black hip of her PVC hot pants.

"He marked you yet?"

Ian smiled, shook his head.

"Oh, so you're still in the the – uh, trial run." She laughed. "He let you talk?"

"Yeah."

"But he told you to wait here for him, right?" She smirked. "Been gone a long time, hasn't he? I think he's up on the roof fucking my sister."

Ian bit his lip and tried to sound polite. "He didn't tell me anything," he said, "I just want him to be able to find me whenever he wants. So I'm staying in one spot."

"Not bad," she appraised. She turned around to face the crowd at the far end of the Quonset hut. Stevik broke through, dragging a skinny bald guy under his arm, both howling loudly.

"Well, your wait's over, it looks like. He's bringing over

the ex for introductions." She looked back over her shoulder at Ian, eyebrow arched. "You must rate."

Stevik and the bald guy tossed her happy nods in passing. They planted themselves before Ian and Stevik proudly slapped the bald guy's chest. His head and torso were a myriad of designs. In the dim light, Ian could barely sort out the intertwined images: an octopus sat on his head, tentacles creeping down the neck. Two figures hung down his pecs, crucified at crossed wrists just above each nipple. Geometric spirals rose out from the waistband of his black leather pants –

"This is what real skin looks like, boy, see this? This is real work! This is the kind of work I do when I give a shit about someone."

The bald guy beamed proudly, his blue eyes sparkling brighter than the glinting four-inch steel spike through his septum.

"Don't take all the credit, now!" The bald guy grabbed Stevik's crotch. He crouched down, confidentially, to Ian. "Stevie, now, he didn't do all this, mind you. But, eh, he got it all started."

"Look at this fag's shit!" Stevik yanked Ian's T-shirt, pulling it up over his head.

"See? He's a little lost tribal boy, look at that. My!" He grabbed Ian's arm and stretched it up high. "A chain around his arm! Tough shit! And wait, there's more!"

He reached over and grabbed the back belt loop of Ian's cords.

"Stand up, fuck," he muttered.

He spun Ian around and pulled down the back of his shorts, exposing the dogpatch hair leading down to Ian's ass. Off to the left side, where the hair faded into pale fawn-down, was an ankh.

"Wook! It's a wittle ankhy-wankhy!" Stevik sneered. "Itn't it twoo tweet?" Stevik howled. His friend belched. Ian stood, patiently waiting.

"Rufus," Stevik said to the bald guy, "this little turd wants me to mark him. He wants me to put my art on the same skin with all this other piss-ass shit." He snorted.

Rufus smiled. "Now why don't you just, eh, cut out those old ones, eh, Stevie?"

Stevik laughed. "Nah, no scars for him yet. Maybe we get Ben to brand him someday. For now I want his skin clean."

Rufus nodded. "Then you'll just have to cover." They stared up at Ian. He held his head bowed.

"Look at me, fuck." Ian raised his eyes to the short, dark man. "You really want to get marked by me? Like Rufus here?"

Ian nodded.

"I had to earn this, you see," Rufus said with quiet pride.

"I understand."

"It was quite difficult."

Ian nodded.

Stevik and Rufus exchanged glances. Stevik shrugged.

"Go let Rufus fuck you, asshole. Head's clear." Stevik jerked his head toward the crowded rear of his space.

"Keep the door open," he called out as they walked away.

Stevik shifted weight in the worn easy chair, his boots propped up on a cinderblock. He watched across the space till Rufus' serpent-entwined arm shoved Ian out through the bathroom door, to the cheers of the crowd. They gathered around Rufus, laughing.

Ian pegged his shorts back up. He looked around the floor by the chair for his shirt. It was soaked with beer and cigarette ash, marked in the middle with a bootprint where it'd been used to swab the floor.

Ian wiped the wet come-muck off his face with the back of his arm. Sticky smears clung to his hairy abdomen.

"Sit down," Stevik muttered.

Ian sat, wrapping his bare arms around his chest. Ian looked at Stevik's boots. He leaned forward.

"Touch me and I'll beat the living shit out of you, right here."

Ian froze.

"Christ, you stink."

"Like you wanna cry. You think about how bad you want me inside you, how you want my dickhead kissing your heart, my cock's shit-smeared blessing. You want it so bad you can't stand it. You think of it and you think you'll just collapse in a big whimpering, slobbering mess, begging for me to do it. Doncha? Doncha?"

He slapped the boy's naked stomach. Ian nodded, dislodging tears that dripped onto his chest, trickled down the sides of his neck. Ian heard Stevik tear open the needle package.

"But you haven't, have you?"

Ian shook his head proudly.

"No, you haven't. You're tough. You never even asked me for it, never went around with your ass in the air like some damn cat in heat." Stevik ran his gloved hand down the side of Ian's face, wiping away the saltwater, the rubber dragging across Ian's lips. Ian kissed. Stevik kissed his clean scalp.

"You already got it, man. You already got it. Everything I'm ever gonna give you – you already got it."

Studying the Alliance of Professional Tattooists manual and the Oregon state regs, Ian imagined Stevik marking him. He imagined Stevik fucking him, till the two fantasies meshed.

The tat machine and Stevik's all-but unseen, imagined, longed-for dick merged – the machine's rabbit ear screwed into the base of Stevik's pubis, its mechanism sticking out from the pubic hairs. The armature bar shot upward as the base of his shaft; DC coil, spring contact points and base all curled into an electromagnetic nutsack. The rubber bands were black neoprene cockrings. A dark brown foreskin stretched out over the armature bar and sanitary tube – it skinned back to reveal a 5-point grouping of liner needles arranged in an "X" like 5 dots on a die, like a man spread-eagled. The red cock-needles shot in and out, woodpeckering Ian's scalp through scaly layer, epidermis, into dermis.

Stevik pushed his cock needles further, standing above, Ian bowed at his feet. The needles mixed Stevik's precome-ink with Ian's head-blood, sucking the serum up into the foreskin tube through capillary action, Ian's capillaries got some action, filling with Stevik's #C Hard Black spunk. Stevik marked deeper, aiming for Ian's fontenels, poking through the skull-joints' cart, past the blood/brain barrier. Ian's whole body spasmed, muscles filibrating with abandon.

Ian's fantasy lost physical specifics at this point. He couldn't visualize or verbalize, only feel a destruction, absorption, union. He imagined a world without images, a world without words. Isn't that what he was looking for? Wouldn't that be home?

Stevik stuffed cotton wads into Ian's ears. Ian looked over at the tat machine in Stevik's hand.

Time slowed down. Ian watched. Current flowed through the coils and the base of the machine. Electromagnetized, it pulled the bar down, pulling down the needles and opening the silver contact points. Opening the points killed the magnet and the spring assembly brought the bar back, causing the needles to move up and contact the points, conducting current and repeating the cycle. Again. Again. A cycle of opposite motions and polarities, endlessly repeating.

The first of the needles broke his skin, the ink penetrated his dermis, hundreds of times a second. A world of words and images began on Ian's skin.

A Ho's Hieroglyphic

Darieck Scott

In the glam times, the good times, when I knew I was a god . . .

The lights of a City. Lights in the windows of the tall buildings, lights that glow like tiles on a vertical path to the lowermost clouds; lights from the cars that cruise by, that glow like animal eyes or like UFOs coming to land; the lights of convenience marts spilling out onto the littered walks; the lights of signs and of planes and of the bay's water reflecting the lights of the buildings and the few stars and the shifting moonlight limpid as a spring or oily, oily like the surface of a minestrone soup . . .

In these lights his face and his body make their appearance, the arrival of a beast or a god. I'm into the simple things. Like the bit of gel in his hair that blackens its blackness and makes the short-cropped crown over his forehead erect, and his pupils as black as his hair and as large as nickels. Oh, I always talk about lips – but, yes, his lips: the lower one, that's where I'll focus, like a cutting from the cup of a tulip, thickened and protruding: a gorgeous pout. Tuft of black hair beneath the lip, beatnik style. Big ears, strong jaw. And the clothes – here's where simplicity does the trick for me: a T-shirt, red, with thick white piping from the V-neck to the edge of the short sleeves. Hangs off solid, worked pecs, and as he walks the shirt sways slightly below and sometimes just above the navel circled by a hedge of black bristles. Army pants hug thick thighs and open sandals show his big feet and big toes that I beg to kiss.

Because whenever I see Darius I wish to become a slave. Some part of who I am, an important, vital part, unnamed because we are not to know (or if we do know, then we are not to encourage) this thing in us, but truly some part of who I have always been, wishes for this and wishes for it almost more than it wishes for love or fame or money or power or peace or joy: to surrender, to bow down, to do obeisance, to be a slave to the physical glory of a man whom I would, in the moment, for the sexual and emotional thrill of it, call my superior.

Is it all about power?

How does it begin?

Far, far back. But I'll begin recently, with John.

WASPy type, big groin stuffed in black slacks, corporate slave: John the poet. He has small ears and gray-tipped brown hair neatly trimmed at the neck and along the back of his head, thick and brushed into a suave and conservatively flamboyant curve across his forehead. Nice lips. Very nice: surprisingly rotund and shapely, a rich, slightly-short-of-purple color. Pretty eyes – can't remember the color: possibly hazel or light brown. He wears a suit and a tie and he makes a lot of money and may be, probably is, a Republican. Married, repressed.

We meet at a dinner party hosted by a mutual friend. John remembers me from some other party more than a year ago. "Caine!" He smiles as his fingertips graze my upper arm. I do not remember him, but he has my attention now. I fancy there is a flow of energy, a charge of the god Eros like a gunpowder trail simmering between us. But this cannot be; it is only the ache of the god Need that I feel, a peeling from His aura shimmering across my line of sight so that nothing else registers. John and I talk of politics, and art, and money, and barely agree, though somehow agreement and a meeting of

minds seem altogether inconsequential. He shakes my hand.
I leave the party. I walk back to my car and the air is heavy
with a deep-bone chill and the stars are naked in the broad,
black sky: Mars is high, showing a faint scandalous scarlet.
Scandalous? The night is quiet, and echoes with emptiness,
with lack of meaning.

John the poet. He calls me. At school, in the office I share
with two other students. I am grading papers. I do not know
what he is doing; I do not know what they really do in those
huge glass buildings when they get behind their desks and
make phone calls and plan meetings. "John," I say whipping
up a froth of phone-enthusiasm though I don't quite yet
recognize which John he is. "Oh. How are you?" He is
chatting about nothing really. I think: he wishes to attach
himself to academia, to literature and the remembered thrill
of learning, in his youth he dreamed of writing poetry.

We are to meet for lunch.

At lunch, during lunch, there comes a point when he
reaches across – across underneath, underneath the top of
the table, the top of the table where the whole world exists in
our conversation, the only world I would ever imagine
existing between us: the world of words, only faintly inspiring, largely dull; and food, much the same. He reaches,
moves, below this world, in the underneath, in the darkness.
His hand falls upon my knee. A light touch.

I register this below, but not above. I keep talking, and
perhaps my eyes flicker away from his for a moment, less
than a moment, as if my attention might go elsewhere. This,
it would seem, is exactly what I ought to do, for his hand does
not retreat. It takes up residence. It moves, slowly but with
iceberg inexorability, higher up my thigh, until it comes to
linger near the marsupial pouch of my crotch. Rests there.
Warm. Unwavering. John the poet.

At length the meal is over. I have eaten all I can eat. He is
not eating. We sit there. I would signal for the check, but I
cannot. Our positions are reversed. Free-flowing me, for-
ever-student me, irresponsible me: I stand (sit) repressed.

His eyes have grown bolder as his hand has become more familiar, and his gaze is now undaunted as he locks my attention on him. "I have an apartment south of Market," he says.

There is nothing more that need be articulated. I feel that I'm in a Henry James version of a porn story or something.

I notice: he pays the check.

In the apartment: he is quiet as he performs his striptease. A tight smile on his nice lips, as if he must hold back words I won't accept. There is something at once poetic and cliché about the unzipping of the pants: the movement of his fingers and of the gray slacks falling below the waist of his silk boxer shorts – like oil moistening a well-worn groove in my brain. Somehow it restores to me some ur-pleasure, the template for all subsequent pleasures: a lazy comfort and tingling arousal similar to what reading the same story aloud each night gives to a child.

It's a big red number. Thick, very hard. I think: he brings his mistresses here. This is a place he's purchased for his mistresses. I am one of these. They're mostly women? All women? He likes his butt licked and the hairy skin between his balls and his muscled thighs lacquered with my spit. He likes to kiss in a hard, probing, untender way, and he likes pinching my nipples. A flood of dirty talk – or, as he says when he shyly warns me of what he likes, "heavy verbal abuse". "Suck all the come outta my balls, eat it, go down on it so my pubic hair's in your nose, bitch, yeah you bitch, suck me, suck me, bitch, bitch, slut, cunt."

John the poet. Hot splattering come everywhere.

After, he is happy to have my nose in his armpit, until he's ready to go back to the real world.

At the end of it, which I dread and long for, I am lying wet under the sheets of the four-poster bed in a room heavy with draperies, fit for a vampire's domicile. I want it up my ass. I'm waiting for it: ass up in the air, waving for him to stick it. But today he only uses my mouth, my face, my tongue. He slaps my ass and the wedding band on his middle finger slides forward because of the sweat on his hands. But he doesn't fuck me. Not today.

He graciously gives me the keys so that I can depart at my leisure, he says. This reasoning makes no sense, but he tosses the keys at the pillow where my head reclines at the same time that he notches the semi-lucent belt (alligator?) around his waist. His arm jerks, his hand, which has been inside me, flicks forward, and from my vantage his hand and the protuberance of his genital package in his gray slacks are level: I see his hand and his bulge together, and the keys appear. I imagine that the keys are the largesse of his penis. His penis as the giver of gifts. The penis that I imagine I am falling love with. (It is a strange thing, the love of the phallus. Rooted in the material, it is nonetheless all smoke, all ephemerality.)

I consider his presumption and his feeble attempt to conceal his presumption a condescending affront, and so I do not say Thank You, but I do smile, for I am amused. John the poet amuses me.

When I hear the door close (and lock – proving the fallacy of his logic), I rise. His "apartment" is no coldwater walk-up, of course, but a mansion-like loft. High high ceilings and sparkling pine floors, tall wide windows that show the upper floor and rooftop of a blue building across the street, over which stoop the lower heavens. Today the lower heavens are like the smoke of a great fire above a rain-forest, shifting and thick. The apartment is sparsely furnished. The black gleam of granite counters makes for a cold kitchen, their emptiness echoed by the lone carton of expired milk and two corked and sealed bottles of white wine too long chilled in the voluminous refrigerator. The bedroom's bed is whorish luxury, but the living area is best suited for dance rehearsals, not living. A couch, an endtable, a coffee table, two lanky lamps, an entertainment armoire. Tasteful, admittedly. A desk: serpentine, sectioned, with a computer and printer and fax machine on one link, empty dust-free surfaces on the others, with shelves and cabinets above and below. Cherry wood.

Does a fuck-toy need a desk? Ours is not to reason and

write, but to lounge upon the couch-cushions swigging champagne and nibbling cheese whilst drumming indentations into the tasteful endtable with our just-painted fingernails as we impatiently await the arrival of Him, who will arrive brimming with appetites, with desires and demands.

No, the desk is his, not for us mistresses. For when he finds work too confining at "the office" (again, an abstraction, for I do not understand his office, it is an empty signifier: men and women in suits are there, I gather, and some of them have sexual drives, though none so inspiring, I suspect, as my John's). I sit in the chair, lean into the high back, rock and let the springs of the chair prevent me from pitching too far one way or another. It holds me like a hand.

I rifle the desk drawers. There is a leather checkbook, with no checks inside (damn). In the ledger there are some hundred or so checks recorded in amounts ranging from a couple thousand to several times a couple thousand. Each to women.

Asha, Sarah, Tanya, Kendra. Clearly he likes women whose names end in ah. Ah: the sound of satisfied ecstasy, of passion fulfilled and come to rest. Or, depending on your pronunciation key, uh – the sound of a grunt, the sound of his push inside you below, though you hear it above your face or behind your head. The sound of thrust and conquest. What then should John seek in me, whose name does not open at the end? Nnn. Not the sound of legs spreading or lifting to gird his shoulders, but a sound that struggles to enunciate a refusal. Or a sound of teeth gritting, of bearing down to endure pain. Perhaps that – the will to make it happen as I lower myself onto the fencepost of his cock.

Is that what he desires? To bend another man to his will, to perform literally what he and his business cronies lust to do figuratively to their competitors day in and day out? My friend Jason works as a bike messenger in the Financial District, and frequently he overhears conversations or pieces of conversations: "We're going in balls out," some gray-haired great-grandfather in Brooks' Brothers' best will say; "He's fucked" "I'm gonna tear him a new asshole" "We fucked him" "Let's fuck 'em!" and other such rallying cries. Must build up a lot of juice, listening to all that, saying all that. A man could work up a thirst.

In another drawer there are files. Most are empty. One, only slightly thicker and perhaps slightly more nondescript than the others, is not empty. In it on thin paper are drawings: Broad-shouldered, well-muscled men and big-bosomed, wide-hipped gals, demonstrating in elaborate, carefully rendered pencil-shades and ink, from a number of perspectives, variations on positions in the Kama Sutra. Long looping lines like oil well explosions, that evoke nothing in my thoughts so much as the image of a cornpone feller in a ten-gallon hat leant back in his chair on a dusty porchfront, striking his knee and yelling out over the sound of the wind tumbling the tumbleweeds: "Lots o' heaping come!" My favorite etching shows a well-endowed gentleman surrounded by seven women overbalanced by their breasts, who kneel at his crotch and each offer tongue service to his inflated balls. There is a broad smile of the Charlie Brown comic strip variety on the man's face. Below in somewhat hieroglyphic lettering is the legend FUCK ME.

I don't know whether this is a title for the picture, and if so, who is supposed to be speaking, the women or the happy happy man, or whether this is the artist's expression of frustration at his inability to capture on paper what his thoughts, his whims and needs, compel him to try to create.

My John the poet.

We know that silence is its own species of language, the refusal to speak an act of enunciation. The absence of words denotes the presence of defiance. Silence says, at minimum, You can't make me. Is there language in the ringing of the telephone? Ring ring ring ring ring. I dial the number John gave me and these are the only words I hear. Surely if this is an office number there ought to be a secretary who answers, or a voice-mail account that's activated? Ring ring ring. Only now do I realize that it was he who always called me. (Which seemed thoroughly appropriate. He was only a stuffed shirt, a suit, it was for him to want *me*, because I, I was . . .)

I could ask our mutual friend, Nancy, but she's a friend of John's wife Kitty, only incidentally a friend of John's. Kitty, once incidentally my sort-of friend, has now become my kinda-sorta enemy. The more so with each passing day of pressing the receiver to my ear and listening; the ringing, somewhere in a room or an office in a house or a building I may or may not have ever seen (it could be one I pass by now, with the cell-phone's signal vaulting up to a hillside antenna, getting caught there as if in a net, then falling down again almost precisely where my foot lands), stokes my desire to speak to Kitty's husband until it becomes a ravening. Of course this is nonsense; I raven in a vacuum, without context or cause. It's an affectation I've acquired, due to a weakness for fantasies. (I don't want him for a husband, I could tell Kitty, I just want him as a . . .)

Ring ring ring ring ring.

Each trill is an island in an archipelago, and somewhere, at the end of its elongated trail, lies a mainland – or an un-plumb'd, salt, estranging sea (Arnold).

So I return to John's apartment south of Market, though I'd vowed I wouldn't without an invitation (but I'd kept the key). It's been chilly all week, our indifferent and unpredictable winter rolling in, but the apartment is unheated, its concrete floors cold. In the refrigerator I find two bottles of Irish beer in a carton with four empty slots. I figure I'll hang out a bit, watch some tube, fiddle around with his computer and his desk, and when he walks in and finds me here – perhaps he'll have a slender woman on his arm, Natasha by name, I'd like that, what a scene that would be – when he walks in . . .

I spend the night. At three a.m. I gather the courage to get from under the sheets and find the thermostat to turn up the heat. (As if there were a miniature electronic security panel John carries in the false bottom of his pocket watch that lights up when one of his possessions is used without his consent, I'd waited, fearing, oh, this will increase his heating bill.)

The next night I order in pizza.

The next I bring clothes from my dorm room, and, once settled on the couch in boxer briefs and a robe, start dialing my friends (but not Nancy). At two in the morning I dial John's number, shaking as I punch in the numbers, for now, surely, he will be awakened from sleep and the number in the caller-ID box will warn him that he'd better answer quickly so that Kitty won't get up. The phone rings and rings.

But the next day as I half-watch *The Young and the Restless* and half-read for class that afternoon, someone rings the doorbell. I hurry over to the intercom, scattering my pens (highlighters of two colors, and a felt-tip) and notebook in my wake. "Yes?" I cry, and choke back *John?* It's only a messenger. Special delivery, from the Board of Directors at Macy's, an invitation to an AIDS benefit fashion and music gala, where for the favor of seeing big name past their prime models like Tyra Banks and Joel West sidle down the runway while Elton John bounces up and down near his piano on one of the runway wings, the wealthy and would-be wealthy can pay a few hundred dollars. John, evidently, has already paid, or has been invited to attend gratis.

Two tickets.

I leave one on the granite kitchen counter, gather up my shit, and scoot out of there with the other safely in my jacket's breast pocket.

I go over to this guy's apartment. I meet him at the fashion show. Well, more precisely in the bathroom at the fashion show. This guy is in the restroom during the middle of the thing, and I have to run out to pee because I've been drinking water like a fiend all afternoon to try to flush the psychic toxins from the last couple of days out of my system. So I bump and stumble and apologize my way over a phalanx of knees and past a line of very annoyed faces feeling terribly embarrassed, since, like, who leaves a show in the middle during the best part unless they're a hotshot industry type in the back or the front row, and I scamper to the restroom thinking I should take a look at my face and see if my eye-sockets are all bulged out and if I look like some haggard witch (this is not one of my finer moments in terms of self-esteem, etc.).

Of course, I don't see John anywhere.

Anyway there's this dude in the restroom, when I expect to be alone, when I expect and look forward to and need the luxury of an entire bathroom all alone to look and feel terrible in just like I could in John's apartment. He's at the urinal. About my height, jet black hair, stocky build, in a purity-clean ribbed white long-sleeve T-shirt and silky-textured coal black jeans, with a silver chain looping from the left back pocket. The chain is vaguely suggestive of a weapon, I think. I think perhaps a sharp silvery knife is attached to the clip at the chain's end, and the blade rests at a slant across the globe of this brown boy's ass, grinning in the darkness of the pocket. Nice ass, too. And he knows it.

The stocky guy looks over his shoulder at me as I enter. His eyes are a magnificent black, under black brows and above a black mustache and a sleek triangle of black hair below his lips, which are both round and long. And wet, as if he's been licking them. I can see one forearm peek from the urinal into the light as his head turns, and long, wispy dark hairs stand out along the nutmeg-colored muscular cords. I plan to make it to the mirror, but I don't make it there, because a few steps later he's turned to show me the whole package, a lotioned-up shiny thick johnson hanging low with a prominent vein running from the foreskin-hooded head down to the base sprouting from a heavy mass of black pubic hair. And if it's him that I smell, that's nice, too: sharp and soft like the mingling of a perfumed candle's burning carbon and sweet jasmine.

He figured only the real hos would come trolling the restroom in the middle of the show, he tells me.

"You're looking for a real ho, huh?" I half-laugh, staring at his dick.

Staring makes it thicken very quickly. "You know how to hook me up," Darius says softly.

"This is what you want," he says.
What is it about me that makes men know they can use me?

"It was good," I whisper, but I'm not really there; I'm off, somewhere, just trying to remember the sensation, stay in it, live it. "But the deep-throating. I don't get much out of deep-throats."
"I do," Darius says, and pushes me down to the floor.

I tell him about John, and find that I focus, for some reason, on describing the apartment: the ceilings three basketball players high, the walls like sheer, bare mountainsides. Darius listens, pulling my fingers through the hair that twists along his flat stomach. He has taken my lap for a pillow.
"So what do you think?" I ask when he doesn't say anything.
Darius declines to comment.
"Do you know a John Lennox?"
Darius kisses me.

He has me between the legs, and I think, this is just what Plato would want us to do, no real violation of the body's orifices, no compromise of seals and barriers, just a fierce and passionate simulation of coitus that goes further than mere copying to become an end in itself, a necessary and compulsively pleasurable enactment of pure desire: It is for us the act that reproduces the state of wanting, desiring, needing, that pretends to satisfy, but doesn't quite, never quite delivers – it leaves us wishing, imagining more. Not that we ever stop there. The intracrural fuck is like a foyer leading into the many rooms of a mansion, because Darius is not going to stop with this between the legs shit, oh no, he's gonna take that big Puerto Rican anaconda and let me know how it feels slithering up inside me boom boom boom.

*   *   *

The room is dark, so dark that I could almost convince myself that it is no longer as I remember it, that the rumpled, always unmade, always faintly musky bed is not in the center, dominating the room's uses and its pleasures, that the desk and the large black PC and its dark screen is gone, done away with, the dresser drawer and corner bookshelf with trade paperbacks piled horizontally and an economy-sized round tub of lube on its top rung have been packed up and spirited away. Darius likes darkness. He likes the way darkness plays with the minds of his seducees, his victims: they might imagine themselves held captive in a basement, their only meals a bowl of pasty gruel and a smelly dick slipped between the cell bars for sucking, 8:16 a.m. sharp everyday. They might suppose they were in another realm, in the maw of a black hole spinning away into the depths of the universe, far from the judgment or censure of any prudish deity's watching eyes, far from the constraints and comfort of inhibitions. The door is shut, and it is locked, and I am incarcerated and he is free to do with me whatever he pleases.

I don't need to be told to strip. It's hot in there. He's turned up the heat. Likes his hos to sweat, he says. He likes, too, I suspect, as I do, the smell of his body as it warms in the contained, limited space that grows smaller when the door is locked and the light is banished; like a flower in a hothouse, Darius blooms in the heat – his aroma is funkier, spicier, his saliva is hotter and wetter, his dick is thicker and stronger.

While kneeling before me, as his breathing becomes more ragged, he slips his many rings from his fingers. So that he can manhandle me freely, without scarring the smooth body he so likes to plunder.

One night Darius is at tae kwon do practice and I sneak back to John's apartment. I consider it sneaking because I don't tell Darius about it, though doubtless he would view my action as less than noteworthy, perhaps give me a lazy spanking just because I have that look in my eyes that says I need one. In the apartment I find the two beers I never touched still untouched, the sheets in the disarray in which I left them, the doors of the entertainment armoire wide open, the TV still thrust out into the midst of the room on its train-rails.

I get to cleaning. I want every trace of me, every molecule of Caine Monroe, removed, banished from the premises. I scrub and mop in the nude, with the heat turned up high, and keep my erection throughout.

As I make my way down the hall, I think I hear the trill of a ringing phone. (But this time I locked the keys in behind me.)

This is one of the things he likes me to do, and what we did today. First he pulls down the shades; the shades have black construction paper taped to the inside of them. I get tied up, loosely, on a very comfortable ergonomic chair he has next to the drafting table. My arms are bound behind the chair's back, and my mouth is gagged, and my shoelaces are tied together because he keeps forgetting to buy more twine or electrical tape to secure my feet to the trunk of the chair. He turns out the light. I wait. Soon he enters from a side-door. I turn sharply. He waves his hand in front of my eyes. There is a ring on his finger with a prominent faux-emerald set in duller army green metal. He removes the gag from my mouth. "Green Lantern!" I cry. "Thank Minerva you've saved me!" Whereupon he yanks the drawstring of his army-green sweats and lets them fall to midway down his hefty thighs, grabs hold of the back of my head, and pushes me down to suck him so that I'm straining against my bonds. "You like that, huh?" he says hotly. "You want more, huh? Don't worry. I'll use my power-ring to make my dick so big it'll reach down to your stomach." And pumping more and more urgently, he comes, spraying down my throat and across my lips. Then he kisses me, sets me free, and walks over to turn on the light. This is the part I like best: In the darkness, I see a phosphorescent prick-shape like a snubbed version of a traffic light's glowing green left-turn arrow, gently bouncing as it moves toward the wall.

(Never have figured out how he does that trick.)

Something is happening now that I've met Darius. Now that I belong to Darius. Last night around nine we were playing the 50s Housewife and Biker Stud game – just a simple lay-there-and-take-it-like-a-good-bitch fuck, where Mr Schindler the middle level executive at IBM or whatever is gone away for a business trip (and probably porking some hooker in a Holiday Inn room), and I, Mrs Schindler, get all hot and bothered watching a gang of bikers revving up in the parking lot of the grocery store and one of them, a dark-eyed fiend with a fiendish goatee, sees me, grins lewdly and says something to his fellow hard n' hairy, chain-around-his-neck-between-his-pecs gangsta guy and they both snicker, so that I lock my four-door sedan down tight like strapping in Frankenstein and cut out for home – with two motorcycles trailing me at a none-too-discreet distance. Of course they bust up in the house and I scream and I get chased, and then while hard n'hairy jiggles his big belt buckle in front of my face and I can smell the heat-baked flesh of his hairy stomach as his dirty T-shirt rides up over his navel just before he unzips and lets it all roll out over my nose and lips and squeezes my cheeks with a rough hand and says, "Do it till I come on your face, you hot bitch," Darius the dark-eyed fiend dressed all in leather presses his cold black soft-metallic body across my back and grabs hold of my tits from behind and pokes his hot-from-the-oven poker right through the resistance of my sphincter. All of this is in my apartment in student housing, and somewhere in my mind I do try to remind myself of this – at least at the beginning – that there are guys out there in the hallway playing rollerball with hockey sticks and their roller-blades creaking on the old floors and a pissed-off RA who keeps yelling at them, and I don't even have any tits that you can grab onto from behind like that and tweak, and there is no one here in this room except me and My Man. It's all words, words we speak together that don't make sense before we do it, words he says in my ear, that he traces in some old language across my chest with his saliva and an old quill pen that tickles and bites, like nipple clamps. Whatever: it works. There is another guy here (C.B. is his name, I think; Darius keeps saying, "Yeah, ride it, C.B.") and he's making me suck his big slobbering precome-loaded dick and I have tits and a pussy and somehow I am getting a royal clitoral orgasm.

(Sometimes when we play this particular game we do the other version: I'm no longer Mrs Schindler, but Darius is Mr Schindler, and he's this big, lanky, pale Germanic type very much like Liam Neeson, and very hung very much like Liam Neeson heh heh heh. It is 1942, I happen to be a Czech Communist refugee, we are in a hidden lair waiting for the arrival of my false identity papers, and Herr Schindler likes to pump me a good one while I lie perfectly still, because he's sort of evil even though he's doing the right thing, you know, and it gets him off to know that I really don't want it but he does and he gets to take it, and he smells like a German in winter, all musky, and the hair under his arms when he smothers my face in his pits as he hunches across me driving toward the last deep-dicking thrust tastes like salt, and the sweat from his pits runs across my face like tears.)

I am drunk. On what, I don't know. Darius, the devil – yes, he is the Devil Himself – he fed me something. The salty taste of his long, thick fingers as he pushed it into my mouth is still with me, still a residue on my lips. I smell it, right beneath my nose. I smell him, my Lord and Master, Darius Lucifer Morningstar, Baal, Angel of Lust and Decadence. I lay upon my stomach on the floor and his feet used my back for a stool; when he wished, I kissed his toes, licked between their knobs like a dog, like a fool. It gave me such pleasure. He wasn't wearing underwear. He looked down at me from on high, and it was like staring into the eyes of an irresistible demon god. I knew his desires and it gave me such pleasure, such indescribable pleasure, to comply. Hair by hair I licked up along his ankles, his strong calves, the backs of his knees, the muscular inner rings of his thighs. He slid forward in his chair and I slavered for him, cleaned the hairs of his dark and dominant ass for him and then he rewarded me by raping my mouth. There was a madness, an insanity in him. I felt amazed to see it, felt a deep reverence for the rapaciousness that seemed suddenly to seize him and make him rabid, and oh, it gave me such a thrill, when he pulled at my head and impaled my lips on his dick and thrust so hard into my throat. Oh, the pleasure of that pain, it was – ecstasy. His come was hot and acidic and burned my throat sweetly. I lay upon my back, spent. I had orgasmed when he gave me his come; the taste of it, the feel of it was enough to send me over the edge, destroy me, uplift and transfix and transmute me. I lay upon my back and he bent over me, a terrible smile upon his face. "Take these," he said quietly, and pushed something – a pill? a pellet? a vitamin? a communion wafer? – he pushed it into my mouth and I tasted him on his fingers. "Go dance," he told me.

In my apartment I fling open the window above the street. The lights are out, the music is low – five CDs at random: free jazz, circuit party anthems, top of the pops – so low that it is a whisper in my ears, a stream of sound more shallow than streams of thought, a tiny thump thump thump I strain to hear and to which I leash the movement of my body, following the faint rhythm as it beckons, obeying as if it were the very words of all mastery.

"You are an apsara."

"What does that mean?"

"It means . . . It's a Hindu nymph. A sex angel for the Hindu gods. I been looking for some legends about them."

"Hm."

Darius touches me lightly on the shoulder. He bends down to me so that our lips almost touch. "Just think of an apsara as a politically correct name for Sex Slave. Cause that's what you are, baby."

Grabbing me by the chin, Darius squeezes my cheeks so that my lips pucker, and invades my mouth with his rough, insistent tongue.

On my back. My neck follows the soft contour of the bed's edge, the top of my head dangles toward the floor. Above, Darius's torso, shaped from the living clay of red earth, webbed with vines and moss, like a cave-wall lit by fire. My mouth is open. It is full. It is empty. Full; empty; full. Blood collects in my temples. I feel that I'm drowning and drawing down breath from heaven.

If I open my eyes again I know it will be there: white columns, the high sun, waxy magnolia leaves, and the thumb-screws. A different game.

Darius is my plantation master, I his house-Negro concubine. Missus don't know what's going on, she up in the nursery playing with the little sickly pale white runts, but massa loves me more than any of 'em, he sneak me upstairs and lock the door and strips off his shirt and make me lick the smelly hairy pits beneath his arms and kiss his navel and wash between his balls and his thighs with my tongue. He calls me "darkie" and shoves his fingers up my butt to see if I been keeping it tight and because he likes to see me squirm. "That wince, I like the wince on your face when you feel pain and lust at the same time," he says to me, pushes the words out from his lungs like dragon's steam (okay, okay, so where does a plantation concubine find out anything about dragons? give me a break, we're play-acting). "Yes, massa," I says and tries to smile. Ass to lick now: it's hairy and dark and I push my nose all up in it to get the full flavor, the whole taste of him and his dirt and his stuff. This is all of him, his ass, and I want it, want to take all of it in me and down my throat. "Ahh, slaaaayyvvah," he says, and it sounds like love to me, don't nobody in the fields believe it, but I say 'tis love true and through. Massa gives my ass a slap so that it burns and then has me bend down with my face in the soft hug of those big white pillows. "Does slavey-boy want his Master's cock in his slave butt?" he says. "Oh, yessa, massa, sah," I says. "Well, wiggle it, then, and show me how much you want it." So I do, and then he grabs hold to keep me still so's he can get down to what he likes to call raping me. "Uhh uhh huh huh huh hu hu hu uuuuuuyyyesssss mah swweeetbllackk booodie!"

Malcom X wouldn't like it, but goddam I do come good when he talks like that.

Like a shackling of my wrists?
    Like a scythe across my scrotum?
    Like a bride crossing the threshold?
    Like a long-broken circle, mended.

In my office I have another round of freshman essays scattered across my desk. The ones closest to the phone vibrate when it rings.

"May I speak to Caine Monroe, please?"

"John!"

He tells me that he has been on business in Hong Kong for several weeks. His voice is soft as he talks about how much he enjoys his visits there, describing for me the voyages of the Star Ferries across Victoria Harbor, the forest of cranes on the skyline, the armadas of ships, the mayhem of neon at night, the melange of temples and shrines. Have I ever been, he asks. I tell him that I have been calling him constantly, but the number never picks up. "Oh!" he says. "I must have misspoken," he says – but offers no correction. He wonders if I'll be attending Thanksgiving dinner at his house with Nancy. I tell him I'm sure that I will. "When we see each other," he says – and I'm thinking again: how soft, how mild is the tone of authority, both he and Darius are the same this way – "When we see each other," he repeats (or perhaps he merely pauses; the words echo in my thoughts, they tell me he is not referring to Thanksgiving dinner) – "I'd appreciate it if you'd bring me my drawing back."

I pause only slightly before promising him I will, and so

our conversation ends. He asks nothing about the fashion gala ticket, but then perhaps he knows nothing about it.

(I won't give him the drawing back, not unless he sends some thugs to beat it out of me. I keep it in a large envelope in the bottom drawer of my desk, under a pile of books. I want it as a keepsake, yes, and more than that. It is not beautiful, it has no appealing aesthetic, it is not, on its own terms, arousing to me. I think of it as something an archaeologist might find in the silt and rubble of some long-deceased buried city – as if it were a polished stone in the shape of a phallus, maybe, with a sinuous loop like a serpent's tail carved along its shaft. It reads to me like a puzzle, a code, in which, perhaps, are encrypted the attributes of my god Need. Extravagant, my god is; do you really need *seven* women to get you off? Reciprocal, my god is, for he gives his gift to them as they give their mouths and the sights of their breasts like panting animals to him; he serves as they service. Profound is his lesson, for isn't the riddle of service the riddle all gods pose? To surrender the ego, and throw open your arms to something Other.)

In this phase of our relationship Darius and I meet in coffee shops, in bookstore cafes. He wears glasses sometimes. They ride high over his crooked Puerto Rican nose – is the crook Indian, African, or Mediterranean? (Tonight it favors Mediterranean. Do you like Mediterranean dick? I imagine I do. I think of being a boy trussed in the boudoir of an Umayyad caliph, my beauty sung by court poets, my virtue plundered and plundered again by a hairy, masterful man who is the servant of God and my absolute monarch. I think of being the slender, ephebic eromenos of a burly, hirsute Athenian citizen whose hot breath bathes my face like the steam of a Turkish bath.) Darius pushes the glasses up over his nose as we discuss Fanon and Stuart Hall. We discuss piercing: I want a new look to better accord with the true me, and so am considering a ring through my navel. Darius avows that he thinks this a fruitless quest, but the ring's not a bad idea.

There is wind in the air about a trip to Mykonos. I've entered a contest and expect to win. He will accompany me? Yes; I'll feel his thick dick pushing into my ass as I lower myself down, relax, relax, as he fills me, the heat of him ah the thickness, it's not comfortable but it's magnificent – and oh the sound of his gasp as the pleasure of violating me flows over and through him, and overcome with it he begins to spear me, and now, now, now baby, don't it feel *good* as it goes in and out, as he goes in and out of me faster faster faster. That's what makes it feel good: the speed. The speed and the thickness together with the heat and the way I've trained the muscles of my canal to flex around the shaft of his dick like biceps announcing their power.

It is all about power.

And it's about the lights, too, through the open window (it is a cool night), and the sounds of traffic, and the little bursts of laughter that climb up the steps of the fire escape and come to peek at us from the outer edge of the wooden windowsill where the paint has flaked away to watch, bemused, my face slack and moist in the throes of the experience of power, as I rise and plunge, rise and plunge, and then hold on while I'm savagely pounded.

The sound of the cars is soothing: wheels, rubber turning as it passes over asphalt is like the sound of waves stroking the pebbles of the beach at night: like an exhalation of the sky. I listen to it, and I listen to his moans and the dirty words *uhh you like getting fucked you like taking it up the ass taking my fat cock you always like it you like it when I hurt you too don't you don't you don't you* and hear my own moans burst from me in answer. And I listen to the cars pass by below, and I see the lights below and above, and I feel the thickness of him stretching me (I relax, I flex, I grip – such a charge, like a surge of fever, a spike in the temperature). And I know: I love life in the Big City. I love My Man.

The glam times, the good times, when I know that I am a god in a human body and why a god would choose to live that way.

Will we go dancing later tonight? He doesn't have to work tonight. (He's a screenwriter-actor wanna-direct-someday, in school, in productions, working for a computer company at odd hours. I study theories of how representation in literature, film, television and comic books shapes the ways we think of the world – I am a perpetual student, moneyed, the inheritor of a cache of ill-gotten money from a mean uncle I was forced to visit frequently as a child. I have nothing truly to do in life but enjoy. I am a god. Was it that big British blowhard Waugh who said, "To know and love one other person is the root of all wisdom"? I believe it.)

We will go dancing. We leave the bookstore café hand in hand. His palm is warm and large and callused at the bottom of his fingers because he keeps forgetting to buy gloves for lifting weights. Tongue. I want his tongue in my mouth, asserting his possession of me. To feel his body pressed hard over mine, exactly when and how I want it (that is, pretending that only he wants it, and I only serve his need).

In the club I slide against his naked torso, and our sweat runs together, down the cages of our abdominal muscles, through the valley ridges along the center of our backs. I'm not even looking at him, really, though I'm always feeling him. We're both looking around, at the flushed faces and the sweating men and the pumped bodies, while the running throb of the music makes happy puppets of us, yanking and twirling our hips and shoulders and feet. Have I ever been happier?

Afterwards I slake myself with a plastic bottle of cold water, pour it down my throat and then pass the wet bottle across my nipples and over my forehead in the air outside, as if it were an ice cube and the midday equatorial sun were beating down on me. We stagger a bit as we walk, our bodies still moving to the rhythm that even now shakes the floors and the rafters of the warehouse. He is not working tonight, but he must report to work by at least noon tomorrow, so we should probably be abed by the time dawn breaks.

In bed I let him fall asleep before I run my finger lightly

through the hair nestled between the mounds of his chest and then the hair nestled between the mounds of his ass. I hear him moan, just slightly, and I move quickly, seamlessly, so that I can place my nose near the parting of his lips and just – inhale.

And listen to the sounds through the open window, and look to the lights through the window that hovers in darkness as if afloat, the guardian angel that witnesses our love and my irrepressible lust, the unblinking Eye of My City.

Certain Shades of Blue Look Green, Depending on the Light

Marshall Moore

Sanjay lies in the median of Interstate 80 looking up at me. Traffic whizzes by, yet we are invisible, shielded from view by the V of our impact-spliced cars. We are somewhere between Vacaville and Davis, California. Nothing for miles in either direction: flat fields, distant farms, the blue suggestion of hills off to the west. Oleander shrubs tower over us: toxic leaves, lethal pink and white blossoms. Only deer can eat them without dying.

It's too early Sunday morning for heavy traffic. What timing.

I cradle Sanjay in my arms and smile down at him. He shouldn't have left me. I will make love to him again. I will convince him to stay. If it's the last thing I do.

"Fancy running into each other like this." Through his pain, Sanjay looks happy to see me. I find this strange. Couldn't he tell I ran him off the road? But he is a generous soul. He may not suspect I did it on purpose. He is injured, perhaps severely; my presence comforts him. He puts his arms around me, but winces: something inside him is damaged. A grimace contorts his face, and sweat gleams on his brow.

"Don't talk," I tell him.

Doctors would caution me against exposing myself to the blood now dribbling down his chin, but so what? I have swallowed how

much of his semen? Had him inside me how many times, raw? I
wipe the blood away from his mouth with my shirt sleeve, then
kiss him. Copper electric taste on my tongue. Him.

"I've missed you," I tell him. "I've missed you so much. I
never would have wanted something like this to happen."

"Have you called 911?" His voice is weak.

"Yes," I lie. "As soon as I recognized your car."

The lie doesn't matter. Someone else will have made the
call. Any minute now, a highway patrol cruiser will
screech to a stop next to our wreckage. Maybe a fire
truck, maybe an ambulance. This is a busy and well-
patrolled expanse of nothingness. It won't take long for
help to arrive.

"Sanjay. I love you so much. Stay with me," I beg him.

The tears welling up are sincere. I do not want to lose him.
It would feel like losing a part of myself. Which is why he
should not have left. He should not have said he'd leave first
thing in the morning to stay with friends in Sacramento until
he could sort everything out, that maybe we ought to take a
break from each other.

"How badly are you injured?" I ask, unbuttoning his shirt,
red linen, red like the blood on his face.

"I don't know. Everything hurts."

"Stay with me, Sanjay," I tell him. "You'll be all right.
Everything will be all right. Help is coming."

I undo his belt.

"What are you doing?" he asks.

"Checking for bruises."

He complies. He lets me unzip his pants.

What few cars are on the freeway at this hour do not stop.
This is good. I slide Sanjay's black jeans down his hips,
exposing his cock.

"You're fine," I tell him, unable to take my eyes off it. I
want to take him in my mouth, but he's not hard. He is
trembling. "You're going to be fine. I think it's just a
concussion."

He looks confused. I suspect he's okay. His skin tone is

healthy – maybe a shade or two off his rich Indian tan, nothing more.

"Stick out your tongue," I tell him.

I caress his cock, his balls. Soft heft. I would taste their salty authority here and now but the cops will arrive any second. Myself, I am aroused to within an inch of my life. Sanjay, in my arms again. I didn't let him get away. I'm so hard I hurt.

It's now or never.

Sanjay has bitten his tongue. I lick the gash made by his incisors – that coppery taste comes again, and I'm thinking *This is what men really taste like* as I slide my own pants down and lower myself onto him. When his cock touches mine, waves of pleasure course through me, intense as the tremors of an orgasm.

"*So handsome* . . ." I whisper.

There's no time to penetrate him, not here, not in the median with cars whizzing by. I grind against him. He probably thinks he's dying. His dick stiffens against me, anyway. We grind against each other, me expecting the cops any moment, my pleasure spiking from the danger of getting caught, him probably too dazed to question making love right here of all places, right after I've run him off the road.

We come in unison, dicks jammed together. Supernova of the flesh.

"I love you," he says. "You're always there when I need you most."

Only that's not how it happened.

Sanjay drives a blue Accord and so does this woman lying on the pavement, coughing up blood. OK, not blue. More green. In the blink of an eye, my vision of Sanjay vanishes. I was frantic to catch up with him, talk sense into him. Then there he was next to me on the freeway, surprise. I just caught a glimpse. The long hair. The dark skin. Late-model Accord; even the license plate numbers are similar. Only the paint color is different. Certain shades of blue look green, depending on the light. And it's not Sanjay.

"I'm so sorry," I whisper to the dying woman at my feet, the woman coughing up bubbles of blood.

She looks through me. Sirens, in the distance, coming closer. For a long moment, I stare at her. Finally, she stops moving. Dead, glazed eyes are fixed on some point in space.

Oh God. What the fuck have I done?

Without another second's hesitation, I rip a handful of leaves off the poisonous hedge in the median and start chewing . . .

Theme and Variations

Edward M. Cohen

Leon Cameron, Vice President in charge of Artists and Repertoire for the American division of a German music company – ordinarily jetting back and forth, wearing out tuxes, air kissing Ned Rorem, *tête-à-têtes* with Yo-Yo Ma – spent the evening at a dreary Carnegie Recital Hall debut of a mezzo who was being promoted by the manager of the label's biggest star. So how could Leon have turned down the invite? But the singer had programmed an evening of Hugo Wolf art songs, tough going under ordinary circumstances, which she delivered with what his mother used to call a "Head in the Toilet" voice – listening to herself, pleased with the echoes, disconnected from her audience, wrapped in an aura of sainthood, eyes crossed so she looked slightly batty.

Nevertheless, he was in his usual seat on the aisle and all in the audience – the manager, the singer's parents, friends, competitors – were measuring his response. If he applauded too vehemently, her stock would go up for all the concert bookers in attendance; if he failed to applaud the word would be out before the final encore. So he had to stay alert and smile and remain seated during intermission to prevent anyone asking what he thought. Those in the know would get the message. On the other hand, he could not leave before flowers were handed across the footlights, and even had to put in an appearance at the backstage reception.

In his immaculately tailored Italian suit, taller than most of the people in the room, his departure would have been easily noticed so he had to stay as long as would be appropriate. And he knew exactly how long that would be and stayed no longer; receiving supplicants in a corner, glass of wine in hand. Up and coming artists, fawning agents, famous teachers, even reviewers kow-towed before him. His favorites got a kiss, or even a hug; he was known in some circles for his warmth and astonishing nurturance of talent. He could be the most wonderful, maternal force in the life of a young artist, it was said. No one knew about his concert pianist past – no one knew much of anything about Leon – so it was claimed that, for a non-musician, he had an amazingly sensitive comprehension of what makes an artist tick.

But there was a camp in the room who knew his other side. Cross him, it was gossiped, and phone calls were not returned, studio dates were postponed, contracts were cancelled, even good tables at restaurants grew harder to come by. Defy him on choice of repertoire, show up late for a session, get too demanding in negotiations, make a fool of yourself at an industry function – and, still smiling at your recitals, even attending the receptions afterward, he would mysteriously cause you to have to return to Europe to jump-start your career.

And, it was said, it was impossible to know how he truly felt. Those who were sure they were deeply loved would be astonished by how abruptly he could drop them. Those on the rise would hunger for any sign of approval and, since he was so hard to read, could always find some hope to hang onto. Those dumped would keep their mouths shut because they could not prove it had really happened and prayed that, even if it had, it could be overcome.

Talk about him was always in whispers like those that followed, as he finally was able to glide from the room, stopping to kiss the head-in-the-toilet mezzo's hand.

When he hit the cool air of Fifty-seventh Street, his whole body rhythm changed. He gasped for breath, heart pounding with the effort. The slight wind caused his eyes to tear. He strode down the street, heading east, no longer silken in his movements. Sudden desire pumped through his veins.

At Third Avenue, he turned downtown; already he could feel the pull of the hustlers hanging out in doorways. Once he passed a few, he felt better, safer; forcing himself to slow down so he could look them over and they could do the same to him. No need to hurry. He often thought that the walking, the shopping, the looking was as exciting as the sex. There was a stretch of dark blocks which he covered one way, turned, came back, gave every boy the once-over; careful to postpone a decision until his breathing returned to normal, his pace slowed, his hunger grew sweeter. He liked the shadows, the secrecy, the movement, the quiet. Arranging matters over the phone would have deprived him of delicious aspects of the adventure.

Twenty-three years ago, when he had given up the piano and taken a job as production assistant in a classical record company, his mother, outraged because he was deserting her – not his – dreams of a concert career, had mailed him a check to stave off such a rash move. The day before the job had started, he used the money to buy a pair of thickly heeled, heavy leather, ox-blood cordovans.

As a concert pianist – and tennis player – back home in Ohio, he had always worn sneakers. A tall, skinny, limber adolescent, he had scooted across the court the way his fingers had raced across the keys; bending low for the ball, scooping it up at unnerving angles, playing so fast sparks seemed to shoot from his hands. He had dazzled his opponents and audiences, blinding with brilliance and speed. He had never been noted for strength; rather for a light touch, for sparkle, for delicacy, for the way he crept up on climactic moments and then pounced, to the surprise of everybody, even himself, and, of course, to his mother's delight, especially when perfection had been achieved.

She had never forgiven him for his deceitful use of her money. But, on the first day at the job, he had been pleased by the noise the new shoes had added to his step. His body had found its density and his pelvis propelled him forward. He filled the space in his tiny cubicle and his fingers pounded out memos on the typewriter with a power he had never experienced at her keyboard.

Now, in his black evening shoes, his legs had turned numb, probably from sitting rigidly for so long. At the reception, everything had been blurred; faces, mouths, hands he had kissed. Striding down Fifty-seventh, he had been trembling. But as soon as he passed the first boy in a doorway, his walk turned from a stride to a slide and sensation returned to his limbs. He was able to breathe, to think, to enjoy the night. As the traffic grew less and the street grew darker, he saw more vividly. He strolled back and forth, passing the same boys over and over, discarding some, swiveling back for another look at others. If he saw a hustler he had already had, he nodded but made it clear he was not interested in a repeat. If he saw another regular john, he would smile; most often they ignored it. But what the hell, he was enjoying himself. Back and forth, from Bloomingdales' to Fiftieth Street, from a slide to a slither, the anxiety lessened, and he could feel himself returning to that golden-boy-concert pianist-tennis sneakered-son.

As he approached a decision, he looked over the finalists, and every detail of every physique on the short list burned itself into his brain. The one he allowed his glance to rest upon was tall. Sometimes he liked them short and compact; little guys were often great in bed because they had more to prove. But this night he wanted tall, taller than himself, someone laid back, available to be adored.

This kid had long, long legs and Leon noted the way his calf muscles strained against the back of his jeans: farm-boy type, like the farm-boy football players he had been desperate to impress back home. The ones that thought piano was for faggots. So was tennis. In those days, so were tennis sneakers.

Maybe he actually was from Ohio, probably not, but the fantasy was inviting; slightly sullen – perhaps it was just that he was stupid. Leon could not recall having seen him on the street before; another plus, besides the halo of his golden hair. Was it bleached? No. Maybe he was from California. And he had huge hands, big feet. Leon dreamed of his other – extensions.

After they had stared at each other for a while, Leon nodded. The boy nodded back. Leon approached.

"Nice night," he said.

"Kinda cold."

"Well, soon it will be Spring."

"Yeah."

Silence. But Leon sensed no danger. This was not a junkie, nor a psycho. Leon had been at this a long time and had learned to trust his instincts. Many times he had walked away because he had not liked the vibes. Not this time. This kid might turn out to be boring, but that was the only threat.

"Very quiet," Leon said.

"Dead as a doornail."

"Well, it's a weeknight."

"Yeah."

The form was as rigid as a sonata and the players knew their parts; only the kid had given away too much with "Dead as a doornail". The hint of a moan had been a concession. His price had already dropped.

A few more beats of silence. The honks of auto horns. Other cruisers danced back and forth. Leon and the farm boy pretended they did not know what came next but the basic theme had been established.

"What's your name?" Leon asked.

"Oscar."

"A strange name."

"Well, it's mine!" replied the kid. Mistake number two. This kid wasn't experienced enough to lie and and, more surprising, was prickly about the accusation.

"What's yours?" Oscar asked, trying to cover his defensiveness – which he never should have done. Leon liked the façade of disdain and the fact that it could so easily be chipped away.

"Hugo Wolf," he replied.

"That's a strange one, also."

They both laughed. Leon liked him. He could already picture him in his high school locker room, slipping into a jock strap. The thought burned into his cheeks. The kid noticed. Balls whizzed over the net.

They caught a cab and he took him home, making sure to greet the doorman.

"Good evening, Rudy."

"Good evening, Mr C," although it was past midnight but Leon was a generous tipper so, looking Oscar up and down, the doorman continued, "Good evening, young man," making it clear he could be identified if there was a robbery in store. It was a carefully rehearsed exchange, practiced and polished over many years.

In the apartment, all went smoothly. Leon offered a drink and made sure to pay before, not after, a courtesy appreciated by hustlers. It made it easier to manipulate them into the bedroom, onto their naked backs.

With Oscar, it got him talking, so Leon had to pretend to listen to the usual lies about being straight. Oscar had been living with a girl back home, he said, but she threw him out for some dude she had met in a bowling alley so he headed for the big city. But he had never figured it would be so expensive and the bitch had their furniture, the bank account, even his clothes because she had locked him out so he hit the streets and, anyway, his heart was so broke, he couldn't go with a woman right now, so that's why he was here.

"Utter drivel!" his mother would say.

People think that giving a blow job is a submissive, passive, feminine act; not when the receiver is as hot and responsive as

Oscar. Not when he responds to your mouth with a gasp and is hard immediately and soon is moaning, despite all his denials, explanations, apologies in advance. His life story, his doubts, the misery with his girlfriend burned up in the bed.

Leon controlled with his teeth, manipulated with his lips: curling his tongue around the head, sliding down the shaft, caressing a pair of beautiful balls. Oscar's body, squirming under the pressure, was forced to surrender, lick by lick, suck by suck, nibble by nibble; tightening, loosening, up and down. It was in the thighs, in the belly, in the pulsing veins of his dick. His eyes closed. His lashes fluttered. He couldn't tell lies when pinned by Leon's mouth to the mattress, legs entwined around Leon's neck.

Even when supposedly straight Oscar got on top and locked Leon's head between his knees, it didn't mean that he was the stronger and Leon the weaker. Leon was the one who was really in charge because Oscar's face was turning flush, his breathing heavy, and there was a look of surprise and, yes, even fear when he exploded in a crescendo and Leon savored the sea-weedy taste of triumph in his mouth.

After the hustler left, Leon showered, remade the bed, put on Horowitz playing Chopin to erase the sounds of the lousy concert, the gossip in the Green Room. He slid between crisp sheets, surrounded by The Master's exquisite fingering, the dazzling rhythmic changes, subtle use of pedal, as controlled and controlling as Leon's brilliant blow job.

Perfection had been achieved.

Divide and Conquer

William J. Mann

A lifetime ago, way back in 1988 in fact, back when I was still a lad with a passion for leather jackets covered with crack-and-peel slogans and boys who shouted themselves hoarse at ACT UP demonstrations, I first had raw, sweaty sex with Mitch Ward.

It's become such a cliche now: two hyped-up screaming activists lock eyes while chanting about the government having blood on its hands and a few hours later are working off that rage by fucking each other senseless. Passion is passion: in bed, later, I pinned Mitch down by his shoulders and called him a privileged little white boy, and he pushed up at me, wrestling me down, pinning me by my shoulders and then kissing me so hard I thought my teeth would break.

"You privileged little Puerto Rican HIV-*negative* boy," he growled, reminding me of the odd distinctions of privilege.

It's not unusual for us negatives to work out our guilt, our fear, our anger at ACT UP demos. At least, it wasn't unusual back in the days when ACT UP was still acting up. A lot has changed in the last few years. ACT UP simmered down. I slept with Mitch again. And again. Both times more out of a growing sense of affection than out of rage. Mitch and I became boyfriends. We fell in love. I slept with his father. I came out to my mother. I had sex with my first man aged over sixty. I might not have been acting up, but I was growing up. I dealt with my own looksism, my own ageism, my own ism-everything, and how limiting it was to sleep only with pretty young buff boys.

Boys like Mitch Ward.

There's no doubt that Mitch is exquisite: strawberry blonde hair, green eyes, a light patchwork of downy white fuzz on his chest, his arms, his legs. Nice definition to his torso: well-rounded pecs from three years of regular attendance at the gym, chunky biceps that contrast nicely against his triceps and forearms, small waist, an outie belly-button. And a dick that won't quit: I never knew white boys to be hung so good. Eight inches – and more if the guy really turns him on, he says. (For the record: whenever he's with me, it's more.)

Dick size runs in the family. His father's pretty big, and his –

Okay, so your jaw is still down on your chest. *Slept with his father?* you're asking. (Have you heard *anything* else I've said since? Oh, yes, the part about the eight inches, I'm sure you heard that.) Yes, I slept with my boyfriend's father. And I'll get to that. But give me a minute. This story isn't just some one-handed reading material about what it's like to do father and son. You can get that in any of those little yellow paperbacks they sell at Gay Treasures. I'll *tell* you what it's like, but this story isn't just about them. It's about me, too. So you'll just have to hear *my* story as well.

My name is Andrew John Rodriguez. Not Andrew Juan, Andrew *John*. I'm Puerto Rican, but I'm not even second generation. It was my grandfather, who I never knew, who was born in Puerto Rico, and my grandmother and my mother are Irish and Italian, respectively, so I can't really claim a lot of Puerto Rican culture. I don't even speak Spanish. But I've never felt entirely white. There's a look some guys get on their faces when they first meet me ("What's your name?" they ask. "Andy Rodriguez," I answer, and *there's* the look). It's a look that says: "Oh, you're different." To be fair, it's not always said derogatorily – it's just an acknowledgment that I'm different from whatever they perceive the norm to be, that I'm "other". Some will back off; others seem to *like* the difference. But no matter how many Irish or Italian genes I've got floating around in my blood, it's clear that to *these* guys, I'll always be different. *Other*.

Sometimes I wonder about difference. I wonder just what it is that makes me "other". My last name? My dark skin? My HIV status in an ever-expanding community of positives? The fact that I'm working class, but not poor? The fact that I'm *not* middle class when queers have suddenly been mass-marketed as wealthy? How many divisions are there among us? What are the divides? And, I wondered not so long ago, is it ever possible to cross them?

Mitch Ward, however, is not what these guys would consider to be "other". He's white to the core. Oh, he got over the arrogance of whiteness fairly soon after he tested positive. I remember going with him to the local clinic when he came down with a mild case of shingles once, and he sat there between a teenaged black girl and a big fat Latino guy, and before long they were all laughing and joking together. It was beautiful to watch.

Just like Mitch.

Okay: let me tell you why I think he's so beautiful. It's not just those blue eyes or the rounded pecs or the white down on his chest or that big old dick of his. It's this:

"Andy," he says, his lips pressed against my ear. "I want to put crushed pears on your chest and lick them off you."

The pears are cold. They're his favorite dessert. From a can, no less. (This is further proof he has overcome the arrogance of whiteness. I can just imagine what his mother would think about him eating canned pears.) He rubs them into my skin with the balls of his palms. My nipples perk up immediately at his touch and the coldness of the pears. (My nipples are my most sensitive area: it's like they're little dicks, they're so much fun.)

Then he really *does* start licking them off. His tongue starts at the hollow spot under my Adam's apple, where some of the pear juice has collected. He laps at it like a hungry strawberry blond kitten, and he looks up at me, with those soul-filled sea blue eyes. His tongue is incredibly agile: darting down between my pecs, sucking up the pears, teasing the increasingly sensitive skin around my nipples, making them arch higher and higher, desperate now to feel his warm slippery tongue, causing me to start to whimper as he circles around and around and around . . .

And finally: contact. He bears down on my right nipple in a triumphant kiss, and I'm so wet now down in my crotch – oozing pre-come all over the place even though neither of us have touched my dick yet – it's like I'm a woman, just waiting to be fucked.

He's straddling me now, his legs on either side of my torso, and I have a vision of what I must look like to him: my erect nipples, bared and vulnerable, stand awaiting his mercy, capping my tight, defined (but not rounded) pecs, my smooth copper skin wet and shiny from his saliva and the pear juice. I'm hard just thinking about it. Mitch is hard, too: his dick is resting alongside mine, in my pubic hair.

Now he gently takes each of my nipples between his thumbs and forefingers, and begins to rub them, in the gesture men make as if to say: "Give me some cash, man." (I'd give him anything at this point.) He summons a wad of spit into his throat in a grossly machismo effort that seems so out of place for him (but which nevertheless turns me on) and he hawks it down onto my chest. Taking it, he lubricates each nipple and continues his work. I close my eyes and groan.

"What am I working you up for, my hot little Puerto Rican Italian Irishman?" Mitch asks, between unmoving, even teeth.

"Give me your dick," I plead.

He grunts. His fingers leave my nipples for a moment as he lifts himself up, pushing my knees up and raising my ass.

Still wet from his spit, he touches my puckered anus with his middle finger, making a circular motion and pressing ever so gently against me.

"In here?" he asks. "You want me to put my dick in here?"

"Yes," I say, between breaths. I want so desperately for his fingers to return to my nipples. Do whatever you want, I'm thinking. Just touch my chest again.

He reads my mind. With one hand he rolls a condom over his dick; with the other, he begins squeezing my left nipple again. It's only a matter of seconds before he's working the right one, too, just as his dick, with little effort (there rarely is, so long as the guy's doing my nipples), slides right up my ass.

Then he says: "You think you're so pretty, don't you? So pretty that you can get all the men in my family. Don't you?"

I groan in reply.

"You little tramp," he says, thrusting all eight inches of his big WASP meat in and out of me, a big eight-inch pole that pokes my prostate and sends me into a deep, hungry bliss, making me feel as if I suddenly need to pee. "You fucking little tramp," he's saying, pinching my nipples harder now, twisting them between thumb and forefinger. "And to think, you did it all for me."

He bends down, stopping his thrusting, leaving his big hard tool embedded all the way up my ass, and kisses me tenderly on the lips. I draw in my breath, feeling the hard warmth of him inside me, filling me up, puncturing my gut. I kiss him back, our lips gently brushing. Then, with my tongue inserted in his mouth and his dick inserted up my ass, he begins pumping again, making sure he keeps his thumbs moving at all times across my screamingly erect nipples.

This, *this,* is why he is so beautiful.

Okay. So the father. Everyone wants to know about the father. So I'll tell you: it was hot. But first — there's more I have to explain.

You know Mitch is positive. And you know I met him at an ACT UP rally, back when ACT UP was still all the rage and it was really cool to go to all the actions and so on and so on. And you know I'm negative. I had to work through all of that: even though I spent two years wearing my Silence = Death T-shirt and yelling at AIDSphobic pigs, I still had to process my own shit about sleeping with somebody who was positive. Mitch was the first (that I know of, of course – there were most assuredly dozens of others). And just my luck: I fell in love with him.

Here's the lowdown on Mitch. He's a rich kid who none of my friends really liked at first. He had this rich boy look, in his too carefully constructed grunge appeal (real lower class kids don't wear flannel shirts with the sleeves torn off), and he had (has) this aloofness that my buddies took as snobbery. I might not be from the projects, but I'm not from Greenwich, Connecticut, either. I'm from a working-class family and although I went to good schools, it was because my Dad broke his back as a salesman and my Mom worked as a phone operator. And they took out a lot of loans. Dad died a few years ago, but Mom still works for the phone company, and she takes a vacation in Florida every couple of years with my aunt. She – and my Dad – worked hard for everything they got.

Mitch's parents didn't.

The Ward family has been in this country since before there was a New York. Now they own a lot of it. Or at least used to, before they sold big chunks of it to the Japanese and made even more money than they already had. Anyway, they have a big house out in the Hamptons and yes, Mitch *does* come from Greenwich – Old Greenwich, to be precise. (Mitch's mother, who is divorced from his father, lives in the Greenwich house; his dad stays in the Hamptons or in a townhouse in the city.)

But you should see the Greenwich house. You can imagine: big and white (very white) with columns and lots of trees and a lawn that just stretches on for days. *Weeks.*

Servants and a big garage and lots of cars and plenty of dogs. Ever notice really wealthy white people always own dogs – big dogs that point with their snoots – and never cats? (I grew up with three cats.)

Rich boy. Rich HIV-positive boy. The first time I put Mitch's dick in my mouth (after cruising him something fierce at an AIDS action at City Hall) I admit I thought about HIV. *His* HIV. I pictured little black viruses that looked like houseflies with mean, bug-eyed little faces swimming furiously out of his slit and boring down my throat. But I got over that. I mean, his dick tasted so good – and in my head, I was repeating the mantra I'd recently read on a safer sex pamphlet: "Sucking is probably safe. Sucking is probably safe." (Of course, it was a Canadian safer sex pamphlet, but I've always trusted other governments more than my own. Not that *any* of them should be trusted, but that's another story.) So I relaxed, and enjoyed the warm silky feel of his cock thrusting in and out of my mouth.

Of course, we use condoms for fucking, and I'll admit, at first, I used to think about those mean-faced little HIVs here, too, every time I unrolled that latex down around my rod (or his). But eventually I decided this divide between negatives and positives was pure bullshit: "I can outwit those little buggers," I said. And besides, the world's too small to exclude positive guys from my sexual stock company. It's the reverse of the song: to exclude guys who are positive would mean so *little* men, so *much* time.

What hit me, though, was another divide: here was Mitch, this big rich white boy, and me, a working-class kid with Puerto Rican blood in my veins, and Mitch was the one who had it. Let's talk about good fortune and bad here: who did life deal the harder hand? When I first met him, Mitch had disowned his family, so he wasn't even really rich any more. They knew he was queer, but not about the HIV. His right-wing father (yeah, yeah, I'll explain how I could do a right-winger) couldn't abide the fact that his son was out there screaming at the government. So instead of listening to his father's harangues, Mitch said: "See ya."

Back in the old days, the Wards owned factories; now they own computer software companies. And other telecommunications stuff. Don't ask me. Mitch never talks about it. But the first Mitchell Cameron Ward way back in 18-something made a fortune and now all the ensuing Wards have been the beneficiaries of it, right down to Mitch's Dad.

Mitchell Cameron Ward III.

(Guess that makes Mitch a Fourth, but I have a feeling he'd be pissed if I brought that up.)

Another cliché: wealthy father disapproves of gay son's lifestyle in the East Village. And still another: when gay son tests positive, recalcitrant father throws open his arms and welcomes him back to the clan. (After much hand-wringing and dealing with ignorance and prejudice, of course.)

That's almost – but not quite – what happened. Just be patient and I'll tell you everything.

But first a little more about me. What I look like, what I like to do.

First of all: I *love* sex. I'm really tired of these prim and proper gay Republican types who go on and on about how we as queers (excuse me, *gay men and lesbians*) shouldn't be fucking in the bushes, how we shouldn't let the leather folks and the topless women march in our parades, how instead we should be trying to convince straight America we're just like them: uptight about sex.

Fuck that. I'm *not* like them. I love sex. In the bushes. In the parades. Anywhere I can get it. Even with a Republican like Mitch's Dad. (I bet your mouth is watering by now. *Who fucked who?* you're wondering. Did the ACT UP boy plow the rightwinger? Or did the Puerto Rican pretty boy kneel and receive his whacks from Big Daddy Republican? You just wait – and there's more. Do you know who *else* I slept with? Mitch's – no, on second thought, you just sit tight and wait.)

It's not like Mitch and I have ever been monogamous.
And certainly not when we go to places like Fire Island or
Provincetown. Let me tell you about this guy I did in the
dunes of Provincetown last summer. It was an eye-opening
experience for me. And it's how everything else came to
be.

The guy looked like a librarian: fortyish, maybe just fifty,
with round glasses and a small, pleasant face. Nothing
remarkable. I don't know why I found the idea of having
sex with him so appealing: probably because I was (am) a
cocky little shit who gets off on other guys getting off on me.
Or maybe because there was something about his strawberry
blonde hair that reminded me of Mitch. Up until that
summer, I admit, I was pretty selective about who I slept
with: they all had to look like Mitch. You know, great bodies.
No fat. And young. Most of all, young.

Mitch and I had come up to the gay resort on the tip of
Cape Cod for a week's vacation. I was tired from my job at
the bank (I'm a teller) and Mitch (who's a writer, or at least
trying to become one) was badly in need of some inspiration.
That day, he wanted to go to Tea Dance (where I'm sure he
found *more* than inspiration) and I wanted to explore the
dunes. Mitch gave me this knowing look: we both knew what
went on there. I surmised that, given the overpopulation of
pretty boys that P'town endures every summer, I would not
have to fend off any trolls in the dunes. "There will be boys
there," I assured myself. "Pretty boys."

Yet somehow, as I trekked through the windswept sand
drifts, the lack of pretty young things failed to discourage me.
The librarian seemed more than adequate. Even desirable. It
wasn't as if I were feeling desperate: I could always have
joined Mitch at Tea Dance, and we could have brought some
young buff buck back to our guest house and done a three-
way. Maybe it was because I *wasn't* desperate that sex with
the librarian seemed so appealing. I was arrogant enough to
know that he would follow me into the dunes. I knew my ass
looked good in the shorts I was wearing. I knew my arms and

chest showed well through my tank top. I stumbled through the brush into the dunes, and could feel my dick getting heavier. Knowing I was turning this guy on really turned *me* on.

He was dressed in loose-fitting beige chinos and a white polo shirt. He wore blue-and-white running shoes that did not match the rest of his outfit. I had always prided myself on always looking hip (notice I did *not* say trendy, although Mitch might call it that, to cut me down to size in that delicious way he has.) I always know which boots are in, what the proper length is for denim cutoffs, the right way to bunch one's socks, how to position my tank top and when to turn my baseball cap around to the back. But somehow the librarian was the picture of sex, despite the fact that he looked like a model from an outdated L.L. Bean catalog, and I wanted his lips around my cock.

He wasted no time. He got down on his knees and awkwardly began unfastening my belt buckle. I had to help. Then he popped open my jeans, and stuck his face into my open fly. I looked down at the top his head: thinning hair, like my father's. It was an odd thought, and what was even odder was that it made my dick get harder. That's when the librarian pulled down my white Calvin Klein briefs and fumbled my erection into his mouth.

I leaned back against a tree and looked skyward into the lacy network of limbs that crosshatched against the bright blue sky. The man's mouth was warm and slippery. He moved up and down my shaft in record time, and I could feel my cock swell and fill his mouth. He licked the underside and then rolled his tongue around the head, pushing at my pee hole, and then took it all again, all the way, into his mouth.

His hands inched up under my tank top to feel my pecs. I instinctively flexed. This was hot. I suddenly had an image of myself: this young stud, flexing his chest, having his dick sucked and being worshiped by an aging, nerdy librarian, who wished with all his life he was as young and attractive as

I was. He pinched my nipples, which drove me wild. I began thrusting jauntily into his mouth, fucking his face.

"Taste good?" I heard myself ask, and he nodded, my dick still lodged down his throat. "Suck it," I said. "Take it all." I laughed to myself. I sounded like a porn star.

In and out of his mouth my dick moved, and I could feel the back of his throat each time I gave a thrust. I was getting ready to shoot, disappointed that I could not bear to contain it much longer, wanting this worship to go on for hours. I was planning to pull out of his mouth and shoot into the bushes – while, I was sure, he would watch in awe – when I noticed a man with a big lumberjack moustache approaching.

A three-way? I asked myself. I felt a moment of panic, and slowed down my thrusting. Nerdy librarians were one thing, but a lumberjack? I flashed on my pretty tricks standing around modeling at the bar; I thought of Mitch's near-smooth, chiseled chest. The lumberjack wasn't fat, but he had a paunch, and tufts of thick black hair sprouted up from under his T-shirt. My dick softened just a bit, the come inside of me retreating back up my shaft. I suddenly became conscious of my breath, how fast I was inhaling and exhaling.

The lumberjack now stood in front of us. The librarian, oblivious, seemed to think it was his fault that my dick had softened, and he was sucking with renewed vigor.

I looked at the newcomer. I was frightened to make eye contact with him, yet I was too intimidated to look away. He had short black-and-gray hair, with a large moustache over thick, full lips. He filled out his jeans well, with strong, round thighs and a basket that seemed unreal. I didn't wear my jeans that tight – it was considered out-of-style – but suddenly I was glad his generation did. Big biceps – and I mean *big*, not the "defined" muscles for which Mitch and I prided ourselves – emerged from his sleeves. His brown eyes had fixed on mine: and I knew then that my time as object of worship was over.

The librarian stood up, checked out the new man, and went back to his knees, hands reaching up to unbutton another pair of jeans. So we'd both get serviced by the librarian, I figured, feeling vaguely unworthy of being given equal status with this man.

"No," the man said, still looking at me. The librarian, confused, stood up again. The lumberjack reached over and placed his large hand on my shoulder, and pressed down. He wanted me to suck him. Yes, I thought, yes, *yes* – and I gladly obliged, falling to my knees. I'll be your boy, I thought. I'll suck your cock.

But he took the top of my head in his hand and pushed me away from his enticing basket, and instead into the flat beige crotch of the librarian. I started to recoil, but his hand was firm. And then, as a new flood of desire washed over me, I thought: yes, yes – this *is* what I want.

I pulled down the zipper of the librarian's fly, and smelled something clean. Like soap. His blue underwear – tacky, I would have called them yesterday – were wet with precome, so aroused had he gotten sucking my dick. Now I would suck him: the young buck having the tables turned, down on his knees worshiping the man who had worshiped him. I took his cock into my mouth.

It was surprisingly big, and I gagged almost immediately. But I persevered: I wanted to give this man pleasure, this man I never would have looked at before today, whose dick would never have been in my mouth except for here, in these dunes. It was an egalitarian place, a place of leveling out the leagues that divide us. That's what I thought about, as I struggled to fit his long cock all the way down my esophagus, struggled to give this man as much pleasure as I could.

"That's a good boy," I heard above me, and I knew it wasn't the librarian talking, but the lumberjack, who was teaching me this lesson. I sucked on the librarian's dick even harder when I heard his voice, and I tasted the salty release of new Drelome. I pulled off his dick, and looked up. The librarian's body tightened, his face contorted, and he drew in his breath – just before coming in thick, forceful spurts, all over my face and hair.

"Yeah," the lumberjack moaned, now stroking his own massive tool, sticking straight out of his jeans. He shot his load all over me, and then I came too into the sand, in rough, violent, eruptions, aware of the fact that the sticky jizz of two men now streaked my face, my hair, my shoulders and my chest.

So I learned a few things that day in the dunes. About how we divide ourselves. And how we can conquer those divides: Young and old. Positive and negative. Pretty and not so.

On our way home from P'town, we drove through Hyannisport. The Kennedys' town. "My parents have a house here, too," Mitch said, and he seemed a little wistful.

"The Hamptons *and* the Cape?" I asked, but it was clear that Mitch wasn't being resentful right now.

I looked at him closely. He kept his eyes square on the road before him, his hands gripping the steering wheel tightly.

"You want to resolve things with them, don't you?" I asked.

He shrugged.

"Let's stop by their house," I suggested.

"No," he spit.

"Come on. See how they react. You've settled down somewhat. Maybe your father has, too."

"Andy, I don't want to see my father," Mitch said. "Maybe, if I could be sure my mother was there, I'd stop. But I don't know whose turn it is to stay at the house."

He looked so sad, I remember, so crunched up and lost, like a little boy who has gotten lost in the department store and can't find his parents. I felt awful, and helpless. I wanted to do something that would make him feel better: I loved this guy, and hated the thought of him being unhappy. I reached over and cupped his basket in my left hand.

"Remember when we first met and I'd give you blow jobs as you were driving?" I asked.

It made him smile.

"Yeah, I remember," he said, and I could feel his cock stir beneath his button-fly.

I slipped a finger between the buttons and popped a few loose. He was wearing his swimsuit, a glistening blue Speedo, under his cut-offs. I began nuzzling the soft shiny smooth material with my lips and nose. His dick was responding.

"Aw, yeah, suck it, Andy," he groaned.

We were driving down Route 6 when I went down on him. After that, I became oblivious to all the turns and stops that Mitch made. His big pole stood straight up from his Speedos and I slicked it wet with my saliva, in and out of my mouth, up and down, the back of my head occasionally knocking against the steering wheel. Mitch moaned and began thrusting himself, taking over some of the work from me. He was big, but I'd learned how to accommodate all of him down my throat. When my lips would close around the base of his shaft, he'd shiver.

"God, I love you," he said, just as I felt the car stop and heard Mitch turn off the ignition. He took his dick out of my mouth and shot high in the air, like Old Faithful, hitting the windshield in the first two powerful ejaculations and then messing up the front of his shirt with the rest.

I looked around.

We were in a driveway. A beautiful summer home in front of us, the harbor a crystal blue vision behind it. Some gulls cut across the shimmering aqua sky, and I heard them call out a welcome – or a warning.

"I'm home," Mitch said.

He told me later that at the moment I'd gone down on him he'd decided he wanted his parents to meet me. At the time, I was too shocked to ask. He got out of the car and went around to the trunk to pull on a clean shirt. I stayed frozen in the car. He leaned back into the window. "It's my father," he said. "I recognize his car. And my grandparents. They're here, too."

"You still want to go in?" I managed to ask.

"My grandfather is just as bad. Worked for Nixon. This could be tough."

I could still taste his cock in my mouth. "We can still leave," I said. "It's up to you."

"No," he said, looking up at the house, a sprawling compound that looked every bit as regal as I expected the Kennedy "summer house" to be. (Except the Kennedys are Democrats, but is there really a difference, when you come right down to it? Wealth is wealth.) "We're here. They may have seen us drive up. Let's do it."

I had no idea then that we would do it, all right. Would we *ever* do it.

So I told you that story about the Provincetown dunes for a reason, not just because it was hot. I have a lot of hot stories in my repertoire, but that one is significant. I learned a lot of lessons. That part I've explained.

But here's the kicker.

Remember the guy I called the lumberjack? Guess who opened the door to the Ward summer house when we knocked?

To say I was blown away would be a major understatement. There he was, all six-feet-three of him, looking even bigger and even more fucking hot (and remember, a few days before, I'd have dismissed his type as leftover San Francisco Seventies clone) than he had at the dunes.

No, no, he's not Mitch's father. Mitch was just as surprised as I was (no, I suppose *that* would have been impossible – let's just say he was very surprised.)

"Uh, hi, I'm looking for—" Mitch paused, swallowed. The lumberjack bore down at him with big, fierce brown eyes. "—Mitch Ward." He paused. "He's my father."

The lumberjack's eyebrows raised up slightly. Then he narrowed his eyes, as if looking for a resemblance. Meanwhile, I'm wondering if old Daddy Ward knows about his manservant's escapades up to P'town.

Of course, I was *assuming* him to be a manservant. A caretaker, perhaps. A chauffeur, maybe, even. What else *could* he be?

"Come on in," the lumberjack grunted, and then, finally, his eyes moved to me. They seemed to register some recognition, but I could tell he didn't place exactly where he'd seen me. But he would. And Jesus, when he did—

I had started to sweat.

We stepped inside and the lumberjack disappeared through the kitchen.

"This is odd," Mitch whispered.

"What is?" I asked, paranoid.

"Dad never had any servants on the Cape." He looked around. "Just a few years ago, I would've come in and out of here at will. Now I'm standing here like a fucking door-to-door salesman, waiting for the mistress of the house –"

That's when Mitch's Dad entered.

And although I didn't pass out, I don't remember the next several minutes. I'm sure anyone who looked at me probably thought I was a ghost, or at least would become one anytime soon.

"Hello, Dad," Mitch said, and I guess, looking back now, his Dad was just as stunned as I was.

So you've probably figured it out.

Mitch's Dad was – is – the librarian.

My librarian. From the dunes.

He didn't say anything right away. Mitch was probably too nervous to notice that his father kept looking at me. Unlike the lumberjack, he clearly remembered exactly who I was.

And what he'd done to me.

And me to him.

"Dad, I hope you will at least listen to me. I want to try and –" Mitch stammered. "I just thought maybe –"

"Mitch," his father finally managed to say, and now the lumberjack was behind him. He was glaring at me, too. He'd remembered.

"Mitch," his father repeated. "Come in, sit down."

We all moved like robots. I couldn't look up at either Mr. Ward or the lumberjack. I could smell Mr Ward's clean cock scent all over again, and remembered how big he was – like Mitch. I noticed the lumberjack's hands, now crossed in front of him, with their sprigs of short black hairs at the knuckles, and I remembered those same hands forcing me down on to my knees in supplication before my boyfriend's father's crotch.

He was *gay?* Mitch's father – his right-wing, Republican, homophobic father – was gay?

For the first time, I wondered about the proverbial other side of the story.

"Dad, please just hear me out –" Mitch was saying. We were all sitting now in the comfortable, modern living room with its big picture windows that looked out over the shining blue harbor, a few idle sailboats on the horizon.

"No, Mitch, you hear me," his father was saying, and he didn't sound like a librarian now. He sounded every bit as corporate America as Mitch had described. He was trying to assert power in a power-threatening situation, but he was frightened. (As, I imagine, most of corporate America really is. Just what dirty little secrets are they hiding?)

"I can explain everything," Mr Ward continued, and I glanced up at the lumberjack, who was staring at me. No, I shook my head. I mouthed the words: *He doesn't know.*

"Mitchell," the lumberjack said, his head snapping to Mitch's father. "You should –" there was the slightest pause "– make sure your parents are settled in first before you –" another pause, almost undetectable, but I caught it "– get into anything here."

Mr Ward was still looking at his son, and then at me. To Mitch, he explained, with the edge gone from his voice: "Your grandparents are here. It's their anniversary. We're going to have a party. Please don't ruin things."

"That's not my intent," Mitch said.

"Mitchell," the lumberjack repeated, clearly wanting him

out of the room so he could tell him that Mitch didn't know about our *ménage à trois*.

Mr Ward nodded. "All right, Marco." To his son, again: "I'll be right back. Will you wait here?"

Mitch nodded. His father followed Marco out of the room.

"Mitch," I said, unsure of what I was going to say, but I knew something had to be said. "Who – how – what are you going to tell them about me?"

"The truth. You're my lover."

I nodded. I could feel the blood returning to my face, and my brain was starting to think again. "Okay. But first, you should know something –"

"Who's your friend here?" Mr Ward asked suddenly, coming back into the room.

"This is Andy," Mitch said. "He's my lover."

"Andy," Mr Ward said pleasantly, turning to me. "Would you mind if I spoke with my son alone for a few minutes?"

"I'd like him with me," Mitch said.

"Well, sure, but for just a few minutes? Besides, Marco could use some help –" Mr Ward was grinning idiotically – "– getting the doors open to the cottage where your grandparents are staying. Would you mind giving him a hand?" He didn't wait for me to give him an answer. He turned to Mitch and said, too quickly, "I hired Marco to do some work around here."

I *bet* you did, I thought.

"Sure," I said. "I'll go help him." I turned to Mitch. "But I'll come back."

Mitch nodded.

"Thanks, Andy," Mr Ward said, his eyes fixing on me, beaming desperate gratitude, dire threat and whatever else.

Kind of a fucked-up situation, huh? Well, it gets better.

So out at the cottage I met Mitch's grandmother ("And who might *you* be?" she asked, seeing me walk down the hill with Marco. "Name's Andy Rodriguez," I said. "Your grandson's lover." Her blue glasses shifted on her nose, and she found an excuse to wander off by the water).

Marco was okay. I was prepared to hate him, but man, seeing him again . . . I think he pulled off his T-shirt deliberately when he saw me approach. I mean, come on: of *course* it was deliberate. It wasn't *that* hot today.

It soon would be, however.

"So the kid doesn't know anything?" Marco asked after the grandmother tottered away.

"No," I said. "I had no idea who you were, who he was. This whole thing is just an incredible fluke."

Marco whistled. "I'll say." He looked up at the sky and I felt my dick, despite myself, stir in my Calvins again. Without his shirt Marco looked every inch the hunk fantasy of the typical straight woman – big, broad shoulders, hairy chest, massive arms, Tom Selleck face. Not my type. Not my type at all. Give me Keanu Reeves any day. But there was – is – something so raw, so basic, about Marco's brand of masculinity that it excited me in a way I'd never known before – except in those few minutes when he'd forced me to my knees in the Provincetown dunes.

I tried not to think about it. I mean, this was my boyfriend's father's – what? Hired escort? Plaything? Lover?

"Who are you?" I asked. I felt I had that right.

"Marco Alberghetti," he said, flashing a devil's grin and extending his big old bear paw. We shook heartily. I told him my name. "Look, Andy," he said, "I think we can be friends."

"I hope so," I said.

He shrugged. "Mitchell's really missed his son."

"Great," I said. "But he kicked him out."

"He did not. The kid left, walked out."

"Because his father is a right-wing hypocrite."

Marco's eyes narrowed. "Don't go flapping your jaw when you don't know what you're talking about. If you want to be friends, you gotta have an open mind."

"The guy's a Republican," I spit.

Marco shrugged again. "Yeah, maybe so. I don't know politics. But I know good men. Mitchell Ward is a good man."

"*My* Mitchell Ward is a good man," I countered.

"I don't doubt he is," Marco conceded, "but so is mine."

I took the cue. "So you're lovers?"

"Yep." Marco smiled. "For the last three years."

"You often go to the dunes together?"

"Sure," he said, grinning wider now. "At least *we* go together."

My turn to narrow my eyes. "Hey, Mitch knows –"

"You tell him about the scene we had together?"

I hadn't. I wasn't sure why. Maybe because it was so powerful for me I didn't want it to suffer any reduction in the telling. Mitch might have said: "You did it with a librarian and an old clone?" No, it needed more context than that. I hadn't brought it up.

"No," I admitted. "But he knows I went. He goes too. We don't believe in monogamy."

Marco studied me. "But you love each other?"

"Absolutely," I responded.

Marco clapped his hands. "Non-monogamous *and* in love," he said. "Shit, we *do* have something in common after all."

And with that he grabbed my face with both of his big brute hands and brought me close to him for a deep, soulful kiss. For a couple of seconds, I rebelled, then melted. It was so incredible to be crushed in this great big bear hug, his sharp moustache hairs poking my skin. It was completely inappropriate, and incredibly stupid, but I kissed him back, and in moments I could feel his pole jabbing at me through his jeans.

"Let's go into the cottage," he rasped into my ear.

"But the grandmother –" I protested.

"Don't worry," he said. "I can lock the place from inside. And the grandfather's on one of his long walks."

"No," I said, but what I meant was: "Persuade me."

It didn't take much. He inhaled deeply, pushing his massive chest into me, and with one big palm he gripped my basket through my shorts. "Don't you want to get what you were so craving in the dunes? My big cock up your butt?"

"Oh, God, yes," I said.

I was too swept away to notice Marco had forgotten to lock the door. Meanwhile, the man I love is up the hill locked in a gut-wrenching and possibly fraudulent reunion with his father. Was Marco manipulating me, neutralizing me? I wasn't so far gone in my lust that I didn't think these things. But I surrendered. I'm not proud of it. Nor am I ashamed. I gave into my boiling-over passion for this man who reminded me of Popeye's Bluto – and discovered there were still parts of me left to discover.

So here's what happened.

As Mitch told me later, his father came across like a dove: let's be friends, let's make amends, let's not delve into too many personal issues right now. Mitch got suspicious: "Hey," he asked, "where's Andy?"

His father feigned ignorance, and tried to dissuade Mitch from going to look for me.

Whether Mr Ward and Marco had quickly hatched a plot to seduce me down at the cottage so that the situation with Mitch could be defused (or neutralized, in the case I was discovered), I don't know. Thinking about it now seems unlikely: Marco would have had no idea that the grand-mother would so easily stumble away on her walk. Maybe he was just told to "divert" me.

He certainly did.

The first thing he did in his diversion was kiss me full on the lips: big, rough lips and a tongue that had more strength, it seemed, than my hand. It pushed into my mouth between my closed lips, as if it were looking for something inside, and I sucked it in as far as I could. His big paws, meanwhile, had grabbed ahold of my ass, squeezing it, clamping it into a grip that seemed to stake a claim of ownership. He smelled vaguely sweaty, as if he really *had* been fixing up the cottage when we arrived, maybe hauling the grandparents' heavy luggage down the hill. I broke free of the kiss, intending to sample his chest, to lick across that hairy mat and suck on his big, quarter-sized nipples. But he resented my boldness: he snapped my head back up to his and kissed me even harder this time, causing me to lose my breath and succumb completely.

"Pretty little boy like you shouldn't be prancing around through the dunes," he mock scolded, and with one fierce movement he lifted my shirt up and over my head. With his rough fingers he clamped onto my nipples, and my knees buckled. He twisted and turned as if my chest were a radio and he was desperate to tune into a far-off station. I groaned.

As such, you understand, I was under his power. Holding onto my right nipple between his fingers, he pushed me down by the top of my head with his left hand, forcing me onto my knees to worship at the denim altar of his crotch. I burrowed in eagerly, my tongue snaking between the buttons of his 501s, as I remembered doing not long before to Mitch. But instead of a skimpy blue Speedo beneath, I found nothing but cock: no underwear shielded the heavy odor of sweat, piss and come that lingered there. In moments, his dick was standing straight out of his pants and I wolfed it down my throat, all nine thick inches of it, in one sudden gulp.

Feeling his tool in my mouth, choking off my air, was more surrender of control. I was getting off on this concept: ever since the experience I'd had with him in the dunes, I had wanted something like this again. That's maybe why I behaved so irrationally, sucking my boyfriend's father's boyfriend's dick just a few yards away from where my boyfriend and his father sat. I'd always been such a control queen: that's why I was in ACT UP, because it gave me the (false, but nonetheless empowering) sense that I had some kind of control over this insane epidemic that was wreaking havoc in our lives.

But with surrender of control comes risks:

"What? What is – What is going on here?"

The voice was new, but decidedly male (that was good: it wasn't grandma). I couldn't see who had entered the room: all my eyes could focus on were the popped-open fly of a pair of blue jeans and the explosion of dark pubic hair that protruded from it. Marco's cock was still all the way down my throat and his hands at the back of my head would not release their grip. Then I heard a shuffle of feet, as if the newcomer had turned to leave, then decided against it. Then I heard a clamp, like a lock sliding into place.

Then I felt two hands on my back, sliding around and under my arms to grab hold of my pecs.

"You'll say nothing," the new man said, apparently to Marco, in the form of an order.

The hands at my tits I could make out only barely: they were not young. I had been frightened only for a second, when I thought perhaps it was Mitch or his father. But this was someone else, and I let go into the sensations of new fingers kneading my already sensitive nipples.

"What a pretty young boy you are," the voice whispered in my ear. Then, to Marco: "And I thought you were a hunk from the moment we arrived."

I sucked on Marco's prick as hard and as fast as I could. The new man's hands began flicking my nipples while his lips caressed my neck. I felt his tongue slide down my spine and to the edge of my shorts, and then his fingers left my pecs and undid my zipper. I raised up my back and pushed my ass toward him for better access. Awkwardly he yanked down my shorts and began kissing my exposed ass, before plunging straight to my butthole with an evidently experienced tongue. I felt its warm moistness thrust in and out of my anus, and I grew sweaty with fulfilled lust: Mitch didn't like to do that, but I craved it, although I rarely asked for it from tricks since some boys were pretty leery about doing it.

Boys.

Therein lies the difference.

This man's tongue massaged my asshole with regular thrusts, and we began performing our individual tasks with synchronicity. When his tongue was in me, Marco's cock was down my throat; when the tongue came out of my ass, I slid up Marco's shaft. And so we worked, the sensations of giving and receiving combining in a climax of pleasure. The man behind me was now working my hard dick as it hung heavily swinging below me: tugging at it, gently then roughly, and I was close to coming.

When Marco shot, pulling his rod out of my mouth and aiming over my shoulder, I was sure he must have covered the back of the man behind me, eating my ass. Maybe he did. He gushed in long, ecstatic spurts, and I caught only the sight of his white jizz flying past me in rapid fire. That made me come finally, too, that and the man's agile little tongue working its way higher and higher up inside me. I came as I had before with Marco, with my dick pointing down, covering the hardwood floor of the cottage with a puddle of milky white water.

"You'll say nothing," the man behind me said again to Marco, and I caught just a glimpse of him as he slipped quickly out the door, pausing first to slide back the bolt that I'd earlier heard him secure. Outside, I heard muffled voices: his, and a woman's. I thought I heard him say: "He's *who?*"

"Holy Jesus," Marco murmured, buttoning up his pants.

"What?" I asked. "Who was that?"

"Holy shit," he said, not looking at me.

"What?" I demanded.

"This is a whole lot stickier than we even thought," he said, now turning his big brown eyes on me.

"What do you mean?" I asked, but I think I was starting to suspect.

"That guy who just ate your ass," Marco said, the edge of a smile tugging at his lips, "was your boyfriend's grandfather."

*   *   *

Okay, let's all take a breather here, shall we, folks? Even my retelling the story gets me all horned out, you know what I mean? Come on, admit it: deep down we're all turned on when taboos are broken. What aroused me was the breaking of the taboo: I had now engaged in sex play with both my boyfriend's father *and* his grandfather.

"Mitchell and his father have never gotten along," Marco said that afternoon, sitting down on a wicker chair and gazing off into space. "Wait'll he hears his father is an asslicker."

"He told you not to tell."

Marco narrowed his eyes at me. "Seems to me we have a dilemma here," he sad. "Your lover is estranged from his father. My lover is estranged from his. And they're all a bunch of fags. What do you make of that?"

"I say it settles that nasty old little debate about nature versus nurture."

Marco smiled. "Maybe. But what are we going to do about it?"

I crunched my brow. "What do you mean?"

"I mean, my pretty young friend," Marco said, wrapping me in those big arms of his, "this is our golden opportunity."

Flash forward one day. To get there, I'll fill you in on some particulars (but not all): Mitch came down to the cottage, a little perplexed about what had been keeping me, and I made up some story about helping Marco get the wicker furniture out of storage. Things with his Dad had gone okay, but tension was still high. His father had invited him to spend the night ("What about Andy?" Mitch had asked. "Sure, sure," Mr. Ward had replied. "We have plenty of room.")

"Should we?" Mitch asked.

"Sure," I said.

So we did. Mitch and I were left pretty much to ourselves, except when his grandmother staggered over to where we sat around the small duck pond and covered Mitch with kisses, completely ignoring me. Mitch put up with it. Then she was gone, and I didn't see her again for the whole time we were there. I'm not sure what they did with her. Maybe Marco locked her in the cottage or something. But she thankfully fades from the scene at this point.

Mitch and I made love under the moon by the pond. "I can't believe I'm spreading my legs for you here, on my father's property," Mitch said, his big beautiful eyes gleaming in the moonlight. His ass was tight, and silky: I slipped in without too much difficulty and felt his hungry hole suck my dick right up to the base of the shaft. In and out, at first slow, then faster, I fucked him with every breath I took. In moments like this, we really were like one being: his heart beating in my ears as my cock pulsed in and out of his body.

Afterward: "I need to tell my father about my HIV status," Mitch said, in hushed tones.

"Yes," I agreed.

"That's when he'll throw me out," Mitch said.

"Try him," I urged. "And whatever happens, I'm here."

I'll let you in one more important detail that I learned from Marco: Mitch's Dad already knew. Some cousin that Mitch had told about a year ago let the news leak to an uncle, who told Mr Ward. At first I was pissed: "And he still kept his distance?" But Marco told me how Mr Ward had struggled with the news, and how he really began learning a lot about the disease, and about the people who have it. He even (much to my shock) had done some volunteer AIDS work, all in preparation of seeing his son again. "So he planned to –?" I asked Marco, who nodded. If Mitch hadn't come by first, Mr Ward would have approached his son.

So the next morning shone bright: a warm (not at all humid) sunny summer day. Mitch and I got up early, and traipsed out to the small home gym and sauna room his father had installed near the pool. We both worked out, pumping our bodies with a fierce energy as if we knew what the day held in store for us. Mitch looked great in his cut-off sweats (I knew there was a jockstrap underneath) and no shirt, the white downy hair on his arms and chest beaded with crystalline drops of sweat. I knew I looked pretty good myself: my tight torso packed into skintight black lycra shorts. I was wearing a jockstrap, too, and my crotch bulged for anyone to see.

And someone *did* see. Was watching us.

I first spotted the grandfather as I was on my fourth or fifth bench press. I detected movement out of the corner of my eye, and I turned, noticing a flash of gray hair slip back behind the half-opened door to the supply closet. Then, two beady eyes peered through the crack of the door and the hinge, and I smiled. When I stood I faced the closet and stretched, displaying my body so that Mitchell Cameron Ward II could see and appreciate.

Of course, the idea that he was spying on his own grandson really pushed the edge of my horniness, because Mitch *did* look so fucking hot. I imagined the old man in there beating off to Mitch's pumped-up pecs, his biceps that strained against his creamy skin with each curl.

I decided that I'd give the old man a show myself: hey, I'm just a nice guy, that's all. So I went down on Mitch: right there, as he straddled the bench, curling with free weights. I pulled down the front of his sweats and began sucking on that big old jockstrap pouch. I swear I could hear a groan from the supply closet.

"That's it, Andy, suck my dick," Mitch said, easing down the weights and leaning back to give me better access. I chomped on that jockstrap, feeling his sizable meat swell and stretch beneath it. I hoped that my timing was right. I needed to work Mitch into a fever pitch of horniness, get him as riled up as possible. I was deliberately teasing him, darting my tongue under the jock but never removing it. "Come on," he said, "suck my dick." But I kept eating the jockstrap instead, and he finally lay back on the bench in writhing ecstatic frustration.

"Mitch," I said, hoping Marco had everything in place, "let's go in the sauna." I said it loud enough so that the grandfather in the supply closet could hear. His presence was an angle Marco and I couldn't have anticipated; his turn was supposed to come later. But I believed in fate – it had led me to Mitch, hadn't it? – and I decided to play with it. Besides, involving him really turned me on. I wouldn't mind his tongue up my butt again.

Mitch agreed the sauna was a good idea. He peeled off his shorts but left his jock on, his dick pushing at the material. When he turned to walk towards the sauna, his beautiful bubble butt, framed by the white straps of the jock, faced his grandfather.

I got to the door of the sauna first. I had one more thing to do. Just before Mitch opened the door, I fell to my knees and began sucking his pouch again. Then I pulled it down and plunged his cock down my throat in one fast movement. He staggered a bit, and I caught him by each cheek of his ass. I had him where I wanted. Then with one last lick up the underside of his shaft, I stood and opened the door.

And inside, buck naked, was Marco, on his knees, sucking Mitch's Dad just as I had been sucking the son.

With both father and son at such peaks of raw sexual excitement, we had counted on there being little awkwardness. Of course, we were overly optimistic: Mitch recoiled at the sight, and tried to bolt out of there, but I stopped him. "It's okay," I said, holding his beautiful blue eyes in mine for a second, then getting back down on my knees and taking his still rock-hard dick into my mouth again.

Mr Ward, for his part, enjoying (what I later learned was) a rare blowjob from Marco (Marco usually played top, and Mr. Ward generally was satisfied with that), hardly stirred. His eyes didn't register the shock Mitch's had (after all, he already knew his son was queer) but he did seem anxious, at least for a few seconds. But either Marco's magic lips or else a sudden realization that truth was better than secrecy made him relax. He closed his eyes and a small smile stole over his face.

So there we were: father and son being blown by their respective boyfriends. I can't imagine what Mitch was thinking, but he seemed to be getting off on it: his dick swelled

bigger than it ever had before in my mouth, and I actually
gagged a bit. When I looked up, I saw that Marco had taken
the next move. He was behind Mitch now, and Mr Ward had
followed, dropping to his knees to service Marco this time.
Marco, meanwhile, had reached around to squeeze Mitch's
freshly pumped pecs – and I thought Mitch would come
right there. I decided to pull off his dick so a premature
ejaculation wouldn't spoil all our moods.

Now Marco was fingering Mitch's butthole. I knew how
much he liked that. Mitch's anus is like my nipples: all
electric sensation. He groaned in pleasure. I was odd man
out suddenly, standing around with nothing to do, until I
noticed Mr Ward's big old dick dangling between his legs, in
that half-hard/ half-soft stage that often occurs when one is
giving head. I remembered how good that cock had tasted in
my mouth, and decided to plunge ahead.

I took a gamble that it would be okay with Mitch.

It was.

He really seemed to enjoy watching me suck his father, and
I thought again about how far I had come. How much I'd
been able to conquer the divides. One hurdle had been with
Mitch, with me being negative and all. Then came the
looksism and ageism and all that "ism" crap that I don't
necessarily buy into: except that a few days ago, I never
would have had Mr Ward's dick in my mouth.

Marco's by now got a couple of fingers up Mitch's butt,
and my boyfriend's groaning marvelously, eyes closed. Mr
Ward's lips are still clamped around Marco's huge tool, and
now I'm on the floor, on my back, Mr Ward's dick plunging
in and out of my mouth. We need one more link to make our
chain complete.

I had left the door of the sauna open slightly. Although I
didn't see him, I was sure that Grandfather Ward was
watching this whole hot scene. Half of me thought he'd be
too freaked to enter, and run off.

Half of me thought otherwise. That half was right.

In he slipped, and for the first time I got a good look at

him: a handsome man, looking more like Mitch than even his father did: chiseled features, startling blue eyes, a full head of brilliant white (not gray, as I had thought earlier) hair. His face was the craggy, weatherbeaten bronze that many rich old men have, after decades on yachts and golf courses. He was wearing white shorts and a light blue polo shirt. Looked like somebody from the old Bush Administration. But who am I, lying here on the floor with his son's dick in my mouth, to play partisan politics?

This time, it was Mitch's father who reacted. I felt him tense, and that's when I heard the old man say: "It's all right, son. I've known for a long time. About you *and* me." A gentle hand on his son's shoulder. Mr Ward (the middle Ward, Mitch's father) then relaxed, and his eyes met mine. I took my mouth off his cock and kissed its head. I smiled, and Mr Ward smiled back.

Now Grandfather Ward turned his attention to Mitch. "You beautiful boy," he said, caressing Mitch's cheek. And then to me: "And such an unbelievably beautiful lover." He was on his knees almost instantly, massaging the big bulge in my lycra shorts. I realized then that I was his type of boy: and I'd play with that.

I heard the tear of cellophane, and saw, over my shoulder, Marco unroll a condom over his big heavy dick. Oh, baby, I thought, grinning up at Mitch, are you gonna get it now. Mitch practically swooned in anticipation. I kept up the sucking on Mr Ward's dick, enjoying its size as he fucked in and out of my face. Grandfather Ward had slid my shorts (with difficulty, they were so tight) down around my thighs, and was now munching on my exposed jockstrap, moaning over and over. I pushed my crotch into his face and he began playing with his own dick down in his shorts.

"Oh, yeah," Mr Ward sighed, watching his lover plug his son's hole. Mitch was being fucked by Marco now, with Marco holding him up in front of him, his right arm tucked under Mitch's stomach. Mitch was backed into Marco's crotch, and Marco was pumping like there was no tomorrow.

It was an amazing scene, made all the hotter by how hot we all were: literally. Remember, we were in a sauna.

Now Grandfather Ward was sucking me, and boy, what experienced lips he had. I felt my whole being go in and out of his mouth. I was knocked for a loop by the expert blowjob, falling off Mr Ward's dick, who made a beeline for my chest. This, of course, sent me into the stratosphere: with Mr Ward licking my tits and his father sucking my cock, I was in a state of bliss that transcended the time and place. I don't even remember now when we all moved out into the weight room, or if Marco actually pulled out of Mitch to do that, or just carried him along in front of him, his big old rod still firmly implanted up his ass. But when I realized that Mr Ward was no longer sucking on my tits I looked around to see that I was on the weight bench, and my legs were in the air, and Grandfather Ward was down there with his tongue up my ass. I just closed my eyes and slipped back into space.

So it had happened I thought – contact between the family had been made. I roused myself from my euphoria to watch what happened next. When I opened my eyes again, I realized I was sucking cock: Marco's now, and Mr Ward was sucking me. I sucked Marco's dick, the dick that had just been up my lover's ass.

Marco withdrew from my mouth and came around to the end of the bench to fuck me. Another condom (where *did* he hide those things, I wondered later?) unrolled around his massive tool, and then up into me he went, and I groaned, remembering how much I had wanted that in the dunes, and that here I was, being plowed in front of my boyfriend by his father's lover.

In seconds, the family had surrounded me. Mitch stood over me and smiled. Then his beautiful dick hovered above my mouth, and I eagerly ate it. He fed it to me, long and thick and full of come, while his father knelt on one side of me and his grandfather on the other, each sucking a nipple gingerly into their mouths. Everyone – and every part of me – was now accounted for. I felt the raw power of Marco's cock ramming up inside me, shaking my body with every thrust. I felt the fullness and love with which Mitch's thick tool slipped in and out of my mouth. And I felt the teasing caresses of Mitch's father and grandfather, their tongues, teeth and lips alternately licking, biting and kissing my nipples. The picture was completed when Marco – amazing, agile Marco – was able to bend over without his dick leaving my ass and taking my throbbing cock into his mouth. He was fucking and sucking me at the same time: thanks to his agility and my length. I had never known such a state of arousal. I felt the come surge from my testicles and travel up my shaft. Marco sensed it too, and he replaced his mouth with long, sensuous strokes from his hand. In seconds, I erupted, shooting wads of come everywhere, streaking over my head, catching Mitch's hair, his father's forehead, his grandfather's shoulder. Everyone let out groans of appreciation.

Especially me.

They all came, each in their turn. Mitch's grandfather was next, shooting all over my chest. (I guess my glorious climactic display had just been too much for him.) Then came Marco, pulling out of me and shooting on my stomach. Mr Ward took his son's hand and pressed it to his lips: "I love you, Mitch," he said.

Marco touched my shoulder. Our plan had worked. Unbelievably, against all of society's odds, it had worked. Things would be equal between them from now on.

They came together, simultaneously, Mitchell Ward jerking himself off. When it was all over, Marco and I backed off a bit, and the three Ward men all held each other, not saying anything. Mr Ward sniffled a bit. Then they pulled on some shorts and took a walk off down by the duck pond. I imagine they processed what had just occurred. Mitch told me later his father had been emotional: "What a jerk I've been," he'd said. He didn't renounce the Republican party or anything, and I guess neither Mitch nor I thought he needed to any longer. But he recognized that he'd been part of the problem:

supporting people who were anti-gay, staying in the closet when his presence as a gay man in political circles, even conservative ones – *especially* conservative ones – could have had such a positive impact. He promised all that would change.

In fact, so powerful was his conversion that I took it to heart, coming out myself along my own final frontier: my mother. She was terrific. "Of course I knew that," she said. "Probably before you did."

Mitch's grandfather, while closer now to his son and grandson, remains closeted: poor old Grandma still doesn't know anything. But that's how he – and so many of his generation – have lived their lives: tea rooms and rest stops and furtive encounters. For them, Stonewall happened too late. Yet he is proof that regardless of one's age or life experience, self-growth can occur: he greets me warmly each time we visit, and he has no trouble introducing me as his grandson's "wonderful lover". (He's changed some minds at his country club: "I've got a son *and* a grandson who are gay," he says. "Bigotry is bigotry. Get over it.") He calls me "Tasty," for obvious reasons: it's a little secret among the five of us.

Mitch's Dad joined a Log Cabin Club this year, and he and Marco now officially live together in New York as lovers. We see them frequently, and we argue about politics still – but in a good way, a respectful way, a loving way.

And all of them – Mr Ward, Grandfather Ward, and Marco – have been wonderfully supportive of Mitch around his HIV status. When Mitch realized that his Dad knew he was positive and *still* didn't freak out when his father's lover went down on him, he saw his father as an intelligent, informed, compassionate man – despite the fact that he's a Republican. "Guess I can't have it all," Mitch laughed, "but I'm pretty damn close."

Nothing like what happened that day on Cape Cod ever happened again. At least, not yet. We don't talk about it much, but it's there, living on fondly as a hot memory. It's there when Grandfather Ward calls me "Tasty". It's there when Marco greets me with a big bear hug. It's there when Mitch and I fuck, and he tells me how much he loves me. It's there each time Mitch and his Dad embrace – and I thank God for that day in the Provincetown dunes, when I learned just what could be accomplished by getting past our divides.

The Bureaucrat

Andrew Holleran

I've never been able to work in an office without belonging to a gym: the sweaty, wordless, physical exertions at the end of the day are the only thing that can wipe out the cerebral, disembodied, frustration of a day spent pushing paper. For a gay man, of course, exercise has other aspects – though the gym I joined after moving here two years ago was not the one popular with gay men. It had just stopped being that, a friend informed me. There were, nevertheless, left-over traces.

The shower room, for instance, was still one large open room with nothing but spigots along the gray walls, and a frieze of naked men washing themselves on both sides. There was even a man who shocked me my first visit by standing in the center of the room with his back to the wall, sporting a large erection as the water streamed down his back and people walked by. Indeed, he was there every time I went that fall, so I presumed he spent a lot of time at the gym, doing just that. Just before Christmas, I was not surprised to see workmen installing plastic panels on the wall of the shower room. This did not solve the problem, however – the open cubicles that resulted apparently allowed men to masturbate to one another from opposite sides of the room. So a few weeks later white shower curtains were added so you could shower in complete privacy.

There seemed, in fact, many things at the gym that could be explained only by an effort to avoid the homosexual gaze. It was as if a regime change had occurred, and all former practices were to be wiped out. A few young men, mostly Indian, for instance, would even undress at their lockers wrapped in towels, the way Europeans change clothes on a public beach, so that no one could see their nakedness. Then they wore their towels into the showers, and pulled the curtain shut, to avoid prying eyes. That there might be prying eyes was still possible because the cubicles on the east side of the shower room had been left without shower curtains. Why this was so I did not know. To shower in a cubicle without a curtain, it seemed to me, could mean one of two things: one had no need for this silly, prudish paranoia, or one wished to advertise one's body. An open cubicle was fine for me, I decided, the curtain seemed excessive, though I never knew if I was doing it to show my contempt for the absurd modesty, or because I did want to exhibit myself. Whichever it was, however, I pretended not to see what was around me as I showered – because I did not want to be asked to leave the gym; the idea was too embarrassing.

The man whom I had seen exhibiting himself in the shower room when I first started going to the gym continued to behave without shame, however: a short, bald fellow, with a large, commanding nose, a salt and pepper beard, and a beautifully compact and proportioned body. He was perfectly built, and had a big dick. Though I blamed him personally for the cubicles in the shower room, he was still there when I went, walking around the locker room naked, with his towel in hand, exhibiting himself.

One day I was sitting on the steps of a friend's apartment building, two blocks from mine, when the man from the gym walked by. My friend told me the exhibitionist (whose name was Daniel) was not only chairman of his co op board, but had a job at the International Monetary Fund. In short, by day he was a financier or economist whom I saw on the street in a dark overcoat, suit and tie. At the gym, however, he was Priapus. He was also, alas, the sort of man I would love to have had sex with, but I was so resentful of his egotism – he was the reason the gym staff had clamped down – that I held him in a sort of contempt.

In fact, the more we passed each other, in the locker room, even after I'd learned his name, the more irritated I felt with him. Perhaps because there were straight men at the gym who sometimes brought their young sons to the gym, I was angry that he cruised so blatantly. Perhaps I was jealous of his dick. Perhaps I wanted him to want only me.

We never spoke. I never saw him speak to anyone. I never saw him even laugh. All he did was walk naked through the locker room with an expression both closed and open, as if he would assumed a demeanor based only on the looks he got from other people. In other words, he was walking a line. Like the blank expression on his face, he seemed to possess characteristics that canceled each other out: perfectly built, but small, handsome but bald, contemporary but ancient. The big aquiline nose, the watchful eyes, the head itself, made me think of a Jewish scholar, or gem-dealer, or banker, in Antwerp, in the Middle Ages. Yet he seemed to be merely an ordinary gay man. One Sunday I took a tour of a local cemetery with a group of gay men, and, halfway through the lecture, noticed him on the other side of a gravestone, in jeans and a plaid shirt, with another man. We did not acknowledge each other. He had a whiny voice, I learned when I fell into step behind him, and a sort of sissy walk – even when he was walking through the locker room with his towel dangling from one outstretched hand. As time went on, I continued to ignore him so fiercely – when we passed each other I frowned, or looked away– that he must have concluded that I disliked him, so that he began to flinch, as if I'd struck him, whenever we passed each other in the locker room.

It is a truth to be universally acknowledged that none of us has any idea whom we have pricked with Desire as we go about our daily lives. So determined are most people to conceal their lust for others, we would be astonished if, at the end of every day, we received, from the municipal authorities, a list of people who wanted to sleep with us, perfect strangers who had seen us in a bakery or post office or museum, or gym. But, of course, there is no such list delivered at the end of every day, so people never know exactly who it is they are torturing; no one ever receives roses, or serenades, or letters, or approaches of any sort. They merely inspire masturbation – that fundamental outlet that makes possible the workings of democracy, that safety valve without which people could not endure life in our impersonal and over-stimulated culture.

I masturbate at home, before the computer screen on my desk. Just before coming I drop to my knees so that my semen will be absorbed by the newspaper I have spread on the floor. The section of the newspaper is always the Classified ads, or the stock market listings: a sheet of grey newsprint – no photographs, or images of any sort, that may distract me when I climax, or make me feel I am disrespecting anyone, remembered on the Obituary page. (Now and then – like people who open the Bible at random to read a passage that will tell them what to do – I pick up the paper to read the classified ad, or stock quotation, the biggest blob of sperm had landed on but it has never given me direction in any way.) After several orgasms this newspaper begins to wrinkle and turn yellow, and I replace it with another. Since the *Times* is published every day, I am never without something to soak up the puddles of precious DNA which end up, along with the newspaper, in the recycling bin in the basement of my apartment building.

I was never able to imagine the man from the International Monetary Fund for purposes of masturbation, however. I was simply not sure what we would do together. One day I saw him walking down the street with a man who was tall, blond, and young. "That's his boyfriend," said my friend, sitting with me.

"Ah," I said, "he likes people taller than himself."

"We always want what we don't have," said my friend.

"Well, he's got it," I said. "I'm not surprised. Someone like that will always have a boyfriend."

"What do you mean?"

"I mean he has a very nice dick."

My friend took a puff on his cigarette, and said: "A big dick is something. But it's not everything."

"Well, it explains the two of them," I said. To be honest, I was jealous of the young man at his side. I was jealous of the young man who was going upstairs to have sex with the exhibitionist. Yet, the next time we passed each other in the gym, my face assumed so annoyed an expression, Daniel blinked, as if I'd slapped him.

When, a few months later, my friend told me that his building was undergoing a crisis – mold had been discovered in the heating system, apartments would have to be evacuated, money would be exacted from each tenant – my friend blamed the man from the International Monetary Fund for the whole mess. He had tried to save money, my friend said, by hiring a maintenance man whose work was sub-par. There was even a young mother alarmed about her baby who was thinking of suing.

On hearing this my disgust with Daniel dissolved; and I felt sorry for him – after all, his real career involved his penis, and petty distractions like this should not be his lot. For a while, he stopped working out and his exceptional body lost its definition and became merely average. But the building was finally cleaned, and within weeks he recovered the physique he had let go during the crisis, and once more, as I watched him walk down the aisle at the locker room, stark naked, with his towel dangling daintily from an outstretched hand, I reverted to my old mixture of envy and desire.

This happened at a time in my life when I'd stopped having sex – a time Cicero described by comparing himself to a slave who has been "freed by a cruel and insane master". Walking around town I felt sorry sometimes for the ones who were still under his whip: the people forced to go to bars, gyms, bath houses, parties, or use the computer to hook up and discharge their loads. Curious word, *load*: something one wishes to put down, to relieve oneself of. That's how it seemed to me: the young men who made a point to not look at me on the street were simply staggering under a burden. They were lost in a hormonal cloud I had exited, but which they, like bees in a hive, or birds in a storm, were still in, beating their wings, without even knowing why they were doing it. One no longer felt compelled to follow people down streets. One could go to bed at night without having to put on one's clothes and go out for one last try at meeting someone. One could look for sex when one felt like it, and not be deeply crushed if one didn't get it.

Then, of course, there was the real reason this detachment was possible – that breviary, that *vade mecum*, that personal prayer book that we turn to when we are alone: the computer, and its endless supply of images of naked men floating through cyberspace at all hours of the day and night. These images had become my family, in a way. I could not live without them. In the early days of the Church most of the populace was illiterate, and so the West allowed pictures of the saints and gospels to be painted for those who could not read (though the East destroyed theirs during the iconoclasm of the 9th century, following the Biblical injunction against graven images). The Church knew the power of images. Now capitalism – advertising, movies, television, the computer – provide them, and my contemplative life, I had to admit, now consisted exclusively of people I had never met whose bodies were floating in cyberspace.

For example, that winter I conducted an affair with two Pakistanis living in Toronto. They did not know each other, yet they were so similar that for a time I suspected they were the same person. Each one wore plaid shirts and jeans, had thick black hair, a moustache, and a hairy chest. One liked the outdoors, hikes and camping, and was pictured nude with his hand on what looked like a modern version of an archer's bow, with a cache of arrows with feathered shafts. The other said he liked man smells and underwear. I liked both men, so every two weeks or so I went to a motel on the outskirts of

Toronto, where the two, whom I had introduced, would tie me to the bed, and then come and go all night, doing with me what they wanted. Because I was face down on the bed, all I heard was the door opening and closing behind me, so I never knew, when I heard the click, who had come into the room. It was only when the penis was placed before my mouth, or into my anus, that I realized which one it was. Sometimes both of them came together. And thus the winter passed, with one satisfying orgasm after another.

Even porn fantasies, however, like real affairs, come to an end, so that one has to look around, take inventory, and say: well, who is not an assemblage of pixels? On Sunday nights the feeling of deprivation was the worst. I would mitigate my loneliness by going down to a museum to hear a concert given every Sunday at seven o'clock. I had become part of that floating world of museum- and concert-goers, the small core who went to everything for reasons probably like my own: loneliness, a desire to get out of the apartment, some wish to transcend themselves. I was living on Art – on music, and paintings. In my isolated state it was quite possible to fall in love with some young man in a painting by Rogier van der Weyden, some youth in a diptych, with his hands folded in prayer and an enormous nose, dead now for many centuries, but still lustrous with youth; and then go home to masturbate to one of the Pakistanis in plaid shirts in Toronto. What was missing, however, was a live human being. Even the exhibitionist disappeared – at least, I had not seen him for so long I assumed he had tired of our gym, and moved to the gay one, where he would have a bigger audience.

Then one Sunday evening I went down to the museum for a concert of 19th-century English art songs, entered the museum auditorium and stopped to survey the crowd to see if the friend I'd agreed to meet there had saved me a seat. But I could find him nowhere, and there were few seats left, so I went to the very back of the room, and sat down beside a quartet of Asian women. Then, after I'd perused the program (a soprano and pianist singing songs associated with the countryside, in conjunction with a show of paintings by Constable), I looked around at the rest of the audience and saw, sitting two rows ahead, in a red and black plaid shirt, with his back to me, the man from the International Monetary Fund. Next to him was a man equally bald, but younger, if the dark color of what hair the barber had left on the sides of his closely shaved head was any indication. They were a perfect match. The head of the young man was almost the same shape as Daniel's, though the young man's skull was dented, with small craters at the back.

The exhibitionist read his program, then looked around, then returned to the program, as did his date, but neither one spoke or smiled or laughed. Then the date looked back in my direction to see where the slide projector for the show was. He had long, curved, black eyebrows, black eyes, a large nose–as big, really, as Daniel's–and a black goatee. He was just the sort of man I was attracted to, but hadn't the nerve to cruise. He was still swimming in the hormonal sea, a dark shark flickering through its dim depths. That, I assumed, was the reason they were together – not because one or both of them loved 19th-century English art songs; they were on a date whose cultural antipasto was merely a pretext for the sex to follow, or had been going together for a while now and were just out for the evening, in real life, not cyberspace.

The date's thumbs were big. His shoulders seemed to be broader than the exhibitionist's. Daniel was a slight, small man, really. His hair was grizzled white at this point, even his beard. His expression, even in profile, was blank, a mere radar screen ready to receive an impression, an organism whose intelligent eyes and enormous nose were all directed toward one thing – the gathering of tribute to his dick. This was the function of the date, I assumed, whose youth was offset by the fact that he had already lost his hair, making him more serious, more masculine, than a man his age with locks. There was something both touching, and comical, about their two heads side by side, sundered by age, united by alopecia (baldness; from the Latin for fox-mange).

The effect of going bald on a man cannot be under-estimated. It seems like a small thing – it does not threaten one's health – but it has huge emotional significance, even if one cannot speak of it without being chided or laughed at. Men who go bald at an early age I suspect are touched in some elemental way by death long before those who keep their hair till they are laid in the coffin. Going bald is a chastening thing, and going bald in one's twenties must be even more so. People love to run their hands through, or grab on to, their partners' hair during sex. Clutching a head of hair is a form of possession, one of the most primitive there is, the way we imagine cave men dragging women off. Women when young wear their hair long, down their shoulders, gleaming and brushed – the flag of their fertility. Then, as they grow older, they cut it short, their days of sexual advertisement over. A bald man has no options. He walks into every room scalped, with a piece of himself missing – looking like a businessman, a banker, a retired accountant, no matter what his temperament. The light gleams on his skull, the cold wind blows across it, he is exposed. The fact that it is caused by testosterone – the fact that the term is male pattern baldness, and many of us find bald men sexy – is of small comfort. One is forced to look like something one does not wish to look like. One is forced to resemble Dean Rusk, or Mister Magoo, or – why not say it? – the head of a penis.

It was just as I was wondering if the logical step beyond fist-fucking would be to insert one's bald head into another man's rectum that the concert began: a young woman in a turquoise strapless gown came out, bowed to the audience, and began singing a song by Ralph Vaughan Williams. Then the accompanist, a short, plump, middle-aged man with glasses and wispy gray hair, went to the lectern, put a slide of a Constable painting on the wall, and gave a talk. With each new song, he changed the slide. For a while I forgot the couple two rows in front of me, and concentrated on the music. Then, halfway through the program, I noticed the date was looking not at the printout of the poems, following along as the woman sang them, but at the program itself. Hmm, I thought, he wants to see what the next thing is. That means he is bored. That means he does not like this music much. That means Daniel was the one who brought him here. I had seen Daniel at two events now: the lecture in the cemetery, and this concert; in other words, he and I had some of the same interests, the interests of educated men our age who enjoyed history and art. His date, on the other hand, was bored. Sure enough, at intermission, both men removed their black leather jackets from the backs of their chairs and stood up to leave: wrapped in the possession of each other's bodies.

The date changed appearance the moment he rose. The well-proportioned young man whose shoulders I had finally decided were broader than Daniel's was actually much, much taller than I had thought. He towered above Daniel by more than a foot. He was so tall his shoulders no longer looked broad, but rather narrow, on his large, ungainly body, whose hips seemed the biggest element in his physique. He was wearing blue jeans, and a thick black belt, he was enormous, and as I sat there watching them walk out, I thought: Daniel will be crushed when they have sex together, there will be no way he can crawl over that enormous torso and even match body parts. Surely they could not sixty-nine. He would be like a monkey climbing up a tree.

As I sat there wondering if the distance between the mouth and the genitals is uniform in every person, I spotted my friend in the third row, reading a book, went up to him and said that while I had enjoyed the songs thus far I could not imagine sitting through the William Walton setting of the Lord Mayor's Banquet, which, judging from the poems printed, would take a very, very long time, and therefore I was leaving.

Out through the gloomy foyer I went and then downstairs to see them walk off together into the night, and thus extend the slim sense of possession I'd had in finding them at the concert – but when I emerged onto the steps of the museum they had already disappeared – no doubt in a taxi, I thought, back to Daniel's apartment, as I walked home alone down the deserted avenue. The porn I'd been looking at that day – Thomas fucks Frankie on www.HisFirstHugeCock.com – would not be enough this evening, nor even the two Pakistanis in Toronto on www.silverdaddies.com with whom I'd gone to the motel all winter, nor Ed and Hugo on the massage table on www.Un-der-wear.com (not even the ecstatic moment when Ed finally lets Hugo inside him, Ed's legs spread wide, Hugo's mouth shoving his tongue down Ed's throat) – so I lay down on my daybed when I got home, and began imagining the two men at the concert together. We assume the taller man is always the top, but it was only when I switched their roles, like a novelist who finally sees where a particular scene should go, and pictured the young man on his knees, gasping, slobbering, and begging for Daniel's cock, that my erection sprang to life. The two men sat in Daniel's apartment – entirely naked, Daniel in a green, high-backed chair, the younger, much taller man, on his knees at Daniel's feet, in considerable distress. The tall, young, darkly handsome, goateed, giant was a quivering mess. Either drugs, or extended foreplay, had raised him to such a pitch, he was slobbering, as he sat back on his haunches, pulling at his penis, while staring, like a beaten dog, at Daniel's dick, which, half-soft, Daniel held loosely in his hand as he sat there with a cold expression on his face, the neutral, inquiring, open-to-any-offer blankness replaced by the cold, haughty mien of the Jewish grandee, turning ever icier with each gasped importunity from the man on his knees before him, who was pulling his penis ever more rapidly, and rising up to kiss the dick Daniel held half-soft in his own hand as he sat there in the armchair, with one leg crossed over the other. Then Daniel spoke. "You stupid pig," he said. "Get up, and go into the bathroom." In the bathroom Daniel peed on the young man's face. Then they went back to the living room, where the young man got on the dining room table, raised his big hairy legs into the air, and Daniel inserted his dick, with a cold expression – like the one I assumed whenever we passed in the locker room. At that point I squirted onto the Classified ads. As I did so I noticed a burning sensation, as if the sperm itself was hot, which made me recall that the Romans believed the best children came from a hot fuck.

The next day I saw Daniel at the gym. He entered the locker room in a beautiful gray three-piece suit and a dark gray herringbone overcoat, carrying his briefcase and a maroon silk scarf, just as I was on my way out. I frowned, then looked at the ground. But before doing so, I could see his face assume a crestfallen expression, as if he could not understand why a perfect stranger could loathe him so.

Blood Heat

Chaz Brenchley

I came in from a sudden summer rainstorm, wet and unready
and late for my shift.

No coat, naturally, and I wasn't going to stand and drip-
dry in the hall. I went straight through to Quin's room, my
fingers rubbing raindrops from my hair; a voice said, "Do
you want a towel for that?"

"In a minute. First things first," and this was always the
first thing: I walked over to the high incongruous hospital
bed, kissed Quin lightly, asked him how he was.

Not so good today, not talking; but he hadn't said much for
a week or two. It still felt important to ask. To ask him. The
day I turned to other people first, that would be the day that
something broke between us, as it had already broken between him and the world.

With no reply but nothing broken, I could turn to the
ledger by the bed, read up the last day's notes; and check the
level in his drip, check the regulator, check his eyes weren't
too dry, grab a temperature reading –

"Wouldn't dream of saying hullo for you, obviously, but I
did do all the rest."

That voice again, amused; so I could smile as I said, "I'm
sure you did, and now I've done it too, so we're both happy."

And so I could straighten up at the bedside there, I could
turn with my hand still on his shoulder where it lay bare and
bony and exposed; I could find the owner of the voice,
leaning in the doorway, deliberately posed with a towel in

his hands, which he must have slipped out to fetch while I was being ritual with Quin.

I'm a hands man, I can't help it. It's the way I was trained. Blame Quin, if you want to blame anyone. If blame attaches, which I really don't believe it does. I think we're hard-wired, to focus on a feature. There are size queens and bottom-biters, there are those who are drawn to a bear's hairy neck or a boi's smooth cheek; whether they look for the same thing every time or whether they go for variations on the theme, everyone finds their point of attraction. You can play it up as a kink if you choose to, but it's a way to say we're all kinky for something. I think it's just the way the system works.

For me, it's always been hands. Oh, I get as turned on as the next man by the fine tight curve of a buttock, and I am as intrigued as the next man by the endless variety of cocks out there, and I do kind of want to play with all of them, just to see, but still it's hands that I look to first. They're what I remember best, how I'd pick a man out in a line-up.

Like this: he held the towel out, and I smiled and thanked him and walked across the room; I took the towel and rough-dried my hair while we introduced ourselves, while we explained ourselves to each other; I was physically and intimately aware of him, my night's companion, my fellow nurse standing in arm's reach as we talked – and yet, when I was done, when he twitched the towel out of my fingers and went away, I'd have sweated to give a description that anyone else could work with.

Blond, yes – except that I doubted the word as soon as it came up. Younger than me, shorter than me, but not so much of either; just an impression, two impressions, nothing that I could swear to. Clean-shaven, I thought. Clothes? Well, God only knew what he was wearing on his legs – see, this is what I mean, I'm never a crotch-watcher first off; but he had a regular cotton shirt on, that much I was sure of, because the cuffs of it were liminal in my mind's eye, stripes of Oxford blue that hid his wrists and emphasised his hands.

Which were broad and strong, a farmer's hands; thick

spatulate fingers with the nails scrupulously short, the way that dentists keep them, waiters, anyone with their hands in the public eye and hygiene a matter of concern. There is no art to tell a man's profession from his hands, but I do keep trying.

They were good hands. Challenging. Robust. What I remembered.

When he came back, those good hands were wrapped around two mugs of coffee, which was also good. He passed me one and went back to where he'd clearly been sitting in the far corner, where I hadn't seen him on my way in. We kept the light dim for Quin's comfort, and he hadn't turned on the anglepoise lamp above his chair; I forgave myself for over-looking him, and took the chance now to look him over, in what extra light spilled in from the hallway through the open door.

Hair the colour of wet straw, as it happened: darkly blond, like shadows at sunrise. Eyes indeterminate at this distance, but light and watchful, more interested than wary, returning my own scrutiny quite unabashed: he might have been shy and wasn't, might have been awkward in this unpredictable company but showed no signs of it.

He didn't look heavy, exactly, but very grounded, secure in his own weight: his body a match for those hands, broad and stocky. Rugby sooner than soccer, I thought, and sooner than cricket too: strength over speed, impact over grace. Legs apart as he sat quietly attentive in his chair, waiting to see what came; there was power in him, and he wore it indifferently, and I liked that.

In honesty, I liked everything I saw. I'm not saying that looking at his hands gave me a hard-on, that would be weird and let's not go there. It's myself I'm giving away here, of course, I know that, but be reasonable. Just because a man's hands are his first line of attack, just because hands are my kink doesn't mean that I imagine every man's hands slicked up and sliding over my skin, seeking finger by blind finger into the tender heat between my buttocks, finding out that hidden pressure that can melt me every time . . .

No. Not every man's hands, not most men's. I don't. And not here. But what this guy's hands said about him, which the rest of his body backed up – well, if this were a nightclub rather than a sickroom, I might have made a move. I might well have been up for that.

When Quin decided, when he decreed that he would do his dying at home, thanks, we all understood what that meant: that we his friends would have to be his nurses. It used not to be a hard duty. In the early days, we did little more than keep Quin company and take some of the pressure off his partner Gerard.

But Quin got sicker, and Gerard's work took him away, often and often. We learned new skills, rewrote the schedule, sent out a call for volunteers. We were always teamed in pairs for a shift; these later days, as often as not I was teamed with someone new, someone who'd never known Quin except like this, a husk, departing.

"So how do we pass the time?" he asked: not bored, not aggressive, not anxious. Certainly not leering: if he'd caught that touch of interest in me, he was quite properly ignoring it. Just curious, I thought, and mature enough to ask, sooner than bully or blunder his way into a gaucherie.

"Oh, however you like. People read, talk. There's music here. Every game ever invented for two players, in that cupboard there. Crosswords, jigsaws. Or there's a TV in the other room."

"But?"

Oh, he was quick. I grinned. "But that's considered heretical by the old guard. Quin wouldn't have one in the house; we only got it a month ago, because some of the kids who volunteered this term just can't imagine eight long hours without it. It's fine if you want to, we don't both need to be in here and Gerard's away, you won't be disturbing anybody . . ."

"But," he said again, as though that was almost sufficient; and then, because it wasn't, quite, "Wouldn't want to be a heretic, my first night on. Backgammon bewilders me, I don't get the point, but I can play chess or go, or half a dozen card games. Or if you'd rather just sit and read, I'm up for that too."

My turn. "But?"

"But, first off, why don't you tell me about you and Quin?"

It had been in the back of my mind, if not on the tip of my tongue, to ask about him and Quin. That might seem to be an invitation to talk about himself, but it wasn't really; it was quite the opposite, a way to interrogate Quin obliquely. There was no Quin-and-him, except for this: a volunteer and a dying man, with never a word passed between them. I would dearly love to know how Quin did that. When he was active, when he was engaged with the world, then it was easy, you could just stand back and watch it happen; kids would hurl all their youth and energy at his feet, and he'd step daintily between them and take whatever he fancied from each, give back whatever he felt like sharing. I should know, I was one among them.

Then he got sick and was suddenly more demanding, having no energy of his own; and that was fine, we were already committed, bought and paid for. It was still and always worth the time and troubles he asked of us, just to have access, to be Quin's Crew, something ineffably larger than the sum of us its parts. We knew, we gloried in it; no surprise, if others wanted in. We made room, and welcome.

Now, though: when he was more than bedridden, body-ridden, caught entirely within himself, when even that voice was lost; what did he have now, to snare them with? Where did the magnetism lie, if it wasn't in the touch of eye and hand, nor yet in the words that came with?

It was, perhaps, in his story, the man of words reduced to a bitter shell and failing, fading fast. I'd have liked to ask; but

my partner tonight had got his question in first, and you
learned to be scrupulous around Quin.

Besides, what he offered was an open invitation. If I'd
asked him, he'd have talked about himself, so that I could
learn more about Quin; because he asked me, I could talk
about Quin directly. Which I don't get to do much any more.

It felt strange, telling tales of the old Quin – the raptor, the
insatiable, the unrelenting – in his own room, in his hearing if
he could still hear me. I had to sit with my back to his bed, my
attention turned away from him entirely; which was why it
needed my co-worker, looking over my shoulder, to say,
"Uh, I think – is he *bleeding?*"

"Oh, damn – is he?" I looked back quickly, for the telltale
dark dribble from his mouth. "Okay, no panic. We've got
him on his side already, so he's not going to inhale it and
choke. It's probably just leakage. You want to deal with that?
I'll talk you through," but it was his chance to prove that he
was fit for this, that blood didn't make him queasy, nor being
intimate with a more or less unconscious body.

He gave me a fairly sardonic glance, recognizing a test
when it was flung in his teeth; and stepped up to the plate, to
the bedside, with no hesitation; and was just reaching for
paper towel when I stopped him.

"No. Gloves first. Always, glove up first. It's like air-
planes, when they tell parents to see to their own oxygen
mask before their children's? Feels counter-intuitive, I
know, but it's crucial. Your safety is Quin's most precious
possession," and I was quoting here, not being epigrammatic
on my own account. "Soon as there's blood around, you
glove up before you touch him."

Technically, we were supposed to glove up before we
touched him at all, blood or no blood. Some people did,
at least sometimes; not me. I could give an old friend a bath,
at least, without being afraid to touch him. I insisted on that.

Good sense insisted on this, though, when there was blood
on the case. I watched him pull on the disposable gloves, and

then told him to do it again: "Double-glove it if there's time. Just to make assurance doubly sure. He bites, you know."

"If he bites me, I'll thump him." But he was obediently working on the second round of gloving when Quin suddenly bucked in the bed, and was choking despite what I'd said before: doing it to spite me, most likely, flooding his mouth with so much blood some of it inevitably backed up into his lungs. And I reached for him instinctively, because I was so close and so ready for it, and there was an arm suddenly across my chest and a voice, "No! You glove up first, while you tell me what to do . . ."

He tossed me the box of gloves, and I took a cold and deliberate pace backwards, not to be tempted.

"Right. Under the bed, there's a bucket. Got it? Right. Just hold his head, and let it come."

"Is that all we do?" Incredulous is what he sounded, as he did that thing and Quin gouted darkly into the bucket, like a teenager throwing up his first bottle of vodka, on and on.

"Pretty much. He'll dry up, or he won't. Give it five minutes. If he doesn't, then it could be his portal vein's ruptured big-time again, and there's nothing much we can do except yell for help. Gill comes round with units of blood and all her doctor-stuff, and sorts him out. If she can't do it, then it's hospital or nothing," which was the choice none of us wanted to make, break a promise or let him die, "but she always has, so far."

Gloved-up and double-gloved, I was fit to help; and usefully so, as Quin bucked and twisted, his whole body seized with the pain of convulsion. Moving hurt him so much; we struggled to hold him still, and never mind if the blood went into the bucket or onto the bed, or all over us.

At last there was no more coming up. Quin sank back slowly into his pillows, into his torpor; I gave him a morphine shot, mostly because I thought he deserved it, and reached for the phone.

In response to a quizzical glance across the bed – hazel, I thought his eyes were, though it was still hard to be certain in this low light and easy to be distracted by the blood-boltered face around them – I said, "I know, he stopped of his own accord. But that was . . . extreme, and I want Gill to have a look at him anyway. She may want to put a couple of units back into him. Besides, frankly, I'm scared he might start again. I'd like to have a professional here, if he does."

So I phoned, and Gill came with blood and bag and back-up, a GP-in-training who was shadowing her practice. We'd barely started on the clear-up, just because I didn't want to disturb Quin now that he'd settled again; before she'd even got to him, the blessed Gill looked us up and down and said, "Good grief. You two just go and get yourselves sorted out, yes?"

"No point," I said. "Not until we've got him cleaned up and the bed changed and so on. We'd only get mucky again."

"Sweetheart, just look at yourselves. Do you seriously think I'm going to allow you anywhere near the clean sheets, or anything else? Or us, come to that? The state you're in?"

We couldn't actually look at ourselves; no mirrors on the walls any more, they'd upset Quin during his last days up and around in the house and we'd taken them all down. So we looked at each other in lieu, him and me, and – well, she had a point.

Besides, it was his first shift. A baptism of fire is one thing, a baptism of blood is something more; it lingers. In your hair, at the back of your throat, on your mind. I couldn't say so, but I did think maybe he'd had enough.

So did Gill. We were halfway up the stairs when she called after us, to say that she'd stay with Quin till the morning team came in.

"Is that normal?" he asked me, on the landing.

"It's not unknown, after an episode like this. Sometimes he just needs professional cover, and she's it. And – well, it's easy to forget, but Gill and Quin were friends for a long time before she was his doctor. She's a volunteer here, as much as the rest of us; I think sometimes she likes to sit a shift with him, just to be there, the way the rest of us do."

"Okay. So what do we do?"

"Shower and change," I said, pushing him into the wet-room. "After that, it's up to us. Stay and talk to Gill; talk to ourselves in the other room, if it looks like she wants to be alone with him. Or go for a walk, go find an all-night café for an early breakfast, go home. Whatever. First off, let's just get clean."

When Quin got sick, when he decreed that we should nurse him at home, when we agreed: that was when we spent a lot of his money, unless it was Gerard's, converting their big upstairs bathroom into a proper wetroom. It was easier to manage him if three of us could get under the shower at once, easier to get him in and out of the bath if we didn't have to worry about spillage. It used to soak through, and drip down the light fitting in his study; now we could flood the floor, and it all just drained away.

Once he got too sick for anything wetter than a bedbath, we were still glad to have it there, just for our own sakes. Some of us liked to shower before a shift, or to wallow in a deep hot bath after; some of us dealt with the stress by running it off, pounding miles around the streets, and then again a power shower was good to come back to after.

And, of course, Quin had days or nights like this, which left everyone in a mess. At these times a really functional wetroom wasn't only a blessing, it was next thing to essential. Oh, we'd have managed without, of course we would – but from this end, it was hard to imagine how.

I pushed him in and peeled off my own stained and sodden clothes with the swiftness of experience: sweatshirts and old jeans, no buttons to fuss with. He fumbled at his shirt, frowned, realized he was still gloved up; glanced at me sharply and yes, I was grinning, and not trying to hide it.

"We all do that," I said. "Not just the first time, either.

It's an occupational hazard. Here," and I stepped up like a penitent to undo all his buttons for him, cheerfully pretending that the gloves had been his only problem. He pulled them off one by one and stared down at his hands, as if startled by their pale still-scrubbed cleanliness; as if neither one of us could see the way they were shaking.

He looked at them, he looked at me. I waited, to see which way he'd jump.

"What," he said, "I suppose this is reaction, is it?"

Good man. I nodded, toeing off my trainers and kicking them into the corner after my clothes.

"Again, we all get it. And again, not just the first time. There's still something about it," *being right up close and personal with an old friend while he spews his blood up*, but I really didn't need to spell that out, "it shakes me up every time. Getting clean helps; I think it's the steam and the heat, as much as the actual scrubbing. More." One thing I'd learned this year, one of the many things: scrub as hard as you like, something always lingers. Blood under the fingernails, something. Even through two layers of gloves, all the protection you can bear. "I hope you like your shower scalding hot."

If he hesitated, it was only for a moment. I encouraged him, by stripping off my underwear; he smiled a little, shrugged a little, unhitched his trousers. Just as well, or I'd have done it for him; you can't *be* body-shy in that kind of intimate nursing. He'd learn.

Maybe I'd get to teach him.

I was already thinking, I might like to adjust my shifts over the next few weeks, see if I could tie them in with his; we'd been interrupted this evening, and I would like to get to know him better.

Significantly better, in one respect at least.

He turned his back to shuck his underpants, and I'd have frowned at that concealing impulse, if I hadn't been so taken by the view it gave me: broad clean shoulders and a pleasing spine, a chunky body all the way but all of it in proportion, good strong legs and a peach of an arse to top them.

I said already, I'm a hands man, but – well, it's good when they come with a package.

Also, all that smug righteousness about not being body-shy? Well, I'm not; but I was suddenly dealing with a whole different issue here, a degree of attraction I didn't feel for anyone else on the team. Now it was me turning my back, heading for the shower controls and slamming them on, dialling the heat way up, buying myself some time, maybe a little concealing steam . . .

Dream on. I glanced over my shoulder, and saw him coming to join me under the hammer of the shower-head; and there was nowhere near enough steam yet to hide his own burgeoning hard-on.

Nor the direction of my eyes. He saw me look, he shrugged; in the interests of fairness, I turned and showed him mine.

Then we both cracked up, and the awkwardness washed away in a flurry of adolescent hooting under a blast of superheated steam.

"Does that," he gasped, leaning both hands against the tiled wall and leaving a streak of pink that diluted as I watched, "does that happen often?"

"No," I confessed, "no, it doesn't – but have you met the other guys on the team?"

That cost me a buffet on the chest that had me reeling for a moment, before he grabbed at me to keep me upright. "Whoo, sorry – you shouldn't make me laugh, I'm not safe out. You okay?"

"I'm fine. Rugby player, right?"

"Stand-off half, but I haven't played much since college. How did you guess?"

"Not guessing. I can tell, from the bruises I'll sport in the morning."

He blew me an infant raspberry, and moved back under the stream of water. I followed, hooking up a bottle of shampoo en route. Squirted it directly into his thick thatch of hair, and worked it like a salon specialist, firm massage at the same time as I washed out all the blood.

One brief moment of stillness, and then he was leaning back into my hands, grunting gently. When he could find words, they were typical of him: intelligent, challenging, direct.

"Seriously – why do I feel so horny? I've shared a lot of showers in my time, and I'm not usually this hormonal."

"Seriously," I said, "it's what you said before. It's a reaction. That happens, down there," directly below our feet, Quin's room was, "and you get through it. Then you come up here and shuck it off, slough it off, wash it off. In here it's a whole different kind of physical, it's an invitation, and your body's not going to turn it down."

"Really? This happen often, does it?"

"Not often, no." I turned him round, and said, "Fooling around, sure. That kind of stress-relief. Release. Locker-room stuff. Not this." His balls were wet and heavy in my hand; his cock was the only slender thing about him, skinned like silk, not cut, and oddly aesthetic on a man whose body was so utilitarian. Even jutting hard, it still had an unexpected grace to it.

"So why –?"

"Why don't you stop talking?"

I kissed him, and his mouth was cool against the burn of all that water sluicing down over his face, over mine. It was a refuge, a place to be; his tongue was a companion.

His hands, those big hands on my body, on my back; cracking my butt-cheeks apart, so that one broad finger could work gently, insinuatingly against the sensitivity of my anus.

Then not so gently. Poking, pushing its way inside me with no more lube than the water trickling down my crack, so that I was the one who shuddered suddenly now.

Also, I was the one – older, maybe wiser, far more familiar with house rules – who had to pull away, hold him off, get out from under the water there; who said, "Wait. Just, wait there . . ."

Over to the toilet, where there's a basket of condoms on the cistern that we always keep topped up; I grabbed an assorted handful, and was halfway back before I had another thought. I could hear him groan in a kind of impetuous urgency, you couldn't call it language but it carried all the meaning that it needed; and even so, I went over to the door and shoved the bolt across before I went back to the water. Just in case.

I dropped the condoms into the soap-tray below the shower head, stuck my mouth by his ear and said, "Glove, and double-glove. You choose."

Under the shower's thunder – the heat and the pressure, as much as the noise of it – it was hard to speak, hard to think. Easy to play, of course, to soap and rub each other, but this was abruptly not about being playful any more. Some harder, more demanding spirit had overtaken both of us: more need than desire, like being so hungry your hands can barely make a sandwich, or so tired that you cry.

Did he knock the shower off, or was that me? I don't know: only that we were wet and warm but that flow of scorching water was gone now, so that the KY didn't wash off his fingers before he could ease them – swiftly, roughly, the opposite of body-shy, but it did still feel easy – past my sphincter and so deep inside me.

When he slipped his fingers out – too soon! – I gulped a protest, but slick as they were, those same fingers were neat and quick to slide first one and then a second condom onto my stiff cock, one and then another onto his own; and then his hands were quick to turn me, quick to guide his cock to where it could nudge like a sniffing dog, curious and intent; where it could press, urge, thrust like – well, like nothing so much as an eager cock.

One of the things about setting up a wetroom for an invalid, there are plenty of grab-handles all over. I grabbed, and hung on hard.

*   *   *

Nothing came off the wall.

When he came, he did it like a gentleman, quietly explosive, and the shiver was in him for a long, bone-melting moment after; and he was ahead of me, and so quickly onto his knees to work with mouth and tongue – and nipping teeth, okay through double rubber – and fingers too until I felt that hot surge draining out my marrow.

I dropped down to join him on the floor, and we sat leaning against the wall in a kind of amicable and mutual exhaustion, just lightly holding hands; and he said, "No obligations, right?"

"Not a one," I agreed, rubbing my thumb across the back of his fingers. *Good* hands, that man has.

"Because I wouldn't want, well, this," his head, bumping lightly against my shoulder, "to get in the way of . . ." A gesture, downwards: Quin, and all that he implied.

"I swear." This might have sprung from that, surely must have done, in all its rampant urgency. I thought it was an affirmation, from one traumatic act of intimacy to another. You cling to life any way you can, wherever you can find it. Quin did it in the shadows of his room, retchingly; we apparently did it in his wetroom, climactically. But I'd nursed Quin through other bleeds, and not felt any need to do this after. I was quite comfortable, then, to grin at him and say, "If I want to pursue you, I'll do it off-duty and outside this house."

"Oh. Good. Um, do you want to pursue me?"

"You'll need to give me your phone number, before we go home," which was as good an answer as any. And then I reached above my head for the shower control, and dialled up a slow warm sprinkle; and got to my feet and pulled him up after me, reached for the gel and said, "Oh, one more thing."

"What's that?"

"Well, only that I wasn't really concentrating, earlier,

when we introduced ourselves," I'd been too focused on those hands of his.

"So?"

"So you'll need to give me your name, too . . ."

PATH

G. Winston James

Who knew that it would take such a long time to fill so few empty minutes? I did, or would have normally. But I guess it's understandable that I might forget when so immediately in the moment, in the heat, crush and press of the moment. The amnesia of sweaty, logic-less seconds compounding so mysteriously, forcing the rational and the remembered to disappear imperceptibly, instantly. Perhaps it was the crush, after all, that caused me to forget how long it can take to silence my lust and to get moving back on my way.

It wasn't a very crowded train that morning – the PATH from Journal Square. Not any more densely packed with commuters than on most days. Still, I knew immediately when I got on that that day's ride would be more eventful than usual. More intimate than the norm. As if there was something almost tangible moving among the passengers. Lifting women's skirts, brushing the denim of men's crotches, stroking everyone's nipples. Resting finally on him. Pulsing there.

Or perhaps it was more that there was something in his half-closed eyes, or in the shine and slow-sliding silent question on his lips, than anything physical about the train itself. There was an energy, a revealing. A pulling. But all of that is relatively unimportant. What is important is that because of it all, I knew. With no rainbow flag pins or protesting pink triangles, nor even the quickest adjustment of his trade, I knew that this man in business attire could be had if I played my fifteen minutes on the rails between New Jersey and New York just right. A short commute too often mitigates the effectiveness of non-verbal communication, but still I had hopes. And there was that energy. Palpable. Vibrating. There.

He was tall. Much like myself, but olive-complected, where I am a deeper brown. As slender as he needed to be to attract me, dressed in a suit of material as fine as it was well-tailored, he was simply handsome. Beyond that, sexy. It was summertime; he glowed. Warm. I wanted to touch him. To feel the color beneath my fingers that a passionless, silent sun had left behind. To stroke him in a way that said, "This skin of yours, it matters. I care deeply about hue." I moved further in his direction.

I'm not sure where he was from – Latino, Arab, Israeli or some multi-culti mix – but at 8:35 in the morning I could see that he would only be more lovely at noon, and someone else's erection by three. I'd have to work fast and be direct, yet somehow subtle. Like a twenty-dollar bill on a dance floor, I hoped I could entice him to stoop low enough to pick me up in a way that none of the others on the train would see.

He was standing to the left of the door opposite the one I'd stepped through. Leaning against the wall and the faux-wood divider at the end of the row of seats. I walked directly towards him. Eyes to his eyes. To others it would look like we were going to speak. If the move worked as I hoped, he would straighten as if he knew me. Focus on me to remember a face he would believe he had forgotten. By the time he realized that he hadn't met me before, it would be too late. I would be inside that sphere of personal space outside of which the rest of the world dissolves into dim shapes, shadow, and murmur. I would be in that blind spot that most men possess, but of which few take advantage in public. If I was right about the energy I felt around him, he would stand stock still in order to time just right our eventual collision.

When he did as I expected, I ran my stare like fingers down his face and chest to his zipper, then back to his eyes as I stood closer to him than was necessary on a leisurely ride like that morning's.

The fact that he didn't adjust himself in response to my nearness was a very good sign. His eyes yawned and fluttered as memories of sleep still held him. He crossed his hands over his crotch. No doubt to test and to draw my attention. I let my right hand fall to within two inches of his knuckles. Waited.

I wondered then whether wishing could make a man rub his dick against the back of my hand on a train. Whether my wanting could cause our trip along the turbulent tracks to rock my fingertips momentarily beneath his testicles. Whether desiring it could make me bold enough to keep my hand there. Kneading his genitals slowly. Surreptitiously. I wondered many things and hoped.

If ever I'd doubted the power of creative visualization before, I became a changed man that morning as he unclasped his hands, put one behind his back (bringing himself closer to me) and moved his feet even more forward. My heart moaned. Blood surged like evening tide just beneath my skin. The man seated at the end of the row next to where we stood heard my blush. He glanced over at my hand lightly grazing the material of my conquest's trousers. I glared at him where he sat and saw jealousy clenching little fists behind his eyes. He was as gay as I am and as desirous. I noticed then that every homosexual on the train had looked up at us at almost the same moment. They knew that sex had uncrossed his muscled legs and was slowly standing in that train. That energy filling the car, obvious and sweaty to anyone who could feel and smell it.

With our faces fixed in the humdrum expression of morning, I rubbed his dick with the back of my hand, and slowly moved my right hip between his thighs. When he could, he stroked my ass. By then we were uncaring, believing that only other homosexuals – creatures specially attuned, like wolves – would see. We were impossibly bold. Cavalier in our not-so-secret touching of balls, dicks, ass, and eyes. It was strangely beautiful to be so unthinking, to feel so free.

When we arrived at the World Trade Center, though, I found myself suddenly in a quandary: to continue to pursue or not to pursue. To get to work on time or to fuck the establishment and blow him as I wanted.

He headed towards the restroom on the first landing, just at the top of the escalators from the train. I hesitated only a second before – as it would appear to any onlooker – I too suddenly realized I had to pee. I couldn't believe my eyes as, entering the restroom, I rounded the corner, hoping to stand at a urinal next to him, and found that at 9:00 a.m., every single, solitary toilet was occupied. Men with eyes darting down and into the urinals next to them. Arms moving when to my knowledge urine needs no external help to be freed. Perhaps they didn't start work until 9:30, but I was not so lucky. I wanted to ask them to leave, but realized as the words touched my lips that I had little right to be so demanding.

Instead of fighting, I motioned with my head that my new friend should follow me upstairs to the smaller restroom behind the escalators, to the left of Duane Reade in the mall. There were three stalls, two urinals and one resident homeless man bathing in the sink. I stepped into the stall for the physically challenged – and wondered for an instant if, all things considered, I might not be handicapped myself in some way. With a quick flick of the hand, I silently asked him to join me in the slightly larger than usual stall.

There was true fear in his eyes then. "We can't do that," he said. "What about the cops?" he asked. Yet each word had somehow brought him farther into the stall. I simply stopped listening, knowing this variation of "Don't stop. Don't stop," all too well. I closed and latched the swinging door behind him. Fortunately, he left his chatter outside.

He shut up, unzipped his zipper, fished in his boxers and spilled his fucking dick all over my arm. "No, ma'am!" I thought. I wanted to call the homeless man in to see. His trade was longer and more girthy even than my own. One of the rarer of treats. With a dick so big and chicken eggs for balls, I couldn't have chanted "Nam Myoho Renge Kyo" enough times in my lifetime to ask for that.

I literally dropped to my knees with a thump. I was looking at his dick, almost waiting for it to speak. He began speaking in sign; one of his hands touched my head and the index finger of the other motioned me to climb on. I opened my mouth and wet it as far down as I could go, then withdrew. I held it in my hands; uttered a requisite, whispering "umm, uumm, uummm"; and licked the parts my restrictive throat and tonsils hadn't allowed me to pursue. Then I sucked his dick like I was late for work.

One hand just as wet as my tongue, following behind my mouth as I let those inches slide in and out. Stroking circles around the head for good measure. I stopped only once to wipe away tears and to make sure that his eyes were glued to the space at the hinge of the stall. I was nervous, in an absent sort of way, as the homeless man's agitated mumble increased outside the cubicle. I hoped his insanity wouldn't attract too much attention. There was already more than enough frenzied madness going on inside my mouth, my hands, and the witnessing walls of the stall. I looked up to make sure that he was vigilant. It wouldn't have done, after all, to be caught by the police on my knees devouring cock in an Armani. He smiled down at me and said, "Just suck my dick. You gonna make me come."

That was the point, after all. When he roughly moved my hand away and started fucking my face, I knew he was close and I loved him as one does trade in such moments.

"You want it in your mouth?" he panted.

"Ahhhh, no," I thought. It's Tuesday morning. I have no toothpaste. No mouthwash. And I'm not crazy enough to think that come doesn't smell like come when it's laying heavy on the breath. I shook my head urgently so he'd know. Thankfully, he understood.

As his streams of come fell into the toilet, I wiped the corners of my mouth and looked at my watch for the first time since I'd first genuflected in the stall. 9:30! Oh my God, I thought, imagining the department heads gathered for the meeting that I had called the day before and should have run. The one that should have begun right then. I didn't know what I was going to do.

My new friend was gone by the time I looked up. Taking his sexiness and my sense of satisfaction with him. I imagined that later he would dry the thin layer of moisture from his dick and wonder if his boxers smelled of my breath, stomach acids, and his come. He would think of me and I would think of him, even though I hadn't seen him leave. Hadn't really cared to watch him go.

Minutes and men, I thought then. Minutes and men. So little to hold onto when encounters with them are done.

I gathered myself and headed home to be sick. From work, of course, though there was the option of feeling better by the afternoon. I really had forgotten that it could take so long to get so little accomplished. As the train doors closed behind me, I realized ruefully that I still hadn't come. I looked at the fellow seated next to me and wondered.

Code Voyeur

Bob Angell

Geek is sexy. Geek is true. Queer geeks will break your heart and they may never know it. It's those little obsessions that get them. Or get you when you least expect it.

My subconscious nature is to overload myself with impossible or nearly impossible tasks that look seductively doable, kind of like one-night stands. Take work, for instance.

There's this new guy, a kid really, works with me in the LAMP pool; that's Linux, Apache, MYSQL, and PHP, or L-A-M-P; decoded that means the computer platform, the web server, the database, and the language that my company, Mutagenic Software Corporation, uses to develop most of our applications.

They put the kid, Juan Ha, into the cubicle across the aisle from me. From day one he pounded on his keyboard nonstop, ten hours a day, a tinny drone often squeaking from headphones clamped over his ears.

You know how you can tell when co-workers switch programs? There's this little moment of silence, maybe a click or three of a mouse? A lot of clicks in a row mean they are shopping or surfing. Short little bursts of typing followed by long pauses usually means they are instant messaging with someone. If they haven't muted their sound cues, you hear every damned reply until it drives you insane.

It was rare that Juan slowed down or changed his clunky rhythm, so I suspected he either didn't have any friends or he was a shark angling for god status in the company.

To tell you the truth, I didn't care either way. I wanted only one thing, and I knew it the moment Shawni from human resources escorted him in and showed him to his cubicle.

Juan was tall and thin, a waif really, and his clothes hung on him like smoke so that you only got a glimpse of his body now and then when he was seated and his shirt and jeans pulled tight across his back and butt. His hands were like spiders, long and more articulate than a Cirque du Soleil contortionist.

His soft hair was a deep chestnut brown that fell around his face in lazy curls. Juan Ha had perfect skin, yellow-tinged, rich looking like the cream on top of non-pasteurized milk, the first blush of a summer tan without the tan lines. I'd bet he had never seen sunlight and, being in the world of code hackers, I'd seen some real vampires in my time.

Shawni assigned Billy Mac, the first guy I'd slept with after joining Mutagenic two years ago, as Juan's buddy. It was Billy's job to show Juan the ropes and introduce him around. She left them in Juan's barren cubicle and sneered at me as she stomped away.

I took that as a challenge, and kept my distance. After all, mystery loves company.

"JJ?" Billy Mac said, leaning in. I pretended I was absorbed in the source code on my screen. "Dude! Hey, JJ!" He tapped me on the shoulder and I jumped appropriately.

"Billy, mon, what's up?" I said, standing, my eyes locked with Juan's incredible bright olive-green eyes, flecked with red and yellow around the black holes of his pupils. Impossibly long, black eyelashes surrounded dangerous, fluttering lids like Venus flytraps. He had perfectly symmetrical and child-like eyebrows.

I gave him my best bedroom smile, the one perfected on so many adults and mentors, and then brought up to weapons-grade in the DC bars.

My aim missed completely. Juan was staring at my screen where colored-enhanced patterns of machine-generated HTML code scrolled like liquid art.

"Nice," he said. "A table, six columns and four rows that I can see, with image slices and embedded links."

"Yeah, that's right."

"And all from a single database call?"

I nodded, wondering if he had good peripheral vision and could see my head.

"Yours?"

I nodded again.

He clasped his hands together, the long fingers engulfing his hands, and I imagined those fingers wrapping around me, playing across my chest. You know what they say about long fingers and thumbs. I had been attempting my own correlation over the years with some success, and Juan's were outstanding specimens, worth an investigation.

Billy Mac caught me staring, and then Juan was reaching for my keyboard. No boundaries on this one.

"That's pretty invasive," I said, wishing he'd reach for something else.

"Oh, sorry. I just wanted to scroll down."

That would be nice.

He backed off, and I said, "I wouldn't do that to you. Ever." Maybe he would take it as a signal of trustworthiness and integrity?

I extended my hand. "JJ," I said.

His fingers wrapped soft around the back of my hand and touched my thumb, sending sparks coursing through my gut. I imagined Juan in a Speedo, all bunched up in there and waiting to dive into anything. His eyes glided up my arm to my face and he stood there blinking.

"His name's Juan," Billy said, "Fresh meat from the university, with a Maryland Center for Cognitive Computing scholarship."

"Nice to meet you, Juan." I shook his hand, and then

peeled mine away, glancing at Billy. "I need to see you later, okay?"

Billy Mac nodded and took Juan out for the grand tour.

Billy and I rendezvoused in the break room. I needed to grill him on the newbie.

"So, what is it with Juan, Billy? Mild autism? Asperger's?

"Shawni said he's over-the-top smart. No other info." He stirred his coffee and shook his head. I looked away from that blond-haired, blue-eyed, and broad-shouldered wedge, and scanned the nearly empty break room. Sara and Josh, the newlyweds, were holding hands and sharing a latte. The poster on the wall behind them showed how to save a choking victim.

"That's all. No personal insights?" I asked.

"Come on, JJ. Since when have you met a great programmer without some form of Asperger's, whether diagnosed or cultivated? We all have our little social blind side and tics."

I frowned.

"How about your helpless appreciation of male beauty?"

"Good point," I said. "But hardly an affliction."

"No? You're an insensitive wet-end, JJ. If there was a door on your cubicle, there would be a lot more repetitive motion behind it."

"Harmless, but productive," I said, grinning.

Billy rolled his eyes and reached for his coffee.

"More cream?" I asked.

"You suck."

"True, and I have other talents of which you are aware, and some you are not."

"Like innuendo?"

"I'd like to get in –"

"Jordan," Billy said, his expression hardening. "Don't take advantage of the kid, okay? Don't break his heart, too."

"You know I won't. I never make the first move. You, of all people, should know that."

"The only move you ever make is walking away from

relationships. You're a conquistador, Jordan Jones, forever tilting at the next beautiful boy." Billy looked at Sara and Josh. The foam head on the forgotten latte between them had collapsed, but they continued whatever intense conversation they were stuck in.

"I don't know what you mean," I said, assuming perfect posture.

"No. I can see that you never will. You're cold, JJ. You worry about other people's social skills just so *you* won't get hurt."

Billy bowed his head, massaged his forehead with his hand while the silence stretched between us. He still loved me, but he might be right; I may never be ready for a relationship.

But what's wrong with that? There were so many men in the world.

Juan was at his desk, black T-shirt, jeans and rumpled hair, hacking away when I got to work. I mumbled, "Good morning," to the padded walls and set my coffee cup on the hot plate. Two of the cubicles around me mumbled back, but not Juan; it was like he hadn't heard me.

I had things to do, so I settled into my routine of email. I started working on the next code block on my prioritized list of functions, and that took me the rest of the morning.

Juan hardly moved. Whenever I'd stretch or lean back, there he was sitting forward in his chair, hunched over in front of his monitor. I could see the back of his head, the bumps of his spine under his T-shirt. There was the crescent of marble flesh between his belt and shirt that was bony and dimpled and delicious. His jean-covered butt was cradled in the mesh of the office chair, and I could see his legs to mid thigh before the jamb cut off the visuals. There were no soccer-developed gams on that boy. Of course not.

Billy popped in and asked me to lunch, probably a preventative strike. We invited Juan, but he grunted something and waved us away. At least it was an interaction.

"Stop it," Billy said.

"What?"

"You remind me of my dog when she was on the leash and saw a squirrel down the street. Her ears would perk up and her eyes would get big like she was trying to hypnotize it. The longing was so obvious."

"Woof."

"Shut up."

Mid afternoon, I was testing a function against the software requirements and decided to take a break. I stood and stretched, then casually walked across the aisle and leaned against Juan's door. He made no notice that I was there at all.

A sandwich wrapper lay crumpled on the desert of his desk beside a can of Mountain Dew. So he was a purist. No Jolt or ginseng-laced juice for this guy.

"Hey," I said, leaning around him.

His slender fingers danced on the keyboard, no mouse action; he was all about keyboard-shortcuts. Code flew from his fingertips onto the monitor and scrolled upward in beautiful asymmetry. The concentration was impressive, and I leaned too far in to read his shirt and broke that concentration, making him jump. He had a RAID Memory Prosthetics T-shirt, classic high-end geek.

"Sorry, man. I thought you heard me come in."

"Uh, no." He looked bewildered, innocent, like he was waking from a nap.

"Just checking to see how you are adapting to the job. How are things?"

He nodded, well, more like his head started bouncing in place. He tipped it toward the monitor and I got the hint.

"Nice T-shirt."

I went back and finished my testing.

About an hour later, the mad tapping continued and I began to wonder if you could get stress fractures from keying too long. I glanced over there.

He was still hunched over, the little peek of hairless skin at his back. But there was a bulge poking up a little ways down the inside of his opposite leg, and further down than I would have guessed.

It couldn't be.

And why was it there? He wasn't surfing porn sites with that much keystroking going on, and the company had all those sites blocked anyway. It must be something else, a Snickers bar? Then it strained like an alien pushing free, and I pushed my chair back to get a better look. I swelled in sympathy, made a critical adjustment, and leaned forward in case someone walked by.

Juan began opening and closing his legs, applying a little friction, absorbed in whatever code he was generating. I wanted to see it, that code and Juan's barometer all at once. So I wheeled a little into the aisle, looked both ways, un-tucked my shirt, and went over to poke my head in.

His legs were getting wild, his fingers flew, and I could see his trouser snake sliding against the fabric of his jeans. I pressed against the edge of the doorway, restraining myself. He stopped typing and leaned back in his chair, briefly exposing a flat stomach with protruding hips on either side. I glimpsed a thin trail of hair running from his bellybutton down to his waistband.

Then he shoved himself under the desk and rubbed his legs together for all they were worth, and he made almost no noise at all.

On his screen, the compiler was running in one window and the file scrolled up in another. The code syntax-coloring made a beautiful moving tapestry and I stared at it, distracted for an instant.

The cubicle shook briefly. Juan had grasped the desk's edge and was shivering, his eyes fixed on the screen where the compilation had finished.

Zero errors.

I bolted back to my cubicle, snugged up to my desk, and forced myself to wait. What had just happened?

* * *

It almost came to me in a dream.

Billy Mac, Juan Ha, and I were in my apartment playing strip poker around my coffee table. Juan was on the long end of the sectional sofa hunched over his cards, wearing an unbuttoned floral shirt, boxers, and one sock. Billy Mac was on the short end, leaning back against the pile of rainbow throw pillows, his cock pushing against his tightie-whities while he dragged his cards up and down his washboard stomach clack, clack, clack. I sat on a folding chair in full-length pajamas with bunny slippers, my back to the TV, which showed reruns of William Shatner playing a game show host.

"I'll see your sock," I said, throwing a slipper onto the pile of clothes on the coffee table, "and raise you a rabbit."

Juan looked hard at his cards, like he was having a vision. The end of Juan's uncut penis slipped out of his boxer leg. The pucker raised its head and looked around, dwelling on the swell of Billy Mac's briefs, then snaked over and started penetrating the pile of clothes while Shatner hooted, "Show me the money!"

I thought Juan's dick was enjoying itself in there, but it was only looking for the remote control. It coiled around the remote and pointed it toward the TV, switching to the source-code channel.

Juan's penis started to get hard. It dropped the remote on my lap, and then hovered by my ear, the foreskin peeling back as his glans swelled to emerge glistening and eager.

The remote rooted around at my crotch for the fly opening and went in. I lay back, letting the remote rub down my penis, then tickle my balls. When it went for a deeper investigation, I grabbed Juan's penis with both hands and forced it to look at me.

It started to soften, but I coaxed it, stroking down the silky cream-colored shaft as far as I could reach. I looked it square in its glistening little eye, kissed the royal head, and was rewarded with a pearl offering which it pushed to my face and smeared fondly on my cheek.

Juan had somehow lost his boxers and fallen back on the sofa, his shirt falling open on a lightly muscled body, chestnut pubic hair trailing to his belly-button, his hands on the boney handles of his hips. He stared at the TV.

Billy Mac, now naked, was masturbating one-handed and cupping Juan's balls with his other. The remote was working its way in and out of my ass while my dick jumped around on its own.

The application code on the TV scrolled faster, and Juan's penis hardened even more in my hands, pulling me out of my chair. I wrapped my legs around it and was carried, bobbing, toward the ceiling. I dry-humped the penis while licking its oozing head.

Tonguing the delicate, translucent membrane under the foreskin drove it wild, and it seemed to want to throw me off, so violently did it wave me around the room. The remote control in my ass was doing its job. Billy Mac was yanking on Juan's balls, stretching them to the floor, and coming all over his chest.

I was almost there, and humped the penis harder. A continuous flow of precome ran down the shaft of Juan's dick, making it hard to hold on, and I slipped up and down the self-lubing shaft in sweet, sticky delight. My pajamas were soaked with ecstasy.

One more swing. One more hump.

Then the penis was deflating, crashing to the floor with me underneath. I tried to hold on to it, hug it close, but it slipped through my hands and down my chest to escape between my legs. It reeled itself back into Juan's crotch. His balls snuggled back in place under the flaccid pout.

I followed Juan's stare to the TV, where the words "End Of File" burned on the screen at the bottom of a familiar block of code.

I knew that code. It would be the key to unlocking the mysterious Juan Ha.

Wednesday morning, Juan was hammering away at his keyboard when I got in. I half expected to see his penis pushing the space bar for him, then shrugged off the thought as I booted up my system.

The files I wanted belonged to an old co-worker and mentor. Sunil was brilliant, and a great friend. Too bad he had been lured away by a director's position at one of our competitors. He left me with his body of work and the understanding that I would continue it, but management had shelved the project to make room for other priorities.

Here it was, a long file of beautiful code that Juan would not be able to resist. I knew what it did, mostly, though I was not sure how Sunil had accomplished most of his tricks; he left too soon, and I had not taken time to dive deep.

I scrolled down to a particularly colorful section and let it sit in a window on my desktop. When Juan got up to go to the bathroom, I would make my move.

"Hey, Juan?"

He was anxious, almost dancing in place. Amusing.

"I'll be right back."

"It'll only take a sec."

He leaned into my office space, blinking, scanning around my cluttered desk, the mesh trashcan, the poster for RAID Memory Prosthetics (yeah, I'm a fan, too), and the photo of my family: mom, dad, and my two older brothers. Then Juan's eyes fell on the screen and they stayed there.

"That's interesting," he said.

"Yeah, I was wondering if you had any staples?"

"Sure," he said, moving toward the screen, oblivious that I was in the way.

I scooted my chair back, and he glommed onto my keyboard and paged down. His hips were right by my elbow, so I had a nice view of his hardening member pushing down his leg. My hunch was paying off.

"Is this yours?" he asked.

"Yeah. Old stuff."

"Nice. Is there more?"

It was forward of me I know, but I shifted in my chair and 'accidentally' brushed the outline of his cock, just to make sure it was real, of course. He straightened up fast and jammed his fists in his pockets. Damned if he wasn't blushing. I guessed what else was flush.

"There's more," I said.

"Um, I got to go. Can I see it later? Maybe you could give me a copy that I could dissect?"

It was the most articulate thing I'd ever heard from him, and I wanted to see more as well.

"No copies. Source code control. You understand?"

He nodded, and shifted his weight back and forth. I grinned.

"Maybe you can explain it to me later?"

"Sure," I said.

He danced off to the bathroom, and was back pestering me about the code in fifteen minutes.

"I don't have time today, got a project deadline to meet. Maybe tomorrow?"

He looked so sad as he shuffled back to his cubicle, and I felt so happy. Time to build up the desire.

Thursday, I caught him peeking out of his door down the aisle as I was walking in. He bounced up and asked me how my night had been.

"Great, thanks. Watched a little TV, played with the remote a little." I let a sly, knowing smile creep onto my face, confusing the boy.

"Can we maybe look over those functions this afternoon?"

"Oh sorry, Juan. I have a project deadline tomorrow and if I don't meet my milestone the boss will have my ass."

"Oh."

Hands jammed into his pockets, he raised his shoulders high and narrow; a perfect pout. I wanted to break down and show him everything he wanted, but I had to stick to my plan.

"Sorry, Juan. Tomorrow?"

Three times is the charm, so when Friday afternoon rolled around, he was practically drooling over my chair as I finished the last test run and signed off on the milestone.

"Juan, I'm sorry. I'm leaving a little early today. Going to my brother's for dinner."

"Monday, then?" he asked.

"Definitely." I started shutting down the system and he turned to go, all hangdog and bummed out. "Unless . . . ," I said.

"What?" He snapped right around.

"I was going to do a code review tomorrow. You could help if you wanted."

"Saturday? Okay. What time should I meet you here?"

"Well, that's the thing. I'm going to work out of my apartment tomorrow."

"I could meet you online?" He brightened, thinking about his privacy, I'm sure.

"Nah, that wouldn't really work," I said. "Never mind."

"I could come over, if you want."

And there it was, the invitation I'd been waiting for. I looked into those liquid olive eyes, the brown locks drooping down around his face, and it was all I could do to keep from going for his thick, pouty lips.

"Come in the afternoon," I suggested.

My entire morning was spent cleaning, and I don't know why, except maybe to waste time waiting for Juan. How messy can an 800 square-foot apartment get? Pretty messy, it turned out.

I found two pieces of unidentifiable underwear under the bed that must have been there for a while, a crusty condom behind the headboard, streaks where come had run down the walls and dried, and an old bowl of vanilla ice cream I'd set on the bottom shelf of the end table last Sunday night and forgot on account of Patty Cornwell's book, *Postmortem*.

And that was just the bedroom. The kitchen was another matter, with a refrigerator to clean, a gas stove to pull out and clean behind, Formica countertops to scrub, and a stainless sink to polish. The pink and white tile bathroom was easier, but you'd be amazed at how much scale accumulates in the shower.

When he arrived at three in the afternoon bearing a bottle of Zinfandel, I was fresh from the shower, my shirt ironed, my jeans loose, and I was exhausted. Juan arrived in sandals, loose jeans, and an oversized T-shirt with a cover from Mental-Floss on it. He offered the bottle, wrapped as it was in his extraordinary fingers. I perked right up.

"What a pleasant surprise," I said, accepting the wine. "A little Zin Sin for later, huh? Thanks."

"Have you started yet?"

This boy had a one-track mind, and I reconsidered that he had brought wine. Maybe I should just chug it now and let him have at it?

"Not yet," I said. "You're just in time. Have a seat." I pointed toward the sectional.

He didn't walk; it was more like skating. He led each step with his head and all his weight went from one foot to the other. Juan slipped around the coffee table, and plopped down exactly in his dream spot. He glanced around and settled on the blank screen of my TV.

I'm on the fourteenth floor and look out across blocks of restaurants and trees. The next building is a half-mile to the west up on the ridge. It's a great view, and what my guests usually notice first about the place. But Juan was all internally focused; it had probably made him nervous to go outside in daylight, much less pick up a bottle of wine.

I set the laptop on the coffee table, and then turned on the stereo and played the latest Grey Area CD, my favorite techno-trance group, very good for setting the mood.

"Anything to drink?"

He shook his head as he reached for the laptop and opened the case.

"It takes a password," he said, looking at the logon screen.

"Yep," I said, ducking into the kitchen. Let him wait a little longer, build up that anticipation until his breathing gets shallow and his pulse quickens at my return.

What was I saying? I was nervous, and I never get nervous. I took him a glass of ice water anyway, sat beside him, and set the glass on a coaster. My hands were shaking as I entered the password slowly so he could see what it was: LoverBoy. Then with a coy glance his way, brought up the editor and opened Sunil's first file.

Juan shifted forward on the sofa right away, leaning into the screen and blocking my view. The back of his neck was long and marbled with delicate veins. I could see his jugular pulsing strong and steady.

"Don't crawl in there, there isn't enough room."

"Sorry," he said, shifting next to me so that our legs were touching from hip to knee, though his legs were longer and skinnier than my own. He was hot against me in more ways than one, and I could feel my heart skipping beats. His breath smelled like bananas, and there was no deodorant masking the aroma of a June afternoon's sweat.

"May I?" he asked, reaching for the keys.

"Sure." I lay back and traced my hand down his backbone. He noticed, evidenced by the slight sideways glance, but he was focused on the screen and the color-patterned code that was flashing page after page like an art show.

"I went to a museum once in San Jose," he said in a low voice. "They only showed photos and engineering drawings of integrated circuit chips. It was the most beautiful thing I've ever seen."

His paginations had synched with the trance-dub beat, and I leaned into the pillows, careful not to break contact with his leg. I started at the top, taking in his wavy chestnut hair, the way it fell across his bony shoulders. There was a rounded grace to his back as he breathed, and the muscles that ran beside the bumps of his spine twitched as he moved.

He was already notorious in my mind for shrinking T-shirts, and this one rode up nicely. I could spend an hour licking the smooth skin, exploring the dimples at the small of his back with the little pad of parallel muscles at the base of his spine. That spot, at the nexus of hips, spine, and butt crack, caught in an accidental glimpsing is one of the sexiest things going to my mind.

I let my hand drop close behind him on the sofa and felt myself hardening. My fingertips were close enough to brush that hard little pad of flesh, to trace the faint blue veins there under the thin skin and explore the groove that slipped so invitingly into his jeans.

No boxers today? Interesting.

"This is interesting," he said.

"Yes. You read my mind?"

"What does it do?"

"I was wondering the same thing," I said, letting my hand randomly touch the exposed skin as I sat up.

He tugged his T-shirt down and pointed at a block of code. "This is yours, right?"

I glanced at his lap and smiled at the bulge I saw there before focusing on the screen. I nodded, trying to remember what that block did, and paged up until I found the function name: erection.

Sunil had been a playful coder, and knew me all too well. He and his wife, Saras, often had me over for dinner, and I had twice taken care of his two kids to give them a night out. We had been good friends, so I regretted that his new job was on the west coast.

This was a little joke Sunil had left for me to find. It named one of the longest stretches of code in the whole application, a kind of recursive size-queen joke in, and of, itself.

"Yeah, well, you'll have to ignore some of my nomenclature tics."

"No, it makes sense, since this builds part of the outgoing webpage code where data gets pushed out to the client in auto-refreshes."

"You got all that in one scan?"

He bobbed his head, shrugging his shoulders.

"That's scary."

"Sometimes I get lucky and just see things, in a general sense," he said, trying to deflect.

Here was one bright kid, toning it down as if afraid it might chase me away. It was like I was seeing his intelligence smile, and it had dimples. The urge to kiss him swelled like the tide. I wanted to push him back on the sofa and wrap myself around him while he talked. I would stroke his hair and explore under his shirt.

"JJ?" A worried expression clouded his face. The lump in his jeans had ebbed.

"Sorry, just spaced a little. I was up late."

True enough; thoughts of Juan had kept me up late into the night, and now here he was.

"So, why did you write this part as a cascading if-then and not a case ladder?"

He was right back on it. I fumbled through some rationale, all the while thinking of a guy in my networking 101 class; I studied with him because he was cute and I wanted to go out, but he was so oblivious even when I was so obvious that I eventually gave up. Those hours with Parker still make me smile because he told me when we graduated how he had lusted after me in those days, and that I could have done anything I wanted.

It was a good lesson, and I noticed the whale had resurfaced on Juan's other thigh, so I let my hand fall on his leg as he went back to scrolling. His hipbone pressed into my forearm, and he widened his legs, stretching the loose jeans taut between his legs and eliminating all traces of his arousal. I imagined his penis roving through the cavernous space formed by his jeans, bobbing around in there, his balls contracting and releasing, the hairs tickling his legs.

I shifted against him so my cock could unfold down my own pants leg and not be so confined. And I wanted it to be obvious; no secrets with this one. What was happening here? I had to find out, so I slid my hand around the curve of his thigh, putting pressure on the tight cloth of his jeans.

He caved and brought his knees together, the cloth falling loose, trapping my hand between his leg and his cock. On screen, he reversed the scroll, and then continued slowly.

"I love this part," he said, his penis jumping against the back of my hand.

"Me, too," I whispered, scanning the outline of his cock.

He glanced down, noticing my own erection, the spreading wet spot there. His hand floated above it. A long finger dropped down to touch the wet denim and trace along my penis.

"You spilled your drink?"

"No."

He rubbed his thumb and forefinger together, testing the stickiness of it, then brought it to his nose.

"It smells good."

He was looking in my eyes. His cheeks flushed in patches like rose petals that highlighted the mole on his jaw. The blush spread down his neck.

I extracted my hand so I could feel his hardness, pushing the cloth around the contours of it. All the while, I searched his eyes for a trace of misunderstanding, and was baffled at my own restraint. This wasn't like me at all.

The cock swelled in my hand as his fingers returned to my wet end and worked their way around. We read each other's face, but otherwise didn't move.

"Have you never been kissed?" I whispered.

He gave the slightest shake of his head.

I put my fingers in his hair, pushed it back around a reddened ear, felt the cheekbone under his hot, soft skin. When my index finger brushed his moistened lips he let them part and made to grasp it, the flesh exploring, inviting.

I thanked Parker and leaned into Juan, pulling his head close so our lips rubbed lightly together, the tipping point of the day.

He crushed our lips together, our teeth clicking, tongues probing, and he wrapped his arms around me, and pushed me back into the pile of throw pillows. My hands slipped under his shirt and up across his back, then down his spine to trace circles from one dimple to the other as he squirmed against me, then rutted against me as my hand slid down his crack to grasp a cheek. My fingers probed his moist, warm nether spots.

Juan gasped and fell to nibbling at my ear, so I slid my hand around his hipbone and into the wiry pubic hair under his penis. He raised his hips to help me, and I felt his balls drop free, so I grasped the swollen eggs, massaging them as his penis slid hot against my inner forearm.

It was only natural that my finger traced the hairless, silky path down the center of his scrotum and then pushed against the embedded root of his cock. As if in answer, a drop of his precome dripped onto my arm and I used it against him, sliding it around while my finger went farther into that nether world, and I found his quivering anus.

His legs were wide, trying to accommodate me and he slipped, tangling us, forcing us to look at each other. I noticed he was shaking violently as he crawled back on top.

"Are you cold?"

"No," he said, "I've never done this before."

He unbuttoned my shirt with palsied hands, then pushed the shirt over my shoulders. I slid out of it for him, and then pulled his T-shirt over his head and tossed it to the floor.

The sun had come down the sky and light was blazing through the window, across the parquet floor, and onto the edge of the sofa. Soon it would be hot on us and help quell Juan's nerves. Until then, it was my job to heat him up.

He was on his knees between my open legs, silhouetted against the bright window. His loose jeans jostled on his shaking hips, and the head of his penis glistened above the waistband. I reached over and wiped the precious ooze, rubbed my thumb and finger together, stretched a sticky thread, then raised it to my nose.

"Nice," I said. "Musky, with notes of walnuts and brie." He smiled at that, but kept his innocent stare fixed on my face.

In that instant I trusted him completely, believed him absolutely, and wanted him badly. I licked his ooze from my fingers while he watched, vibrating in place.

"Hints of cumin and fish sauce." I winked. "And wonderfully sweet. Please, sir. Can I have some more?"

I unbuttoned his jeans, slid the zipper down as the singer in the trance-dub sang "slowly, slowly, slowly" against a swelling beat. The cock fell through and pointed to me, and I worked the jeans down his hips until he took the hint and stood to pull them off.

His long fingers flew at my jeans. For all their dexterity, they fumbled at the button. In two easy movements I had them undone and shoved down my thighs. He just stood there, his eyes riveted on my cock.

"Pull them off for me?"

I leaned back against the pillows and put my arms over my head, waiting. Juan grabbed the legs and tugged them around my ankles, stepping back into the wash of sunshine as he pulled the pants from my legs. The sun flashed on his golden skin, in his dark hair, and fell obliquely across his angular face.

His chest and stomach were flat, his shoulders boney, and his ribs showed clearly. Two veins rose from his pubic hair and dissipated up his chest. Juan wasn't the usual muscular boy I liked; but there was something most appealing about this boy with his spindly legs, his almost alien fingers, and that insistent cock that arced toward me and corkscrewed slightly in a perfect imperfection.

I opened my arms and he crawled toward me from the foot of the sofa, pausing to rub his hands in the patch of my own goo. He made to taste it but I grabbed his wrist and pulled his hand to my cock and caught my breath as he cupped my balls with one hand and encircled my shaft with the other. The tips of his fingers tickled under my scrotum. One slipped toward my anus, then finding it, pulled quickly away. His eyes fixated on my penis, drinking it in as his hands explored, experimented, tugged the taught skin up over my glans with some difficulty.

"I'm circumcised," I said, then got up so we were both on our knees, his legs between my own. Our cocks were together and my balls rested on his thighs.

The skin of his penis was much looser than mine. I grasped his shaft and easily slid the skin to cover his glans, then released it and watched the head emerge, revealing another glop of clear liquid. It smeared easily around the purple dome, and he bucked against me.

We locked our arms around each other and trapped our oozing cocks between us. We kissed hard, licking at each other like cats. He pushed closer, his back sweating in the flood of sunlight that now washed over us. He was no longer shaking.

Juan slid his penis against my stomach, reached around and grabbed my ass to pull me into a better position. I felt our balls tumble and merge, and I leaned back and clasped our penises together, blending our fluids as I polished our knobs.

Then he spit in his hand and put his long fingers around us, encircling us perfectly, and began a long, slow pump. I eased my hand off, curious what he wanted, and leaned back for the ride, my hips moving together with his. His other hand joined the first. More spit, more ooze, his tightening grip pressed our cocks together and slid, pounding with our hearts.

Our breathing became a freight train in the room; our hips moved involuntarily together; our balls crushed and slipped among themselves, squeezing their loads into action. We tensed, eyes on one another as the heads of our penises erupted together throwing ropes of come in a white-hot fountain between us.

I had met my match.

We fell back on the sofa in a fierce hug, and in the glow he said, "We should stick together."

"We are," I said, sliding against him.

"No, really."

In a blink I knew that's what I wanted, too. But I had to figure out how to tell him it wasn't my code, and hope that he could forgive me, and that he would stay anyway.

All the World's a Game Show

Gregory L. Norris

I have this theory that life is really just one big game show. The Almighty's the host of this extended half-hour of nail-biting drama, while the rest of us are contestants forced to endure an ongoing series of stunts, challenges, pricing games, eliminations, and multiple choices. Take a spin on the wheel. Get your hand on the buzzer. Buy a vowel. Deal or no deal. Just make sure your answer is in the form of a question or you will get voted off the island.

Whacky, sure. But if you stop to think about it, it all makes perfect sense.

"I guess I could suck a tit," I tell Joe.

Joe is my straight thirty-year-old roommate who knows I am gay, but that doesn't stop him from firing off one morally corrupt question after another, testing my boundaries because he can't quite wrap his mind around the idea of me wrapping my lips around another man's erect cock.

Looking sexy in the same T-shirt he's worn for two days, a pair of sweat socks he's probably had on for the same amount of time, and army fatigue cut-offs that showcase his hairy athlete's legs like the works of art they are, he lays across from me along our sofa, on his back, with one knee arched. A goofy grin breaks on his mouth, which is stubbly with a couple of days' worth of dark scruff.

"So you'd do it? You'd suck on some hot chick's jug?"

Answer, the Daily Double: "Well, yeah, if you'd just titty-fucked her and your jizz was dripping all over her nip."

"Aww, fuck, dude," Joe grunts, kicking at the empty air above the sofa with the foot of the knee that's bent, sourness creeping over his classically handsome face. "You sick fuck!"

"You asked."

"Now I know you're sniffing my dirty underwear when I ain't here."

"Sometimes, but I prefer your sweaty socks."

I get the reaction I've sought: Joe throwing a good-natured tantrum on the sofa in our shitty one-bedroom apartment in Culver City. He chuckles a blue streak of expletives, gags.

"To repeat, you asked."

"Yeah, real glad about that."

One hand masturbating the remote control's channel changer, he calms down and resumes his line of questioning.

"If you were forced to have sex with one of the Three Stooges, who would it be?"

Now, I do the groaning.

"Give it up, dude. Are you a Moe, Larry, or Curly sort'a cock-smooch?"

"You only gave me three choices," I fire back. "There were five in all. What about Shemp or Joe Besser, the much-aligned Fifth Stooge? And you haven't taken into consideration Curly-Joe DeRita, who joined up with Moe and Larry when they started making features."

Joe should know better than to fence with me about such things; I don't know why he does it. I am, however, completely convinced that Joe and I – before his killer good looks land him his first big TV or film contract – he and I are going to have real sex. Not the drunken kind we never talk about but often find ourselves exploring after he knocks a few cold ones back and opens up to me about his true feelings, cries on my shoulder, humps me through his pants, and then begs me to blow him. Which I do, while he conveniently pretends to pass out, meaning to him that it never really happened. On those kinds of nights, which we experience with more and more frequency, we dress up in costumes just like contestants in that sappy 70s game show, *Let's Make a Deal*. It plays here on GSN, the Game Show Network. Only instead of face paint and feathers, Joe wears the invisible mask of one man secretly curious and denying his attraction to another of his own gender. Me, I play somebody who only needs the occasional mouthful of a stud's jizz in his diet to remain content. Not romance, love. Not something real.

So I blow Joe when he gets drunk and needy. I lick his hairy, sweaty balls, sometimes shoving my tongue behind them and up into his asshole. I lick the cheesy-smelling sweat from between the long, flat toes of his big, sexy feet, and I nurse the seed out of his cock, greedily guzzling every drop. Once, I even took his drunken beer piss down my throat as he clung for dear life to the towel rack in our shitty bathroom in our shitty apartment.

I love Joe, and that's the problem. I always fall for the wrong guys. One day, probably sooner than he suspects, he is going to declare his true love for me, and there won't be a drop of alcohol involved in this revelation.

Less than a minute to go in Double Jeopardy, Joe, so please choose your category quickly.

He will passionately explore his love for me, oblivious to the many future challenges that must inevitably arise, like revealing the truth of our union to his folks. Joe hails from a big Irish Catholic Family. And after Hollywood comes knocking on our shitty apartment's front door, he'll have more people than his parents and brothers and aunts and uncles to explain *me* to.

No, Joe is going to dump me, take up with a blonde-haired actress with huge tits, deny ever knowing me, and break my heart. It's happened once before already. He doesn't know it, but Joe is Bachelor #2.

"So which one?"

"Which one what?"

"Which Stooge would you sleep with if you had to pick one?"

From the loveseat where I sit, I gaze to the sofa, narrow my eyes while drinking in Joe's magnificence as he absently scratches his nuts, gaining access to them along the left pant leg of his massacred cammies.

Let's get ready to play the Feud . . .

"You. You're the only Stooge dick I want to suck."

Joe's handsome face, his emerald-green eyes; black hair, perpetually bed-headed; his strong, stubbled jaw locks with a look of almost religious bewitchment, like a spark has gone off in that space between his ears where the rest of us have brains. The spark becomes fireworks, a nuclear explosion, a supernova. In that bottled gaze, I know what is happening: Joe is considering the possibility of a life spent loving only me.

The limerance is brief. Joe blinks himself out of it and the hand tugging at his nuts, one now drooping visibly at the fray of his cut-offs (Joe's balls are that big and hang that low, and as I learned years ago, he mostly goes commando – not for the convenience, but because he only has a few intact pairs of boxer-briefs and he hates doing laundry), reaches lower. He peels off one sock, then its twin, balls them together, and pitches them at me with the same perfect aim I've seen him toss around a baseball when he plays with his team of other struggling jock-actors on Saturday afternoons over in West Hollywood.

"Suck on this," he growls good-naturedly.

I pick up the socks, whiff deeply of their hot, buttery stink, and fall even deeper in love with him.

"Fuckin twisted, dude," he admonishes from the other side of the living room. I focus on his feet, which look sexy and god-like, their second toes slightly longer than the big ones, like on the feet of classic Greek statues. I sniff his socks. He flips channels with the remote. My God, we could be so perfect together if not for that damn final spin of the wheel that is going to doom us by landing on "Bankrupt" once Joe gets discovered.

"Hey, look, it's your show."

Half-high on the heavenly odor of Joe's dirty socks, I glance up and see that he's made it past the cooking channels, all the way up the dial to GSN.

"That show you were on a few years ago, right before we met."

"*Buy 'Til You Die*," I grumble.

"Wouldn't it be a pisser if it's your episode?"

"It isn't," I say, studying the screen, which is presently focused upon the show's host, J. T. Roberts. Like Joe, J. T. is a Neanderthal who cleans up good for the camera, but at home hangs out in the same sweaty socks for days, scratches his balls, pees standing up, picks his toes, secretly tastes his own fingers sometimes after he jerks off, fucks best from the dawgy position, and speaking of which, probably, at one time or another, let the family dog lap at his balls during a private horny moment when there was nobody else around to do it. He-man. All-man. A real beer-drinking, red meat-eating tough guy.

"How do you know it's not your episode?"

I shift my gaze from J. T. Roberts, his short black hair in a neat athletic brush-cut, his sparkly blue eyes hypnotic, one cheek dimpling as he flashes that patented game show host smile, over to Joe. My insides crash and burn, ache. Back to J. T. for more of that practiced smile for the cameras before the show takes a commercial break.

"He's wearing a maroon paisley tie," I answer. "The day I was on *Buy 'Til You Die*, he had on an open collar shirt under his blazer. You could see his hairy chest."

"Bet that made you moist," Joe jokes.

"Fuck off."

"I mean, he's a stud, that guy. Though a bit of a loser."

"Why do you say that?"

"Shit, dude, look at him! He could go anywhere with his looks, but he's hosting the crappiest game show on TV. They only give you prizes, not money. Nobody cares about winning kitchen appliances. People want money and cars when their names get called to '*come on down*'."

"If it wasn't for that show, we wouldn't be sitting here on this sofa and loveseat and watching that TV," I remind him. "And maybe he likes his job."

"Yeah, right. I'm just saying he could score bigger and better projects with that face of his."

It's back to the action, with two teams fighting for the chance to shop for a prize in the show's mall-like set, which looks more like the insides of a warehouse when you actually stand inside that cavernous sound stage. One couple is a husband and wife combo, judging by their coordinated outfits of plum-colored polo shirts and blue jeans. The other is comprised of two Asian women who look meek and nowhere nearly as aggressive as their opponents.

"Turn it up."

"That's turn it up, *Sir*," Joe corrects.

"Yeah, yeah, whatever. Daddy. Sir. Master. Stud."

In response, Joe blasts the volume, hoping for a rise. But the mere sound of J. T.'s gravely voice numbs my senses. Not getting the reaction he expects, Joe thumbs the remote's volume back down to a decent level. J. T. is discussing a buyer's challenge in which the two Asian women must dress each other up as characters from a generic Science Fiction movie using pieces of costumes scrambled together in a bin – in under a minute if they want a chance to win the big *Buy 'Til You Die* challenge. J. T. glides across the screen, dress shirt, maroon paisley tie, black sports coat, matching black dress slacks spray-painted onto his tight, muscled ass, loafers on his big feet. And for a second of splintered time, I'm there again with him, approaching the dressing trailer, taking that fateful walk through Door Number One where I'll find both ecstasy and agony on the other side.

Door Number Two, sitting on the sofa, snaps me back to reality. "Yeah, I bet you wanted to hum on his dick."

"No," I say. I didn't merely want to. Truth was, I *did* hum on J. T. Roberts' hairy, above-average game show host's boner. Repeatedly, as a matter of fact, over a run of several days the same summer I was a contestant on *Buy 'Til You Die*. But I've never talked about it with anyone, not even Joe. Until now, I've been the ultimate Secret Square when it comes to kissing and telling.

So what happened between J. T. Roberts and me? That's the 64-thousand dollar question, isn't it?

That whole, *if you live in the greater L. A. area and would like to be a contestant on* Buy 'Til You Die *thing,* I discovered, is because lower-echelon game shows are too cheap to fly you out to attend a taping after you make it past the tryout stage.

I lied, said I was living in the Greater Los Angeles area, and flew out there on my own dime a month before the actual taping. Unknown to the brain trust at *B 'Til You D*, the address I gave was a bug-infested motel with industrial cinderblock walls on the corner of Hollywood Boulevard and North Whitley. I picked up a rechargeable cell phone in town, which necessitated me getting a 323 area code, and for a month, with little money in my pocket, I ate bologna and mustard sandwiches from supplies I bought at the corner groceria, refrigerating the leftovers in buckets of ice cubes from the machine on my floor.

You see, my master plan all along had been to relocate to Hollywood, anyway. I attended three tapings of *The Price is Right*, but never made it to Contestants Row, so I didn't get to play Plinko, punch the Punchboard, or spin the money wheel for a chance at winning the Showcase Showdown. *Who Wants to be a Millionaire* had switched to a daily format, but that was back in New York City three thousand miles away. *Jeopardy* was entrenched in the midst of Ken Jennings' monumental win streak, which was about to be interrupted for two weeks by the college crowd, and Pat was giving the wheel its final spins, adding a thousand dollars to every consonant, while Vanna tapped letters magically into existence out in Hawaii before *Wheel of Fortune* took the show on the road to Las Vegas. I made it to a tryout after the show returned to tape in L.A., but the line of hopeful contestants stretched around the block.

The best I came up with between working on sample scripts of existing TV series and my own original screenplays was my upcoming appearance on the bottom feeder of all game shows, *Buy 'Til You Die*.

I met Cabot Burch in line at the *Wheel of Fortune* tryout. He was short and effeminate, and he was there to fulfill his ultimate dream in life of appearing on the show. Enthusiasm poured out of him for the first few hours we waited to be called into the studio, our bodies steadily evaporating into the steamy air behind a line of thousands that moved forward at a maddeningly sluggish pace. We had plenty of time for idle chitchat.

"I'm going to be on *Buy 'Til You Die* next week. You know that one?" I absently offered.

"What a comedown," he snorted haughtily.

I didn't know Cabot, but I sensed I wouldn't have wanted to be his friend in the real world. "I still need a partner. I lied about having one. They didn't pick up on it when I said it would be me and my pal, a Mister W. Martindale."

"You mean *Wink*?" And then he did.

"You want to go on the show with me?"

I think Cabot thought we were going to roll out the barrel back at my place after the tryouts, that he was going to get into my pants for his own private *Match Game* session played among the bed sheets.

"Sure. That show's host is really cute. So're you, my new friend."

Soon after that, I begged off waiting to be cattle-called into the studio and returned to the motel. Feeling dirty, I took a long shower and called the show's producers to say that my buddy, W. Martindale, had been called up for guard duty and wouldn't be joining me in the *Buy 'Til You Die* mall. My other pal, C. Burch, would instead.

A week later, we met in the Green Room, slightly made up so that our shiny faces wouldn't glare for the camera, sizing up our surroundings and the competition.

"Cheap bastards," Cabot bitched. He was referring to the spread laid out on the table for us to help ourselves to, which basically amounted to a box of stale donuts and an urn of coffee that tasted bitter, burned. No real milk or cream to soften it, just the powdered crap. "At least at *Lingo* they put out a bowl of fruit. I could use a banana."

At first, I figured the banana comment was another veiled attempt to get into my pants. Then Cabot mentioned his tendency for low blood potassium levels, the toad.

Our opponents were two large ladies, busty on top, voluminous in the caboose, who looked like sisters but weren't. *Friends,* they said.

Yeah, of the lezz-be-friends variety, said a voice in my thoughts.

A pair of dykes versus a couple of homos. This left us at a serious disadvantage. The dykes would work in unison as a team, overcompensating everything and determined to leave with a new fridge, some gardening tools, and a shitty trip to Palm Springs in their pockets. Their opponents were a rich troll/mamma's boy looking to get laid and a broke-ass wannabe screenwriter who didn't really know what he was doing here.

The two positives on our side were the size of their *backsides.*

I didn't really want or need the things we had the potential to win. By applying to the game shows, I was merely hoping to make connections. I didn't know anybody in the business, or how I'd go about making those all-important connections. Fuck, this sure wasn't the way, but like many cocksuckers who grew up watching game shows, it had seemed a fitting means to my end.

Cold sweat broke out over every inch of my skin. I wasn't just going in front of the cameras to be seen nationwide on the lousiest game show on the airwaves, but was also about to suffer the added humiliation of being trounced by a pair of stone-cold butches.

I was headed in the direction of the nearest exit when the Green Room door whooshed open, and in walked J. T. Roberts.

His scent carried on the wave of air set into motion by the opening door and swept up to greet my next panicked breath. Like soap on bare skin, a trace of deodorant, no heavy cologne to gag upon, J. T. Roberts smelled the way a natural, real man smells when he's freshly showered. And he looked divine in his ass-hugging dress slacks and sports jacket over a polo shirt whose open collar clearly displayed the thatch of dark hair sprouting where his neck met his chest.

Cabot and the lesbians were closest to the Green Room's door when he entered, so he shook their hands first. But after he made it past the big butts and lascivious, sex-crazed toad, he gave me one of those double-takes that tells you a chemical connection has just sparked, one with the power of a super-nova. It burns white-hot, consuming every atom. J. T. Roberts' eyes met mine and his mouth instantly curled into that five-alarm, phony smile he makes for the camera when he's trying to seduce the viewing audience. His hand came out, big and strong, squeezing mine in a way that amounted to a kind of foreplay.

"You must be the writer," he said.

I didn't know it then, but he had marked me, and I was smitten, all before the opening jingle.

"He's a screenwriter in search of his first big break. He's a game show fanatic who dreams of winning big time. They could both be granted their fondest wishes – and experience the time of their lives on . . . *Buy 'Til You Die!*"

One sofa and loveseat combo. A TV. A full set of overpriced cookware. A garden bench. A Music Land gift card.

By the time all was said and done, the dyke-namic duo tanked during the ring-toss competition that pitted our two teams against one another for the big buyer's challenge.

If it's one thing we dick-lovers know how to do, it's toss our holes onto a spike.

I got the sofa set and TV. I gave Cabot the rest and told him never to contact me again.

*   *   *

Someone who's about to get laid just knows it. Maybe it's the way your skin prickles when another set of eyes undresses you from across the room, when another man touches you with overly familiar caresses (not that I minded!) like rubbing your neck or petting the small of your back, or when he pulls you aside just as you're about to exit the studio through the private security door.

"You got a moment?"

"Sure," I answered.

"Not here. Come out back with me to my dressing trailer."

J. T. escorted me over to the air-conditioned sixty-footer outside the stage where *Buy 'Til You Die* was taped. Warm air gusted through the lot, carrying with it a sexy, hot smell born of the sun, the laurel trees growing nearby, and a senses-stirring trace of *him* as he walked ahead of me.

It didn't strike me as unusual that the star of a game show was taking me into his dressing trailer to talk, probably because I knew I was about to get stuffed full of his hard cock. I saw its outline briefly, swollen and prominent, bouncing in his dress slacks as he hopped up the metal steps and unlocked the trailer's door. My mouth felt like the desert. My own dick had reacted similarly, but unlike J. T.'s, which swung big and free at the front of his pants, mine was pinned uncomfortably by too-tight underwear and suffocating blue jeans.

Chilly conditioned air poured out, along with a host of my host's scents: masculine deodorant, air freshener, and the sweetness of beer mixed with the sourness of foot odor and the musky ghosts of endless past ejaculations. A pair of dirty socks and a nastified pair of cross trainers greeted my eyes just inside the living area, along with a small plastic trash can loaded down with a lifetime's supply of used condoms. My already-galloping heart raced even faster.

"So what's up?" I dumbly asked.

"That guy you were with . . ."

I felt my face flush with embarrassment. "Oh, puh-leeze. I'm not *with* him."

"Good. What a loser. You seeing anybody else?"

"Nope."

His eyes locked with mine, and J. T.'s contrived smile for the camera disappeared, replaced by a serious scowl. "Suck me."

I drew in a deep breath of the male-smelling air, convinced I was going to pass out at any second.

"Go down on my dick."

And it happened just like that. I fell to my knees on the trailer's carpeted floor and unzipped his pants. From within emerged a meaty man's cock, the shaft pitted with dings and ridges, the head rising mightily up, deep crimson in color, gorged with blood, demanding to be worshipped. Two fat balls covered in lush dark hair soon followed it out of the cover of his slacks and boxer-briefs.

"Yeah, that's right . . . do it," J. T. ordered. "Hum on my dick!"

I took him between my lips, and until attaining the first of what would amount to four ejaculations that afternoon, I didn't stop suckling on J.T.'s boner.

I let J. T. fuck me. Twice. Once, doggy-style in the trailer's surprisingly comfortable queen-sized bed.

I studied his magnificence in the big mirror that hung above the bed; the sculpt of his chest, the dark hair that superimposed a T-shape over it, one bar cutting him across his pecs, the other slicing him in a treasure trail evenly down the middle. J. T. rode me with one of his strong, bare jogger's legs arched onto the bed. Through the near violence of his lovemaking and the veil of sweat dripping into my eyes, I kept returning to the reflection of his hairy leg and big, naked foot. I hadn't yet licked his toes, but knew I would eventually. Attraction to a hot guy's feet is written into my genetic code.

I didn't fall asleep in the dressing trailer's bed so much as I passed out, helped there by my own orgasms and the gentle cadence of J. T.'s snores. I jolted awake sometime just before sunrise unsure of my surroundings, which slithered out of focus under the eerie glow of the alarm clock and the streetlamps outside.

"Morning," J. T. growled. His sleepy voice anchored me back to my location.

"Morning, yourself," I answered.

J. T. leaned over and kissed me. I tasted day-old asshole on his breath. He'd eaten me out like a starving man turned loose on an all-you-can-eat buffet, and while he hadn't shown that same kind of attention to my front side, it hadn't stopped me from erupting courtesy of his fierce fuck-thrusts or his roaming hand doing the old reach-around, jerking me off while his tongue was playing my asshole like a rusty trombone.

That night, we had bought every vowel in the alphabet, howling them at the limits of our lungs.

"I'm not supposed to crash here overnight, but I do sometimes," he whispered, a shadowy presence to my right. He took my hand and maneuvered it between his spread, furry legs. J. T.'s cock was up again at full mast, and not because he needed to piss. "Come on, babe. Gimme some more of that awesome mouth of yours . . ."

I slid under the covers, ignored the stale stink of old sex on the sheets, and opened wide. J. T. was completely hot. A real he-man. A stud. I could get used to this, I remember thinking.

Breakfast that first morning consisted of the most delicious potato, egg, and bacon English muffin sandwiches and cold juice from the Kraft Service truck. J.T. vanished into the head to brush his teeth while I innocently checked out the rest of the trailer. Bedroom, full bathroom, a living area whose surfaces were piled high with scripts from the show and empty food wrappers, and a kitchenette. All the comforts of home.

He emerged dressed in a T-shirt, track shorts, and bare feet. God, those feet, so big, so perfect, each long toe capped by a dusting of dark hair. I watched him slide them into his nasty old cross-trainers, minus socks.

"I usually go for a jog in the morning."

"Cool," I said.

"Naw, not cool, *hot*. My feet are gonna be sweaty and smelly when I get back. My nuts, too. Really ripe."

I smiled.

"Figured you'd like that by the way you were sniffing and licking me last night, balls-to-toes."

And they were, after he returned from his run around the studio lot. Ripe and musky and sweaty and wonderful. And mine, all mine.

"I'll put in a word for you with the writing staff," he groaned as I tongued the sweat from between his toes. "Get you a job with the show, your first big break."

I spit out J. T.'s big toe. "You can do that?"

"I'm the fuckin star of the show," he smirked.

"But you'd do that for me?"

"Sure, if you stop licking the stink off my feet and get up here and sit on my dick . . ."

Another dead, come-filled soldier went into the trash can.

"I need to shower," J. T. moaned. "My call to the set's in half an hour."

"I could use one, too. Want to conserve water?"

J. T. scratched at his nuts. "Naw, my dick's raw."

"I didn't mean —"

"I know you didn't, but if I see your butt in there, I'm gonna want to devour it, then fuck it. I'd be rawer than I am now and late for my set call." He rose from the sofa and spanked my naked ass. "You can go in after me. You parked in the lot?"

"I don't have a car. I took a taxi."

"I'll have my driver take you home."

J. T. vanished into the bathroom. He emerged a few seconds later with a toothbrush in his mouth and a circle of rabid-dog foam around his mouth. Sort'a sexy, I wasn't quite sure why.

"I don't have a home. No car. No job. I'm living in a hotel

off Hollywood Boulevard, but I can't afford to stay there past the weekend."

J. T. ceased brushing, narrowed his gaze, revolved, spit. When he righted, he said, "I'll get you the car, the job. Why don't you go back and pack up your shit. You can stay here."

"In your dressing trailer?"

"Sure, why not?"

J. T. folded his arms over his hairy chest. His meaty cock was half-hard again, hanging openly over two swollen nuts that had fallen loose in their sac thanks to the dual forces of gravity and arousal.

A wave of emotion for him rushed over me. It felt like love. Looking back, I see there was some of that as well, but it was mostly relief. Two hours later, I was back at the trailer permanently, with my suitcase and laptop and all that I owned in the world. Well, as permanently as things like what we had could be in Hollywood.

So where would I put a plasma TV and a living room suite in the trailer?

That was one of the burning questions that plagued me over the next week, when I started to believe J. T.'s dressing trailer was home. And for that brief and wonderful stretch of days, it was.

When I wasn't typing away feverishly on one screenplay or another on my laptop, I explored every corner of the oblong metal castle deep in the protected space of the studio lot. I found stacks of J. T.'s professional black and white headshots behind Door Number Three in the kitchenette's cabinetry and guiltily jerked off while looking at them – when I wasn't sniffing his sweaty, dirty socks as a means toward the same end, or going down on the real deal, that is.

We ordered takeout and expensed it on his account with the show.

We made love every day, explored every kind of love, from the purely missionary to the grossly kinky. It's like we were living the fuckin *Newlywed Game*.

"How're things coming with that job?" I asked early into our second week together.

"Working on it. Hey, I can't stay over tonight. Got things I have to deal with back at home."

Home. He was referring to his one-story bungalow in the Hills. It was the first real challenge to my illusion about the trailer being our home.

"Okay," I said, somewhat disappointed. On his way out of the trailer that morning, J. T. gave me a peck on the cheek, not the deep, passionate full-on-the-lips variety I'd grown used to. And when I wished him a good day, I got that practiced game show host smile of his, the one meant for the cameras.

That was the second hint, and it should have been enough to tell me that things were about to go sour between us.

"I've set up a meeting for you with a friend of mine at one of the studios. He's an executive producer for *America's Craziest Families*, that show on Sunday nights. Thinks he can make room for you on their writing staff."

The news was delivered without any direct eye contact.

"What about the job here on *Buy 'Til You Die?*"

"We're going on hiatus in a month, so they won't be hiring until after the break. This could get you in the door. His name's Jerry Jenkins."

"Cool," I said. "So let's celebrate. Can you stay over tonight?"

"Sorry, babe. I've got shit to deal with at the house. He'll meet you for lunch at that sidewalk café on Hollywood near your old motel. The Green Room."

"I don't have money for a taxi and lunch."

"You can take the car," J.T . sighed, his voice huffy. He whipped out his billfold and tossed a hundred onto the counter. "Here's the number of his cell. Call him *today*."

And then he slammed the door on his way out of the trailer.

"Turn around," I said.

"What?"

We were halfway to my meeting with Jerry Jenkins when I had the overwhelming urge to return to the dressing trailer.

It could have been raw nerves; after all, I hadn't left our little fortress for fourteen whole days, and apart from the driver and an endless succession of delivery men, I hadn't seen a human face other than J. T.'s in that strange, mystical stretch of time.

"I forgot something. Turn around."

We drove back to the studio lot.

I had J. T.'s driver park near the laurel trees, told him to wait, and exited the car. Walking the two-dozen steps to the dressing trailer felt more like a million. My legs turned to lead. My guts tied themselves into knots.

The trailer, *home* . . . something was wrong. It still looked like the oblong metal womb I had been reborn inside of, but it had altered. Not physically, you understand, but in a way that was felt more than seen. My heart raced, unleashing a succession of cold tickles across that sensitive spot between my balls and asshole.

I made it to the metal steps, up them, and finally to the door. Using the spare key J. T. had loaned me the day I collected my stuff from the motel, I entered quietly.

And from the hallway, I saw the malaise I'd been feeling given form.

J. T., naked from the waist up, was bent over the queen-sized bed where we'd made love, his handsome face buried between two shapely legs. A *woman's* legs. He was tongue-deep in some blond chick's cunt, loudly slurping on her the way he'd devoured my asshole a week earlier.

She caught sight of me and let loose with a piercing shriek. J. T.'s head catapulted out of her pussy and spun around. At first, his expression mirrored the look of horror on my face. But then, with cunt-juice dripping down his chin, he shot me his trademark smile. That look of his that seemed to say, *you are the weakest link.*

Goodbye.

        ★   ★   ★

I was twenty minutes late meeting Jerry Jenkins at the Green Room on Hollywood Boulevard. I'd called him on my cell and lied about getting stuck in traffic, but he saw through me immediately, perhaps due to the fact I'd showed with a suitcase in tow that had obviously been packed in haste and a devastated expression he surely must have recognized.

"Let me hazard a guess. J. T. just fucked you over royally," he said bitterly, a sharp smirk on his face.

My lack of a response to the question was the perfect answer.

"Sit down, have a coffee. Or something stronger if you need it." He waved me toward the other wrought-iron patio chair at the little outdoor café table. "You aren't the first, you won't be the last. I'm Number 1,031, I think. That was a good seventy or so warm bodies ago."

The look on my face betrayed the violent cyclone twisting unseen through my insides.

"Don't take it personally. And don't confuse what you had with him as being real love. J. T. only loves J. T. You accept that, the pain will go away quicker. We exist only to suck his dick and service him. J. T.'s just a big boy who hasn't grown up, and like any boy, when he gets bored with one toy, he moves on to another."

Jerry waved the waiter over. I ordered Eggs Benedict and fried potatoes and forced them down.

"So I hear you're a writer. I could use a capable story editor. What shows have you worked on?"

I shook my head. "I haven't. But I have some scripts . . ."

He gave me the job anyway, partly out of pity, the rest, I imagine, strength in numbers. No matter what he said about J. T., I think part of Jerry Jenkins, deep down inside, still loved him, too.

There was a bulletin board outside the Green Room's head, where I yarked up my Eggs Benedict. Among the ads for open mikes, low-budget casting calls, and porn companies seeking both male and female actors for high-paying daytime work, through waterlogged eyes I spied: *Roommate Wanted* . . .

It had been the best and worst day of my life. I'd lost the man of my dreams, but gained the job of my dreams writing for Hollywood. I'd lost a home, but wound up finding two others, one on the set of *America's Craziest Families* for two full seasons, the other after scaling three flights of metal stairs outside a shitty apartment building in Culver City.

I found the door with the right number and knocked.

A few breathless seconds later, the door opened, and standing on the other side was a tall, youngish man, truly the handsomest I'd ever seen in my life. Black, bed-headed hair. Dressed in a white wife-beater and camouflage cut-offs. Hairy legs. Big, sexy bare feet. I knew without being told he was a laid-back surfer type, total jock, a real guy's guy.

"Hey," he growled as he crunched on a stalk of celery stuffed with peanut butter. "You the dude that called about the apartment?"

"Yup," I stammered.

His startling green eyes zeroed in on my suitcase. "You want the place so badly that you packed for it?"

"I'm sort'a fucked at the moment. I don't have anywhere else to go."

"Then you'd better come in."

The first thing I noticed was a lack of furniture. It was a shitty, typical cinderblock apartment, not much different from the motel room I'd rented for a month. There was only a small portable TV propped up on a cardboard box and two folding chairs in the living room.

"I haven't been out here long. I'm Joe, by the way."

I took his hand, marveled at its strength, and shook back as firmly as I could. "Nice to meet ya," I said.

"I only got one bedroom, but if you're paying half the rent, you can have it. It's a mess right now."

The bedroom consisted of a sleeping bag on the floor, an army-issue duffel bag, some sports equipment, notably a baseball bat and a glove with a large dirty-gray jockstrap cupped in its palm, and the requisite pile of dirty sweat socks in clear view that all single, macho mostly-straight men seem to come outfitted with. I was smitten.

"You can keep the bedroom. I'll take the living room."

"You got a bed?"

"No, but I just won a sofa, loveseat, and a widescreen plasma TV on a game show."

Joe's noncommittal face unfroze. "No fuckin way! Hey, you said you're gonna be working on that show where people send in their craziest home videos?"

"Yeah. I have a meeting tomorrow at the studio to make it official."

"Sweet! I'm an actor."

"I'm gay."

Joe ceased crunching on celery and straightened. A confused look swept over his handsome face. "That's okay, I guess. You're not gonna, like, suck my dick when I get wasted, are you?"

"Only if you want me to." I fished the hundred-dollar bill J. T. had given me out of my front pocket and offered it to Joe. "Consider this a deposit, if you don't mind waiting for me to cash my first paycheck. That's if you want to be roommates . . ."

Another commercial break, and an ad saying that *Lingo* is coming up next on GSN. That's the show that features the blonde English chick Joe wants so desperately to fuck.

"Dude, I'd so cunni-*Lingo* that whore."

I glance in his direction and see Joe is still tugging on his balls. One hairy, itch-red nut hangs out of the left pant leg of his cut-offs. "You're a pig."

"And you love it."

He's right. I do.

Joe continues to toy with his balls. I steal a look at his crotch to see he's tenting in his cammies, a wet spot already formed where the head of his cock is pressing upward, begging for release.

"I better fuckin get laid tonight," he growls, shoving a hand into his shorts, the remote control abandoned.

There's a six-pack of beer in the fridge. "Oh, you will, I guarantee it," I whisper.

J. T.'s voice booms out of the speaker. "Be sure to tune in the next time our shoppers go credit-crazy on *Buy 'Til You Die*."

He flashes that phony smile again for the camera, but I don't respond to it. I only feel nothingness for him now.

I turn back toward Joe, who is quietly masturbating his cock in his cut-off cammies, and what I feel for him burns with overwhelming passion. We have been together for three years, as close as two men can be.

Before I can stop the words, I say, "I love you."

Joe's eyes narrow into gun sites, pinning me in their crosshairs. "Huh?"

"Let's not do this anymore," I say. I slide off the loveseat and kneel between his legs, place my hand over the hand he's stroking his cock with. "I love you, Joe."

"Dude, I'm not gay," he says weakly, making no attempt to shirk my touch.

"I know, babe. I know."

He slides his hand out of his pants, tosses his arm over his face. I catch sight of his emerald greens from under the wrist, watching me without blinking as I unzip his pants and haul out his magnificent cock, which is fully erect, its pee hole oozing clear liquid. As I lower, taking him between my lips, Joe tells me he loves me, too.

And he doesn't phrase it in the form of a question.

Gut Reaction

Barry Lowe

I should have known I wouldn't make it. That's the problem with eating new cuisine: you don't know how your gut will react. Well, I knew now. After trying that new Kyrgyzstani restaurant, recommended so volubly by the local food guide, I had decided to walk home in an effort to shed some of the *avoirdupois* that had settled on my already portly frame. My dinner companions had very wisely taken the car.

My mouth had loved the new flavors and food textures but my stomach, the final arbiter of all things cuisinetical, was now remonstrating sourly that a car ride would have been the better option. It was rumbling like Old Faithful in Yellowstone National Park. And was likely to be as projectile as said geyser if I didn't hurry. Fortunately, as someone who did not like to publicly expel any bodily fluids from any orifice of my body, I was nearing the local park set up by the city council in an effort to capture the green vote by dedicating a former industrial estate alongside a major freeway from the airport. To date it consisted of hardy weeds and spiky bushes which thrived on the carbon monoxide and particulate rubber from the passing stream of motorists. Grass, however, was attempting to impose its authority on the landscape without much success. And dominating this forlorn excuse for green space was the brick toilet block of such utilitarian architectural ugliness the more environmentally sensitive members of said council had attempted to disguise it by planting a number of trees and native bushes grandly labeled an urban forest.

Those of a less party political bent said the urban forest was merely a ruse to disguise the folly of the park that remained steadfastly underutilized by the locals who had a healthy concern for their respiratory well-being. Regardless, the single-storey brick garage of a building with opaque glass and wire mesh windows and a doorway on opposing sides, one labeled men and another wimin, not a tribute to the vagaries of council political correctness but more correctly to feminist vandals, is patronized. In the late afternoon by dog lovers who can release their pooches to cavort, shit and piss freely without the Gestapo tactics of the poop scoop brigade. But even they flee the advent of darkness. As the sun sets they desert the oasis of dust and toxic fumes to make way for that most ubiquitous of all life forms, the cockroaches of gay and closeted humanity: beat queens. These are the people who live on scraps of sexual experience away from bright lights, scuttling from contact to contact, disappearing at the slightest hint of trouble, and so widespread and adaptable are their earth-wide foraging fields that they, too, like their insectoid counterparts, would probably survive a nuclear holocaust.

Beats: a necessary part of gay life and, in fact, for many people of my generation in particular, the only gay meeting place for our early sexual and social experimentation. I spent many an exploratory teen year undergoing rigorous oral examinations unknown by my high school examiners and about which my parents remained resolutely mute. I think a strong case could, and should, be made that the United Nations declare beats the sacred sites of gay culture.

But my stomach was in no mood for such philosophical niceties. It wanted my mind to concentrate on from which orifice I was going to expel rancid food particles that were bubbling volcano-like in my gut as there was no way I was going to make it home before the expected eruption. That had been my initial plan. You see, I'm modest about body functions in public. I don't mind flashing my dick in circumstances that are likely to have it (a) sucked, or (b) inserted in someone's rectum; for everything else I find a cubicle to give piss a chance. I piss in the street only (a) when my bladder is about to burst, (b) a sex partner has an uncontrollable urge to be humiliated publicly, or (c) I wish to show my contempt for some extreme examples of modern architecture. And if I'm coy about public pissing I'm downright obsessive about public displays of projectile vomiting.

I gave belated thanks to the misguided council apparatchik who had created the park and headed for the block. It was dark and my way was guided by the peripheral glare of the halogen beam that emanated from the tall concrete pole. The other five park lights had long since given up in despair, or homophobia, so that all that remained was this brave little park light that cast its happy smile on nothing more edifying than a few clumps of fly-blown dog shit and the occasionally rotting carcass of a bird or marsupial that had been clobbered attempting to cross the freeway and had limped or dragged itself to the comparative safety of the park only to expire.

Or perhaps the happy little light knew precisely what it was doing. There were rumors that shots had been heard in the vicinity the night the first lights went out: those that focused their sticky-beak illumination on the toilet block and the surrounding bushy urban forest. Just as the internal lights in the toilet had been rendered sightless within the first week of their existence. A half-hearted attempt to replace them had led, ultimately, to the sockets being wrenched from the walls. No one had been foolish enough to go against the obvious wishes of the park's constituency and the amenities remained resolutely dark, lit only by the odd beam of a car illegally chucking a U-ey on the freeway or the rheumy wintry glow of the moon.

Hoping for some privacy I went to the women's toilet. But the grate was locked. I rattled it and all I got for my disturbance was a drunken slur: "Piss orf, we're full up." Full in at least two senses of the word.

At the darkened entrance to the men's toilet I bumped into a figure standing guard – occasionally the police would roar across the park with their lights blazing and siren screaming and the denizens of the sex pit would scatter – I begged his pardon and his reply was a surly "Watch it next time, mate." I groped my way inside and paused to give my eyes time to adjust. I basically knew where the cubicles were, the position of the urinals, and the odd positioning of the wash basins. I expected the smell of stale piss, sperm and urinal cakes although most of those had disintegrated long ago and had never been replaced, I suspect, because they were too *Princess and the Pea* lumpy for those of a sensitive disposition who lay in the stainless steel urinal.

Nor was the smell that of rampant testosterone. I sniffed again.

"Some demented queen has adorned the place with air fresheners," a voice beside me whispered.

"Mm, sure is minty fresh," another hissed, not altogether in approval.

I could see vague shadows now and that there was activity afoot, or rather aknee. In fact, the guy who had commented on the freshness of the air had a kneeling head at crotch level apple-bobbing frantically on his cock while others watched, expectantly awaiting their turns. I stumbled to one of three cubicles all of which had their doors closed. I knew they weren't secure because the locks had been removed. Not by council but by beat queens who had bristled when recreational drug users discovered they were an ideal shooting gallery. This had been tolerated as long as the drug users stuck to their hours and removed the paraphernalia afterwards. But they hadn't and, in the ensuing stand-off, locks had been removed and police, who were more than amenable to arresting drug addicts (it looked good on their arrest record) than randy queens, were tipped off. They relocated to a more amenable abandoned sports block within walking distance to the methadone clinic.

The drunks were much more amenable. They only used the toilets in winter when the temperature outside threatened to freeze their balls off and beat queen numbers declined. An unofficial memorandum of understanding proscribed the women's toilet for the exclusive use of the alcoholically addicted during winter and that they could use it and lock the iron grate door against invasion.

I pushed on the cubicle door. Someone was leaning their weight against it. Ditto the second. Voices hissing angrily "Wait your turn like everybody else," were not about to dissuade me from my purpose. The third door opened unexpectedly because the occupant, a young man kneeling on the floor ministering to the obvious needs of an eager penis engorging through the expertly drilled and sanded glory hole, was too engrossed to bother wedging his hand or foot against the door. He hadn't time to push me out before I had my pants down round my ankles and my ass over the stainless steel bowl, and contemptuously continued his oral gymnastics. I wanted him to leave and whispered that I needed privacy for what was a very private experience for me. He either didn't hear or didn't understand because he burbled something about, "Wait a minute and I'll get to you as soon as I've finished with this one."

I didn't want a turn. And I couldn't wait. All I wanted was privacy. I toyed with the idea of rushing out and squatting among the pine needles but my gut made the decision for me. The fart was L-o-n-g. LOUD. And Very Toxic. Fermented. The young man didn't miss a beat in his vacuum action until the stench reached his nostrils. He paused. Looked at me. Sniffed. Let out an "eeyeeeew" which was followed seconds later by a chorus of similar from the other side of the cubicle door. The cock that had been poking through the glory hole was withdrawn as quickly as a bank deposit in a shonky bank and I heard a chorus of zips zipping and hasty exits. Ah, at last, I was going to be alone for my business. Yes, the circumstances were embarrassing as half the denizens of said toilet block were daylight-hours respectable men who would now avert their gaze from me on the bus we took to our places of employment each workaday morning. I had soiled not only myself but also my reputation in their eyes. It was worse than being rejected in public by butt-ugly straight boys who would normally plug their cock in any orifice within spitting distance.

It was much worse, even, than being rejected publicly by Him! Him was God incarnate! We had all tried. And all failed. Built like a brick shithouse, the looks of a young Billy Idol with platinum blond hair and a platinum blond sneer. And a platinum blond cock carved from the most magnificent platinum blond marble on Mt. Olympus. The gods of all religious persuasions had smiled indeed on this guy. I consoled myself the night I had been rejected publicly with the simple maxim that I wasn't turned on by blonds anyway so there . . .

But right now I was attempting to hold the cubicle door closed with my foot while perched over the bowl expelling wads of fetid foodstuffs while the front entrance guard was banging on the door telling me that there had been complaints I was using the toilet to shit in. Did I know that was a breach of Paragraph 6, subsection 15A, lines 27-35 of the beat queen's charter? My response was a curt "Fuck off, I've got diarrhea." "Well fuckin' take it outside like everyone else," he huffed. "There's a section in the pine grove for that sort of thing. There's even toilet paper supplied along with a small shovel." I thanked him for his concern and excused my behavior on the grounds that I was not a regular. "Yeah, that's as obvious as the nipples on a watermelon," he muttered and gave me a few minutes to tidy myself up and get out or he'd come and get me. He even tossed a few scraps of paper over the door. I was thankful because otherwise I would have had to resort to using my handkerchief, which I was extremely reluctant to soil as it was the only remaining memento from my long-dead grandmother. I was cleaning up as best I could when I heard the guard say: "I wouldn't go in there, mate. Not until the air fresheners have done their job."

Obviously the newcomer took no notice because I heard the scrape of running shoes on gritty concrete. Then the first cubicle door slammed open. He had been expecting resistance and there had been none forthcoming. Similarly the second. When he reached mine I was about to call out that I was in no fit state to receive visitors when the door banged part open, slamming against my knee. I was about to scream a string of curses when I realized that my previous dump had been merely the first in what was to be a long line of boweletic evacuations. I realized simultaneously that standing witness to my predicament was Him himself! Without thinking I pushed the man of universal wet dreams out of the cubicle and slammed my foot against it. I shat in abject humiliation. My life was at an end. There was no way I could ever catch the bus to work. I would have to leave the country.

I cleaned up as best I could and decided my exit strategy would be to walk out as if nothing had happened and return at least one sheet of the toilet paper to the concierge at the door. Alas, the best of intentions . . .

I rushed through the entrance and toward the clump of trees hoping to cover not only my embarrassment but the yards needed to make it to the outside latrine. A hiss of spray took my place in the toilet and I detected the subtle aroma of lavender before a voice called, "Okay, girls, it's safe to come back now." A stampede of shadows almost knocked me down but at least the urban jungle was free. I found the rather well concealed, but well planned, latrine with its shovel and bucket of sluice water and a rather lovely textured toilet paper cut into equal sized strips with just a hint of . . .

I had my jeans down round my ankles and was squatting unceremoniously over a small hole I had dug sniffing a sheet of paper. I couldn't quite make out the scent.

"Jasmine and jojoba," a voice said from the dark.

Shit! On top of everything else that had happened that night I had been caught sniffing toilet paper. Was there no end to my disgrace? I looked up and, of course, it was Him. Was ritual disemboweling now my only option?

"You rejected me," he said ominously. "No one's ever

rejected me before. That's my line. But you pushed me and slammed the door in my face."

There wasn't a lot I could do if he intended attacking me. My life flashed before my eyes. And my stomach lurched in terror.

"You know what your rejection did to me, mate?" he said. I nodded weakly as he moved closer. "It made me so fuckin' hard!" He unzipped his jeans. "Nobody's done that me in yonks. Made me so hard."

He held my head and began to push his cock rhythmically in and out of my mouth, his shaft headed toward the back of my throat. Big mistake. My gag reflex is usually something upon which I pride myself. But not this night. Not with a stomach full of acid and raw vomitous. He pushed. Too far. And too often. I could feel reflux in my throat. I pushed him hard enough that he tumbled over backwards just in time for me to deposit the contents of my stomach all over his cock and balls. Not once. But twice.

I wiped my mouth and fled the scene, tugging up my jeans as I went. "Hey, fuckin' get back here!" he called. I couldn't determine whether it was anger, murder, or mutilation in his voice.

I stumbled, rather than ran, along the footpath hoping that in the glare of the headlights of cars whizzing along the freeway he would injure me only slightly. I was too weak to struggle so when I heard the thud of footsteps I decided to confront my fate. When I turned he was smiling. "That's the second time you rejected me! Fuck man, that's so cool. All the other guys are so fuckin' annoying, chasing after me cause I'm so good-looking. And a cock courtesy of God Almighty. It's all too easy. But you, you fuckin' rejected me. How great is that?"

I knew better than to tell him I'd rejected him only because of a mammoth attack of food poisoning and that in reality I was another of those annoying stalkers. "What's your name, mate? I'm Wayne." I revealed my name as he walked slowly alongside me and I glanced at the guilty wet patch at the front of his jeans where he'd attempted to wipe my chuck off with the sluice bucket. "You got a phone number?" he asked. "I mean, only if you want to give it to me. I won't be one of them annoying stalker types. You know, I'll only ring if you want." I gave him my number as *faux* reluctantly as I dared. "You've got no idea how boring sex is when you can have whoever you want," he moaned. No, I didn't have any idea and I was never likely to. "Makes it hard to get excited." There was a very long pause before he stopped and looked at me. "You wanna do me?"

I tried to look as if I was wrestling with the answer, hoping my stiffening cock wouldn't give me away. "Well . . ." I said, mustering every ounce of my acting ability to sound as offhand as I could.

"Come on," he pleaded. "Let's go back to the park and I'll let you do me in front of them bastards. Really piss them off"

"I dunno . . ." I stared at my watch, insinuating I had somewhere better to be, all the while gleefully anticipating that this one act would wipe out the total humiliation of the night thus far and lend me an aura of sexual supremacy.

"I'll drop you off if you have to go somewhere. I got my car." He was so eager.

I allowed him to cajole me into it. Reluctantly, ever so reluctantly, he brought me round. He was getting off on it and it made the anticipation all the hotter.

"Come on back to the park and do me!" he commanded finally.

So I went back to the park. And did him. I did him good!

The Other Half of Me

Jim McDonough

I groaned as the alarm buzzed. I wasn't ready to get up. I was never ready to get up.

I nudged my boyfriend Paul who was sleeping soundly to my left. The man was able to sleep though just about anything. I nudged him again and got no response.

"Paul, Paul. Wake up. You'll be late for work again."

I then crawled on top of the sleeping hunk with whom I shared my bed, my thoughts, my hopes, my dreams, and the past four years.

"Wake up. You're going to be late."

Paul groaned and rubbed his eyes.

"Huh?"

"Time to get up," I repeated. "Don't blame me if you're late for work again."

I reached under the blankets and tickled him. He squirmed like a fish flopping on dry land.

"Okay, okay. I'm up. I'm up."

He pushed me off him. I pulled the covers back over me as he headed off to the bathroom. Paul paused at the bathroom door. He turned and flashed me the smile that made me fall in love with him over and over again.

Paul looked so damn good standing naked at the bathroom door. Just looking at him with his broad shoulders, his beefy pecs that were covered in a swirl of dark hair and his flat stomach that was just a few crunches short of being a total washboard was giving me more than a few ideas.

"What time is your shift at the store?" he asked. Paul scratched at his balls, totally unaware just how much he was getting to me.

"I go in at ten," I said.

"Bastard," said Paul.

I rolled over, feeling a bit frustrated. I pulled the covers over my head and grabbed Paul's pillow, pulling it close to me. I lay there for a few minutes, listening to the sound of the water running in the shower and Paul's off-key singing echoing off the tile bathroom walls.

When it became apparent that I wouldn't be able to get a couple more hours of sleep, I hopped out of bed, figuring that I could get some stuff done around the house before I had to go in and play the helpful salesclerk at Crate & Barrel.

I padded into the bathroom to take a leak and brush my teeth. Paul was still singing. It was another one of the many things I loved about him.

"Justin, what are you doing out of bed?" he asked over the sound of the water. I briefly thought about shucking my jockeys and joining him, but I knew if I did, one thing would lead to another, and I'd get blamed for making him late for work again.

"I'm going to take a shower and do a few things before I go to work. We need groceries and I can stop by the cleaners and pick up your shirts."

Paul turned off the water, got out of the shower and grabbed a towel. He stepped closer to me, smiling as he approached.

"Well, it's all yours then," he said.

Paul stood in front of me, still damp from the shower. He rubbed the bright yellow towel through this thick wavy hair and then wrapped it around his middle.

I turned and smiled. Paul stepped even closer and gave me a look. He smelled fresh and clean and I was filled with nothing but dirty thoughts.

He grabbed his toothbrush and squeezed a big dollop of toothpaste. Sometimes I could just lose myself as I watched

Paul doing the simplest things. I particularly loved the faces he made in the mirror as he brushed his teeth. He scrunched up his face and squinted his eyes as he continued brushing. I chuckled quietly to myself as Paul began to foam at the mouth.

"What?" asked Paul. The bright red toothbrush was sticking out of his mouth.

"Nothing," I said.

Paul shook his head and rolled his eyes at me. Sometimes I wondered if he really knew just how much I loved being with him.

"Are you going to take a shower?" he asked.

I shrugged. Paul stepped closer. He wiped his mouth with his forearm.

"You know, I could go in a little late," he said.

"I know," I said, gulping.

I looked quickly at Paul and then diverted my glance.

"You could go in late, too," he said. "Or maybe not at all."

"I could," I said. I knew that wasn't going to happen. We had played this game before.

A few seconds passed. They seemed like forever.

"You going to shower, or what?" asked Paul.

"Or what," I said. I could feel myself smirk.

Paul dropped the towel and it puddled on the floor around his ankles. He flashed me that smile again and I immediately tented my shorts.

It was a mad dash back to bed. We collapsed in a heap on our old down comforter in a fit of giggles. Paul pulled me close and his lips brushed my cheek.

He pulled back slightly and grinned. "You need to shave," he said.

"You need to shut up and kiss me," I said.

Paul pressed his lips to mine and locked his arms around me, pulling me tightly to his still slightly damp body. He tasted of peppermint and smelled of Ivory soap. I ran my fingers through his damp hair and kissed him harder.

We rolled around the bed several times until I was finally

able to pin Paul's shoulders to the mattress while I repositioned myself on top of him.

We both tried to catch our breath. I sat on top of Paul, just staring into his brown eyes, occasionally catching a glimpse of myself reflected in his pupils. I was smiling. Lately I was always smiling. In a million years I could have never imagined myself so happy. And Paul was the one who was most responsible for that happiness.

We had met at a party, introduced by mutual friends who thought we'd be perfect for each other. Had I known I was being set up, I would have stayed home, and I suspect Paul would have done the same. He was shy and awkward at first, and I'm sure he sensed my own resistance at being set up, but before the end of the evening we were off in a corner totally unaware of the party around us.

The first clumsy date led to the second, the second to a third. Friendship led to familiarity, familiarity led to comfort, and comfort to closeness – and finally to love.

"You know, I still have to get to work," said Paul.

"So, then you're only looking for a quickie?" I asked. I rolled off Paul and laid next to him, wrapping my arm around him and snuggling close.

Paul reached over, stuck his hands in my shorts, pulled them down around my butt and then finally off before depositing them on the floor. He laughed and I kissed him again. Paul pulled me close and kissed me harder. As he hugged me tight, I thought just how comfortable my naked body felt pressed against his.

I noticed Paul watching the alarm clock. I hoped he really wasn't concerned about the time. Most often I was the one to instigate our morning romps. He was the responsible one. He was the one with the well-paying job that paid the mortgage and most of the bills. I, on the other hand, jumped from retail job to retail job and took a couple of evening classes, hoping I'd be able to figure out what I wanted to do with the rest of my life besides lying in Paul's embrace.

Paul didn't seem to mind that he carried most of the weight

when it came to the finances. His friends had told me that he seemed much more at ease since we moved in together. Even with that knowledge, I sometimes felt guilty about not doing my fair share.

He was a catch. All my friends told me that. He was classically handsome, with his dark wavy hair and deep brown eyes. Even with the demands of his job, he made a point of getting to the gym on the nights I was in class. He didn't have to work too hard to stay in shape. He'd played soccer in high school and college, and still enjoyed the occasional weekend game with his friends.

While Paul kissed me, I ran my fingers across his back and broad shoulders, playing with the drops of water that he hadn't toweled off. I wished that we could spend the entire morning in bed together. It was so rare that we got to do that, given our crazy schedules.

Each kiss left me wanting more, but I knew Paul was pressed for time. I would have to work fast. I began to kiss the nape of his neck and worked my way lower and lower.

When I kissed Paul's shoulder, he closed his eyes and let out a deep breath. I flicked my tongue across his nipples and then continued my way down to his taut belly.

I teased and taunted Paul with my tongue. When I finally took him into my mouth, Paul sighed. I could feel his entire body relax as his cock got harder.

"Oh, Justin. Don't stop."

I kept on going and it wasn't long before Paul was gasping for breath and on the verge of coming.

I knew he was really close, so I let up on sucking his dick and took him in my hand and with a few slight jerks, Paul shot his load all over his belly.

"Oh, fuck," he groaned.

Paul gasped for breath a few more times. I sat there and stared at him, happy, knowing I'd send him off to work with a smile on his face.

"What are you grinning about?" he asked.

"Oh, nothing," I said.

Paul repositioned himself on the bed and leaned up against the headboard.

"Your turn," said Paul.

"You're going to be really late," I said.

"Well, I can't leave you like that," he said.

I looked down at my erection and chuckled. I could have taken care of the problem myself while Paul cleaned up, but I generally let Paul get his way.

"If you lose your job, don't go blaming me," I said.

"I can get another job."

I rolled my eyes at that comment. Paul loved his job. He was probably the only person I knew who truly enjoyed going to work.

Paul scooted down the bed and positioned himself between my legs. I closed my eyes, lay back down with my head on the pillows and sort of drifted off as Paul went down on me.

There was something about sex with somebody who truly knows me that I really enjoy. I had done my share of tricking before I had met Paul and it always left me cold. I even had a few failed attempts at relationships, but I had never found anything like what I had with Paul. It was like the man could read my mind or sense my every feeling. He knew exactly what I liked, what made me feel so good. I often wondered if he thought the same of me.

"Oh shit, that feels great. Don't stop," I groaned.

I opened my eyes and glanced at Paul. He looked up at me and grinned. Our eyes locked. I watched as Paul licked his lips slightly and the corners of his mouth turned up.

"You like that, don't you?" he asked.

He knew I did. Before I could protest one more time, Paul worked his way even lower and I began to squirm.

"Oh stop. I'm getting close," I said.

Paul ignored my pleas and continued to work his magic. I tensed up and thought I was going to lose it. I sucked in a deep breath and tried to relax. I wasn't ready to come just yet.

I found myself looking around our bedroom, trying to

distract myself so it would last. I never told Paul, but I loved when we got a little carried away in the morning, which more often than not led to his rushing to work. I loved the idea of Paul sitting at his desk thinking about us together; I got lost in thought that way often enough while I was at work.

I focused on a pair of Paul's well-faded jeans that were rolled in a ball at the foot of the bed. He'd dropped them there right before he crawled into bed with me the night before. He never put anything in the hamper, the slob. Next to the jeans were a pair of his bright white boxer shorts and a pair of his tube socks.

Next, I focused on a photograph of Paul and me that was sitting on top of the dresser. It was taken while we were on vacation in Palm Springs the year before he asked me to move in with him. Paul was standing behind me, his arms wrapped around my middle and his head nestled on my shoulder. We were both sunburned, but smiling. Years later, I was just as happy as the afternoon that photo was taken.

I got to the point where I was no longer able to hold back. Paul was making me crazy. I let out a soft groan and felt a familiar wet gush across my belly.

Paul gently kissed me on the shoulder. He then scooted up the bed and lay next to me. He kissed me softly one more time.

We lay there for a few minutes in silence. Paul glanced over at the alarm clock which was ticking away the minutes.

"I am going to be so late," he said.

"I told you."

Paul hopped out of bed and made a dash for the bathroom.

"Just tell them you got stuck in traffic," I said. I turned on the radio and fiddled with the dial, trying to catch the traffic report.

"That's what I always tell them," he said. "I guess I should come up with a new excuse."

"You could tell them the truth," I said.

Paul laughed. Somehow I couldn't imagine him telling his boss he was late because he was screwing his boyfriend.

"Better save me some hot water," I said.

Paul stopped at the bathroom door. He turned and flashed me that smile once again.

"Well, you coming or not?"

Dear Drew Peters

Harry Thomas

I just read a review of your new film, *Deception Part 2* on the Internet. Apparently, you get fisted in it. The reviewer gives this movie four stars. I also read a review of *Skateboard Sliders 3*. In that film, you reportedly get fucked by two guys at the same time. Not one in front, one in back Chinese fingercuffs style, but DP, double penetration: two pegs, one hole. This only rates three and half stars. (Everyone, it seems, is a critic.)

But really, Drew, fisting? I've been watching your movies for years now. I've seen you on your knees, on all fours, on your back. I've seen you suck cock, I've seen you get fucked. I've seen you in handcuffs and blue Speedo swimsuits. I've seen you seduced with fresh strawberries and champagne, I've seen you strapped to a wooden cross and whipped until your back was raw. I've seen nine or ten guys fuck your face in a jail cell while they called you "Ratboy". I've seen a roomful of straight Marines jerk off all over you. I've seen you smile and sit effortlessly on cocks so terrifyingly huge they are more scientific anomaly than turn-on. I've seen you get fucked by all manner of hideous but horsehung tops, men so consistently, unrelentingly ugly they couldn't possibly deserve you, men so ugly they look like they should be in straight porn. But I've never seen you get fisted.

I don't know anything about the porn industry, Drew, so when I imagine your life in my head your supporting cast is pretty sleazy. Did a fat man with a wheezing laugh who takes

a cut of your profits tell you that you were getting boring?
Did he tell you that everyone's seen you suck cock and get
fucked a thousand times already? Did he tell you that people
were tired of that? Well, don't believe him. This career
trajectory might be true for other porn stars, but those
meatheads are just mere mortals. We the sleazy tire of
watching them just suck and just fuck because when they
do, it's just that: just sucking, just fucking.

You don't just suck cock, Drew. You worship cock. You
slobber on cock like a man who's been starving for it, like a
boy who's facing ten to twelve years of cock drought ahead of
him. You suck cock like it was the last cock on Earth, like you
were the Platonic ideal of cocksucker, like whatever dick
happens to be between your lips and down your gag-reflex-
less throat was the king hell bastard of all cock, the dick to
end all dick.

And you don't just get fucked. You squirm and you whine
and you moan and you screw your pretty face up so we all
know just how much it's hurting you and how much you need
it. You don't get fucked, you get drilled, you get nailed, you
get plowed, you arch your ass up and stick it back, asking for
it, begging for it. Men fuck you the same way I used to dig
holes to China in my backyard, convinced that if I just got
down in there deep enough, I'd break through to another
land, to some mystical place where everyone wore silk and
funny hats and where my parents would have no rule over
me.

But seriously, fisting and DP in the same year, Drew?
What's next? Where do you go from here? 'Cause, soon
enough, we'll be tired of fisting, too. I won't be, of course,
but that fat man will tell you I am, and you'll believe him.

It's not a question of not being able to have you. I know I
could have you. The Internet assures me it's as easy as calling
303 329 8242, the number for Boys Next Door, the "escort"
service that books you. Their homepage assures me that you
are "available for travel", so I guess a plane ticket and three

hundred bucks is all I need. The three hundred's for you of course, that's what you make in an hour, just to "escort". That jumps up to fifteen hundred if I want you to stay overnight.

I called the number of course. Not that I had my credit card out and ready to charge or anything, but I had to see if it was real. So I called. Someone named Greg answered the phone: "Boys Next Door, this is Greg." Who the fuck is Greg, Drew? Do you know him? Has he met you? Does he have your contact information, your home phone number? And what kind of life does Greg have anyway? Who's more pathetic, me for calling to order you up like a pizza or him for being there to process my request?

Don't answer that, Drew.

Of course I hung up on Greg without saying a word, but what if I had ordered you? I wonder how it works because while I'm devoted, I'm also poor. I mean, I own most of your videos – all of your good ones anyway – but I always rent before I buy. They're fifty dollars a pop after all and fifty dollars is a lot of money to me, not to mention six times that for an hour of the real thing. Like any well trained American (read: consumer) I like to know what I'm getting before I buy.

Thank God then for the Internet. Is the Internet American? Did we invent it? We must have, because what could be more American than a means of communication which lets anyone bitch and whine about the products they consume, even when one of those products is you, Drew. Oh, I'm not kidding: I found a website where johns review their hustlers.

Of the four reviews of your (ahem) work online, the "oral bottom" liked you the best. His review said he hired you in San Francisco, during November of 2000. He said you live in San Francisco. He said you work part time as a lifeguard at a YMCA there. The mind boggles just to hear this, Drew, and even though I know that truth is always stranger than fiction, I still wonder if any of it is true. After all, it's your job to make anyone's idiosyncratic sexual fantasy seem like exactly what you wanted to be doing morning, noon or night, so doesn't it figure that you also know how to tell people what they want to hear?

Mr "Oral Bottom" said a lot of things about you online, Drew. He said, "Drew made out with me like we were going down on the Titanic." He said you arrived "on time, freshly showered and full of come". He said you were "safe, honest, reliable" and "sweet". He said you were "humble". He promised prospective customers of yours that you wouldn't leave them "unsatisfied". He then went on to complain a little. Just a little. He said you were "a bit too businesslike, a tad bit aloof, but only very slightly." He said you "absolutely got the job done", but that you were not "the boy to have a crush on".

Well, it's a little late for that.

And damn it makes me angry, him calling you "business-like." I mean, my God, he was paying you to fuck him. It's like walking into a bakery and getting mad because they aren't giving the bread away for free. It's a bakery, not a soup kitchen, you know?

Still, most of the reports were positive, Drew. Three out of your four online reviewers give you a "Recommended" or better rating. The last guy said you flaked on him, said you never showed up for the appointment. This would be the "39-year-old Caucasian top", from March of 2001. He said:

I called Boys Next Door, Drew's agency, to make a booking for the following night. I was suitably impressed that within a few hours Drew himself called to make the arrangements. We arranged to meet at my hotel the following evening at 8 p.m. After reading the reviews on this site and talking to him, I was really excited about the meeting. 8 o'clock rolled around, 8.30 [sic], no Drew and no phone call even. I called Boys Next Door and they said they would try and contact him. They never called back. I called again and they said they had been unable to reach him but would try again. Once again, they never called back to let me know what was happening. By the time 9.30 [sic] came and still no Drew, I gave up. I tried to call a couple of other escorts, but of course at this late stage they were unavailable. I went to the Nob Hill Theatre and ended up paying too much money for appallingly bad sex with a model named Enrique. I was very disappointed with my experience with Drew and Boys Next Door. I still think Drew is the hottest guys [sic] around and when I am in San Francisco again in June I will try again hoping I have better luck.

Well, nobody wants to have sex with someone named Enrique when they could have had you, Drew, and your behavior here seems anything but business-like. So, like the rest of these ads, it leaves me wondering what the truth is, wondering what really went down in The Ramada Inn or The Four Seasons or whatever lonely hotel room you met these guys in. All of the reviews begin with fast facts: What you look like, how much you charge, how big your cock is, if you're willing to kiss. Reading over them, comparing the little discrepancies is like looking at slightly different maps of a place I've never been. Guy number one says you have an eight inch cock, Mr "Oral Bottom" says seven. Did you lose an inch? Gain one? Are you an "earnest youth" or a flaky, overpriced disappointment? And if you're more the latter than the former, how come Mr "Caucasian Top" – that poor schmuck – is going to keep on trying?

Okay, even I know the answer to that one.

Still, I wonder which Drew I'd get if I ordered you. And don't get me wrong, I would order you. I don't wonder if I'd pay three hundred for an hour of your time, but I do wonder what I'd do with it.

Okay, I admit it. On my list of things to do with you there's definitely the part where I buy every buttplug and dildo and arm-long set of anal beads in a twelve-square mile radius of Christopher Street and shove them all up your ass while you

whine and whine and whine like the beefy blond bitchboy of
my dreams, but then I think about actually having to do that.
Like, without the advantage of video editing. Like, all the
prep time and poppers and showering and the seventeen
enemas beforehand and, ugh. I don't want to deal with all
that embarrassing, potentially messy real-world stuff. I don't
want to have real sex with you, Drew. I'm twenty-five years
old, for God's sake. I'm a single, not hideously disfigured fag
who lives in Manhattan, and even if I did have a boyfriend
you could bet money we'd have an open relationship like
every other radically aspiring and commitment-terrified
homo-couple that parties south of 14th Street. I can have
real sex. I mean if I flat out had no taste I could have real sex
every night of the week and twice on Sunday! For free, no
less.

But I don't want real sex.

I think about you all the time, Drew. Not just sexually. You
are totally my pretend boyfriend. Like, I wonder about your
life. I wonder where you live. I wonder who you spend your
time with, who your friends are. I wonder what's in your CD
collection, if you even have a CD collection. I wonder if
you're happy, doing what you do. I wonder if you do drugs. I
wonder if you have AIDS.

And see, that's so fucked up. I mean everything I have ever
seen you do is safe. But still, I'm all sex-negative about it.
Like, okay, my biggest Drew Peters fantasy is that you are
this abused, fucked-over, exploited kid from some middle of
nowhere town in the Midwest. I imagine that your family
kicked you out and that you hitchhiked out to the West Coast
and that you were curious about leather or submission or
control or Daddies or whatever and that some creepy old guy
told you he'd pay you what you thought was a lot of money
but really wasn't and then boom, you're in, you're a porn
star.

But why do I think that? Why do I imagine you're so sad?
Why do I assume everyone you work with is some huge evil

asshole? Is it just because your line of work involves showing your asshole? That can't be it. After all, your asshole isn't evil, Drew. It's amazing.

And I don't want to be one of those Human Rights Campaign Rainbow Platinum Visa Card queers that thinks that all we need to do is settle down like straight people and get married like straight people and have babies like straight people and live in the suburbs like straight people and work shitty corporate jobs that make us miserable like straight people, you know? I mean, I think queer ought to be something different. Being an upper middle class white gay dude who can take his boyfriend to the office Christmas party is nice, but it's not the same thing as freedom. Liberation ought to be about widening the whole definition of what's "okay", not just shrinking us until we fit inside theirs, don't you think?

So then why am I all sex-negative when I imagine you, Drew? Why does their value system about sex, their system of how bodies are to be regulated and maintained color my field of view when I close my eyes and picture your work, your life? Why is my big fantasy you being all fucked up and sad, just so I can rescue you? I mean, I've been friends with enough addicts and depressives and compulsive behavior artists, I know perfectly well that you can't save or change or fix anyone. But even worse, even more wrongheaded than that – I think – is my idea that you need fixing at all. After all, way back in high school I decided to mark myself in terms of my sexuality, in terms of its deviance from what most people consider normal. If I felt – even then – that sexuality was something important, something not to be lied about, then how come some part of me must still think that that sex is the dirtiest, most degraded thing one person could do to another?

I found a picture of you online, Drew. Okay, I found lots of pictures of you online, but this one I'm talking about is the best one. You're sitting on a white counter or a washing machine, I can't quite tell what it is, you're just sitting there,

nude, and you're smiling. But it's this natural, easy, unrehearsed smile. And you're just sitting there, that's the point,
that's what's hot about it: You're not doing anything. You're
not grabbing your dick or leering at the camera with put-on
"Fuck Me" eyes or spreading your ass cheeks or any of those
other dumb porno poses. You're just a boy, a beautiful naked
boy, smiling at me, free and easy and unrehearsed. There are
no better pictures of you. That's the best picture of you ever.
It's the best picture ever, actually. As far as I'm concerned,
they can go ahead and stop making cameras.

I showed my friend Bard that picture. He said you look like
the kid who would pump my gas and wipe my windshield if I
was on a road trip through the Dakotas. He says you could be
a gas station attendant from the scary, rural Midwest. He
says you look like someone took one of those *Children of the
Corn* kids and ran him through the West Hollywood clone
machine. I told Bard to shut up. I told him you lived in San
Francisco, not L.A.

I love that you live there, or that you say that you do. In my
head you are all punk and alternative even though I know
that "alternative rock" was an evil thing and that you're a
porn star and that as such you probably go to The White
Party and The Hotlanta River Raft Cruise and Circuit-Jerk-
It or whatever they call all those parties that just make me
want to die.

It kills me to think of you there: at some dumb circuit
party, whacked out on coke and E and K while a bunch of
Muscle Marys who are mainlining Viagra into their dicks line
up to fuck you in the steam room. It hurts me, physically. As
Bard would say, it hurts my heart.

God, Drew, I'm sorry I'm so stupid. But I am. Stupid, I
mean. Like, I wonder if you're on steroids. As your film
career goes on, you keep getting bigger, keep getting buffer.
Is it possible you hate your body the way I hate mine? (Even
I'm not crazy enough to think you could love my body the
way I love yours.)

Listen to me, like I'm not part of the problem. I mean, I

love your muscles. I totally do. When I found you again, after I thought I'd lost you, when you changed your name from Drew Stevens to Drew Peters, when you made the jump from low-budget leather porn to high-end studio stuff, when you reappeared more bleached and more buff, after the cheesy tribal armband tattoo, after you got your fucked-up front teeth fixed? Fuck, I shot over my head, even if what you'd made your body into was the body of people I hate.

But no matter what you do, your ears are still your ears.

There's no easy way to say this Drew, but well: your ears are big. But I love them. I love them because the rest of you is perfect and your ears make you perfect for me, they make you human, they make you seem sweet. I mean if you watch your videography, and believe me Drew, I have, watching your body over time is like watching this obsessive-compulsive, fanatic, Nazi-esque quest for perfection. In the early stuff, you're more chicken than beef and, as you bottom your way up the porno food chain to where you're at now, working for Falcon Studios, the best of the best, you're more and more intentionally plastic. But no matter what you do, you still have those ears. Those big, huge, jug-handle ears. Those fucked up rural scary Midwest farm boy ears.

I have a fantasy that you really, really hate your ears, Drew. But I love them. They're just human. I love your dick too. But not in the way you might think. I mean, sure it's long, but it's pretty thin, especially by porn standards. I love that. It makes you human: it's just a dick.

Watching your movies is like watching a boy go to war with his own body. It's like you are on a slow but steady quest to root out imperfection, to tear up aberration, to grind all that I love about you into the ground. To break it up and smash it and tear it apart and scatter salt on the fields that gave birth to such offending, imperfect parts.

But no matter what you do to your body, your eyes are still there, looking out from inside of all that homogenous homo perfection, looking like the eyes of a scared little boy and leading me into the delusion that we – that you and I, Drew –

are having some kind of connection, like you're telling me something that you're not telling anyone else, telling me something you'd never tell all those "roided-out, fake-baked Joe Average faggots who get to fuck you on camera, telling me something you'd never tell all the 'Oral Bottoms', all the 'Caucasian Tops'," all the fat, dirty old men who no doubt fuck you off camera.

But isn't that what you're making everyone think? Here I am, hoping and hoping that we – you and I, Drew – are going to have some kind of connection. Hoping that with me, just with me, just this one time, that it's going to mean something to you, that you're going to open up, that you're going to tell me your real name, that you're going to tell me secrets, facts about your life I don't know and can't find on the Internet.

That's another one of my big fantasies: interviewing you. I don't care about publication. No-one else even has to see it, Drew, just as long as you'd sit in a room with me and talk, as long as you'd tell me your real name, where you're from, what your parents are like, if they know what you do and if so, how they feel about it. Aside from the copious amounts of whining you do on video, there's not a whole lot of your speaking voice to listen to, so I wonder what it sounds like. I wonder if it's high and queeny like in the beginning of *Untamed* or if it's all little-boy-lost like when you're begging for it in *Cock Slavery*. I fantasize about coming home with a micro-cassette with your name on it, putting my headphones on, firing up the transcription machine and having you all to myself for hours, your answers to everything I ever wanted to know mine to rewind and replay and never, ever record over. That isn't a jerk-off-to-it kind of fantasy, but it's a fantasy nonetheless.

My friend Joe laughed at me when I told him about that. He laughed harder when I said that maybe that's what I'd do with my hour with you, with my three hundred bucks. I said maybe I'd just interview you. I said it was true, I said I wanted to be sweet to you, Drew, I said we wouldn't even have to fuck. When Joe finally caught his breath, he said only

I could be so stupid as to think that interviewing you would be sweeter, less violent, less exploitative than sticking everything but the kitchen sink up your ass.

I don't want to admit it, but of course Joe's right. Still, I meant what I said: we don't have to fuck. It might be nice just to spend an hour with you. Maybe we could just go out. You could actually, literally escort me somewhere. I could take you to a Le Tigre show and you could tell me that they're your favorite band too, or maybe it'd be your first time and I could stand beside you and watch your face crack with smiling while Kathleen Hanna rages above us, melting down our eardrums with anger and joy. Or we could stay in, we could just talk. You could volunteer to tell me about your life and secretly violent as I am I'd want to put a tape recorder on, I'd want to write it down and take it for my own but this is fantasy, we are in fantasy land now and so I would resist. I would abstain from preying on you. I would buy you plaid pajama bottoms that were just a little too long so you had to cuff them and you'd put them on fresh out the shower and stay shirtless without my even having to ask. Each and every piece of music or movie or TV show or book, each of our personal favorite things we mentioned would be an instant match for the other, a pure and brilliant connection like a hand out of the dark you didn't even know you were reaching for. We could spoon.

I wouldn't make you wear a collar. You wouldn't have to squat on a huge black rubber dildo while you played with yourself and babbled about how badly you wanted to suck my cock. You wouldn't have to call me Daddy or Master or even Sir. If your ass is sore or if you have a yucky stomach flu or if we're out of lube or if you just plain 'ole don't want to, we don't even have to fuck. I wouldn't spank you, or tie you up, or put you in a cage. I wouldn't even bring my handcuffs. I wouldn't hurt you at all Drew, I wouldn't do bad things to you.

Not unless you wanted me to.

Pleasingly

Matthew Rettenmund

I never let myself go, I just *went*.

Actually, if you ask *me*, I didn't really go very far, just spread out a little. I'm not "obese" or "fat" or anything, just soft around the middle, blurred around the edges. I'm . . . *Rubenesque*.

You learn a lot when you gain weight. Like how big a turn-off spare pounds are to your gay brethren. One week, you're right in the thick of things, cruising and flirting up a storm; the next, you don't get noticed unless you make a funny sound or ask an untoward question . . . like, "How's it goin'?"

Being chubby in a skinny fag's world leaves you with lots of time to look around unnoticed, to see things. Important things like what's passing for glamorous these days, what makes all the guys' heads turn. When a musclebound, sha-ven-headed, earringed, *faux* macho-man struts past, the other guys are so busy craning their necks for a second look that they don't even realize *you're* checking *them* out, puzzling over how something so homogenous could elicit such ravenous interest.

I may be chubby, but I haven't lost interest in sex. I've never been much of a slut, always the big talker and seldom-doer. Until last weekend, I'd only ever slept with three guys: two steady boyfriends I ended up seeing for almost two years apiece, and one one-week stand in between them, with a snarky undergrad when I was a graduating senior and old enough to know better. The latter left me with genital warts, quite a feat considering we both wore condoms at all times. Did the fucker have them on his *tongue* or something? Sheesh.

Don't listen to anyone when they try to get you to, "*Relax* . . . we're having *safer* sex." Safer than what? Not having sex at all? Yeah, but still not safe, not ever 100 per cent safe. Sex is always dangerous. One way or another.

I was probably thinking about sex when I first bumped into Christopher. I *always* think about sex; I'm thinking about it right now, even as I'm trying to describe all the things that led up to the most incredible sex of my life, with Christopher, last weekend.

I had been on my building's elevator for so long I was almost convinced it was stuck. Visions of Keanu Reeves appearing at the vent overhead, pulling me to safety, evaporated when the ancient door slid open: Ground Floor. Hooray.

I stepped out and made a beeline for my mailbox, hoping desperately that I'd received my copy of *Entertainment Weekly*. The weekend just isn't the weekend if I haven't devoured everything that just got done happening the week before. Besides, I'd heard that there was a Barbra Streisand cover story, and though I *hate* that woman (I'm sorry, but where's the *pizzazz?*), there was a 50/50 chance for a photo of her luscious son by Elliott Gould (go figure).

Standing at my box was this guy, this big, chunky guy, trying in vain to force open my mailbox with his key. The nerve! I couldn't believe it was happening, and started to pipe up just before he glanced over at me and flashed me the pearliest grin I think I've ever seen.

"Hiya," he chirped, as nonchalantly as a person not trying to steal my mail, "How're you?"

"OK."

He'd straightened and was facing me now, allowing the full effect to sink in. I'm not one for physical attraction; I mean, I get turned on by just about any guy, whether he's classically studly or charmingly nerdy, just so long as he's "cute". But this guy – *whoa!* – this guy was unwittingly pushing every button on my panel without even lifting a finger.

He was my height, 5ft 9in, give or take, and roughly my build, except maybe even a bit chubbier. That would make him about, what? 220? Shut up, already – we've both got broad shoulders and big bones; 220 isn't the end of the world, even if it *is* nearing the end of the scale. He had short, dirty blond hair, a slight scruff on his round cheeks, and a Kirk Douglas puncture wound (read: dimple) in the middle of his chin. His eyes were sort of hazel, and they were looking at me with keen interest. It was like when you catch the attention of a cat – you get the feeling that no matter how hard you try, they're not gonna stop staring at you until they're good and ready.

"I'm having a hard time with my mailbox," he shrugged, "I'm new."

"You might have an easier time if you stuck the key in the right box," I said playfully, pointing first to the "6-E" on my mailbox, and then to the "6-E" printed on my key. He did a double-take, checked his key, then flushed scarlet and stammered an apology.

"It's no problem," I laughed, enjoying his cute discomfort, "Any time."

When he retrieved his mail – success! – it turned out he lived in 7-E, just a few feet above my head.

"I'm dying of embarrassment," he said, squinching up his face like a nine-year-old might. A great big, cuddly nine-year-old in a twenty-nine-year-old body.

"Really," I replied, "it could've been worse – you could've been trying to get into my apartment." We both laughed and then I took off to the store with my mail peeking out of my backpack. As I walked away from him, I had that familiar desire to be able to suck it in – not my tummy, but my love handles – for his benefit. I miss the days of feeling like I was doing someone a favor simply by turning around and walking away, gifting them with a pleasant view. But as I left the building, I turned slightly and saw that he was standing in the same place, watching me leave. Not so shabby after all, I guess, or was I just imagining things?

Later that evening, I found out.

I shopped, came home, put stuff away, and dropped. I'd been working thirteen-hour days trying to finish a mailing list at work, and now that it was over, I felt every lost hour of sleep and relaxation coming back with a vengeance. I thought I could sleep for days lying there on my folded-up futon mattress. I didn't even bother spreading it out, or changing into more appropriate clothes, I just . . .

. . . woke up with the shock of submersion. I was dripping wet, suddenly awake, and too annoyed to do more than exclaim. It was pitch black ouside; I'd been asleep for hours and had only woken up because a light but persistent stream of water was drizzling on my face from the ceiling, where it was condensing in a two-foot patch.

Oh, shit. All I could think of was that the new (cute) neighbor had left his tub running and taken off for the evening. I was going to have to call the super and get him out of bed to come over, get into the apartment, and wade across the upstairs neighbor's living room to incapacitate the tub.

I dashed out of my room, out of my apartment, and up the two small flights of stairs to seven, pounding on the door to 7-E.

"Anyone there? C'mon, open up!"

To my surprise, someone did. It was the new guy, and he was wearing an enormous white robe, just like Madonna in *Truth Or Dare*.

"What's up?" he asked, warming to the intrusion.

"Water. Is. Pouring. Out. Of. My. Ceiling," I seethed, "What's the problem?"

"It is? I mean, I don't know, I have no idea . . ." He stepped back inside his apartment and I followed him to the bathroom, but there was nothing overflowing anywhere. It could only be a burst pipe, and that would be a major pain in the ass to fix.

"Call Juan," he said, handing me his phone, "he'll have to come right over."

Juan did, and was taking his sweet-assed time digging around in the tub and under the sink while Christopher – we'd finally exchanged names – and I sat around watching E! and criticizing Bianca Ferrere and Steve Kmetko. We really hit it off like that, just joking around with each other like old pals, no awkwardness at all. The whole time, Christopher was still in his diva robe, affording me a look at his hairy chest and even hairier legs. He smelled fucking terrific, too, like he'd used some amazing bath gel in the shower, or maybe it was just a killer shampoo. With his hair dripping in his eyes, he looked like young Marlon Brando, except doughier, blonder, and more approachable.

"It's fixed," Juan barked on his way out. "Don't be so rough on the pipes."

"Oh, OK," I called after him, "Next time we take a shower we'll do it real gentle-like."

Now came the weirdness. Up until that point, Juan's presence made the evening harmless. Now, I was alone in the room with a sexy guy who was wearing only a robe and a sheepish grin. He was sitting on the couch, and I was sitting on the couch's arm, feeling like Tweetie Bird balancing on the swing in his gilded cage.

"I better go, eh?" I chattered, getting up to leave.

"No," Christopher said, taking my arm. "Stay."

I'm not lying when I tell you that this kind of shit *never happens to me,* but the next step was complete facial gridlock. He pulled me over on to his lap, holding my jaw and kissing my face like a lonely dog. When he got me on the lips, he had his tongue in my mouth before I was aware my mouth was even *open.* Just the way he pulled me over on to him made me weak with wanting it – he was so aggressive.

I ground my ass into his crotch, my knees at my chest, his arms around my torso and pulling me closer. He kissed my cheeks, licked my neck, nibbled the skin at my shoulder-blades – in no time flat I became shirtless without a care in the world that my belly would be exposed. When he reached up and manipulated one of my nipples, kissed it and flickered his tongue over the tip, I nearly lost it – not only did it make me instantly unafraid that my fleshy body wouldn't be appealing to him, it just so happens that with me, it's *all* in the nipples.

"Oh, yeah, I *love* that," I muttered, forgetting that dirty talk usually does nothing for me. This time, it wasn't contrived dirty talk, it was stuff I was saying because I couldn't *help* myself.

"Suck my tits, lick my tits." I bounced in his lap, luxuriating in the attention he paid to the most sensitive part of my body.

Christopher swirled his tongue around my nipples, ran it from tit to tit and back again, chewed them until they were so raw every touch felt like ten. He was really hard under me – I could feel his prick beating against the underside of my thigh.

I was reluctant to give up the nipple work, but there was more to be had. I stood up and unbelted my jeans, pulled them down and off, leaving the underwear intact. Mental note: use more bleach.

Christopher sat still, expectant, smiling, and winked at me while I got completely naked. I wouldn't learn until the next day that he secretly loves to leave the underwear on, to work around it.

My next move was to open his robe. I don't know why gay guys are so afraid of a little meat on a man's bones, but if anyone could persuade them to change their ways, it's Christopher. He is a hunky, meaty man with a large gut and rounded pecs and just about the most beautiful cock I've ever seen. It wasn't porno-huge – they never are, are they? – but just perfectly fat and artistically veiny, and it was leaking pre-come like my ceiling leaks pipewater.

Condoms.

He had some, thank God, because who knows what I'd've done without them. Sandwich bags? Or just asking lots of sexual history questions and taking the gamble? I pulled a

tight one on him and another on myself. He was admiring my
dick, too, stroking it so firmly I had to ask him to lay off –
seeing his sexy body all naked and glistening from his
shower, not to mention the most loving pec job of all time,
had me ready to squint and spritz.

I went down on him in one big gulp, wishing that instead
of mint they made condoms taste like dick, with a hint of precome. But rubbing my lips over the shape of his dick was
exciting enough for now, at least until we could make a trip to
get tested. And the feeling was mutual: Christopher just lay
there in awe, mouth agape, eyes closed.

I got a major rise out of him when I licked and suckled his
nuts – the most sensitive part of *his* body – and a loud roar
when I nipped my way from the tip of his cock to the
underside of his scrotum. When I lifted one of his legs he
almost stopped me, thinking I'd suck his asshole. Now would
I do that? In flash, actually, but under the circumstances, I
was going to settle for faking it.

I buried my face in his ass, licking his crack and teasing his
perineum with my tongue. He smelled great, very musky
despite the scent of Ivory soap everywhere. I love the smell of
a man's ass, and under safer circumstances, I love, love, *love*
to tongue a big man's asshole, make him cry like a baby with
so much nasty pleasure. I rolled my face in the crack of his
ass, hoping to absorb that scent on my cheeks to smell later,
when the lovemaking inevitably ended.

He pulled me back up to kiss me, dropping his hands to my
ass, which he squeezed mercilessly. He bunched my cheeks
up in his fists and worked them back and forth, with and
against each other, my asshole burning from the friction. I
hadn't been fucked in a year, and hadn't ever wanted to get
fucked as badly as I wanted it right then. He worked his
forefingers toward one another until they massaged my
butthole from opposite angles and slipped into me up to
the first knuckles.

"Aw, *fuck*," I gasped, wiggling on his fingertips. "I gotta
get fucked, man, I have to have it tonight . . ."

He shushed me, "I know, I know . . . I'll do it, I'll do it to you good and hard like this asshole" (rubbing the rim of my hole furiously) "needs to be fucked." I hadn't showered, wasn't clean like Christopher – I could smell my sweaty butt and balls, getting all riled up with his touching.

I rubbed his condomed cock with ForPlay, unable to resist jerking it tightly enough to constitute the beginnings of a handjob. He looked like he would've settled for that quick relief, but I couldn't let that happen so I stopped, applied more lube to my butt, and positioned myself over his erection, squatting over it there on the couch. I was preparing to lower myself onto him, but he beat me to the punch. He'd loosened me enough that when he shoved his fat cock upwards at my asshole, it sank halfway in, no problem at all.

"Oh, mother*fuck!*" I called out, seeing stars and losing control. He started pumping up and into me while I held onto the back of the sofa, just squatted there and let him nail me from below. He held my love handles, pinching them hard enough to burn, while he thrust his hips up, fucking me frantically. Toward the end, he was leaping almost off the cushions to get me as deep as he could, and I felt it, baby, I *felt* it.

"I'm gonna . . ." I stood up on the couch, his prick slipping out of my ass and into his immediately jerking fist. I shot come onto the bricks of the wall, working my meat with my left hand until I didn't think I would ever come again. By the time I'd collapsed into his lap, he'd spilled all over the coffee table (here's hoping he'd already read that poor issue of *Out*) and was losing his boner, half asleep and satisfied.

"That was so great," I murmured. He agreed, hugging me gently and whispering things I couldn't make out. I looked him in the eye and he looked back, rubbing my belly with one hand, holding me in place – close to him – with the other. I knew then – and I'll let you know if I'm right when the time comes – that I was gonna be with Christopher for a long time.

I think he could tell I was thinking that, because he smacked my butt affectionately and kissed my nose.

"Chubby," he whispered to me sweetly.

And then we split a pizza.

The Last Time

Timothy J. Lambert

The cast party was in full swing when Oliver showed up. The Leading Man had just spilled his drink on the Lady in Waiting's skirt, and a bartender threw a towel to a nearby cocktail server to mop up the mess. The towel soared through the air and, as I followed its arc, I saw Oliver standing across the room. He was shaking snow from his hair and unzipping his coat, stamping his boots on the slushy carpet just inside the door of the bar while smiling brightly and greeting the person working coat check.

He was adept at multi-tasking.

The theater company had begged the cast to contact our friends and tell them about our performance, hoping to fill all the seats on opening night. I had a very small part in the play, a role as a messenger, and was only on stage for five minutes in a three-act drama, but I had invitations printed touting my "pivotal role" with fake quotes about my "tour de force performance" and mailed them to my friends, promising them "a night in the theater like nothing you've slept through before"!

I'd sent an invitation to Oliver. On a whim, I added a postscript inviting him to our cast party. I never thought he'd show. We hadn't seen each other or spoken since I'd broken up with him a year earlier. As soon as I sent the card, I tried my best to forget about it. Still, every now and then, I'd wonder why I bothered? What did it mean? What would he do when he saw my name on the return address? Would he open it? Would he throw it away? More importantly, was he still handsome?

Yes, I thought. *He's quite arresting, actually.*

I watched him lean across the bar so the bartender could better hear his drink order, and my gaze lingered on his ass. The bottom of his grey sweater slid up as he leaned forward, revealing taut muscle encased in dark blue denim. Oliver obviously still loved his yoga. Despite the woolen sweater, in my mind I could see his body underneath. It was like a road I'd traveled so many times I could easily navigate it even in the thickest fog. I knew his sweater concealed love handles on his midsection, which I thought were sort of sexy. I could pinpoint the place where four moles formed a line beneath his left shoulder blade. I remembered unbuttoning his jeans once and kissing the scar located midway between his navel and his cock.

He stood by the bar and took a sip from his drink. The rim of the glass rested on lips I'd kissed countless times. Oliver was often very charming. He was always complimentary. His smile was mischievous, as if he knew everyone's secrets and was on the verge of having them published.

As he drank, his eyes roamed the room. Always multi-tasking. I couldn't decide if I should stand up and wave to him or let him notice me on his own. I was sitting on a banquette in a corner and was slightly embarrassed when I realized I'd unconsciously arranged myself into the sort of casual pose affected by nine out of ten actors portraying a rebel without an appearance clause. Worse, my hand was resting on my crotch and I was fondling myself without realizing I was doing it. Although it felt good, I looked around to make sure nobody else had noticed.

Oliver always had that effect on me. I wanted his hands on me. I wanted to be literally touched by his presence. It was easy to put our arguments out of my head and only think about how we clicked together in bed. The first time he kissed me, I knew instantly that we'd have good sex. Later, when he pulled out and came on my chest, I barely had to touch myself to do the same. Everything about him turned me on: his large hands, his smooth chest, his straw-colored hair, and especially the way he touched me.

He finally spotted me and cocked his head in a rakish greeting, like a film star in a forties movie. He walked toward me and I stared directly at his crotch, hoping to unsettle him. If it worked, he didn't let it show.

"Hi," he said.

"You came," I replied.

"Not yet," he teased.

I filed that thought away for later use and said, "I wasn't sure you'd come." I hastily added, "Show up to the party, I mean."

"The invitation you sent was too cute to ignore. Pasting your face over Sara Bernhardt's was funny."

"Thanks."

"You were great in the play," he offered.

"I was hardly in it. It's hard to be bad in a play when you have three lines."

He frowned. His disapproving glare made me shrink into the banquette. This was familiar territory, the way he could make me feel like a child who'd misbehaved. He set his drink on the table and calmly stated, "You know what I'm going to say."

"Thank you," I said, as if reading a line from a cue card. I hated it when he thought he was authoritative.

"That's better. Still can't accept a well-intended compliment?"

I stared at his crotch again and said, "Still dressing to the left?"

He glanced at the people around us to make sure they hadn't heard me, and I smiled somewhat sadistically. I liked that he was embarrassed, that I could still affect him somehow. Of course nobody was listening to us. Everyone was too drunk to care about our petty drama.

"Why don't you sit down?" I asked.

"I really can't stay," he said quietly.

"Hot date?"

"No."

"Did you see the play alone?"

"No." He looked uncomfortable. This time it didn't amuse me.

"Oh? What's his name?"

"Does it matter to you?"

"Yes."

"Darren," he said.

"Is he in advertising?"

"What?"

"Nothing." We weren't in synch anymore. "What does he do?"

"He's an illustrator."

I'd been replaced by a cartoonist. I pictured a nerdy guy with ink stains on every article of clothing in his closet. Because of his persistent adenoid problems, he probably bleated like a lamb when Oliver fucked him.

"How long have you and Durwood been together?"

Oliver grinned and shook his head, having the good sense to look abashed for thinking me witty. He was back in my groove.

"You're not funny," he lied.

"I know. I'm a crashing bore. And I'm slightly drunk."

"Slightly?" Did he look hopeful?

"Okay, very drunk," I amended. I pointed to his glass and asked, "What's that you're drinking?"

"Ginger ale," Oliver answered. He smiled. I knew he was pleased that I was concerned that he might be drinking again. "Can I walk you home?"

"Am I leaving?"

"I am."

"Home to Dagwood? So soon? You just got here. Wait. The play ended over an hour ago. Why are you just getting here?"

"Come on," he urged. He offered his hand and helped me out of the booth. His hand was warm, smooth, and I shivered, wishing it was gliding over my bare back and pulling me against him in bed.

Outside the bar we pulled our coats tight against the cold and walked together, our boots crunching over the snow on the sidewalk. It was late. There were hardly any cars on the streets, so the sound of our footsteps echoed in the crisp, clear night. We passed an alley and I thought about better days, when Oliver might push me into the darkness between the two buildings and shove his hand down my pants while nuzzling my neck with his lips.

Instead, he spoke.

"I had to build up the courage to see you. I walked around for a while after the show."

"What were you afraid of? Did you think I'd get drunk and make a scene?"

I caught a glimpse of his smirk and added, "I may be drunk, but I didn't make a scene."

"You were building up to it."

"You don't know that," I challenged.

I whimpered slightly when he pushed me against the door to Small's Ice Cream shop and held my arms tight, shaking me slightly. My head bumped the glass in the door and I turned away from his angry face, looking at a flyer taped to the doorframe. Somebody had lost a cat.

"I know what you're doing. For a minute, back there in the bar, I thought maybe you'd changed. I know you. Don't forget that," Oliver growled. Flecks of his spittle hit my cheek and mixed with melting snowflakes. "I loved you."

I turned back to look him in the eye and said, "That's wrong. I think you mean love. Present tense." His grip on my arms softened, so I added, "That's why you're here, isn't it? That's why you came tonight. And why you were afraid to see me."

Oliver pushed me against the door again and his lip curled, then he started to walk away. I'd struck a nerve.

I scooped up some snow from the ground and formed it into a hard ball. I threw it, aiming for his head, but it missed

by an inch, sailing in an arc by his ear. He turned back,
looking incredulous and enraged.

"What's the matter? Why don't you finish what you
started?" I asked.

"What you started," Oliver corrected. "Why did you write
to me? I've moved on. I suggest you do the same."

"Moved on," I said, mocking him. "If you'd really moved
on, you wouldn't be here with me. You'd be at home with
Dickweed."

"Darren," Oliver said, "is a better man than you'll ever be.
You're still playing games. You're still fucked up."

"And you're still here."

I was taunting him. It worked. He grabbed my arm and
pulled me around the corner. I slid slightly on the slick
sidewalk. My clumsiness seemed to fuel his anger with me.
He flung me into a dark corner behind McGinty's Bicycle
Shop and then pushed me behind a wooden staircase that led
up to somebody's apartment. I hit a brick wall and bit my lip.

Oliver turned me around and kissed me roughly. His
mouth tasted sweet. I tried to unbutton his shirt, but he
held my hands back. I wrested them free from his grasp and
tried again, and that's when he struck me. The back of his fist
caught my cheekbone. I lost my balance and fell against the
wall for support. My face stung. I felt dizzy and somewhat
giddy.

My chin grazed brick when he grabbed my neck with one
hand and pressed me against the wall so he could rip my coat
off with the other. The flesh on my chin burned and I
laughed, wishing I wasn't quite so drunk, so I could better
appreciate the sensations I was almost feeling. He began to
unbutton my jeans, but I pushed away from the wall and
knocked him backward into the stairs.

"Not so fast," I said and punched him in the stomach. Not
hard, but enough to keep him angry.

Oliver grabbed my hands and we did a clumsy dance as we
fought for control. One of my hands broke free and I pulled
him against me, our hips banged together and I felt his hard

cock against mine. I rubbed against him and groaned softly, enjoying the friction. I reached under the waistband of his pants and scratched at the flesh of his buttocks.

Oliver held my waist with one hand, maintaining our contact, and grabbed my jaw in his other hand. His thumb rubbed the raw flesh wound there, making it sting. He drew my face to his and kissed me again. Then he bit my chin. His other hand moved up my back and then sharply downward, raking his nails over my skin. I cried out and grinned wickedly.

"You're enjoying this," I noted.

His expression changed. His eyes clouded, turning cold and determined. He drew his foot back and kicked me hard in the shin. I fell forward and he pushed my face into his crotch. I opened my mouth and massaged his cock through his pants with my lips. He unbuttoned, unzipped, and drew out his cock. I took it into my mouth and ran my tongue over its head, drawing it to the back of my throat. He pushed forward and I gagged slightly. Holding my head in his hands, he drew his hips back and forth, fucking my face roughly. I breathed through my nose as the slick smoothness of his skin slid back and forth across my lips.

When he pulled out of my mouth I gasped in frustration. I liked giving him head. Oliver's cock was long and thick, and fit perfectly in my mouth. I'd longed for it for months. He pulled me up and unbuttoned my pants, dragging them down to my knees. The skin on my bare ass dimpled in the cold air and I shivered. I willingly turned and faced the wall, placing my hands on the brick.

Oliver's breath tickled my flesh and warmed the air around my right buttock as he grazed his lips over my skin. I shuddered when his mouth connected with my asshole and he began to rim me. The pleasure came in waves as his tongue pushed in and out of me like a small dick. After a few moments I heard him spit into his hand and I steeled myself for what was about to come.

His cock entered me roughly and I fought my instincts,

trying to relax and breathe through the pain. I sobered quickly. As always, I was taken back to the first time. The fear, the ravaged nerves, the violence, the pleasure, all mixed together. Oliver's hands were on my waist and chest, pulling me against him, and his mouth was next to my ear.

"This is what you wanted?"

"Yes," I grunted.

He fucked me fast and hard. I was crying. The pain was agonizingly blissful. My forehead rested against the brick wall, thudding slightly against its cool hard surface with every thrust. I reached down with one hand and masturbated. Oliver brought his forearm to my throat and squeezed, choking me. I began to feel lightheaded and when I came, glints of light flashed around my head and my vision started to close up like a telescope.

Oliver let go of my throat and pulled out of me. I felt empty. My entire body felt like it was burning. I dropped to my knees and heard Oliver gasping above me. His semen fell to the ground around me, disappearing into the gritty snow.

I looked up at him and said, "I'm glad you came."

He tucked himself into his underwear and zipped up quickly.

"I hate you," he said.

"I love you, too," I replied.

He buttoned his coat and turned to leave, but then he turned around and kicked me.

"Don't ever call or write to me again. You're fucking sick, Joe," he said and walked away.

I laughed. That's what he said the last time.

Eden

Steven Saylor, writing as Aaron Travis

ONE

I was eighteen that summer, just out of high school. All my money was tied up for college in the fall; there wasn't even enough left over for bus fare to Los Angeles. But I wanted to visit someone there.

I decided to hitchhike. My father ranted and raved. My mother said she wouldn't be able to sleep at night. I told them I sure as hell wasn't going to stay in Austin all summer.

It took me three days to get out of Texas. I looked at the map I was carrying and started to worry. The desert looked awfully wide, and my roll of bills had already grown appreciably thinner.

I was standing at a truckstop outside Clovis, New Mexico. There was a cafe, a bar, a motel. It was three in the afternoon. The temperature was 97. I stood about a hundred yards down the highway from the motel, duffel bag beside me, with my thumb hooked. I had showered and changed into a fresh white T-shirt at the truckstop – the shirt I had been wearing since morning was soaked with perspiration, and I figured I'd have better luck keeping a ride if I smelled like soap instead of sweat.

My hair was cut short back then, black and wavy. My skin takes a good tan, so the sun wasn't frying me. I was singed, but not burned. The sun had cleared the acne off my forehead and cheeks, and bleached the sparse hair on my forearms.

A big truck pulled out of the parking lot and wheeled onto the highway. The cab was high off the ground; I couldn't see the driver as the truck pulled closer, but I guess he saw me.

There was a low rumbling as the truck shifted down a gear, then the hiss of brakes. The truck slowly passed me and stopped about twenty yards down the road. I grabbed my bag and ran to the cab.

The driver opened the door from the inside and reached out to grab my hand. His arm was strong; he practically lifted me into the cab. The first thing I saw of him was his hand – a big hand with thick fingers, a little grime under the nails – and the back of his broad forearm, thickly muscled and covered with dense, dark blond hair. I stared at his forearm as it twisted to show the underside, where the flesh was pale and long veins ran over the muscles. His wrist was thick and solid.

I was in the seat then, glancing up to his flexed biceps and the single vein bisecting it, then at the subtle smile on his face.

He had blond hair streaked with a darker blond, hanging tousled and windswept over his ears and onto the back of his neck. He had about ten day's growth of beard; its color matched the darker blond of his hair and his eyebrows. He had narrow eyes, long eyelashes, and a smooth broad nose.

He didn't say anything as he started the truck into motion again, and I settled my bag on the grimy, tool-littered floorboard. The cab smelled of motor oil, tobacco, spilled beer. He stared at the road. I stared at his profile – the wild hair, the proud nose, the curves of his finely shaped lips amid the stubble. He was wearing a short-sleeved shirt. It was a summer shirt, red and white plaid, untapered and made of thin cotton – I could see the clinging undershirt beneath, defining his true shape: a broad chest with two big swells of hard muscle hanging over the narrow band of his midsection.

A brown western belt cinched his waist. His pants were cowboy jeans, boot-cut, tight above the knees. His muscular ass and thighs, pressed flat against the seat, looked about to burst the heavy seams. He was wearing heavy-looking lace-up boots.

I watched his feet move on the clutch and gas pedal. I watched his arms, one working the long, ball-topped stick shift, the other controlling the big, freestanding steering wheel. I guess a man gets strong arms and shoulders from fighting that wheel for ten hours a day, keeping two tons on a steady course. His arms were hairy and knotted with muscle. Every movement produced a ripple somewhere.

He told me his name was Reed. I told him mine was Alan. I said I was headed for Los Angeles. So was he.

"Well, you keep up your end of the conversation and don't be a pain in the ass, and who knows, maybe I'll get you all the way there." He smiled, and I realized that needling me was his way of being friendly.

Neither of us was very talkative. The day was too hot. My T-shirt was already wet in the pits. Reed concentrated on driving. I watched the flat New Mexican scrubland and the bands of mountains scattered here and there on the horizon. Occasionally I glanced over at Reed, seeing things I hadn't noticed at first glance. Like the fact that his left arm was darker than the right, more exposed to the sun from the window. His eyes were green, the green of a tabby cat's eyes. His face was weather-lined, but young. I figured he was in his late twenties.

I also noticed – couldn't help but notice, because his pants were so contoured to his crotch, and he kept reaching casually down to scratch it – that there was a lump the size of a Big Mac between his thighs. I finally stared at it outright, trying to figure out what was balls and what was cock. All I could tell was that something massive and thick was trapped inside his jeans at the point where all the seams met.

The fact that he looked to be hung like a horse didn't start my mouth watering. Not yet. At eighteen I didn't have any definite preferences about sex – except that I was pretty sure I preferred men. I was no size nut. I really hadn't been close enough to that many cocks; one was the same as any other. There was only one cock, other than my own, that I had really experienced. Its owner was my reason for going to LA.

His name was Bill, and he had graduated a year ahead of me and gone off to USC on a track scholarship. We had been close friends from childhood; our parents knew each other, we went to the same church, snuck out of the same Sunday school classes, went hiking together every fall in the hills around Austin. I played quarterback on the football team to his tight end.

Off the field the positions were reversed. I was Bill's tight end. That's what he started calling me, after the first time.

We started sucking each other off when I was a sophomore and Bill was a junior. That's about all we did for a year or so. Then, the next summer, Bill talked me into letting him put his cock up my ass. He wasn't particularly big (though I didn't have any standards of size then), about like me, six inches – but it hurt like hell that first time.

I didn't stop him though, and I tried to enjoy it. By that time I had developed a first-class crush on Bill. He was one of the stand-outs in the school, an early bloomer – tall, handsome, blond, a star athlete, good in his studies, my older sex buddy. I would have done just about anything for him. I got through that first fuck, thinking how strong and beautiful Bill was, and how much he wanted to take my cherry.

After that first time, things changed between us. It was like his cock in my ass had changed me into a fag – that's what Bill thought, I guess – but he was still the All-American stud. Like he had taken a part of my manhood away from me and added it to his own. He started acting real macho when we were alone – swaggering, scowling, keeping a tight lip. All of which made me more infatuated with him, and more submissive and eager to please him. We were assuming roles, something I was too unsophisticated to fully grasp.

Bill stopped sucking me after that. He was the one who

showed his hard white cock, and I was the one who got on my knees and sucked. He wouldn't even touch my cock. If I wanted to come, I had to beat off while he stood over me with his cock in my mouth. He became more aggressive about it, too, telling me how to do it – "Suck harder, man" – "Slow and easy, Alan" – "Eat me, buddy. Eat your big buddy's meat." Or taking over when he felt like it, holding me by the ears and pumping his hips, fucking my face. Sometimes he even called me names – cocksucker, faggot. His tight end. That was the worst part, the names.

It was all very different from the gentle, mutual sucking of the year before. Bill was the horny stud, I was the kid who took care of his dick. A lot of it bothered me, but I was crazy about him. I even let him screw my ass six or seven more times that year. I never really got off on it, but I wanted to give him whatever he wanted.

We were still friends as well as sex partners. He didn't lord it over me except when we were alone and he was horny. Still, I went through a lot of shit for Bill. I had lost interest in girls about the time I took up with him. He kept his regular girlfriend, a big-busted brunette cheerleader. Everybody knew Kathy was letting him fuck her. I was crazy with jealousy, and that made me all the more anxious to be whatever Bill wanted.

Then Bill graduated and left for California, and I spent my senior year masturbating and thinking about him. We wrote each other occasionally – nothing intimate, and no substitute for having his lean, hard body above me on the nights I lay in my room and beat off for hours. When I graduated I called him and asked if I could come visit. He said yes.

The week I spent getting ready was full of fantasies. Bill would open the door, smiling. I would step inside and throw off my duffel bag. Then he would take me in his arms and kiss me – for the first time, because we had never kissed. He would undress me, and when I was naked, he would push me to my knees. I would look up at his face, so happy to be back – he would take out his cock and tell me to suck it. I could close my eyes and see it. After such a long time apart, he would want to reclaim my ass. I could tell him, honestly, that no one else had had it, as I walked naked to his bed to lie face-down, spreading my legs for his cock . . .

It wasn't really Bill's cock I was lusting for. It was Bill. His cock was just the part of him that he gave me to love.

Now, riding in the cab of Reed's rig, thoughts hovering between Bill and the big man beside me and the sun-bleached New Mexican flatlands, I noticed Reed's basket and stared. It was curiosity more than anything else. I didn't know yet what a man and his cock could do to me. Bill had taught me about being in love. Reed would teach me about something darker and deeper.

Bill didn't fade from my thoughts as I studied the blond truckdriver. In my slight experience, Bill and sex were the same thing; I couldn't think of one without the other. As I looked at Reed, so big and silent and so close I could smell his body, I thought of Bill's hands in my hair, and Bill's strong thighs pressed against my face.

I was too shy to send any signals to Reed, and probably too naive to pick up any signals if he were sending them to me; but I think he was as cool as I remember. I sat there with the constant hard-on only an eighteen-year-old can maintain, woozy and horny from the desert heat, trying to keep my hands off my crotch – and Reed drove, hardly noticing me. I looked down at the boner outlined in my pants, and saw how small it looked compared to the soft bulge in his. He kept reaching down to grope himself – his crotch was itchy with sweat like mine, I guess – and that made me want to touch him there, to explore the difference for myself.

Then I noticed the diamond ring on his left hand. I sank inside.

Reed glanced over. He smiled. I felt like I had to say something to cover how turned-on I was, and distract him from the hard-on down my pants leg.

"That's some wedding band," I said.

He looked puzzled, then glanced at the ring and laughed.

"Shit, that's no wedding ring. No woman gonna tie me down 'til I'm too old to hit the road and take my pussy where I find it. That's my security ring. My daddy always said, Reed, invest some money in a ring, so you'll always have something on your person to pawn. Claims that's what saved his skin one time when he got his rig stolen in Oklahoma. I've never had to use it, but I always do like daddy told me to."

I just nodded.

After a couple of hours, Reed pulled the rig over in the middle of nowhere. He said he was busting to take a leak and couldn't wait for the next stop. He left the engine running, got out and walked around to my side of the truck.

I tried to sit still, but my curiosity got the better of me. I poked my head out the window and looked down at him, hoping for a look at his cock. I couldn't see much – then Reed looked up and saw me staring.

I must have had a strange look on my face; certainly the look he shot back at me was odd enough. He turned his hips toward me, still pissing, and I caught a glimpse of the big thing he had in both hands before I jerked my head inside, hot with embarrassment.

After a few moments the driver's door opened. I was going to keep my eyes straight ahead, but from the corner of my eye I saw that something had changed. Reed had taken off the cotton shirt. He balled it up and tossed it on the seat between us, then settled back to start rolling again.

I tried not to look. He seemed as straight as they come, and I was always afraid that men could see through me to the cocksucker Bill had made of me. But after a few minutes I began stealing hungry glances.

I could see the whole length of his arm now, the way the muscles flowed up and crescendoed in his brawny shoulders and neck. I glimpsed the wispy dark hair of his armpits, frazzled with heat and leaking streams of perspiration down his sides, and the curly, dark blond hair that showed above the low neck of his A-shirt. The fabric clung to his moist flesh, molded tight to the twin mounds tipped by nipples that pressed like shallow cones against the cloth. The shirt had pulled free of his pants and rode in tight folds over the contours of his stomach and lower chest. A single ridge of abdominal muscle was exposed in the gap between his belt and the hem of his shirt.

He glanced over and saw me staring at that naked strip of skin; saw too, I'm sure, how quickly I looked away. "Too hot for that damn shirt," he said.

I thought – hoped – that he was teasing me. But if he was, the message was going straight over my head.

The heat and the tension made me groggy. I dozed, dreaming something about naked muscle and dark blond hair and thighs framing my face, until Reed's knuckles, poking my ribs, awakened me.

"Hey, you were starting to snore," he said.

I blinked my eyes. "Oh. Sorry."

Then I realized that my right hand was in my lap, closed around the bulge of my erection. I snapped it away, wondering if he had awakened me because I was starting to get carried away and worrying about talking in my sleep.

"If you're awake now, why don't you reach in that glove compartment and find me the route map, the one that says A on it."

I opened the compartment door and searched through the crumpled receipts, half-used matchbooks and empty Marlboro packs. I also noticed a couple of well-thumbed paperbacks.

Any teenage male can recognize a porno book ten feet away. They come in solid colors. One of these was green and the other was hot pink. I held my breath and turned them so I could read the spines, hoping to uncover a secret. But the titles told me what I didn't want to know.

The green book was called *His Oriental Slavegirl*. The pink was *Truckstop Whore*, with the subtitle, "They Tied Her Up and Took Her Three Ways". I shoved them to the back of the compartment and hurriedly found the map.

Reed checked the route and saw that we were only a half

hour away from the Mountain Rest truckstop outside of Santa Fe.

"That's the end of my day," he said. "I'm gonna eat at the diner and take a room at the motel for the night. You got enough money to split the room with me?"

I nodded, and felt my pulse quicken.

"Well, you seem to be an alright kid, even if you are a little quiet, and I get tired of these long days on the road alone. If you wanna go all the way to LA with me, we can probably work something out."

"Yeah, thanks man. That'd be a big help to me."

He looked over and grinned at me, then scratched his crotch. We reached the truckstop. Reed parked and put on his shirt, then we went in to eat.

When we finished dinner, I looked through my duffel bag for my money roll.

It was gone.

It must have been stolen that morning, before Reed picked me up. I tried to think back and figure out how it had happened, but I was so angry I couldn't concentrate.

"What's wrong?" Reed asked.

"Oh, shit. Somebody robbed me. Must have been back in – whatever the hell that fucking truckstop was called. Back in Clovis." I shook my head. "What am I gonna do now? I don't even have enough cash to pay for my meal."

Reed sat back and folded his arms. I could tell by the look on his face that he was genuinely sorry for me.

After a moment he leaned forward and touched my forearm. "Look, don't sweat it, kid. Not tonight, anyway. I'll take care of the check. And I'd be paying for the room anyway. Hey, cheer up. Smile for me."

I tried. It wasn't too hard, with his big hand still resting on my forearm.

He paid at the cash register. I wanted to use the change in my pocket – all I had left – to cover the tip, but Reed wouldn't hear of it.

I waited outside the motel office while he got the room. He

said a single rate would be cheaper than a double, so we ended up in a room with only one bed. I tried to steel myself for the excitement – and the frustration – of sleeping next to him.

We put our things away. Reed said he wanted to hit the bar at the cafe for a couple of drinks before he went to bed, and invited me along. I was flattered that he would want my company, but I wouldn't have felt right having him buy my drinks; I said no.

The motel room was like any other, a big bedroom with a tacky print over the bed, and, at the far end of the room, a recess with a dresser and mirror, a closet with sliding doors, and a bathroom tucked in the corner. I took a long hot shower and tried to forget that I was hundreds of miles from home with only four quarters and a dime in my pocket. Tonight, at least, I had a full stomach and a roof over my head. And I was with Reed. He made me feel protected and taken care of. And he was beautiful.

After the shower I put on a fresh pair of undershorts and paced the room, horny and bored, but afraid to start jacking off in case he came back. I parted the curtains and looked across the parking lot, where I could see the bar and another row of motel rooms.

The door to the bar opened. Reed stepped out. He held the door open. A woman with long dark hair followed him out.

They walked down the row of rooms, talking and laughing. I felt a stab of envy, like I had always felt about Bill and Kathy. I couldn't stand it if I was going to have to lie awake and think about Reed and the brunette in her motel room, his big cock shoved hard and deep up her cunt, while I was stuck with just my fist for company.

They stopped at one of the rooms. The brunette took her keys out of her purse and unlocked the door. Reed tried to follow her inside, but she pressed her hand against his big chest and stopped him. They stood in the open door, talking and kissing. Finally she slipped inside, leaving Reed alone on the doorstep.

I watched him slap his fist angrily against his thigh, then turn to cross the parking lot. I let the drapes fall shut and got on the bed.

After a few seconds the lock rattled and the door swung open. Reed muttered something about "fucked-up women". He said it to himself, not to me, so I didn't answer.

He noticed me on the bed and gave me a friendly smile. "Don't ever bother to buy her a drink if she's got a wedding ring on her finger," he said. I just looked at him blankly, then reached for the chamber of commerce magazine on the bedside table.

"I'm gonna wash up now, okay?"

"Sure," I said.

He started stripping, right in front of me. I watched him over the top of the pages. First he shucked off his boots and socks, then he peeled off the tight, sweaty jeans that were molded to his skin like warm plastic.

He unbuttoned the red and white plaid shirt and shrugged it off. Then he turned his back to me as he pulled the clinging undershirt over his head and pushed his underwear over his thighs until they dropped to the floor.

My cock was getting stiff again. His nakedness was an energy, charging the whole room. I had been dreaming all day of his body. Now I saw.

His legs were sturdy and thick, with no smooth contours – knotty with muscle and veins. The cheeks of his ass, like his pecs, pushed out big and round without a trace of fat; the skin looked smooth and hard as marble. From the waist down he was creamy white.

From the waist up he was only slightly tanned, except for his brown arms, the left one darker than the right. His back was broad in the shoulders, narrow in the waist, divided into two rippling planes by the deep, silky crease down his spine. There were two dimples in the small of his back.

He walked toward the bathroom, and for an instant I saw him in profile – the opposing thrusts of his pecs and ass, the width of his arms and legs above and below the incredible thinness of his waist. And I had a second glimpse of the thick ropy muscle that swung between his thighs.

I heard the water start running. Steam billowed from the bathroom – he hadn't bothered to close the door. I threw the magazine on the floor and turned over on my stomach. I gripped the top edge of the mattress and pressed my body against the bed, closed my eyes and thought about him naked in the shower, slick with soap. I ground my hips into the mattress. I could still hear the shower running, and felt safe to fall into a steady rhythm of rubbing my whole body against the bedspread, making my hard cock feel good inside my undershorts. I shut my eyes tight and imagined a cock before my face. I parted my lips and made a moan to help the fantasy.

Suddenly I felt his hand on my back.

He had returned to the bedroom – forgotten something, I guess. I froze, horribly embarrassed that he had caught me that way. My whole backside must have blushed red. I wondered how long he had been watching me, and if he somehow knew that I was thinking about him. I kept my eyes closed and my face hidden in the pillows.

Then his other hand was on my backside, pressing against the thin cotton. "Don't stop on account of me," he said in a low voice. I caught a whiff of the bourbon on his breath. He pressed his hand rhythmically against my buns, and I understood that he wanted me to keep humping the bed. Slowly, heart pounding, I rubbed my groin against the mattress. My cock seemed to have grown more sensitive with his hands touching me, and the pleasure took over my inhibitions. I masturbated against the bed, faster and harder as he held me down and squeezed my buns.

Then he grabbed the waistband of my shorts and slowly pulled them down to bare my ass. The elastic caught on the bottom edge of my cheeks and stayed there.

I became incredibly aware of my exposed ass. His hand returned. The callused palm brushed softly over my naked cheeks as they tightened and flexed. Then I felt the solid ridge of his fingertips press into my crack, not quite touching my asshole.

Time seemed to have stopped. I kept my eyes shut and hunched the bed in jerks until I was on the verge of coming. Reed stood over me, pressing me flat with his left hand between my shoulder blades while he rubbed his right over and around the slopes of my contracting ass, gingerly slipping his fingers into the hidden cleavage.

Suddenly his hands were gone. I heard a loud breath expelled above me, and once again smelled bourbon. He left me like that, shamelessly humping the bed with my naked ass reared up. I dared to open my eyes and caught a glimpse of him before he disappeared into the bathroom. The thing between his legs had grown even bigger. It stood out stiffly from his belly, white and smooth as a branch from a birch tree. It was the first part of his body to disappear around the corner.

I got under the covers and leaned against the headboard with my knees bent, fisting my cock under the tent made by the bedspread. I listened to the sound of the water rushing over his body and kept myself on the edge of shooting. I could still feel his hand on my ass, as if his touch had singed me.

The water stopped, and I froze. I listened to him drying off. Then I saw his shadow cast onto the sliding closet door opposite the bathroom.

The shadow was broad and elongated, making it look like it was cast by a giant. It emphasized the width of his shoulders and the symmetrical mass of his thighs. Then he turned sideways, and I saw his profile in shadow – a tall, lean column of a man. The shadow of his cock, like a splinter from the main body, stood out from the narrow shadow at a steep angle, long and thick.

I watched as he bent slightly at the waist – he must have been standing over the toilet – and gripped the shadow club in one hand. He stroked himself, first slowly, then faster and faster. The shadow cast by his cock grew bigger. Then he took it in both hands, so that I could no longer make sense of the silhouette. He bent over. I heard his breath from the bathroom, ragged and short. Then a stifled moan, and I knew he was coming.

I slipped low in the bed, completely deflated. He had considered me and rejected me, preferring to use his own fist.

I pretended to be asleep when he came into the bedroom, but I watched him through barely opened lids. He had dressed in a fresh white undershirt and white underwear – I guess that was what he had come back for when he discovered me humping the bed. I wondered if he didn't ordinarily sleep in the nude, like I did, and wore them for my benefit.

But the effect was more erotic, to me, than his simple nakedness. The A-shirt was like the one he had worn in the truck, tight and sheer. His briefs were breathtakingly small. I had never seen anything like them – I didn't know they made such sexy underwear for men. They were cut very low below his navel. I saw why his basket rode so high and compact inside his jeans; the briefs barely contained his genitals, hugging them tight and firm. There was a bulge in the front like two clenched fists. In back, the briefs couldn't contain his ass. The waistband managed to hide the beginning of his crack, but the bottom third of each meaty cheek was exposed. The hem of his shirt and the top of the briefs didn't meet. A circular strip of flesh showed two inches above and below his navel. The fair skin looked dark, framed by the clean white cotton.

I must have convinced him I was asleep. At least he acted as if I were. He flicked off the light and joined me in the bed.

I lay quiet and stiff until I heard him snoring softly. Then I slipped out of the bed and tiptoed to the bathroom. I closed the door and turned on the light.

There were gobs of come still clinging to the underside of the raised toilet seat. I clutched the hard-on inside my shorts and scooped up a string of the stuff with my fingers. I stared at it till my eyes hurt, thought about the man it had come from and the cock I still had barely seen. I put my hand to my mouth and licked up the cool, congealed semen.

Bill's come had always had a bitter tang that made me choke. Reed's tasted strong and smooth and rich. I dropped to my knees and licked a gob from the rim of the toilet bowl. I held it in my mouth; it melted and turned slippery on my tongue.

I switched off the light and knelt in the total darkness of the small room, holding Reed's load in my mouth, trying not to swallow, wanting to keep it there. When I had taken the full taste of it I raised both my hands to my lips and let the spit and semen dribble out. I took my cock out of my shorts and smeared it with Reed's come.

Suddenly the darkness was not complete. A strip of light showed under the bathroom door. He was awake.

I froze and listened to the silence. Then a rustling sound, as if he were getting out of bed. I panicked. I stuffed my cock back inside my shorts. My heart jumped into my throat, thick as a fist. I had to do something. I scrambled to my feet, clumsily opened the door and stepped into the soft light.

I stepped around the corner and saw him sitting up in the bed, covered by the bedspread from the waist down. The look in his eyes flustered me. I dropped my eyes to his chest, then to the bulge in the bedspread between his legs, slowly being kneaded by his hand.

He reached over and flicked off the light. The tall neon motel sign outside, alternately red and blue, penetrated the drapes and filled the room with vague, colorless light.

I stood still, letting my eyes adjust to the dimness. Then he spoke. He was like a stranger on the bed; I had never heard that voice before.

"Come here," he said.

I walked the length of the bed, miles and miles, until I stood beside the dark mass of his body.

TWO

I was dizzy suddenly. Tension, excitement, apprehension. Points of light whorled across my pupils like skittering electrons. They faded as my breath returned and my eyes adjusted to the darkness of the motel room.

The mass of Reed's torso, propped against the headboard, grew more distinct. His white A-shirt seemed to glow softly, like dying radium.

My own body radiated warmth, as if the heat of the day, baked into my muscles, was escaping through the skin. I stood beside the bed, my knees trembling, and looked down at him.

He turned on his side and looked me up and down. He stayed half under the covers, squeezing his hidden erection through the sheets. He stared at me for a long time. Finally he spoke, in that same strange voice that made me feel as if it were a total stranger on the bed.

"Take off your shorts."

I tried to take a deep breath, but my chest was tight, as if there were a band of iron around it. I slid the shorts over my thighs and down. As I bent over I felt the tip of my cock jab against my belly. I avoided looking at it, embarrassed by its hardness.

Reed stared at me. I was naked, shivering with excitement, with fear. Then he reached out and took my cock in his hand. I closed my eyes and moaned, hoping he would stroke it, wanting him to rub his wasted come, that I had scooped from the toilet seat and smeared over my cock, deeper into the silky flesh.

But he only squeezed it, as if he were testing the size and hardness. At the same time he squeezed his own erection through the sheets. Then he released me and leaned back.

Again he stared at me, rubbing his meat. I was afraid to touch myself with him watching. So I stood, painfully aware of my nakedness and the hardness of my cock, and waited for Reed to tell me what he wanted.

I tried to look at anything but his body; but the constant, subtle kneading of his hand drew my eyes to his crotch. The curvature of his hand defined the thickness of his cock, thick as a baseball bat. I tried to see the exact outline beneath the covers, but the darkness and the folds of cloth defeated me. Then he squeezed the end of his cock and smoothed the sheet down the length, molding it over his hardness. I saw the shape and the massiveness. I sucked in my breath and looked up at his face. He was watching me to see my reaction. He smiled then, and patted the far side of the bed.

"Lie down. Here. On your belly."

I hesitated, then began to crawl over him to take the place he indicated. But when I was above him, on my hands and knees, he stopped me with his hands and pushed me down, so that I lay across his lap with my legs over the edge of the bed. My crotch was on top of his. I felt his erection through the cloth, like an arm beneath my belly.

My ass was raised up, right under his nose. I flushed hot again, embarrassed at being exposed like that before a fully covered man.

I grabbed the far edge of the mattress and tensed my body, hiding my face from him. Then I felt his hands on my ass. At first his touch was tentative, almost shy. He trailed his fingertips over the muscles, pressed against the firmness, laid his palms flat and spread his fingers. I reacted as he had wanted me to before, flexing my cheeks and pressing my groin down – not against the bed now, but against his hard cock.

His touch grew more confident and aggressive as he took possession of my backside. Using both hands he pressed the cheeks together, then pulled them wide open, grabbing handfuls of flesh and mashing, digging his fingernails into the skin, slapping gently. It hurt. It didn't hurt. I ground my crotch into his, thinking less about my own cock and more about his. I stroked his erection with my groin, and surrendered to his hard hands on my ass.

He stopped for a moment. His hands left me. I heard him

draw a deep breath. Another pause. Then he slapped my ass, so stinging hard that I cried out and lifted my head. My body went stiff again. Reed's fingertips played on my ass, almost tickling. I relaxed. I felt his cock beneath me. The heat in my ass spread through the middle of my body. Soon I was hunching him again.

He drew his hand back. I clenched my teeth, knowing now what would come next. I felt my buns draw up tight like nuts on a cold day.

He took his time. My ass began to tense and relax, all on its own. Then I felt his touch, and flinched. But his hand came down softly, massaging me till I melted again.

Suddenly his arm flashed up and down. The blow, more painful for all the anticipation, made a loud crack in the darkness. I writhed across his lap, giving up to him completely.

He paused again. I waited for the next slap. Instead, he reached to the bedside lamp and switched it on.

The room seemed brightly lit after the darkness. I wanted him to turn it off, so I could feel protected and secret again – not exposed and naked, stretched over a strange man's lap and letting him beat my ass.

But he left the light on. He made me open my thighs and lift up while he pulled my cheeks apart. Then he probed the crack with his fingers and tugged at the short hairs, examining my asshole under the lamp as if he had never looked at one before. I don't think that he had ever fucked a man, but he had figured me out and knew I would let him. But first he wanted a good look at the opening between my cheeks before he stuck his big cock inside.

It made me feel helpless and degraded, like it was all up to him. If he felt like sinking his meat into me, he would do it, expecting me to take it whether I wanted it or not, whether it hurt or not. Something made me give in, just as something had kept me stretched over his lap while his hand stung my ass, and kept me there while he inspected my backside. I felt the heat of the lamp on my skin – or perhaps it was the burn of his handprints.

I felt his finger slick on my asshole – he must have wet it with his spit – and figured he was about to throw a bone up my asshole, the way that Bill sometimes did before fucking me. But Bill had never slapped my ass. And Bill's cock was nothing like the long, thick ridge I felt throbbing through a layer of sheets and sheer nylon briefs.

At that moment I realized how badly I wanted Reed to fuck me. Bill's six inches had been enough to screw me to the locker room wall, to make me bend over and open in submission. I sensed Reed's cock beneath my belly, huge and warm. I knew it would split me open, wreck me, pound me till I was quivering meat inside, release the part of me that I loved and hated, that was groveling and submissive. At that moment, I knew how badly I wanted it.

But his finger didn't enter me – he just slid it all around and over the hole, pressing gently, teasing me. Gathering more spit from his mouth and spreading it over my buns to make a loud sharp crack when he slapped. I worked my hips and ass, a little at first, then more and more as I got into it. Begging with my body the way I wasn't yet ready to beg with words. Asking him, please, to fuck me with his finger.

Suddenly he pushed me onto the other half of the bed, on my back. Then he was over me, straddling my waist with his knees. I saw only one thing, the massive relief of his hard-on, cradled sideways inside those sheer white briefs. I reached for it with both hands. My fingers closed on its giant curve. I felt its bulk and its heat through the slick nylon. I opened my mouth and sobbed.

Then I groaned in frustration as he grabbed my hands and pressed my arms along my sides, trapping my wrists between my hips and his knees.

I looked up. I took him in with my eyes. All of him. His wild blond hair, the beard beginning on his jaw. And the look on his face – eyes narrow, lips parted, an out-of-it look, dangerous. And his body, rearing menacingly above me, so powerful – I was flat on my back, and the low angle of my vision accentuated the way his chest and shoulders flared up and out from his flat belly. His cock looked thick as his corded forearms, still hidden from me, just as his sculpted chest and stomach were hidden beneath the tapered muscle shirt. His clothing made me acutely aware of my nakedness again, and of my exposed cock, lying rock hard against my belly for him to see. I couldn't even cover it with my hands.

He stared at my cock – I felt it soften from embarrassment. Then he took it in his hand, not to stroke and pleasure it, merely to examine it in the light, the way he had examined my asshole. He looked displeased and I softened more, as if my cock were cringing. I thought of what he was used to, his own cock in his hand, in both hands, and how small mine must feel to him, how little there was of it – and I wanted at least to be hard and as big as possible as he weighed me in his palm.

But Reed had no interest in my cock. He lifted up for a moment, still keeping my wrists trapped by his knees, and told me to open my legs; then he stuffed my shaft, soft enough to bend now, between my thighs.

"Close your legs tight," he said. "Hold it there, out of sight. Where it belongs."

Reed stared down at me, naked below him with my arms trapped at my sides and my cock hidden between my legs. His breath came ragged and heavy and a glaze fell over his eyes, making them look distant and determined. He squeezed his basket, two-handed, and blew out a sharp gasp, baring his teeth.

Then his strong hands were on my body, stroking the triangle of wiry hair above my downturned cock and the inner curve of my thighs, running over my belly and onto my hairless chest, pulling the muscles up in generous pinches, shaping and kneading them, mashing my nipples into peaks and flicking his fingernails over the sensitive tips grown erect from his touch.

I had always been self-conscious and shy about my chest, ever since my body changed in adolescence. I had been skinny as a kid, but in junior high the parts of me that had been thin and angular fleshed out in what I thought was an almost feminine way; my pecs had grown full and firm with a rounded, smooth look, and my nipples had become large and pointed, like shallow cones. Later I would learn that other men liked to touch them, especially the nipples. But they had always embarrassed me, so obvious and large in a T-shirt, different from most of the other boys with their flat, narrow chests. Now Reed fondled my pecs, and I knew he was touching them the way he would touch a woman's breasts, and I flushed with embarrassment, because I wanted it. He spat into his hands and rubbed his mucus glossy and thick into the triangle of my pubic hair and all over my tits until the two mounds of muscle glistened in the light.

Reed circled his big hands around my neck and crouched low atop me – I felt the bulge of his cock press into my groin again, and his mouth on my pecs, stroking long and slick with his tongue, wetting them all over with his spit. Then his mouth moved to the tips to kiss my nipples and nip with his teeth. A good feeling spread through my chest, warm and deep, like the ache in your legs after a long run, or the satisfied feeling Bill had always left in my throat after he fucked my face. The pleasure was pierced when Reed bit the nipples – a sharp, sweet pain then, in the midst of the pressing warmth.

He bit harder and moved up to the very tips of the brown cones, till the mixture of pleasure and pain was unendurable and my body resisted on its own, twisting and bucking against his attack.

In the thrashing, my hands worked free. I grabbed his hips and sensed the power waiting there, and ran my hands up the sides of his chest. I knew he was broad and massive, but only with my eyes. I wanted to know by touch, wanted to feel his bigness. Then I took his face in both hands, wanting to pull his mouth up to mine, wanting him to kiss me, like Bill had never done, while he made love to my tits.

He sank his teeth into my nipple, so hard I squealed from the pain. Then he released it and looked up at my face. There was anger, or something that looked like anger, in his eyes. He grabbed my wrists and pushed them down, caught them again between my hips and his knees.

"Hands off, cocksucker." He growled the words. Then he laughed, I guess at the shocked expression on my face. He grabbed my hair in his fist and pushed my head back. He leaned low and flat, pressing his chest down on mine, and stared into my eyes. When he spoke I could feel his breath on my face, still tinged with bourbon.

"Yeah, I knew five minutes after I picked you up. Knew I had a genuine little cocksucker in my cab." He forced my head back and ran his fingertips over my throat and collarbone. "Yeah, I could tell by the way you kept staring at my crotch. Musta looked pretty good to you, the way you kept licking your lips and swallowing. You could tell it was a big one, couldn't you? You guys can tell just by looking, can't you?"

He squeezed my throat. "This where it goes? This where you'd like me to put it? How's a young guy like you develop such a craving for cock, anyway? How long you been sucking dick?"

He stared down at me, gently pressing my distended throat between his fingers, waiting for an answer.

"I don't know," I whispered. "About three years."

"Three years, huh? Musta sucked a lot of cocks in three years."

"No. Not really. Just one. One guy."

Reed ground his hips into my groin and pressed his hand over the ridge of my throat, framing it between his thumb and forefinger. "So. You suck him regular?"

I thought of Bill, of the hours I must have spent over the years with his cock in my mouth. "Yeah."

"You like it?"

"Uh huh."

"You let him come in your mouth?"

"Uh huh."

"You swallow it?"

I didn't answer. I couldn't think about Bill any more. All I could think of was Reed, holding me down and crushing me with the weight of his muscles. Yanking my hair sharp and sudden, speaking through clenched teeth.

"Huh? You swallow it when he'd shoot in your mouth?"

"Yes," I whispered.

Reed shook his head and curled his upper lip, as if what he heard disgusted him. "He suck you back? Was he as queer as you are?"

"At first . . . no. Not like me. He was more like you."

Suddenly I was mad. Reed had no right to interrogate and insult me. I didn't like being called names. I hadn't liked it when Bill did it – but it had never stopped me. Bill had said things that made my ears prickle with heat – but even as he called me faggot his cock would be in front of me, sticking hard out of his jeans, slick with mucus dredged up from deep in my throat.

Reed was different. Taking his pleasure with my body, as turned-on as I was, the way he handled me. But depriving me, not letting me touch him, keeping his cock out of reach – and labeling me the queer.

I caught him off guard. I wrenched my arms free and pounded my fists against his hard body. We wrestled on the bed. I wanted to hurt him, but he was too strong and solid. He just laughed at me. He cuffed my ears and shoved me around, and in a few moments I was back under him, arms trapped and chest heaving. He pushed my cock back between my legs – it was rock hard again, it hurt. Suddenly I was afraid – naked in a strange place, miles from home, breathless and sweaty beneath a man stronger than me in every way. I had never felt such helplessness. I was close to crying; I tried not to let it show on my face.

Reed smiled. "You're pretty feisty for a cocksucker."

"Shut up!" I yelled.

His smile faded and he slapped my face, just hard enough to make me obey. I felt a single tear run down the side of my face.

His smile returned, just to the corner of his mouth, twisted. "I know what would calm you down. A big pacifier. Something big and warm for you to suck on."

He sat back on his haunches, giving me a chance to catch my breath. He ran his hands over his chest, making the muscles in his arms stand out. He squared his hands around the lower edge of his pecs, making the nipples push against the taut fabric. He slid his palms over the ridges of his stomach, onto the naked strip of flesh below his navel.

Then he wrapped both hands around the ridge lying sideways in his briefs and squeezed, pumping it till I could see the exact outline within the nylon – the curvature, the veins, the head.

He peeled the briefs down, letting his cock snap free. He snagged the tight waistband beneath his balls, pushing the sack up and out to press against the bottom of his shaft.

I had seen it before – he had tauntingly allowed me to see it when he pissed against the truck, when he walked naked into the bathroom – but only from a distance. Now it was exposed and hard, huge and real in the light, inches from my face. The waistband pushed it straight up, so the head rested in the indention between the second cluster of muscle above his navel. I saw the whole length of it. To me, at that moment, it looked like anything but a man's dick – a club, a mallet, an animal cock.

The head was big but only slightly thicker than the shaft, resting on top like a German helmet, blunt and smooth at the tip where the slit was slightly parted, leaking pearly fluid. The shaft was the same shape and width all up and down its length, like a perfectly sculpted column. It was oval in shape, except for the tube, thick as a finger, that pressed out from the underbelly. A few thick, widely spaced veins coiled around the shaft, blue-green and throbbing. The whole thing had a swollen, rubbery look, as if it would be soft to touch despite its firmness.

Everything was in symmetry. There was no blemish or hair, no knotty wrinkles of flesh on his cock. Smooth and white as marble. As if nature had decided not to be careless for once, and make a cock as perfect and powerful and huge as its owner. It was beautiful, the way a face or an arm or an ass can be beautiful.

I wanted it. I wanted to touch it with my hands, my lips, my tongue. I wanted to taste the translucent liquid that leaked from the tip and ran in thin trickles all the way down to his balls.

And I wanted it to touch me, wanted to feel it everywhere on my body – against my face, in my armpits, between my legs, lying heavy on my chest. And inside me – as far down my throat as he could force it, and up my rear end, buried deep in my guts, stretching the hole as wide as my wide-open mouth.

He spat in his hand, rubbed the saliva over the head of his dick and stroked, just the last four inches. He breathed in long steady draughts. His belly contracted to show his rib cage, his chest expanded with pleasure.

"Pretty, ain't it?" He looked down lovingly at his cock as he slowly stroked it. "And big, huh? About as big as they come." He looked me in the eye. "But I'll bet you like 'em big, don't you? That's what they say. Say you queer boys just can't get enough of a good thing. Like 'em as big as you can find 'em, right? Want that meat to cram your throat."

I didn't answer. I was either too turned on, or too angry to speak. Angry not at him any more, but at myself, because what he said was true. My cock was hard between my thighs, and I wanted his cock in my throat, bruising and impossibly huge.

"That guy – the one you been sucking regular for three years – he got something this big to cram down your throat?"

I stared at Reed's cock and shook my head.

"Then maybe you're not ready for it. I figure it's the kind you have to work up to. Meet a lot of whores along the highway – some of 'em pretty inexperienced I guess, cause I like 'em real young, about your age. It's made more than a few of 'em throw up. Yeah, lean over the bed and vomit, man, cause they couldn't take it the way I wanted. 'Course I get pretty rough sometimes." The twisted smile reappeared in the corner of his mouth.

He hawked another load of spit into his hand and stroked his cock, angling it down so it pointed straight at my face. I raised my head and opened my mouth, straining to reach it. It hovered over my belly and chest, glistening with spit.

He leaned over to turn off the lamp. The movement brought his cock a few inches closer, until my lips made contact with the spongy flesh of the head. I pressed my tongue into the moist slit. His cock gave a twitch and rewarded me with a squirt. The taste was the same as the oozings I had scraped from the toilet seat. I held the tip of his shaft between my lips and sucked for more. He turned off the light and leaned back, drawing his tool out of range. I strained to follow it, my mouth open and my tongue curled over my lower lip.

His shaft was like oiled ivory now, bathed in the vague light of the neon filtering through the drapes. The only sound was the slick passage of his fist stroking the long cock from head to base, then sliding up to stroke again.

"Reed," I whispered.

No answer. Only the sound of his stroking fist.

"Reed —"

The rush of his heavy breath joined the slick crackling.

"Reed," I whispered again. Plaintive. Groveling.

"What you want, cocksucker?"

What I felt left no room in me for anger. His cock was growing larger before my eyes. The veins were swollen, casting shadows over the surface of his cock, the color of the moon. So beautiful it hurt to look at it – better to take it out of sight, hide it down my throat.

"Please," I said.

"What you want? Cocksucker."

I gathered the strength to say it. "Please, Reed. In my mouth."

He ran his middle finger, the one with the ring, over my

lips, then around the inside between my lips and gums. He slowly pushed his finger in to the knuckle, then pulled out.

"And you'd swallow it, when I shoot? There was a bitch in Dallas –" His voice was heavy with pleasure, his breathing ragged. "Turned on her side and spit it out. Spit out my come. I had to whip her ass for that. I had to fuck her up the ass. Then I made her suck it again, made sure she didn't waste it."

I didn't know if I could take it all in my throat. But I could lick it all over, and I could fit the head in my mouth, I could take it when he shot. "Yeah," I said. "I wouldn't waste it. Come in my mouth, man. Let me swallow it, Reed —"

He silenced me by stuffing his fingers in my mouth, all four. He threw his head back and his chest expanded. He stroked faster – then began to jerk and moan. His head fell forward, eyes shut, mouth wide open. He crouched low and convulsed.

His fingers left my mouth, letting me release a sob of frustration. He cupped the palm of his hand over his cock-head, catching the long ejected ropes of semen. His face and his body twisted violently, then slowly relaxed.

He rolled his eyes up and stared at me, smoldering and crazy. The he slapped his dripping palm over my mouth. Masses of his come, thick as hawked-up gobs of spit, ran into my mouth.

He smeared his slippery fingers all around my lips, up my nose, over my chin, onto my neck, covering my face with come.

His cock kept shooting, uncontrolled by his hand. I felt it throb against my belly, felt the spidery tracers of his load splash hot on my chest. With his hand still feeding me come, he scooped the wasted ooze from my pecs, rolled off me and slid his hand between my legs to smear his come over my downturned cock.

He rubbed his greasy palm up and down over the top of my shaft, and slid his other hand into my mouth, letting me snake my tongue between his fingers to lap at the webs of fluid trapped there.

Suddenly a final, unexpected jet of semen shot from his cock and splattered onto my thigh. My body shuddered and my cock exploded. His hand slipped down to catch my load and smear it everywhere between my legs – over my cock, my balls, the inside of my thighs and deeper, up the crack of my ass to the hole.

Now I convulsed while Reed watched with narrow, lazy eyes and held me between his two hands – one hand speared between my legs, covering my cock and balls and asshole all at once, the other speared into my open mouth. As the tremors subsided, I looked into his eyes and I imagined that a ring of energy joined us, banded across his broad shoulders and down his right arm, entering me at the groin and running through my belly and chest to come out my mouth, and flow back into his hand and arm to his left shoulder. Then his hands withdrew and the ring was broken.

Reed rolled onto his back, crossed his hands over his chest and closed his eyes. His cock lay across his belly. His balls, loose and empty now, hung like heavy fruit over the edge of his briefs.

His shaft looked obscene. Bloated and soft but still massive, veins distended across the loose skin, throbbing with contentment, covered with a gloss of drying spit. But no come – all his come, and mine, he had left with me.

My hands were free now. I reached over to touch it. Soft, warm, alive.

He felt the contact and pushed my hand away with a sleepy growl. He didn't open his eyes.

I slowly got out of bed and walked into the bathroom. I didn't turn on the light – not because I didn't want to bother Reed. Because I didn't want to see myself in the mirror. In the darkness I wet a hand towel with warm water and cleaned the mess between my legs and on my face. I considered rinsing my mouth, but decided I would hold his taste there as long as it would linger.

I walked back to the bedroom. Reed was as I had left him, except that his balls and cock were stuffed back inside his briefs. His breathing was even and deep. I slid between the sheets to join him. I closed my eyes and released a long sigh, knowing sleep was far away.

Suddenly I was tumbling to the floor – Reed shoved me out of the bed. He threw a pillow after me.

"I won't sleep in the same bed with no faggot," he said matter-of-factly. "Something else my daddy taught me." Then he laughed slightly. "Hell, you might molest me."

He chuckled again, while I crouched on hands and knees on the floor beside the bed, close to tears. But I didn't cry. I tried to make my mind a blank, and stay completely still. I held my breath and listened to his, easy to hear in the darkness, waiting for him to go to sleep.

His breathing settled. After a long time I was sure he was asleep. I did cry then, but just a little. Afterwards I felt better, clearheaded. I stood up and looked down at him, trying to decide what to do.

I told myself I should leave. Reed despised me, his words were clear enough. I wanted to despise him, but I couldn't.

My money was gone, stolen. Getting to LA was out of the question. Start hitchhiking then, in the middle of the night, try to make it back to Austin without eating. It was impossible. But how could I stay with Reed? How could I bear to wake up in the morning, on the floor?

I suddenly saw the solution. His billfold was on the dresser. I had seen that he carried plenty of cash. A fifty would be enough to get me home.

But I couldn't take his money. It wasn't the dishonesty that stopped me. No. I felt that if I took his money and left, after what had happened, that would make me another whore, like the women he talked about.

I was too tired and upset to think any longer. I just stared down at Reed's body and his face, beautiful in sleep. I looked at the bulge inside his briefs – always a bulge there.

Very slowly, I walked around the foot of the bed to the side where he slept. I stared down at him. I dropped to my knees.

Slowly, silently I lowered my face to his crotch. A heat radiated from his cock. I opened my mouth, touched my lips to the nylon and felt the mass of flesh inside. I pressed my tongue against it and felt warmth.

In his sleep he spread his legs and raised his hips, and his cock hardened. It moved inside the briefs. I felt its uncoiling with my mouth.

I pressed my face into it, wanting naked contact. I opened my mouth wide and clamped it over the width. I ran my lips and tongue over it, till the cloth was dark with spit. I wanted to pull his shorts down, lick it to steel hardness and swallow it whole.

One of his balls had slipped out of his shorts – I felt it against my chin, soft and covered with silky hair. I drew back and stared at it. Then I bent down and took it in my mouth. It was big, bigger than my own two balls together. I felt it jerk inside my mouth.

I reached down to my cock and squeezed it with both hands. I masturbated on my hands and knees while I held Reed's ball in my mouth.

I stroked it with my tongue, gently pressed it with my lips, worshipping it because of the taste it had put in my mouth, because it was the only part of him I could have and it was enough.

The room was very still. I squeezed my cock, as quietly as I could, afraid to break the silence. I came without a sound, shooting against the side of the bed. My body contracted and his ball slipped out of my mouth.

He must have been awake, at least at the end. As soon as I was through he turned onto his side, away from me.

I waited again, until I was sure he slept. Then I went back to the far side of the bed, where my pillow waited on the floor, and laid down on my back. I had intended to put on my undershorts, not wanting to wake up with a naked erection. But I forgot. I fell asleep instantly.

THREE

I woke the next morning with a weight on my groin. Something heavy pressed down directly on my cock. I responded to the pressure, unaware of anything but the warm shell of sleep still circling me and the fact that my cock was hard. I spread my thighs and raised my hips, hunching upward against the weight on my shaft. The weight responded by moving back and forth over the length of my erection. It glided smooth as felt over the dry, taut flesh.

Slowly, without opening my eyes, I began to remember where I was. In the motel room Reed had rented for the night – somewhere in New Mexico, or maybe Arizona, on the way to LA. The room where he had made me strip and lie naked across his lap, punished me with the palm of his hand, made my ass hot as a bed of coals inside and ready for what I thought we both wanted.

The bed was scratchy and hard. For an instant I imagined I was lying on a pool table instead of a bed. Then I remembered that I wasn't in the bed. I was on the floor, where Reed had put me.

I opened my eyes and saw him looming above me. He sat on the edge of the bed, wearing only his jeans – a fresh pair, dark blue and very tight, not the sweat-stretched jeans from yesterday's drive. His belly was a stack of hard ridges, foreshortened from my angle and looking incredibly dense with muscle. Above the ridges was the well-defined plateau of his chest. His head was bowed between broad shoulders, looking down. His blond hair, damp from a shower, pressed in flat rings across his forehead and the sides of his face. He still hadn't shaved; the dark blond shadow across his jaw was beginning to look like a beard.

Reed was looking down at me with a vague smile on his face.

It was his left foot that pressed on my cock, covered in a soft gray sock. The inner curve of his arch moved over the underside of my cock. I was stiff with a morning hard-on.

My face and chest flushed red. He had a way of embarrassing me, making me painfully self-conscious of being naked and hard in front of him. I pushed myself up on my arms, and realized how asleep and groggy I still was, and how stiff from sleeping on the floor.

Reed raised his other foot and brought it down on my chest, forcing me to lie back flat on the floor. There was no sock on his right foot. I felt the callused balls of his feet against my skin. The smile on his face vanished.

"Good morning, cocksucker," he said quietly. His lips, shaping the word, curled back obscenely.

I closed my eyes and bit my lip. I was back where he had put me last night. Two feet held me down. My cock filled with blood again.

The naked foot on my chest was like the base of a pillar, unmovable and rigid. His other foot, heavy and soft inside the woolen sock, rubbed sideways over the length of my cock, gently pressing my balls at the end of each stroke. He lifted the sack with the back of his foot and studied it, then let it drop and began stroking again.

"Hey," he said softly. He kept his voice low, as if there were someone else asleep in the room. He licked his lips and raised one eyebrow. "Hey. You think you can come this way?"

I watched his eyes. "Yes," I whispered, matching the secretive tone of his voice. "I think so —" I began to say; but at that moment Reed pressed his foot sharply into my diaphragm, emptying my lungs. The words ended in a rush of air. He pumped his foot against my chest a few more times, making me huff and grunt. He raised his foot into the air, and I expected a jab strong enough to make me faint. Instead he put it down softly on top of my diaphragm.

"Okay, then," he said. "Come for me."

I shut my eyes tight and swallowed. Almost immediately, I knew I couldn't do it. His foot wasn't enough. The pressure and motion felt good, but only the bottom of my cock was being stroked. It wasn't the same as a fist wrapped all the way around and squeezing blood into the head.

I reached up and circled my hands around his calf to control the pressure and guide his movements. I was startled at the size and the hardness of the muscles there, gently flexing as he moved his foot back and forth in steady rhythm.

Reed grunted angrily.

I let go of his leg and dropped my arms to my sides.

I kept my eyes shut, feeling hopeless, then ridiculous. I wanted to tell him to stop, but the awkwardness of everything paralyzed me.

Then a sharp hint of pleasure shot through my groin like a premonition of orgasm. I knew it was possible. I would have to put all of myself into it – and I wanted to, because Reed wanted it. I would have to ignore the paralyzing sensation of being exposed and observed, and give my body to the premonition. I concentrated on the fleeting sweetness in my cock, concentrated until I was my cock, throbbing under Reed's foot.

I clutched the carpet with my hands, tightening the muscles in my arms and chest. I opened my legs wide, clenched my cheeks and curled my toes. My hips began a slow rotation in countertime to his foot.

I strained after the climax Reed wanted from me. My head fell back and my jaw dropped open. I heard strange panting noises coming from my throat. I began to tremble and sweat, despite the air-conditioned coolness of the room. Sweat ran down the sides of my face and gathered between my thighs. I was getting there, slowly, almost by will alone.

I knew, suddenly, that I would make it – and as suddenly felt a fear that Reed had grown bored with all my straining, that he would stop and leave me on the cusp, naked and panting on the floor with my cock sticking up like an unwanted handle.

I opened my eyes narrowly and looked up at him. His face was tense. His eyes were roving over my body, watching me twist and sweat to please him. I imagined how I must look, how the two of us looked, the shirtless trucker sitting on the bed and the dark-haired kid he had picked up the day before, stretched out naked and slick on the floor, grunting like an animal.

I rolled my head on the carpet and released a long, loud sigh. I was there.

Suddenly Reed lifted both feet and drew them back. I raised my hips and thrust my cock high in the air, trying to follow. Then I began to shoot.

I looked up at him again and saw the grim fascination on his face. This was what he had wanted to see: my body jackknifed on the floor, untouched – hands and feet clutching the carpet, stock-still above the waist while the bottom half of my body writhed out of control. My cock jerked in the air like a fish out of water, slapping my belly and shooting jets of come against my chest while he watched.

After the last spasm, my arms and legs turned to clay. I settled slowly to the floor till I was flat as a silverfish. There was a moment of breathlessness, when I thought I would pass out for lack of air. Then a kind of relaxation I had never felt before spread through my body, turning the clay to warm jelly. There was a sensation of lightness in my limbs, as if all their weight had been drawn into my cock and released into the air along with the plumes of semen trailing warm and wet across my chest.

Reed rose from the bed and stood over me. He took a step and straddled my chest. He stared down at me, his eyes and his mouth half-open. His left hand went to his crotch. He stretched the web of skin between his thumb and forefinger across the width of his cock. It ran down his pants leg like a well-muscled forearm sprouting from his crotch.

Reed braced his right arm against the wall and ran his bare right foot over my chest, avoiding the cooling pools of come. He pinched my left nipple between his toes and laughed at my squeal of surprise. He cupped his foot against the side of my face and patted me. Then he put the end of his foot into my open mouth, pushing until I held all five toes between my lips. I sucked on his foot.

Once again, I wanted it to be his cock, instead of his hand

or foot, that he chose to put in my mouth. Then I could return the favor. I could make Reed come – hear his breath quicken while I held mine, watch his face twist up, the muscles in his arms and chest swell hammer-hard, make his hips fuck back and forth – fucking my face, cramming his cocksucker's face, the way Bill used to do. Fucking till everything drew to a point and he filled my mouth with come.

Reed read my mind – or saw the way I was staring at the hard-on in his jeans. I must have looked as wild and slack-jawed as I felt. He pulled his foot from my mouth, using his toes to pull my lower lip down. "Shit," he said, shaking his head and smiling just enough to show his two front teeth. "You got it bad, don'tcha?"

I didn't answer. I pushed myself off the floor and pulled my knees awkwardly beneath me, staying down beneath his legs. There was an arc of unseen energy there and I wanted to stay inside it. I put my hands over his feet and pressed my mouth over the broad bulge down his right pants leg. I licked at it, sucked on it, rubbed my face against it.

Reed let me for a moment. Then he hit my forehead with the butt of his hand, gently knocking me back.

"Cocksucker," he said.

I kept my eyes on the hard ridge of his erection. The shape was clearly defined. I went for the head, bit it with my lips and flattened my tongue against the rough dry denim.

Reed knocked me back again.

"Crazy for it," he said. His voice was oddly detached, as if he were observing from somewhere high above, far away from me, far from the hard cock in his jeans.

I pressed back, wanted to make the cloth all wet around his shaft. I wanted a response, a movement in his hips. I wanted him to bend at the knees and rub himself in my face.

He grabbed me by the hair and pulled me off. He kept my face down, close to his crotch. He shook me till my teeth rattled.

"Faggot," he said. He jerked my head back and slapped

me, hard, as if he were trying to tattoo the word on my face. "Faggot with a hard-on," he muttered, staring down between my legs. I felt the tip of my cock jab my navel. I was already stiff again.

"That make you hard?" he said, slapping me again, more cautiously. I didn't answer. "You always hard? Huh? Or is it something about me?"

I caught a glimpse of the fear at the back of his anger, not fully understanding.

Our eyes were locked. I think he read the glint of comprehension in my eyes. He pushed them out of sight, shoving my face back into place between his legs. I bit the hard nub of denim where the seams converged.

"You still want it, don'tcha?" Reed growled. "I can slap your face and call you a cocksucking faggot, and you still want it, don'tcha, huh? Goddamn."

He was grinding my face into his crotch, crushing my nose and cutting the inside of my lips on my teeth.

"You know," he said, breathing harder, "you know, when I was in high school . . . back in Midland . . . there was a kid like you. Except he didn't need no encouragement, you didn't have to lead him along, no sir, he was a cocksucker and he wanted every guy in school with a big cock to know it. Yeah, he didn't like to suck just anybody, he had a craving for guys on the football team, like me, he just wanted to suck their cocks and make 'em feel good. That's all he wanted, all the time, he wanted to be down on his fucking knees with a big piece of meat down his throat."

Reed twisted my skull, bending my neck back so far that I could hardly breathe. Slowly, his hips began a grinding, fucking motion, burning my lips with the rough denim.

"I mean, he was an all right guy most of the time, he wasn't a pansy or anything. He was alright looking, he looked like everybody else, except he wore real tight pants and walked with his cute little butt stuck out. He was real smart, too, he'd help you with math and stuff. But shit, he didn't think twice about asking for it right out loud. He could really blow your mind. 'Come on, Reed,' he'd say, 'why don'tcha pull it out and let me. You're the biggest, Reed,' that's what he'd tell me, 'you're the biggest, I've seen it and you've got a fucking horse dick between your legs and I wanna suck on it.'

"But I never let him. You know why? Cause I figured you had to be a little queer yourself to get off on a cocksucker's mouth, you know what I mean? That's just the way I figured it. Maybe the other guys didn't think so, they liked it, but I just couldn't see it, it was still doing it with another guy. What do you think?"

He jerked my head back and made me look up at him. All I could see were his forehead and eyes. The rest of his face was blocked by his chest, two slanting mountains of muscle with a deep valley between.

"I think he was right," I said. "You're the biggest, Reed. You're a horse, Reed. You've got a cock like a stud horse."

"Yeah," he whispered. He closed his eyes and pursed his lips, and shoved my face back into his crotch. "Yeah, that's what Reggie said. He was a cocksucker like you, and he wanted it just as bad. He didn't mind if I got a little rough, either. No, he liked that, that turned him on. Like he enjoyed the chance to show you just how low he'd go to get a cock in his mouth. One time, I remember, one time . . ."

Reed's voice trailed off, and was gone a long time. In its place was the sound of his breathing, ragged and shallow. Then he began speaking again, in a voice that might have come from the moon.

"One time, one night after a football game or something, a few of the guys had Reggie in the bathroom. I walked in on 'em – you should've seen 'em jerk and start shoving their cocks back in their pants. Then they saw it was me and relaxed.

"They had Reggie sitting in one of the stalls, on the toilet, stark naked. They'd made him take off every stitch of his clothes, and thrown 'em out the window. They were taking turns making him suck their cocks. They were whopping him up the side of his head and calling him names, cocksucker, queer boy, faggot. He was crying, real soft like, I could see the tears on his face all the way down to his chin. I could see where they'd dripped down and got his chest all wet. Shiny and wet, he had a smooth little chest, not a hair on it.

"But he didn't try to get away. Or maybe he'd tried to before, and finally gave up. There was nowhere for him to go without his clothes, anyway. They kept using his mouth and slapping him, over and over, I could hear him gagging like he was gonna throw up. And he kept looking over at me, and his eyes were real shiny with the tears, and his eyes . . . he wanted something. He didn't want me to stop all those guys. I probably could have, but that's not what he was asking for. He wanted me to join in. I could tell he wanted me over there with the rest of 'em, whopping him across the mouth and calling him names. So I didn't break it up, I just stood there and watched and threw a boner in my pants. I couldn't help it, the way Reggie kept staring at me, looking at me sidelong while his mouth was stuffed full of some other guy's dick.

"And I remember, toward the end, after everybody had shot, one of the guys, his name was Robin and he had black hair and the thickest legs you ever saw, he was a real son of a bitch, real good-looking and stuck-up . . . he said something like, 'Well, if the goddamn faggot won't get off the toilet, I'll just have to piss on him.' Which wasn't true cause there was plenty of other stalls . . . but everybody laughed anyway, like he was making sense . . . and he stood over Reggie and pointed his cock down and let go, all over Reggie's lap. And Reggie stared up at him like he was some kind of god and his cock stood up real stiff, wet and stiff. Then Robin grabbed his head and bent it way back and said, 'You want a kiss, baby?' And he spit right in Reggie's face.

"Robin zipped up and walked out after that, smiling real big like he was proud of himself, like he'd put on a good show for everybody and shown 'em what a stud he was, and the other guys went too. They trailed out of the bathroom, laughing and talking dirty. One of 'em noticed I wasn't going and said something about 'looks like Reed wants some time alone with the cocksucker. Yeah, looks like Reed has to settle for what's left.' And they laughed and talked about how they'd fucked Reggie's throat so much it was loose as a Mexican's cunt, but maybe I could stretch it out some more. My ears burned, but I stayed there till everybody was gone, and I couldn't hear 'em out in the hall any more.

"It was real quiet then, all I could hear was Reggie sort of moaning, sitting on the toilet with his legs open and his head thrown back. I pulled him off the toilet and walked him to the sink and helped him rinse off. He smelled somewhere between a urinal and a sweaty jockstrap, his breath smelled like a greasy cock, cock breath, that's what he had. I had my fingers crossed nobody would walk in on us.

"Then I asked him where the hell his clothes were and he told me, and I went outside and got 'em while he waited. Then he got dressed and I gave him a ride home.

"On the way – I mean, he was really strung out, he looked all pale and weak as a kitten – but he started coming on to me. I got real mad and told him he was a goddamn whore, a goddamn fucking whore. I told him I ought to beat his fucking ass. But he said he knew I wasn't really like that, that I was different from the other guys. That I wasn't mean like they were. He said they were a bunch of punks, but I was a man already. He said –"

Reed gasped and began riding my face, burrowing hard with his hips as if he were hunching a pillow.

"Reggie said he was in love with me. That the only cock he really wanted to suck on was my cock, because he knew it was the biggest, and I was the best-looking guy he knew, and I was nice. He said he wouldn't want any of the other guys' cocks if he could just have mine. He said he knew, he could just tell, that my come would taste real good, sweeter than anybody else's. I told him he had rocks in his head, I wasn't different from anybody else . . .

"Shit, he finally got to me. I was horny, I guess, I was always horny back then, I'm still horny all the goddamn fucking time. I took him to the place I went parking with girls, and I took it out and showed it to him. He started taking off his clothes, and I told him to stop, but he said he wanted to be naked like back at the toilet.

"I guess he wasn't really such a great cocksucker after all, cause he couldn't get much more than the head inside. That was okay by me, cause it sort of turned me off, thinking about all those other cocks he'd had in there earlier. So he just licked it all over, all up and down. And he sucked my balls in his mouth, cause he said he wanted to hold my come in his mouth while it was still inside my body. It felt real good, but I couldn't shoot that way, so finally I just beat off, and Reggie caught it in his mouth. And he said he was right, it was smooth and sweet as cream.

"Then I took him home. He was really beat, he fell asleep on the way, I had to wake him up. He wanted to kiss me but I wouldn't let him. That was all we ever did, just that once. He kept after me, but one time I really told him off in front of some of the guys, and he stopped after that. But he never stopped looking at me . . . that way . . .

"He was an okay guy, really. I mean, I really did like him in a way. I heard he went off to college and made a lawyer or something. He's a big shot in Austin now. Can you believe that? And I ended up being a trucker like my daddy, huh, I guess that's the difference between having a big cock and a big brain —"

Reed went stiff suddenly and held me close with hands like a vise. His cock was pressed against my face through the denim. I felt it pump, felt wetness seep through and touch my neck.

His grip relaxed. He released me and I sat back on the floor. He looked down at me for a moment, breathing hard. I watched his big chest rise and fall.

Then he turned away and started pacing the room like a wired mountain lion. He got a towel from the bathroom and wiped out the inside of his pants leg, then used the towel to mop his armpits and the small of his back, where the sweat glistened in the dimples. He pulled on his thin white A-shirt and a short sleeve plaid cotton shirt, and put on his boots. He grabbed his keys and his wallet and stuffed them into his pockets.

He glanced over at me and frowned. I hadn't moved or taken my eyes off him the whole time.

"Hurry up and get dressed if you want some breakfast," he mumbled. "I'll meet you in the café."

There was a hand-lettered sign in the cafe window that said: BEST BREAKFAST ON INTERSTATE 10. The place was crowded, mainly with men – truckdrivers, travelers, a few farmers. A group of locals in cheap business suits sat at a long table at the back, talking about politics and high prices.

Reed had found a booth for us. He was already eating.

"Sorry, couldn't wait," he said with his mouth full. "Hungry."

There was a big platter of scrambled eggs, ham, and pancakes in front of him. My stomach began to growl. The waitress brought me a menu. I tried to find something I could afford with the small change I had left. The pickings were slim. I had just enough for a small glass of milk and a sweet roll.

Reed was eating too fast to speak. I hid behind my opened menu.

The waitress came back and I started to order. Reed cut me off.

"He'll have the same as me."

The waitress nodded and took my menu. I noticed the smile she aimed at Reed. He smiled back. Something he must do a dozen times a day, I thought – accepting their admiration, acknowledging it.

"Milk instead of coffee," I called after her. My nerves were strained enough, and I didn't need waking up. The waitress turned her head and nodded, and smiled at Reed again. He didn't see. He was busy shoveling pancakes into his mouth. The pancakes dripped with syrup. I wondered how he kept his bright white teeth and his hard lean stomach.

I cleared my throat. "Reed, you know I haven't got any money."

"Shit, I'll pay," he said, swallowing and raising his coffee cup to his lips. "No big deal. I can't expect you to starve yourself just because you were dumb enough to let some jerk back in Clovis rip you off."

I was grateful. I was more than grateful; I felt like crying. I wished I could tell him how I felt, but I couldn't. There was still a kind of wall between Reed and me. Looking at him across the table, I could almost believe that we were nothing more than what we appeared to be, just a young truckdriver and a kid who happened to be hitching with him.

Reed certainly acted as if that were the case. There were no deep looks, no secret smiles. He didn't seem interested in anything but eating. I told myself he had come three times in the last ten hours or so; maybe he was free of whatever crazy energy kept flowing back and forth between us. But I had come three times myself, and I wasn't free of it. It was all I could think about while he ate. I stole glances at Reed and thought what an animal he looked, shoveling in that food and smacking his lips. I thought about the way you could tell his body was big and hard everywhere, even through the clothes he wore. I thought about how heavy his cock looked when it was hard. I ate my scrambled eggs and imagined eating them off Reed's cock.

The energy filled me up and spilled over into the cafe. I looked around at all the men starting out the day freshly showered and shaved. I wondered how the more attractive ones looked without their clothes, and how big their hidden cocks were, and if any of them ever made it with guys.

Reed finished before I did. He sat back and stretched his arms. His biceps mushroomed and filled the loose short sleeves of his shirt. "We'll make LA this evening," he said, yawning.

"So soon?" It had taken me days to get from Austin to the New Mexican state line. Now after two days with Reed I would be on the West Coast.

"You never been this far from home, have you?"

"No."

"Well, it looks mighty big on the map, but once you hit the highway and keep going, this country's not so big, you know?" He smiled. "Unless you have engine trouble."

I hoped we would. I had a vision of Reed, shirt off and dripping sweat, standing on the front bumper bent over the engine, sun beating down on the rippling planes of his back.

"So," I said, looking down at the half-eaten stack of pancakes on my plate, "what will you do when we get there?"

Reed shrugged. "There's this hotel I usually stay at. In a sort of seedy part of town." He smiled faintly, remembering something. "They got a big parking lot in the back where I can put the truck. Tomorrow, maybe tonight, I'll rent me a car. Come Monday, I'll take the truck to the warehouse and unload it. Then I head back to Texas."

"What's today?" I had lost track.

"Friday, sap. All day long." Reed grinned and nudged my leg under the table. There was nothing suggestive in his touch – more like a friendly jab of knuckles in the rib cage.

"So you'll be in LA over the weekend."

"Yeah, a little lay-over. I been gearing up for it all week. Big town." He changed the subject. "And of course, I'll be needing to drop you off sometime. Or it might be easier if your friend picked you up at the hotel. You can call him soon as we get in. You can be sleeping at his place tonight."

I tried to conjure an image up of Bill in my mind. All I could see were the mangled pancakes on my plate. Reed saw that I was troubled.

"I mean, that's what you're wanting, isn't it? To meet up again . . . with this guy."

"Bill," I said. "His name's Bill. Yeah, I guess so."

"Hey." Reed's face turned serious. "You'll be okay with him, won't you? I mean, you two are close enough, he'll take care of you till you can get some dough, right?"

I nodded.

"Cheer up." Reed touched my arm, as he had done last

night when I discovered my money roll was gone. I knew that if I looked up I would see his face as I had seen it then: concerned, reassuring . . . and untouchable, at least in the way I wanted to touch it. Not like this morning. Or last night.

"By the way," he said, brightening, "if you're not gonna finish those pancakes, why don't you slide 'em over here."

We made good time that morning. The day started warm and dry. By noon it was blazing hot.

Reed stripped down, as he had the day before, to his white A-shirt. Soon the thin cotton was soaked through and clung to his skin like wet muslin. The moving muscles in his chest and shoulders pulled it up till it bunched in tight folds over the hard clusters of his abdomen. His naked arms worked the big high wheel and the ball-top stick shift.

Nothing happened. Reed drove the rig. I sat three feet away and stared at the monotonous desert flatlands west of Phoenix. The sun was behind us, casting the shadow of the truck far ahead.

Across the California line, in a little town of about twenty motels called Blythe, we stopped for lunch. It was after one. The place was almost empty.

A couple of guys at a table caught my eye as we walked in. They were about my age, wearing perforated nylon football jerseys, the kind that stay bright and cling to the skin. Reed took a booth in a back corner, next to a window that opened onto the parking lot. I faced the window and watched rippling heat rise from the asphalt. There was only one car in the lot, a blue Camaro. I had to move in a few inches to get out of the glare from the windshield.

The waitress handed us menus. She smiled at Reed; he smiled back and scratched his chest. I studied the menu glumly. When she came back with water, Reed ordered a plate of Polish sausage and cole slaw.

"Sounds good to me, too," I said.

"How're you gonna pay for it?"

I stared at Reed across the table. He was looking straight at me with his arms crossed, one eyebrow slightly raised.

"I'll just have a glass of milk. And some toast," I said, trying to put steel in my voice. Reed seemed to be amused, but he didn't say anything.

"That's it, hon?" The waitress pursed her lips and raised her penciled eyebrows in perfect semicircles.

"Yeah," I said.

I wolfed down my lunch and watched Reed slice into the sausages. They popped and leaked juice as the knife sawed through. He put a big bite in his mouth and smiled at me as he chewed. I stared back at him angrily, amazed at how childish and stupid he looked.

Then I felt his foot against my leg, rubbing gently. A current cold as ice ran up to my groin.

His foot followed it up. He pushed my knees apart, then propped his heel on the edge of the seat between my legs. He straightened his leg. I felt the sole of his boot against my crotch. My cock started to stiffen. He kept pushing, pinning me back against the seat.

Reed smiled and kept eating. His foot began pumping against my crotch, very slow and steady. I looked down at the empty glass and saucer before me, suddenly under his power again. I closed my hands over the top of his boot, trailed my fingers over the thick laces, pressed my thumbs into the worn brown leather. I pulled his foot into my crotch and pushed back.

Reed kept eating, paying no attention except with his foot. I sank deeper and deeper, until I felt nothing at all but the point of contact. I didn't seem to exist above the waist.

Reed picked up one of the sausages between his thumb and forefinger. He leaned across the table and held it in front of my face, pointing the blunt tip at my mouth.

"You want some?" he said in a low voice.

"What?" I batted my eyes, trying to keep them open.

"Open your mouth."

Reed ran the round end of the sausage over my lips,

smearing them with grease, coaxing them open. Then the sausage was sliding past my lips. Reed was propped forward on his elbows, head tilted to one side, watching me through narrow eyes. The heel of his boot pressed hard into my balls.

The smooth, warm casing slid over my tongue. I started to cut it with my teeth.

"Don't bite," Reed said. "Cocksuckers never bite."

He pulled the sausage almost out of my mouth. Then he slid it back in, stretching my lips into a circle. Out again, and in.

Beyond Reed's shoulder, through the plate glass, a movement caught my eye. It was one of the high school boys I had seen eating when we came in.

He was standing behind the open door of the blue Camaro, staring at me. His hair was blond. His skin was gold from an early summer tan. His forearms were thick and covered with golden hair. The muscles of his torso were well-defined beneath the sheer nylon of his loose jersey. His number was 74.

That was what Bill looked like. I remembered.

I stared back at him. Reed was pumping the sausage in my mouth, pumping my crotch with his foot. I dug my fingernails into the unfeeling leather.

Number 74 looked shocked. Then a weird grin spread over his face. He stuck his arm into the car, gestured and said something, never taking his eyes off me. His friend, in the opposite seat, leaned over inside the car and looked. They peered into the cafe as if they had spotted some kind of rare bird.

Suddenly Reed pushed the sausage beyond the stricture at the back of my mouth and into my throat. The other end slipped inside the circle of my lips. Reed pulled his hand away.

I held it in my mouth and throat for a moment. I looked at Reed, not at the young men outside. My throat began to spasm. I leaned over. The sausage slid, very slowly, heavy and thick, past my lips and onto the empty saucer, trailing a string of spittle to my lips.

"Oh, Reed," I whispered, too low, maybe, for him to hear. "Oh, Reed. You're making me crazy."

I had come in my pants.

FOUR

Back in the truck. Back on the road. The views were spectacular. First the endless cactus-strewn stretch of the lower Mojave, like a scene from a widescreen Western. The long winding climb up the San Bernardino Mountains, the engine churning, Reed's strong right arm steady on the stick shift. Then the steep descent into the irrigated lowlands, where the world abruptly changed its face. Dense acres of orchards. Undetermined fields of green in the distance. Palms along the highway. RV dealers. Billboards.

That strange transition must have impressed me strongly. I can see it vividly in my memory. But at the same time it was all lost on me. I was whirring like the truck engine inside, smooth as eggshell on the surface. I would say, now, that I was being quietly hysterical. I didn't know what to call it at the time. I couldn't name it – I was inside it, I couldn't look at it from the outside and see where it began and ended. My whole body, even my face, was tense. Reed was a presence beside me, solid as iron, like magnetized iron, and I was a delicate body made of metal filings, trying to resist the pull, trying not to fly to him and break into a thousand pieces.

The accumulated tension and the heat finally made me drowsy. Reed noticed I was nodding off.

"Sleepy?"

"Yeah." There was an anger in my voice that I hadn't intended to be there.

The sound of the engine. The sharp rush of a car passing in the opposite direction. Then one of Reed's voices. Not the comforting voice, or the moon voice, but both together.

"Why don't you lay your head in my lap?"

I closed my eyes and ordered my body not to shake.

"And take a nap," Reed added, as if he thought I might have misunderstood.

"Okay," I said. Not looking at him, I lay across the seat and settled my shoulder against his thigh. His cock was below my cheek, big and soft.

Reed's erection came and went. Soft and pliable beneath my face, then hard as rope against my cheekbone. I put my hand across the head. It filled my palm like a billiard ball. The vibrations of the engine rumbled through my face and neck, shaking the knotted muscles loose. Occasionally Reed moved his feet on the clutch and brake; the muscles in his thighs regrouped beneath the denim. When his right hand wasn't busy shifting, he rested it on my kneecap and squeezed. Later, he touched my hair. I believe he thought I was asleep.

I did sleep, off and on. The rest of the time I dreamed.

The heat in the cab was like strong dope. I imagined a thousand things. Each fantasy built on the last until my head began discovering things on its own. New thoughts came from nowhere but within.

I imagined sucking on him this way, here in the cab while he worked the rig. My cock was hard. His cock was hard. I wouldn't be able to do it any better than Reggie, I would have to settle for the feeling of it against my tongue and my lips. There was so much of it to lick, to kiss, I could go on doing it forever. The ridge around the corona was thick as a finger. I could bite it, sheathing my teeth behind my lips. I could explore its curvature for an hour with my tongue. It wouldn't make him come. But I could hold his come in my mouth while it was still warm inside him, I could fit a ball in each cheek.

I imagined him telling me to strip down, because he liked me better naked in the heat when my body sported a glistening coat of sweat. I would curl up beside him again and nuzzle his cock.

I imagined his hand on my flank, the calluses rough where I was smooth. He would reach over me and open the glove compartment, take out the jar of Vaseline, gritty and black around the rim. Dip his fingers inside, then reach between my cheeks, fingers searching, probing – then suddenly rough – skewering me . . .

He opened me. I was open, everywhere. I felt my throat open like a rose. I lifted my head and drew a breath, face poised over his upright cock. My lips were like waves rushing over the ridge of his crown, breaking like waves and rushing down to the very base. Reed was in me, in my neck. He would come that way and the taste would be like heavy cream. It would keep coming for minutes while I drank and drank. Then he would soften and recede from my throat till I could hold all of him in my mouth without choking.

Soon he would need to piss. I would be there. No need to stop. Reed would let go and I would swallow as I had swallowed his come, for long, long minutes. He would never have to stop for a leak, we could drive on and on, past LA, up to Canada or maybe down to Mexico. We could roll up the windows, drive into the ocean, live undersea in the cab, naked together in the green darkness, holding each other naked, eating and drinking from each other's bodies forever.

"Santa Ana," Reed was saying. He was shaking my shoulder.

I opened my eyes, and shut them. The dream was too sweet to leave.

"Hey, get up and look. Dust devils."

I pulled my head off his lap and sat up. The highway was taking us through a corridor of high trees. The trees stretched on as far as I could see. They whipped in the wind.

"Blow you off the fucking road," Reed said. From the way he grinned, I was sure there was no danger of that.

I never knew where Los Angeles began. The city insinuated itself into the landscape, detail by detail. The open spaces receded. The freeways multiplied. The sun was setting in our faces, blood red through the haze.

Once I was there, I never knew just where I was in Los Angeles. I looked at a map in Reed's glove compartment, but it was too big to unfold in the cab. I'm sure I could never find that hotel again.

It was far off the freeway. I couldn't see why Reed stayed there, instead of a motel, unless it was cheaper. He had said it was in a seedy part of town. I wasn't sure what seedy meant. The buildings were low, gray and old. The hotel was five or six stories. The facade was Spanish; a lot of the decorative work above the windows and archways was damaged or gone altogether, leaving oddly shaped patches of unpainted plaster behind. There was a huge parking lot in back, surrounded by a high chain link fence.

The lobby was dark. There were lots of fake marble columns and brass railings that needed polishing. The place had a musty smell. In one corner were some old sofas clustered around a black-and-white TV set. The set was on, but no one was there to watch it.

The desk clerk was a bald man about fifty with lots of hair on his forearms. He was reading a dog-eared copy of *Hustler* magazine.

"Goddamn, would you look at that?" he said, holding up a picture of a naked woman who appeared to be smoking a cigar with her asshole. It was the grossest thing I had ever seen, but the clerk seemed to love it. He held the magazine back and leered at the picture. Then he set it down on the counter.

"You guys need a room?"

"Just me," Reed said. "The kid won't be staying."

The clerk looked at us suspiciously. "Sure."

He gave Reed a key for a room on the third floor. "Hey," he shouted, as we turned toward the elevator. "You guys be needing company tonight?"

"Not tonight," Reed said. "We'll find our own."

"Yeah. I bet." The clerk scowled at us. Reed didn't look back. I saw him clenching his teeth while we waited for the elevator. "Asshole," he said under his breath.

The room had white louvered doors. The furniture was old, probably older than me. The walls needed a paint job, bad.

Reed started unpacking his overnight bag. "Why don't you call your buddy?"

I didn't want to, but I did. I rummaged through my duffel bag and found my address book. The clerk downstairs put the call through – I recognized his gravelly voice. I listened to the phone ring and hoped Bill wouldn't be in.

But he was. I was amazed at the effect his voice had on me. It was just the same. Everything came back, all the memories and fantasies that had sustained me before I met Reed. Bill sounded glad to hear my voice. I didn't say anything too intimate; I figured the clerk was the type to listen in.

Bill said he could find the hotel, but couldn't make it for an hour or so. He said not to eat; he'd feed me at his place. My heart sped up, imagining a double meaning. It would be good to be with him. He would know what I wanted, and he would give it to me.

I hung up and told Reed I'd have to hang around for a while.

"That's fine," he said, not looking at me. "Listen, I'm going down the street to a rental place I know, stays open late. Get that car so I'll have it in the morning." He headed for the door. "Uh, look, if you don't see me again – I mean, your buddy might show up 'fore I get back . . . why don't you give me a call here at the hotel sometime tomorrow or Sunday. Just to let me know how you're getting along. You know, the money and all."

He opened the door. He glanced at me. I nodded.

"I'll do that, Reed."

Then he left. I stared at the louvered door for a long time.

I took a hot shower. I lathered the soap around my cock and got horny. My memories swung back and forth between Reed and Bill. Up against a wall with Bill in my ass, calling me his tight end. Flat on my back with Reed's bare foot on my chest. I thought about that kid Reggie, naked on the toilet with a bunch of jocks fucking his face.

I dried off and walked around the room, beating my cock, glad to be alone. I looked through Reed's bag and pulled out a pair of his skimpy white briefs. I tried them on. We were the same size around the waist, if nowhere else. I looked in the mirror at the way they fit snug across my ass. I decided I would keep them to beat off in.

I moved around the room, getting myself hot, beating off in the chair, on the bed, in front of the mirror. I noticed Reed's keys on the dresser and got an idea.

I dressed and went downstairs. I walked through the lobby, feeling my hard-on with every step. The clerk looked up and flashed a flat, meaningless smile.

I walked to the truck, noticing how dirty the sky looked at twilight. I unlocked the passenger door, stepped up and opened the glove compartment. I found the porno books I had seen the day before.

Back in Reed's room I stripped again. I relaxed on the bed and started reading, holding a book in one hand and squeezing my cock through his briefs with the other. The books were straight, but I figured I was horny enough to get turned on by anything with hard cocks in it.

I could see why Reed liked *Truckstop Whore*. The hero was a big blond trucker with a huge dick who traveled across the country screwing big-chested waitresses and motel maids. I imagined Reed as the trucker, and the story got me off. Some of the sex got pretty rough. The women were crazy for the guy's dick, but most of them couldn't take it. It was too big. One of them even gagged on it and threw up.

The story began to sound vaguely familiar.

The trucker had a sadistic streak. Most of the women took it for a while, just for the chance to be close to his dick, before they had enough and ran off. Then he found a girl at a truckstop who couldn't be humiliated enough. The trucker and a friend spent the last half of the book tying her up and screwing her.

Then I came to something that stopped me cold. I read the page over and over. The trucker had the girl naked and tied up. He was making her suck him off. After he came, she spat it out. That made him furious. He slapped her around, the fucked her up the ass while she begged him to stop. Then he made her lick off his cock and suck him again, making sure she swallowed it.

I had heard that story before. Yesterday. From Reed. He had told it while he beat off and teased me with his cock – told it as if it had really happened, between him and a woman he met in Dallas.

His Oriental Slavegirl was straight, too. It was about a serviceman in Southeast Asia who wins a slavegirl in a card game. But there was a scene near the end about a gay GI named Smith, the "regimental cocksucker". A group of soldiers cornered him in the barracks latrine, stripped him and forced him to sit naked on the toilet. Then they took turns fucking his face and calling him names – cocksucker, queer boy, faggot. One of them even pissed on him. Then the hero came in and broke it up. The gay GI wanted to give him a blowjob in gratitude, but the hero declined and went off to use his slavegirl instead.

I laid the book on the bed. Some of the phrases Reed had used were right there, in the books. I couldn't tell how much of what he had told me was real, and how much imagined.

He wasn't the perfect, untouchable stud I thought he was. He was a fake. I felt anger, the special anger you feel when an idol falls. There was something pathetic in it, but I fought those feelings off. I preferred to be mad instead of depressed.

He had lied to me, pretended he was telling me something secret and special, and all the time he was just stealing scenes from a couple of second-rate porno books. The idea of spending the night with Bill, some place far from Reed, seemed better and better.

There was a knock. I opened the door, still half-hard inside the skimpy briefs, hoping it wasn't Reed.

It was Bill. We said hi and looked at each other for a long time. I didn't mind him seeing me in the briefs. I just hoped he remembered, and liked what he saw. I thought about sucking him off right there in the room, but I didn't want Reed walking in on us.

I dressed fast, eager to leave with Bill and get away from Reed to some place where I could be myself and think clearly. He had made a fool of me, acting like such a stud and waving his cock in my face, always out of reach. He had had the nerve to call me a faggot. What was he? I had no idea. All I had was a pack of lies. For all his big, beautiful muscles, he was hollow at the core.

I followed Bill down to his car in the parking lot. I felt the tension drain out of me. Laughing came easy. Bill had a lot of questions about people back home. He kept saying how glad he was that I'd come.

I had meant to leave a note for Reed. I remembered in the parking lot. I decided not to go back. I also remembered that I had left the paperbacks out in plain sight on the bed. Let him find them, I thought. Let him figure out that I'd seen through his stories.

As Bill wheeled his secondhand Ford into the street, I looked back at Reed's truck, sitting almost alone in the parking lit, a vague, hulking shape in the gathering darkness.

The drive to Bill's place took forty-five minutes. I was amazed at the size of the city. We talked about that, and the smog, and a lot of other unimportant things. I was glad just to be in the car with him, soaking in the old familiar feelings.

His apartment was in a huge complex next to a Safeway. There was a swimming pool in the central courtyard, lit by a ghostly blue night light. I followed him up a flight of clanging stairs, toting the duffel bag over my shoulder.

The apartment was very small. The door opened into a small living room separated by a small bar from a tiny kitchen beyond. There was a girl in the kitchen.

"Hi," Bill said. He walked over to the girl and kissed her.

She was a little shorter than Bill, very slender, with large breasts and wide hips. She wore sandals and a white cotton summer dress belted at the waist. Her hair was long and black, parted in the middle. Her complexion was olive, her features very delicate. She looked Polynesian, I thought, or Asian. *His Oriental Slavegirl*, I thought, groaning inside.

Bill introduced us. Her name was Anne. She shared the apartment with him. Dinner was ready. Anne had to run – a night class. Back by ten.

Bill talked about her all through dinner. "She is wild," he said. "Wild, I tell you. I can't believe the stuff she does in bed. There sure weren't any chicks like her back in Austin. It's something about the climate out here."

I smiled, nodded, tried to keep up a front. Inside I was cracking. The euphoria I had felt when I left the hotel evaporated. In its place was an absolute vacuum.

After dinner, I helped him rinse the dishes and load them into the washer. Bill brought some beers from the refrigerator and we sat side by side on the sofa watching TV. I was glad to have the television to look at. I was having a hard time looking him in the eye.

We talked about this and that. Bill kept changing the subject back to Anne, going on about how fantastic and uninhibited she was in bed. Every time he mentioned her name the blood rushed in my ears, droning above his voice. I wanted to touch him. I wanted something to happen. But I couldn't make the first move, and it seemed that Bill didn't care to.

Somewhere in the middle of that miserable night, Anne came in the front door. She sat on the floor at Bill's feet. He rolled a couple of joints. We smoked and listened to records far into the night. Neither of them seemed to notice how edgy I was. They were too wrapped up in each other. Maybe they did notice, and tried to put me at ease by ignoring it. I decided Anne wasn't so bad. If she hadn't been Bill's girlfriend, I could have liked her.

Finally, they went into the bedroom. I was left to sleep on the sofa. I settled down on my back, pulled the blanket up to my chin, and stared at the dark ceiling. Then I heard her. They were fucking in the bedroom.

She was the loud type – probably one of the things Bill liked about her. I could hear everything through the thin, cheap door. She grunted. She moaned. She called out his name. She called him Billy. I got tears in my eyes. I also got hard, listening, knowing how strong Bill's hips were, remembering how his cock felt inside.

I sat up on the sofa and pulled off my underwear, Reed's underwear, wanting to be naked in the grayness. I spat in my hand and smeared the saliva over my cock.

Bill began moaning along with Anne. I recognized that sound, and knew he was coming. I wanted to come too, I wanted to sleep, but somehow I couldn't. I sat there on the sofa, beating my meat long after the groans and sighs died away.

I was like that when the door to the bedroom opened and Bill stepped out. He saw me and grinned, thinking he understood. He raised a finger to his lips and spoke in a soft voice. "What did I tell you?" He shrugged and gestured to the bathroom door at his right. "Gotta wash off."

I stared at his face, trying to tell him everything with my eyes. Wanting him to understand, to save me somehow. His grin vanished. The look on his face told me he hadn't forgotten the old days after all. He took a hesitant step toward me.

I slid off the sofa, onto my knees. I wrapped both hands around my cock and opened my mouth. I stared at his cock.

It hung from his crotch, slick and pale, still heavy with blood, veins pushed to the surface. It looked small after Reed, but it was beautiful and I wanted it.

Bill took another step. He parted his lips and sucked in a breath. Then he stepped toward me, cock swinging. He stopped just short of my mouth and looked down at me.

"Damn," he said. "Same old Alan."

I leaned forward and swallowed his cock. He gasped above me. "Oh yeah. Same old Alan." His shaft filled until it was half-hard. He touched my ears with his fingers.

"Yeah," he whispered. "Suck the juice off that cock. Been making my woman feel good. I was gonna wash, but hell, if you want it . . ."

I tried not to hear. I ran my fingers over his legs and filled my hands with hard muscle. I pressed my palms over the cheeks of his ass. They were smooth and sleek as marble.

I held him in my mouth for a long time. He never got fully hard, but it felt good just to have him there, just to be on my knees in front of him. He started to pull out. I tightened my grip on his ass and held him fast.

"I gotta go," he whispered.

I held him tight.

"Hey. Alan. I gotta take a piss."

I remembered the waking dream of that afternoon. Reed in my mouth. Never having to stop.

Bill tried to step back, but not too hard. There was a long dark silence. He said it one more time.

"Alan. I need to piss. Now."

I drew back, just enough to turn my face up. I looked into his eyes, just long enough to show I understood. Then I swallowed him again. His cock had grown harder.

I waited. Then it began. Erratic at first, then rushing out. I didn't mind the taste. I simply swallowed, and stroked my cock with both fists.

Afterwards Bill pulled free. He was rock hard. I wanted to suck him. But he stepped back, toward the bedroom, looking at me over his shoulder with a strange look on his face.

A few moments later, I heard Anne murmur in her sleep. They started fucking again.

The door to the bedroom was slightly ajar. Perhaps Bill had left it that way on purpose.

I walked to the door and peered through the crack. A beam of moonlight illuminated their bodies. Anne was face-down on the bed, spread-eagled. Bill was on top of her, pinning her down. His legs were stretched over hers. His hands held her down by the wrists. Her face was pressed into the bed, obscure behind the tangle of her hair. Bill was whispering into her ear, biting her neck. I watched the hard, lean muscles in his ass tense and contract. He was screwing her ass.

I returned to the sofa. I sat motionless, cock limp, emotions drained. They came again, both of them moaning.

Then silence. Then the sound of their breathing, steady and deep.

I got up and closed the bedroom door. I went to the wall phone in the kitchen. I lifted the receiver. By the pale white light of the dial I found the hotel in the phone book.

The desk clerk answered. He sounded like he was in a foul mood. I started to ask for Reed, then realized I didn't know his last name. But I remembered the room number.

The phone rang and rang. Finally the clerk broke in.

"Alright already, he's not in. You wanna leave a message or what?"

"I guess . . ." I tried to think of words.

"Wait a minute," the clerk said. "The big blond guy that checked in this evening, right?"

"Yes," I said, my heart beating fast.

"Yeah, that's him. He's just getting in. Looks like he picked up something hot off the strip, too. Hold on, I'll call him over. I wanna get a look at this broad."

I listened to distorted sounds over the wire – the phone laid down on the counter with a clunk, a distant ringing sound, the phone picked up again. Then Reed's voice. I could hear him smiling.

"Yeah, who is it?"

"It's me, Reed."

"Oh . . ."

"Reed, I want you to come and get me. It's no good here."

I heard a woman giggling in the background, heard the clerk bark with laughter. Somehow I knew he was holding up that horrible photo of the woman with the cigar.

"Well, look," Reed said, "I'm kinda tied up right now . . ."

"I don't care. Give her some money and tell her to go away. I want you to come get me. Now. Please, Reed."

There was a long pause. I counted my heartbeats.

"Okay," Reed said.

I gave him the address. He promised to be there in an hour.

I gathered my things. I left a note for Bill and Anne, a simple good-bye. I knew I wouldn't be coming back, whatever happened.

FIVE

I waited a long time in the living room of Bill and Anne's apartment. The only light came from the blue spot in the swimming pool in the courtyard below. Blue lozenges of light wavered across the curtains in weird, changing shapes.

I began to think that Reed had gotten lost, or had an accident on the freeway. Or worse than that, he had changed his mind and decided not to come for me after all. I wanted him so badly I could feel the need. It was a hollowness in my chest, a thickness in my cock, in my throat. I felt the blood pump inside me, heavy as mercury in the veins. I imagined it beating in time with the languid veins that covered Reed's cock like clinging tendrils submerged beneath the skin.

I paced the room. My cock went stiff. I pulled it out of my jeans, spat in my hand and pulled on it. It felt good in the darkness. I opened my hand when I felt the climax approach, waited for the sensation to subside, then stoked again. I didn't want to come until I was with Reed again, until he was there to watch me and touch me.

I let go of my cock. I softened immediately; the day's exhaustion poured through me like lead. I touched myself, and the thought of Reed opened a dark, bottomless well of energy inside me. My cock sprang up hard as marble.

I oscillated in the darkness, from raw excitement to a weariness like death. Each state seemed to feed the other. My body was a battleground, torn, open, vulnerable, barren as a turned-up field before the seeding.

I stepped around the bar that separated the living room from the kitchen and checked the clock on the oven. Two hours had passed since I called. I stared at the phone on the wall.

There was no point in calling the hotel. I went through every step in my mind. I would press the buttons, listen to the distant ringing. The clerk would answer. Whaddya want? No, he's not in. You the same guy that called before?

Or Reed would be there. In his room. Asleep. His body pressed against the naked whore he had picked up on the boulevard. You again? Jesus, what time is it?

I closed my eyes and spoke the words aloud, to no one but myself. "Reed. Please. You said you'd come."

My cock went stiff again. I needed Reed at that moment more than I had ever needed anything, ever. If I couldn't have him in the flesh, I needed at least to hear his voice.

I picked up the phone. The buttons lit up. The phone book was on the counter, still open to the hotel listing. I found the number, pressed the buttons and listened to the tones they made.

A distant ringing. My breath grew short. My cock softened. It was going to be harder than I'd thought.

The phone was picked up in mid-ring. It was the same clerk. I tried to clear my throat, and realized the muscles in my neck were frozen stiff.

"Whaddya want?" the clerk said.

Above the pounding in my ears, I thought I heard a knock at the front door.

"Who is this?" The clerk was getting angry.

There was a second knock, very soft, but I was sure I heard it. I gently placed the receiver back into the hook. The soft click sounded loud in the darkness.

I crossed the room and unlatched the chain on the door. My hands were shaking; I dropped it. It rattled against the wood. I turned the knob and opened the door.

The walkway was dim. His face was in shadow, but I knew the silhouette of Reed's body. His hands were stuffed into his pants pockets. He was tapping one foot impatiently.

"Hell," he growled quietly. "This fuckin' place must have three hundred units in it."

I made a sound in my throat, closer to laughing than crying. I stepped forward and slipped my arms around his chest.

His body was stiff as wood, but he didn't push me away. His shirt was half open down the front. I pressed my face into the hard, deep cleft between the muscles.

I hugged him harder, wanting him to respond. I tried to squeeze the breath out of him, but the sides of his chest were solid bands of muscle, stronger than my arms.

I loosened my grip and dropped to my knees, still holding him, keeping my face against his body. He didn't move. I hugged his thighs and kissed the worn, faded place where his cock rode inside his jeans. I opened my mouth and kissed it over and over, till it began to grow beneath the denim.

"Didn't get enough from your boyfriend?" Reed said. He sounded angry. I looked up at him, confused. His face was hidden in shadow. He moved his head, peering into the dark room.

"Where is he, anyway?"

"In the bedroom," I said. "Asleep."

Reed's voice was flat as a tombstone. "Thought I might get a chance to meet him. Well, get up off the floor and get your things." He pulled free of my arms, turned and headed down the walkway, hands in his pockets.

I scrambled to my feet, grabbed my duffel bag, and followed.

He had rented a big car, a Cutlass or something, the kind of metal monster straight guys count on to impress a woman. It was spotless inside. The upholstery was maroon. It seemed all wrong for him. After the high cab of the rig, the Cutlass seemed to skim just above the asphalt, silent and flat as a stingray. The freeway was brightly lit, almost deserted.

He had hardly glanced at me as I followed him to the car. He didn't look at me at all during the long ride across town. I was so happy to be with him, I couldn't understand why he wasn't happy, too.

I was also tired. I lay down across the seat and rested my head on his lap. Reed didn't touch me, but he didn't stop me. I put my mouth across the long, high ridge that ran from the bottom of his fly halfway down to his knee.

A long time later, the motion of the car indicated that we were leaving the freeway. The car began stopping and starting, turning at sharp angles. There was a wide, wheeling turn and a slight sensation of ascent. Gravel crunched beneath the tires. After a short, straight drive the car slowed and came to a full stop.

Reed cut the engine. Keys jingled above me as he pulled them from the ignition. His hips rose and pressed against my face as he slipped the keys into his pocket.

I expected him to open the door and step out. Instead he settled back and spread his legs.

I pictured the big parking lot of the hotel around us, dark, still, almost empty; Reed's rig nearby, perhaps beside us. I kept my mouth on his erection. I would stay that way for the rest of the night if I could.

Reed hooked his hand between my legs. He jerked my ass up and toward him. My knees slid forward to press against his right thigh. He pushed my mouth off his cock, shoved my face into his crotch and clamped his thighs together.

My neck was twisted and bent; I could hardly breathe. I had to arch my back stiffly, raising my ass up high.

"Pull down your pants," Reed said.

I snaked my hand between my belly and thighs, found the button and undid it, unzipped the fly. With both hands I slid the waistband up and over my buns, then down to my knees.

I was wearing the briefs I had stolen from him. When he touched my ass, the sharp-edged calluses on his hand snagged on the sheer nylon.

"I wondered where these got to," he said. "I don't know if I like the idea of some cocksucker wearing my shorts."

He slid his fingers inside the briefs. He pried the waistband down with the back of his hand, till it snapped against the bottom of my cheeks. His hand moved over my ass again. I felt the rough calluses. My ass turned to gooseflesh.

He slapped it. Then, with two fingers, he pushed the cheeks apart.

"Looks dry," he said. "I don't think your hole's been used

tonight. Didn't your friend fuck it?" He slapped my ass again, then loosened his thighs around my head, enough to let me speak.

"No," I said.

"No? What, he use your mouth instead?"

I didn't answer.

Reed slapped my ass again. "Huh, he give it to you in the mouth, cocksucker?" He sounded mad enough to kill me.

"Yes," I whispered. "A little."

"A little?" Reed's voice was thick with sarcasm. "What the fuck is that supposed to mean?" He was breathing hard. His voice came back husky and low. "Either he put his dick in your mouth or he didn't. You swallow it when he shot?"

"No," I said. The sound of my voice, twisted and strained, embarrassed me. "He didn't even come. Honest."

"You fuckin' liar." Reed's voice shook. He hit my ass again, so hard that tears welled up in my eyes. "Goddamn lyin' faggot. You want to know what I think? I think that guy showed you his dick, and you got all quivery inside and got down on your knees, like a good little cocksucker. I think he made you kiss it, and lick it, and then he shoved it down your throat and made you gag on it. I think he fucked your face and shot his load down your throat."

"No, Reed. I didn't even suck him, not really."

He clamped his knees together, like a vise. I thought my face would split. I put my hands on my leg and tried to pull free. Reed held me tight.

"Shit. All you faggots lie that way? He just put it in your mouth, huh? You just held it there, got his dick all hot and wet. Then what happened?" He spoke through gritted teeth. "I think you better tell me. Now."

I listened to my heart beat. Five times. I gathered my strength, pushed against his leg with my hands and pulled back with my neck.

For an instant I thought I was going to tear my head off. I even thought I heard a tearing sound in my neck, but it was only the tendons snapping taut.

Then I was free. I flopped back against the passenger door. The door handle stabbed me in the back. I struggled up to my knees. The briefs ripped open. My cock sprang free and slapped against my thigh.

I glared at Reed. "Stop calling me a faggot, you redneck shitkicker. You want to know what Bill did? I'll tell you, damn it!" My voice broke, but I went on, shouting hoarsely. "He pissed, that's what he did!" I had to stop and catch my breath. "In my mouth," I added. I looked him straight in the eye.

There was a long silence. I flinched, expecting Reed to start hitting me and never stop.

"What?" he said. His voice was strange, frightening. "What did you say?"

I tried to swallow. My throat was sore. I looked away from Reed, at the fancy dashboard, at the maroon carpet in the floorboard. "He'd just finished fucking his girlfriend," I said. "She lives there with him. They went to bed. I could hear them in there, fucking. Then he came into the living room. I took him in my mouth, I don't know why. He didn't even get all the way hard. Then he said he needed to take a piss . . ."

There was a silence so complete I couldn't even hear his breathing.

"Goddamn," he finally said. "So he just did it, huh?" I couldn't tell if he was angry or excited. "He just – did it. Right in your mouth. A couple of fuckin' freaks."

"Reed, I –"

"Is that why you called me?" He looked at me sharply. "You wanted to get away from him after that?"

"No, Reed –"

"So whose idea was it? Yours or his? Did you ask for it?"

"No. Not exactly. It just happened."

"Did you like it?"

I stared at the floorboard and didn't answer. I felt his eyes bore into me. From the corner of my eye, I saw his hand move to his crotch. He groped himself. Then he got out of the car and slammed the door.

I rubbed my throat and watched him cross the parking lot.
I didn't follow yet, fascinated by the unexpected beauty of
that moment, of the sight of Reed's body, tall and broad in
his tight jeans and his loose cotton shirt, casting a long
shadow across the deserted parking lot as he walked to the
hotel. Man and shadow receded, rounded the corner of the
building and disappeared.

My legs were cramped beneath me. It took me a while to
straighten out and pull up my pants. I got my duffel bag from
the back seat and walked to the hotel. Reed was waiting
outside the front entrance. He gave me an odd look, then
walked inside.

The desk clerk was lying on one of the ratty sofas in the
lobby, watching an old Jack Benny show on the television set.
He laughed. The soundtrack laughed. The noises sounded
hardly human, the way they echoed through the room. The
clerk didn't even notice us.

Reed took the stairs, three at a time. I followed him up to
the third floor, lugging the duffel bag.

The bed in his room was a mess. Sheets tangled and
dragged onto the floor. I knew why he had been so late.
He had taken the streetwalker up here after all, used her
before he came to get me. I could smell her in the room – her
perfume, the odors she had left on the sheets.

Reed stripped down to his briefs. I stood at the dresser and
watched, unable to make a move. Reed sat on the edge of the
bed and peeled off his socks. He looked up at me. His face
was very serious.

"Why don't you come over here and get out of your
clothes?" he said.

I walked to the bed. I stared at the floor as I pulled my T-
shirt over my head, kicked off my shoes, unfastened my pants
and stepped out of them. I pushed the torn briefs to my feet
and stood up. My cock began to harden. I sank to the floor,
exhausted, and sat cross-legged at his feet.

Reed cleared his throat. He took a deep breath. "Look up
at me, okay?" His voice was uneasy.

I looked in his eyes. The emotion there confused me. I looked instead at his chest, at the smooth creases in the skin just beneath the firm, rounded swells of his pectorals, at the firm folds of flesh bunched over his hard stomach, curving down to the waistband of his white nylon briefs. I looked at his cock, half hard inside his briefs, straining against the cloth.

"You make me so fuckin' mad, you know that?" There was something like hatred in his voice, something like desperation.

I nodded. "I can tell," I said. For some reason, a smile was trying to force its way onto my face. I fought it.

"Damn it! You ask for it, you know that?"

I nodded again.

Reed took a deep breath. His voice came back steadier, but still agitated. "I mean, you don't put up any resistance, you know. It's like I could do any fuckin' thing I wanted to you, anything that came into my head. And you'd probably like it. What am I supposed to do?"

His voice was changing again, to a tone it had approached before. All pretense was submerged. His words emerged like thoughts unspoken.

"Always wanted me somebody I could . . . I could fuckin' use, man. Like an animal. Like a fuckin' slave or something. Somebody I could kick around a little, step on every once and awhile when I feel like it. Somebody with a mouth like a goddamn hole, you know, just a hole for my dick, hungry for it twenty-four hours a day. Let me fuck it like a cunt, listen to it gag and just keep fucking, keep feeding it dick. Maybe I'd of found that bitch by now if my cock wasn't so damn big. What do you think?"

He reached for it, grabbed it sudden and hard as if it might fly off. The sheer nylon stretched across his cock like a second skin. I stared at it, amazed. He squeezed it and shut his eyes. "That's what I look for, all the fuckin' time. Shit, I'm not bad looking. I got enough money, not a lot, but enough. You'd think I could find me one goddamn bitch . . .

There was one, that blond I told you about, in Dallas, that one I used to fuck in the ass . . ."

Reed opened his eyes and saw the sudden doubt on my face. I looked down at the floor. He had thrown the porno books beside the bed. They were almost hidden by a tangled fold of sheet.

"Yeah, I know you did some jack-off reading earlier tonight, cocksucker. And you probably thought you figured out some stuff, didn't you? But Carla was real, all right. Maybe I got the idea for it out of a story, but she spit out my come one time and I taught her never to do that again. She spit it out on purpose. She was asking for it, just the way you ask for it, all the fuckin' time."

His body went tense – a flash of sudden beauty in every muscle. But his face was twisted with anger. I flinched, thinking he was going to hit me, and not knowing why.

He took a deep breath. His body relaxed. His voice was bitter.

"She was the one. She could've been the one. She was a rich bitch, all that shiny blond hair and those pretty clothes. She thought I was real lower class, she thought I was scum, but Carla liked slumming, she dug getting it from a guy with muscles and a big working-class dick. Oh, she liked to suck it. She liked me to slap her face with it."

Reed pulled his cock out of his shorts. He held it at the base and beat it against the air. Both of us watched it, fascinated.

"But Carla, she had this rich old man who didn't approve of no common dick getting into his little girl's cunt, soiling his little darling's sweet lips. That motherfucker could've ruined everything I had, he could've taken away my rig with a snap of his fingers. One of these days I'm gonna kill that son of a bitch. He married her off to some fat lawyer friend of his who keeps her locked up in a big house in Highland Park, got a burglar alarm on every door and a gun in every room.

"I had to kiss that bitch goodbye. I had to go back to taking 'em out and buying 'em drinks, and then asking 'em real sweet, say please lady, can I pretty please stick my big dick up

your cunt. I'll be real gentle and sweet and I'll buy you pretty
things and treat you like the sweet innocent thing your
momma raised you up to be, and I won't shock you by
whipping your ass or fucking your face or anything like that,
no sir. Goddamn!

"I had to go back to picking up whores off the street and
finding out a week later they had a nest full of crabs between
their legs that the last fucker left, who knows who the hell he
was, probably some greasy fat rich turd like Carla's old man.

"I just couldn't find that hole I was looking for. That
hungry hole. I even started looking at fags on the street. I
know the places they hang out, here in LA, back in Dallas.
I'd look at 'em and wonder if they were all like Reggie, if
they'd get all choked up if I was to show 'em the piece of meat
between my legs. Yeah, cocksucker, Reggie was real too,
everything I said about him except the part in the men's
room. But he was real all right, back in Midland, and he
wanted my dick bad. Reggie would've done anything I
wanted, he would've crawled on his belly like a snake if I
told him to.

"But Reggie scared the shit outta me. I told myself no sir, I
wasn't gonna go down with no queer, and I told myself the
same thing when I'd see the guys hanging around outside the
queer bars, all sweaty with their shirts off, kissing each other
on the mouth."

Reed looked down at his cock and squeezed it. He pumped
it up and clutched it like a club. He looked me in the eye.

"And then you come along, with your smooth little chest
and your pretty face, and your goddamn pretty ass. And your
cock's always hard, and it's kinda pretty too, you know that,
even your cock looks nice. I actually like looking at your dick.
But I like it better when it's pushed down between your legs
and you're all smooth there."

Reed rubbed his bare foot against the inside of my thighs.
He put his foot over my cock. He stepped on it, pinning me to
the floor.

"And I knew you were trouble, the first time I saw you

standing there on the side of the road. A voice in my head said, drive on by. Even while I was putting my foot on the brake, I said, Reed, you are asking for a whole slew of trouble. Reed, your dick is gonna want that.

"So I thought, I'll just give in to it a little. Just a little. But you kept sucking it up like a sponge. So I thought, slow down, Reed, this kid's as crazy as you are, this kid's infectious. And this evening, when I came back from the rental place, you were already gone. I figured I'd seen the last of you. A part of me was relieved, like it was over and I could just forget about your pretty ass. But another part of me felt stupid, like I'd had a chance to do something I wanted and I didn't take it, like some uptight bitch who's afraid to do it with the lights on 'cause she thinks it's dirty.

"And I was mad." Reed's voice turned a shade darker. "I got mad thinking about you and your buddy. About you sucking his dick and taking it up your ass, loving it, begging for it, forgetting all about me. And wearing those underwear you stole from me, letting him see how sexy you look and getting his dick hot, letting him take those shorts off you. Is that how it was?"

He twisted his foot, grinding my cock into the carpet. I gritted my teeth and pushed his foot away. "No, Reed. I told you. It wasn't like that. He didn't want me any more."

"Then he's a crazy son of a bitch," Reed looked down at my hard cock and gave me a crooked smile. He grabbed his cock with both hands, one atop the other, his fingers not quite reaching around the width. Another handful projected beyond the circle of his fist. His smile faded. Reed hissed and narrowed his eyes. I watched him, enthralled. He was not a man. He was a cock, looking for a hole.

"You weren't here," Reed said. "You went off with your buddy. So I went out and picked me up a blond with big tits and brought her back here. And you were on the phone, just waiting for me. And I thought, this is fate, Reed, give in to it. The kid wants your dick, give the kid your dick, make the kid happy.

"But I'd already paid the whore half, and the clerk was standing there watching, so I brought her up here and screwed her, real quick, real hard. I don't think she liked it. But I didn't care. I was thinking about you."

I shook my head, not knowing what to say.

"I was thinking about you, kid."

Neither of us spoke for a long time. We watched his cock.

Reed reached out and touched my cheek. I turned my face and kissed the palm of his hand.

"Guess what I needed all along was a good cocksucker," Reed said softly. "You're gonna be my cocksucker, aren't you?"

"Yes, Reed."

He nodded. There was excitement in his eyes. "Yeah. Starting tomorrow. I'm gonna have me a cocksucker. You're gonna learn how to suck my dick. I won't expect you to be able to take all of it the first time. But you'll learn. Carla learned to take it, all the way to my balls. Then you're gonna learn how to take it up your ass, squeeze it and eat it with your ass."

He narrowed his eyes and squeezed himself. "I'm gonna tie your hands behind your back and whip you with my belt. I'm gonna treat you real mean, just the way you want it. I got a lot of imagination, you'll find that out. A lot of imagination, and nowhere to use it, till now. Now I got me a cocksucker. I got me a real cock-crazy faggot." He looked down and shook his head. He smiled crookedly. "Oh, baby, look at the way your dick stands up."

He slid his fingers into my hair, made a fist and jerked my head back. There was a rush of air through his nostrils. His face stiffened. He held my head in place and pushed two fingers into my mouth.

"I'm gonna piss in your mouth, too. Three times a day."

He pulled the fingers from my mouth. "Did you come with that guy?" He twisted my scalp. "Did you shoot while he was pissing down your throat, cocksucker?"

"No."

His grip relaxed. "Good. Then you can come now. I want to see you come for me."

I put my hands around my cock. Reed pushed them aside with his feet.

"Not that way. Push it down between your legs like a good girl. Hold it between your legs, hold it there and squeeze it. Rub your hands over your thighs, over your belly. Come like a bitch."

He pulled his hand from my hair. He stroked himself with both hands. I leaned forward and opened my mouth.

Reed pushed me back. With my knees locked together, I almost lost my balance. "Not yet," he said. "That's tomorrow. Right now, just do like I say."

Reed stroked himself with one hand and touched my chest with the other. I rubbed my legs together. I pressed my fingers into my groin. Without thinking, I reached out and clenched my fist in the empty space between my legs, expecting my cock to be there.

"I like your tits, boy. You got beautiful tits. All big and round and firm, smooth brown nipples, all hairless and sleek. You look real good in a T-shirt, you know that? The way your chest fills it up. Makes me want to reach out and touch. One for each hand."

He pinched my nipples. He pushed his fingernails into the flesh and pulled, till the nipples were an inch from the muscle beneath. My cock stiffened between my thighs. I leaned forward, following his fingers. My face brushed against his cock.

I came. The warm wetness shot downward, splattering the back of my knees. The stimulation in my nipples turned abruptly to pain. I convulsed and moaned.

Reed released my nipples. He doubled over and hugged my head, rubbing my face against his cock.

Then he sat back and pushed me gently away. My cock, softer now, was still between my thighs. My groin still shuddered in the aftershock. I pressed my hands into the V between my legs.

"That's it," Reed said. "That's beautiful."

He held his cock with one fist and waved it slowly before my face. "I got a dick between my legs." He smiled. "What you think about my dick, boy."

I stared at it. I studied it. "It's so big, Reed."

"Yeah?" His breathing was turning ragged. Tenseness spread through his body. "Carla always said . . . she said she figured my genes got mixed up somehow, and I ended up with a horse dick." He began to pump it. "One time she said I had to be a bastard. Said my mother must've had a thing for getting screwed by donkeys. But maybe she was just trying to get a rise outta me."

His smile broadened to show his teeth, but only for an instant. He winced. There was a great tension from his body, from his cock, huge and upright, hard as steel. I wondered how his briefs had ever contained it.

"Go ahead," he said, "kiss it, boy, kiss a man's dick."

I leaned forward and pressed my lips to the moist, open slit at the tip of Reed's cock. The shaft jerked. Reed held it fast. He came, and filled my mouth with semen.

When it was over, Reed stuffed his cock inside his briefs, pulled himself onto the bed and collapsed on his back. He turned off the lamp.

The heavy white drapes were coppery with the first light of Saturday morning. I was completely exhausted. I lay back on the floor and stared at the ceiling. For a few moments I felt and thought nothing. I simply studied the pale rays of sunlight angling in above the drapes, flooding the stained, cracked ceiling.

Had I finally seduced Reed, or had he seduced me?

He had wanted me all along. He had initiated the first contact, continued it, cut it short and begun again. I had thought he was tormenting me. He had been afraid of me.

Tonight he had been angry. Not because I was a cocksucker, tempting him. Because he was jealous.

A lightness, cool as helium, spread through my limbs.

"Reed," I said.

"What?" He sounded almost asleep, and his voice sounded distant, drifting down form the bed to the floor where I lay.

"What happens Monday?"

"I head back to Texas." He yawned.

"Will you take me with you?"

"Huh? Yeah, sure." The sleepiness made his voice sound gruff and noncommittal. I wasn't fooled. "I'll even buy your meals if you turn out to be a good cocksucker."

I shook my head. He was a mystery to me; the words he used to brand me were a part of the mystery.

"I don't want to go back to Austin," I said. "Not 'til the fall, anyway."

"Maybe I could hire you for the summer," he murmured. "Get you loading cargo. Gives you strong arms. Drives women wild."

I smiled, not knowing why. Where could it all possibly lead? I wanted to figure it out, but I was too tired to be any place but in that moment, in a sleepy gray room with Reed, at dawn on a Saturday morning.

I knew I had accomplished something – I wasn't sure what – prevailed over something, stumbled onto something unexpected and inexplicable by all the rules I'd been taught to expect from life.

I got up on my knees and stared at Reed until he opened his eyes.

"I can't sleep," I said. "I'm all shaky. Maybe if you held me for a minute."

Reed stared at me for a long time. Then he closed his eyes and stretched out his arm. I crawled under the sheets and pressed myself into the warmth of his chest.

About the Authors

Bob Angell was born under a full moon, a telling detail. As a Libran, he is always seeking balance; he rides a unicycle and wishes he could juggle better. You may have seen his work in *Asimov's*, *The Baltimore Review*, *Gargoyle*, and various anthologies, such as *Best Date Ever*, *Distant Horizons*, and others. Find him at www.rrangell.com

Chaz Brenchley has been making a living as a writer since he was eighteen. He is the author of nine thrillers, most recently *Shelter*, and two major fantasy series: *The Books of Outremer*, based on the world of the Crusades, and *Selling Water by the River*, set in an alternate Ottoman Istanbul. A winner of the British Fantasy Award, he has also published three books for children and more than 500 short stories in various genres. His time as Crimewriter-in-Residence at the St Peter's Riverside Sculpture Project in Sunderland resulted in the collection *Blood Waters*. He is a prizewinning ex-poet, and has been writer in residence at the University of Northumbria, as well as tutoring their MA in Creative Writing. He was Northern Writer of the Year 2000, and lives in Newcastle upon Tyne with a quantum cat and a famous teddy bear.

Alexander Chee's first novel, *Edinburgh*, is the winner of a Lambda Literary Award, the Michener Prize in fiction, and the Asian American Writer's Workshop Literary Award. His short fiction and essays have been anthologized in *Loss*

Within Loss, Boys Like Us, His 3, Take Out, Best Gay Erotica 2002, Men On Men 2000, and *The Man I Might Become.* His poetry has appeared in *Barrow Street, LIT, Interview,* the *James White Review,* and *'XXX Fruit.* His journalism and reviews in *TimeOut/NY, Out/Look, Outweek,* the *Advocate, Out, Bookforum* and the *San Francisco Review of Books.* He received a Story Magazine Short Short Fiction Award, a Holt, Rinehart and Winston short fiction prize, the Paul Horgan Prize in short fiction, the Michener/Copernicus Fellowship Prize, the 2003 Whiting Award, a residency from the MacDowell Colony and a 2004 NEA Fellowship in Fiction. He lives in Massachusetts.

Edward M. Cohen's stories have appeared in *Harrington Gay Men's Fiction Quarterly,* the *James White Review, Evergreen Chronicles, Christopher St., Carleton Miscellany, Evergreen Review, Stories, Confrontation* and *Nuvein Online.* His novel, *$250,000,* was published by Putnam; his non-fiction books by Prentice-Hall, Limelight Editions, SUNY Press and Prima.

Jameson Currier is the author of the novel *Where the Rainbow Ends* and the short story collections *Dancing on the Moon* and *Desire, Lust, Passion, Sex.* His work is anthologized in *Men on Men 5, Best American Gay Fiction 3, Certain Voices, Boyfriends from Hell, Men Seeking Men, The Mammoth Book of Gay Erotica, Best Gay Erotica, Best American Erotica, Quickies 3, Circa 2000, Rebel Yell,* and *Making Literature Matter.* His reviews, essays, interviews, and articles on AIDS and gay culture have been published in many national and local publications, including *The Washington Post, The Los Angeles Times, Newsday, The Dallas Morning News, The St. Louis Post-Dispatch, The Minneapolis Star-Tribune, The Philadelphia Inquirer Magazine, Out,* and *Body Positive.* In 2003, he was a recipient of a writing fellowship from the New York Foundation for the Arts. He is a member of the board of directors of the Arch and Bruce Brown Foundation and currently resides in Manhattan. More at www.jamesoncur-rier.com

Trebor Healey is the author of the 2004 Ferro-Grumley and Violet Quill award-winning novel, *Through It Came Bright Colors* (Harrington Park Press), and a poetry collection, *Sweet Son of Pan* (Suspect Thoughts). His short story collection, *A Perfect Scar & Other Stories*, is forthcoming from Harrington Park Press in fall, 2007. His erotic fiction has appeared in *Best Gay Erotic 2003, 2004, 2006* and *Best of Best Gay Erotic*, as well as in *Best American Erotica 2007*. He lives in Los Angeles. www.treborhealey.com

Greg Herren is the author of five mystery novels set in New Orleans: *Bourbon Street Blues, Jackson Square Jazz, Murder in the Rue Dauphine, Murder in the Rue St. Ann* and *Mardi Gras Mambo*, as well as a collection of his gay erotica about *Wanna Wrestle?* He has edited numerous anthologies, such as *Upon a Midnight Clear: Queer Christmas Tales, Shadows of the Night, Frat Sex*, and *Love, Bourbon Street: Reflections on New Orleans*, and works as an editor for the Haworth Press. He lives in New Orleans with his partner Paul J. Willis.

Andrew Holleran is the author of the novels, *Grief, Dancer from the Dance, Nights in Aruba*, and *The Beauty of Men*, as well as a collection of stories, *The Changing Light in September*, and a collection of essays, *Ground Zero*.

Daniel M. Jaffe's novel, *The Limits of Pleasure*, was a Finalist for a ForeWord Book of the Year Award and excerpted in *Best Gay Erotica 2003*. His personal essays and short stories appear in numerous literary journals and anthologies, such as *Found Tribe, Bearotica, M2M: New Literary Fiction*, and *Identity Envy: Wanting to Be Who We're Not*, and have earned him a Pushcart Prize nomination. Read more at danieljaffe.tripod.com.

G. Winston James is a Jamaican-born poet, short fiction writer, essayist and editor. He holds an MFA in Fiction from Brooklyn College, City University of New York, and is the author of the poetry collection *The Damaged Good: Poems Around Love* and the Lambda Literary Award nominated collection *Lyric: Poems Along a Broken Road*. He is also co-editor of the anthologies, *Voices Rising: Celebrating 20 Years of Black Lesbian, Gay, Bisexual and Transgender Writing* and *Spirited: Affirming the Soul and Black Gay/Lesbian Identity*. His work appears in numerous anthologies, including *Freedom in This Village: Twenty-Five Years of Black Gay Men's Writing, 1979 to the Present; The Road Before Us: 100 Black Gay Poets; Fighting Words: Personal Essays by Black Gay Men; His 2: Brilliant New Fiction by Gay Writers; The Mammoth Book of Gay Erotica; Shade: An Anthology of Fiction by Gay Men of African Descent;* and *Waves: An Anthology of New Gay Fiction*. His poetry, fiction, and essays can also be found in *Brooklyn Review; Callaloo; BLOOM Magazine; Kuumba;* and other magazines.

Timothy J. Lambert is the co-author, with Becky Cochrane, of *Three Fortunes in One Cookie* and *The Deal*; together they're also editors of the anthology *Moonlight & Roses: Men Romancing Men* forthcoming from Haworth Press. As one-fourth of the byline Timothy James Beck, he co-authored *It Had to be You, He's the One, I'm Your Man,* and most recently, *Someone Like You*. His solo stories have appeared in the Best Gay Love Stories series, and he selected the stories for Best Gay Erotica 2007. He lives in Houston, Texas and can be found online at www.timothyjameslambert.com

Michael Lassell is the author of a collection of short stories, *Certain Ecstasies* (Painted Leaf Press); three volumes of poetry: *A Flame for the Touch That Matters* (Painted Leaf Press), *Decade Dance* (Alyson; winner of a Lambda Literary Award), and *Poems for Lost and Un-lost Boys* (Amelia); and a collection of essays, stories, and poems titled *The Hard Way* (Masquerade). He is the editor of several anthologies, including *Men Seeking Men* (Painted Leaf Press), *The Name of Love* (St. Martin's Press), *Eros in Boystown* (Crown), *Two Hearts Desire: Gay Couples on Their Love* (with Lawrence Schimel; St. Martin's Press), and most recently, *The World in US: Lesbian and Gay Poetry of the Next Wave* (with Elena Georgiou; St. Martin's Press). A former editor of *L.A. Style* and *Interview* magazines, he is the articles editor for *Metropolitan Homes* magazine. He lives in New York City.

Shaun Levin lived in Israel for many years before moving to London. His *Seven Sweet Things* was published in 2003, and a collection of short stories, *A Year of Two Summers*, came out in 2005. He is the editor of *Chroma: A Queer Literary Journal*.

Barry Lowe is a Sydney writer whose plays have been produced world wide including *Homme Fatale: The Joey Stefano Story*, *The Extraordinary Annual General Meeting of the Size-Queen Club*, *The Death of Peter Pan*, *Seeing Things*, and *Rehearsing the Shower Scene from "Psycho"*. He also co-wrote the screenplay to *Violet's Visit*. His short stories have appeared in *The Mammoth Book of Gay Erotica*, *Flesh and the Word*, *Boy Meets Boy*, and others. His book on the life and career of Hollywood cult icon Mamie Van Doren will be published in 2007.

William J. Mann is the author of the novels *The Men from the Boys*, *Where the Boys are*, *The Biograph Girl*, *All American Boy*, and *Men who Love men*, and of the biographies *Wisecracker: the Life and Times of William Haines*, *Kate: the Woman who was Hepburn*, and *Edge of Midnight: the Life of John Schlesinger*. He selected the stories for *Best Gay Erotica 2005*.

David May is the author of the book, *Madrugada: A Cycle of Erotic Fictions* (BadBoy). His work, both fiction and nonfiction, has appeared in periodicals such as *The Harvard Gay & Lesbian Review; Advocate Men; Cat Fancy; Drummer; Frontiers; Honcho; Inches; International Leatherman; Lambda Book Report*, and *Mach*. His work also appears in the anthologies *Kosher Meat; Bar Stories; Midsummer Night's Dreams: One Story, Many Tales; Cherished Blood; Flesh and the Word 3; Meltdown!; Queer View Mirror*, and *Rogues of San Francisco*. He attended the University of California at Santa Cruz where he studied dramatic literature, specializing in medieval religious theatre.

Over 65 of Jim McDonough's erotic stories have been published in more than a dozen dirty magazines, on the web and in anthologies such as *Quickies, Nature in the Raw, Droom Jongens, Latin Boys, Saints & Sinners* and *Friction 7: Best Gay Erotica*. A short film, from his screenplay *Waiting For the Ball to Drop*, screened in film festivals in San Francisco, Austin, Tampa and Albuquerque. He is currently working on a novel and serves as webmaster of the GLBT writer's resource QueerWriters.com. E-mail him at jim@queerwriters.com

Tom Mendicino's work has appeared in three *Best Gay Love Stories* anthologies as well as in *Best Date Ever*. He's still celebrating his birthdays with Nick Ifft.

Robin Metcalfe has been a gay activist and journalist for the national and international gay press since the mid 1970s. His fiction, poetry and essays have been published in four languages on four continents; in more than fifty magazines, including *The Body Politic, First Hand,* and *Mandate,* and in many anthologies, including the first *Mammoth Book of Gay Erotica, The Second Gates of Paradise,* and the original *Flesh and the Word*. He has worked for twenty years as a critic and curator in the visual arts and organised the 1997 exhibition *Queer Looking, Queer Acting: Lesbian and Gay Vernacular*. He lives in Halifax, Nova Scotia, where he is Director/ Curator of the Saint Mary's University Art Gallery.

Marshall Moore is the author of two novels, *A Concrete Sky* and the forthcoming *An Ideal for Living*, and the story collection *Black Shapes in a Darkened Room*. He can be found at www.marshallmoore.com

Gregory L. Norris is the author of the baseball-themed gay novel *Hardball* (Alyson) as well as *Ghost Kisses: Gothic Gay Romance Stories* (Leyland Publications). He also worked as a screenwriter on two episodes of Paramount's *Star Trek: Voyager*. For two years he wrote the monthly "Channel News" column for *Sci Fi*, the official magazine of the Sci Fi Channel, and he freelances widely for periodicals such as *Cinescape, Soap Opera Update, Genesis, Smoke, Heartland USA*, and others. His stories also appear in *Best Date Ever, Travelrotica, Best Gay Love Stories – NYC*, and *Ultimate Gay Erotica '07*, among many other anthologies.

Andy Quan is the author of two collections of short fiction, *Six Positions: Sex Writings* (Green Candy) and *Calendar Boy*, and the poetry collection *Slant*. He is also the co-editor of *Swallowing Clouds* (Arsenal Pulp Press), an anthology of Canadian-Chinese poetry. He has also recorded two albums: *Take-off and Landings* (1999) and *Clean* (2002). More info at www.andyquan.com

Kirk Read is the author of *How I Learned to Snap*, a memoir about being out in high school in Virginia. He has worked as an HIV counselor, phlebotomist and volunteer coordinator at St. James Infirmary, a free health care clinic for sex workers. His forthcoming collection of essays is called *This is the Thing* and he is in the middle of a novel and a second memoir about sex work. He can be found at www.kirkread.com

Rick R. Reed is the author of the novels, *Obsessed, Penance*, and *A Face Without a Heart*, and the short story collection, *Twisted: Tales of Obsession and Terror*. In 2007, his novels *IM, In the Blood*, and *Deadly Vision: Book One of the*

Cassandra Chronicles will be published by Regal Crest Enterprises under their Quest imprint. His short fiction appears in nearly twenty anthologies. He lives in Miami with his partner and is at work on a new novel.

Matthew Rettenmund is the author of the novels *Blind Items: A (Love) Story* and *Boy Culture*, now a major motion picture from TLA Releasing. He is a magazine editor, has published books on popular culture and maintains the blog www.boy-culture.typepad.com

Paul Russell, named a *Granta* Best Young Novelist, is the author of *The Salt Point, Boys of Life, Sea of Tranquility*, and the Ferro-Grumley Award-winning *War against the Animals*. A professor at Vassar College, he lives in Poughkeepsie, NY, USA.

Steven Saylor, writing as Aaron Travis, is the author of *The Flesh Fables, Beast of Burden, Slaves of the Empire*, and other volumes of gay erotica. As Aaron Travis, he was editor of *Drummer* Magazine. More info on Travis can be found at www.stevensaylor.com/AaronTravis. Under his own name, Saylor is the author of the acclaimed Roman mystery series featuring Gordianus the Finder. He lives in Berkeley, California, USA.

Lawrence Schimel is a full-time author and anthologist, who's published over 80 books, including *Two Boys in Love, The Future is Queer, Best Date Ever: True Stories That Celebrate Gay Relationships, The Drag Queen of Elfland, His Tongue, Kosher Meat,* and *Vacation in Ibiza,* among others. His *PoMoSexuals: Challenging Assumptions About Gender and Sexuality* (with Carol Queen) won a Lambda Literary Award in 1998, and he has also been a finalist for the Lambda Literary Award ten other times, including for *The Mammoth Book of Gay Erotica*. Born in New York City in 1971, he lives in Madrid, Spain.

D. Travers Scott is the author of two novels: the Lambda Literary Award winner, *One of These Things is Not Like the Other*, and *Execution, Texas: 1987*. Deemed "funny and disturbing" by David Sedaris and "halfway between Flaubert and Straight to Hell" by Robert Glück, Scott's work has appeared in venues such as *This American Life, Harper's*, and the *Best Gay Erotica* and *Best American Gay Fiction* series. Currently he is pursuing a PhD in Communication at the University of Southern California. More info at: www.dtraversscott.com.

Darieck Scott is the author of the novels *Hex* (2007) and *Traitor to the Race* (1995), and the editor of *Best Black Gay Erotica* (2004). His fiction has appeared in the anthologies *Freedom in This Village, Black Like Us, Shade, Giant Steps, Flesh and the Word 4*, and *Ancestral House*. He has published nonfiction essays in *Callaloo, GLQ, The Americas Review*, and the anthology *Gay Travels*. He is assistant professor of English at the University of California at Santa Barbara, where he teaches African American literature and creative writing.

Don Shewey has published three books, including *Out Front: the Grove Press anthology of gay and lesbian plays*. He has written extensively for *The Village Voice* and has taught theater at New York University. He lives in New York City.

Harry Thomas's fiction has appeared in print in *Best Gay Erotica 2004* and online in *Lodestar Quarterly* and *Six Little Things*. He holds an M.F.A. in Fiction from the University of Alabama and is currently working on a Ph.D. (focusing on American literature) at the University of North Carolina at Chapel Hill. Appallingly enough, his mother read "Dear Drew Peters" and reported that she loved it.